Mendis Vakon believed in no gods—Old Gods, Seeker gods, or otherwise. The only thing that interested him about the Seekers was that they were rich.

And mean, he added to himself, glad he'd slipped a dagger into a pocket in his leggings. It's so damned dark, he thought. Why doesn't Hederick light a torch? There's no one here to see . . . no one.

The mayor of Solace turned and ran back the way he had come. His slippers skidded on the incline. Hands caught the knotted cord that belted his shirt, and Vakon crashed onto his knees, tipping forward and hitting his head on the slimy stone. Desperate, he felt for his dagger.

Hederick laughed knowingly. "I already have it, Vakon."

The priest was surprisingly strong. Vakon felt himself being rolled across a slight rise, and suddenly the air was not merely stale, but fetid. He sprawled on uneven slabs of rock as a lock clicked with foreboding finality.

Something stirred in the blackness within the chamber.

Rats . . . ?

Saga

From the Creators of the DRAGONLANCE® Saga

VILLAINS

Before the Mask
Volume One—Verminaard
Michael and Teri Williams

The Black Wing
Volume Two—Khisanth
Mary Kirchoff

Emperor of Ansalon
Volume Three—Ariakas
Douglas Niles

Hederick, the Theocrat
Volume Four—Seeker Hederick
Ellen Dodge Severson

Lord Toede
Volume Five—Fewmaster Toede
Jeff Grubb
Available Summer 1994

DragonLance Saga

VILLAINS

Volume Four

hederick the theocrat

Ellen Dodge Severson

DRAGONLANCE®
Villains Series
Volume Four

HEDERICK, THE THEOCRAT
©1994 TSR, Inc.
All Rights Reserved.

This book is protected under the copyright laws of the United States of America. Any reproduction or other unauthorized use of the material or artwork contained herein is prohibited without the express written permission of TSR, Inc.

All TSR characters, character names, and the distinctive likenesses thereof are trademarks owned by TSR, Inc.

Random House and its affiliate companies have worldwide distribution rights in the book trade for English language products of TSR, Inc.

Distributed to the book and hobby trade in the United Kingdom by TSR Ltd.

Distributed to the toy and hobby trade by regional distributors.

Cover art by Jeff Easley. Interior art by Karl Waller.

DRAGONLANCE is a registered trademark owned by TSR, Inc. The TSR logo is a trademark owned by TSR, Inc.

First Printing: January 1994

Printed in the United States of America.

Library of Congress Catalog Card Number: 93-61433

9 8 7 6 5 4 3 2 1

ISBN: 1-56076-817-7

TSR, Inc.
P.O. Box 756
Lake Geneva, WI
53147 U.S.A.

TSR Ltd.
120 Church End, Cherry Hinton
Cambridge CB1 3LB
United Kingdom

This book is lovingly dedicated

to the memory of

William Olm

and

Max Earl Porath

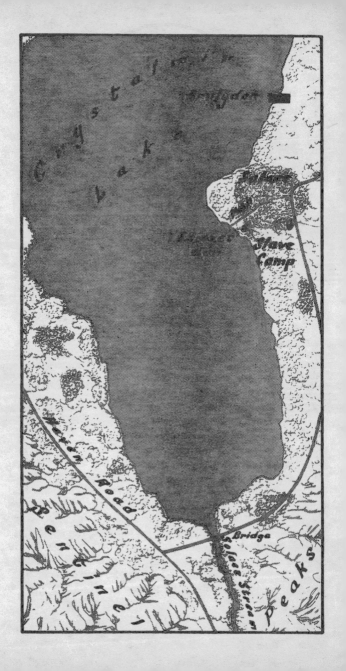

Prologue

Astinus, leader of the Order of Aesthetics, surveyed the three apprentice scribes before him. The historian's face, as usual, wore the expression of a man taken unwillingly from his beloved work for something annoyingly trivial.

The three scribes, a middle-aged woman and two younger men, shifted from foot to foot beneath his gaze and darted cautious glances at each other. Each was sure the other two possessed extraordinary training and expertise. Each was sure that it was his or her mere presence in the Great Library of Palanthas that had brought the dissatisfied gleam to Astinus's eyes. They all were convinced that their own appointments as apprentices to the premier historian on Krynn would soon be found to be a mistake. All that work, all those years of preparation and study, would be found inadequate. They were unworthy. Each steeled for disappointment, afraid of being sent home in humiliation to

1

become a store clerk or street vendor.

In truth, Astinus was not annoyed with the apprentices but merely anxious to be back at work, writing down the history of Krynn as it occurred. Even as he stood here assessing the guarded expressions of these three, details of fact were going unrecorded in the scrolls of the Great Library.

It was difficult to catch up once one was behind, as Astinus knew only too well; it was almost better to skip what one had missed in one's absence and go on to pen whatever was happening at the moment. Unlike the other scribes, who worked in shifts, Astinus had never been known to sleep or to step away from his work for more than a few minutes. There were some among his helpers who whispered that Astinus was no mortal, for hadn't his name been found upon scrolls dating back thousands of years? Unless, they speculated, every chief historian's name, since the beginning of time, had been Astinus.

Actually, Astinus was well-pleased with this crop of apprentices. These three, however they quailed before him now, had come on the highest recommendations of Astinus's far-flung advisers. They needed only seasoning, he'd been told, before they could take their places among Astinus's dozens of assistants in the Order of Aesthetics.

What was needed was a task that would test their ability to cooperate as well as to chronicle history, Astinus thought as the three suffered silently before him. It must be something, of course, that the historian could check for accuracy against his own knowledge of events as they unfolded. He narrowed his eyes and nodded as he surveyed the trio.

"Hederick," he murmured. "That's it."

The scribes exchanged more glances, each wondering which of the others was named Hederick.

"Sir?" the middle-aged woman finally ventured. She had the pale ashen complexion common among those who spent their lives prowling through the dimly lit corridors of libraries. She was of medium height and average build and wore her brown hair gathered with a simple length of blue yarn at the nape of her neck. She wore the same type of sleeveless, togalike outfit that the other two wore—indeed, that Astinus himself wore. "Sir," she said again hesitantly, "is there something we . . . ?"

The remaining two apprentices lost no time interrupting the woman's query. In this competition for a coveted position in the Great Library of Palanthas, none wanted to be left at the starting line. "You have a task for us, master?" broke in the younger of the two men, a tall, red-haired youth with creamy skin, copious freckles, and blue eyes.

"We stand waiting to serve you," interjected the other man. He had eyes as black as his curly hair and skin the color of cinnamon, marking a sharp contrast to the youth beside him.

Suddenly, all three apprentices were speaking at once.

A new frown descended over Astinus's already stern features, and the three apprentices faltered in their chatter. "You are delaying me," Astinus declared in irritation. "Give me your names, quickly, that I may sort you out and assign you tasks. And be brisk about it."

"Marya," replied the woman.

"Olven," the dark-haired man said proudly.

"Eban," the redheaded youth answered last.

"Fine," Astinus said, noting their names for inclusion in his history of the Great Library. "Your task, then, is this: to chronicle the doings of a man named Hederick, recently named High Theocrat of Solace. I believe the scheming of this man will someday have great import in Krynn." His penetrating stare raked the three aspiring historians. "First you will research Hederick's past and set it out. You, Eban, will take charge of that." The youth stood up straighter and cast a triumphant look toward the other two.

Astinus went on, "All of you are students enough to grasp that without knowing a man or woman's past, it is impossible to understand that person's present."

"Oh, yes," said Eban.

"Certainly," Marya chimed.

"Without a doubt," Olven added.

"You two"—Astinus thrust his chin at Marya and Olven—
"will concentrate on recording the present exploits of High
Theocrat Hederick." He pointed to a wooden desk in the corner
of the library. "One of you—and you, too, Eban, when you com-
plete your research—will be seated at that desk at all times, day
or night. This spot must never be empty."

Three pairs of eyes widened, but the historian continued
speaking regardless of their surprise. "History occurs in times
of darkness as well as at noon, as you all know. Even now,
events are sweeping on unrecorded as you dally here."

Eban gasped and swept up a scrap of parchment and a quill
pen from a counter. He scurried between two stacks of books and
was gone. Astinus marked the red-haired youth's industry.
Surely the background material would be ready soon at that
pace, he thought with satisfaction.

Astinus made his way to the door of the Great Library. "I
leave it to you to decide how you will divide the day," he said
over his shoulder to Marya and Olven. "Whoever is not recording currently transpiring events should help Eban with his
research, for that must go first in your written account, of
course. Now I must return to my tasks."

"Ah . . . sir?" Olven said quickly. "A question? Quickly?"

Astinus halted, his hand on the doorjamb.

Olven cleared his throat and looked embarrassed. "How will
we know what's happening now, so that we may record it?" the
man asked.

"After all, it hasn't been written down anywhere yet," Marya
added helpfully. "And it appears that you want us to stay here.
In the library, I mean."

Astinus, expressionless, gazed at the two for a long, silent
moment, then the briefest of smiles crossed the historian's face.

"Sit at the desk," the historian said. "You will see, soon
enough. If you are meant to work here." Then he was gone.

Marya looked at Olven, who gazed back at her. They both
swiveled about to thoughtfully survey the padded chair drawn
up before the desk.

"It looks ordinary enough," Marya said in a small voice. "Just a chair."

Olven nodded. "Magic, do you think?" he whispered. "Has Astinus ensorceled us without our knowledge?"

Marya shrugged, but swallowed twice before going on. "Maybe. You go first."

Olven bit his lips, took a deep breath, and slid into the chair.

Chapter 1

The scream invaded Hederick's very bones and blood, coming from nowhere and everywhere.

The sound reverberated again. Hederick raced across the prairie toward a grove of trees, where his sister Ancilla had hidden ten years earlier. He was still quite a distance away—too far, by the god Tiolanthe! Feet pounded behind him, and with them, thunderclap after thunderclap from the approaching storm.

Time after time, Hederick stamped on jagged rocks and stumbled over upthrust roots. Bloodstained footprints marked his passage.

Then trees loomed. Hederick dove into Ancilla's Copse as though it were a church and Hederick a penitent—as though whatever tracked him dared not enter such a holy place.

His lungs burned. His ribs ached. The boy landed face-down in soft dampness and tensed for the cry that would tell him the creature was upon him. But there was silence; only an intermittent popping sound broke the hush of the glade.

Hederick sat up warily and peered around in the flickering light. Large trees with rough bark towered over him, interspersed with saplings that thrust upward through the ferns. The rich smell of hickory mingled with the odors of fragrant moss and moist soil. Surrounded by dark shapes that seemed to dance in the wind of the approaching storm, the boy fearfully scanned one shadow after another.

The yellow eyes of a gigantic lynx glared at him.

The dappled brown beast was easily ten feet from nose to bobbed tail. The great cat crouched fifteen feet above him, wedged in the crotch of a tree. Its eyes were enormous, forelegs heavy, padded feet huge.

Thunder shattered.

The lynx and Hederick screamed at the same instant.

"Begone!" A sword appeared above the boy, interposed between his crouching body and the giant predator. Red light played on the weapon's edge. A gauntleted hand grasped the hilt; an arm corded with muscular sinew held the blade steady. Hederick sat, powerless with fear.

The lynx screamed again, and the hand tightened on the hilt. "Leave us, cat!" came that same booming voice. The lynx tensed to spring, and the man swore fervently, invoking gods Hederick had never heard of. Just as the giant feline leaped, the man's other hand swept up, raising a flaming torch.

Light exploded. Red and yellow sparks burned pinpricks into the ferns. The lynx twisted away in midleap and crashed through a maple sapling and onto the ground off to one side. The man dropped the torch and whirled to meet the cat, sword ready, his body between the boy and the lynx.

Then Hederick was up. His left hand caught up the sputtering torch from the wet moss, and he ran to the man's side, bellowing a battle cry. Hederick threw anything and everything his right hand could grasp. Rocks, branches, leaves, mud, moss—all were hurtled toward the snarling lynx.

His tall rescuer remained poised with his sword. "By the New Gods, the boy's feisty!" the man said.

The only thing left was the torch; Hederick prepared to throw that as well. The man swore again, fumbled at his belt, and tossed something at the cat just as the boy released the fiery brand.

Another explosion of scarlet and topaz flashed through the trees. Bigger and louder than the last, it knocked Hederick flat on his back. When the smoke cleared, there was no sign of the lynx.

"Did we kill it?" Hederick could barely get the words out. His tongue seemed stuck to the roof of his mouth.

The man sheathed his sword and laughed uproariously, then shook his head. "By the New Gods, that pussycat must be halfway to the Garnet Mountains by now! If her feet touch the ground every six furlongs, it'll be a miracle."

Hederick shook uncontrollably. Blood streamed into his eyes from a cut on his forehead. "It's still out there?" he wailed. "It's not dead?"

"Not dead, lad, but she won't be coming back here soon." The man extended a hand to help the boy up. Hederick's knees shook so that he could barely stand. "I can't imagine what the she-cat was doing so far from the Garnets," the man mused, "but who knows how great a distance the creatures travel to hunt? Perhaps she sought food for kits."

"But it was hunting *me!*" Hederick shrieked.

The man shrugged. "You escaped."

Wordless, Hederick studied his rescuer. The man couldn't have been much more than twenty. His face was long, with a dark beard neatly trimmed to a point and gray eyes that seemed both humorous and kind. A rough brown robe stretched to cover powerful shoulders.

The man submitted to Hederick's frank inspection without embarrassment. "By Ferae, you're a small one! How old are you? Eight? Nine?"

"Twelve," Hederick muttered.

"Your name, son?"

"Hederick."

"I'm Tarscenian," the man said. "Let me invite you to supper, young Hederick." Tarscenian placed a strong arm about the boy's still trembling shoulders and guided him deeper into the grove, where a small campfire blazed cheerily. The fire popped as they approached, the sound Hederick had heard as he entered the copse. Tarscenian urged the boy to sit against a fallen log and handed him a wooden trencher. Three pieces of meat swam in greasy juice.

"You can dine like a theocrat on fresh roast rabbit," Tarscenian said, "and then tell me how in the name of the Lesser Pantheon you ended up alone in the middle of nowhere."

Soon Hederick had all but licked the trencher clean. The hare's picked bones blackened in the fire. Tarscenian lounged on a blanket across from the boy, watching with amazement. "Whatever you take on, lad, whether it's lynxes or supper, you certainly do it wholeheartedly," he commented.

Hederick bristled. The man had offered him dinner. What was he supposed to do—admire it until it congealed? The man laughed and held up his hand. "Calm down, lad. I mean you no insult. You showed more spirit in facing that she-lynx than many full-grown men would have."

Mollified, Hederick leaned back against the log, regarding his rescuer with awe. Tarscenian was a far cry from the men of Hederick's isolated home village of Garlund. The young man's eyes glittered with life, his gaze was direct, and his movements vigorous. If the god Tiolanthe ever took human form, he would look like Tarscenian, Hederick decided.

"So, Hederick, what were you doing alone on the prairie in the dark of night?" the stranger asked. "Assuming that you weren't hunting lynxes, that is."

Tarscenian listened with growing astonishment to the boy's story. Hederick told him about his mother and father, Venessi and Con, who, after walking for weeks due east from their home city of Caergoth, had founded the village of Garlund just south of Ancilla's Copse. Their purpose was to provide a place where they and their followers could worship Tiolanthe, the god that regularly appeared to Venessi and Con, but only to them. Then Hederick had been born, the first baby delivered in the new village.

Two years later, when Con disagreed with Venessi over some matter of Tiolanthean doctrine, Hederick's mother had ordered the people of the village to kill her husband. Hederick's sister Ancilla, fifteen years his senior, had fled Garlund moments after Con's death.

"She promised to return for me, but she never did," Hederick said simply.

Tarscenian interrupted only once—when the storm broke and the pair took shelter under oiled canvas stretched from tree to tree. Each sat wrapped in a gray woolen blanket that smelled of incense and horsehair. Hederick talked until he could barely put words together, he was so sleepy. "And now I've been banished," Hederick said, "by Venessi."

"Your mother sent a twelve-year-old into the prairie alone at night?" Tarscenian demanded with a frown.

"I must learn *humility,* she said," Hederick explained, his words slurring. "And then the lynx came after me, and I ran to the only place I could think of—Ancilla's Copse. This is where Ancilla hid when she left Garlund, when I was two."

"You must not remember very much about this sister," Tarscenian said sympathetically.

"Oh, no!" Hederick exclaimed, shaking himself awake. "I remember her well. She had eyes as green as grass, and she was pretty—oh, so pretty, Tarscenian. She knew all about plants and herbs and things, and when Con beat me for sinning, she would give me things to take away the pain. Ancilla was wonderful."

"But then she left."

Hederick's face fell, and he nodded. "She was afraid the villagers would kill her as they had killed our father. So she left. And then she forgot all about me. I . . . I guess I was too sinful to come back for."

He remembered the night before Ancilla had left. For some minor infraction, Con had beaten young Hederick mercilessly. Ancilla, achingly beautiful at seventeen, defended him and treated his wounds. Hederick had begged her to stay with him. "You won't ever stop being my sister, will you?" he'd cried.

"Close your eyes, little brother," Ancilla had answered, rocking him by the fire. The little boy, safe in the comfort of his sister's arms, resisted sleep. She murmured words Hederick had never heard before, tenderly stroking his face and wispy reddish-brown hair. She fed him cold tea from a spoon, and when he tried to speak again, covered his mouth with a gentle hand and hushed him.

Once she rearranged the blanket to cover Hederick's feet, then she spoke fiercely. "I promise you this, little Hederick: I will always be your sister. *I will never hurt you.* I will protect you with every power I have. I will do all I can, even from afar, to keep Con and Venessi from turning

11

you into . . . into what they are. You need never fear me. That I vow."

That memory was too holy to share with this stranger, however. And besides, Hederick was so tired; he felt himself sinking into sleep. Then Tarscenian's voice roused him.

"This village of yours, is it large?" the stranger asked. "Large and wealthy?"

Hederick shook himself awake. "Sixty people, maybe."

"Prosperous?" the man asked.

"Venessi has plenty of food stored in the barns, but the people don't know that. They're restricted to two meals a day. No one in the village is well-fed except my mother, but *she's* in Tiolanthe's graces. Other than the food, there's nothing but a few candlesticks in the prayer house, and some icons."

"Steel icons?" Tarscenian asked quickly. Since the Cataclysm, steel had been the most precious metal on Krynn.

Hederick nodded. Tarscenian didn't speak for a while, and Hederick thought he'd fallen asleep. The boy had nearly followed suit when the man's deep voice resounded again.

"Lad," he said, "I believe it's time for me to rest in my travels. And it's time the people of Garlund learn about some new gods."

Hederick jerked upright, bumping the oiled canvas and sending a splash of cold water down his left leg. "New gods?"

Tarscenian smiled impishly and extended his blanket to cover the boy's soaked leg. "You've not asked me about myself, lad."

The man had rescued Hederick from a lynx and given him dinner . . . and listened to his long tales. Wasn't that enough to know about someone? "You're a trader," Hederick said. "Or a mercenary."

"I'm a Seeker priest."

A priest! Hederick struggled to his knees. The blankets snared him around the ankles, and he tore at them with clumsy fingers. He didn't know what a Seeker was, but no matter. The man was a heathen and a priest!

"I speak for the New Gods, son."

"No!" Hederick shouted angrily, feeling betrayed by the man he'd begun to think of as a hero. "There is only one god. The Old Gods deserted us in the Cataclysm, and every god since then is just pretend, except for Tiolanthe. He speaks to my mother. And I'm not your son, you fraud." Tears streamed down his cheeks.

Tarscenian carefully gauged the boy's heated denial. Some of the friendliness left the gray eyes. "Who do you think saved us from the she-lynx, Hederick? Who frightened her off . . . me? You and your clods of moss? Some higher power? Or this Tiolanthe—while we're speaking of frauds?"

Hederick refused to look at him. "You did," he said sulkily. "You had the sword."

Tarscenian cocked his head. "My blade never touched the lynx, son. And what about the explosions?"

Hederick had no answer.

Tarscenian's hand locked around the boy's thin wrist, pulling him near. "The New Gods interceded, Hederick," the priest said gently. "Can your mother do that, by calling on her god? Can this Tiolanthe himself, for that matter?"

"N-no," Hederick mumbled.

"Well, then, perhaps the New Gods have a plan for you, son." Tarscenian's voice grew insinuating. "Perhaps I'm a part of that plan. Who are we to question the will of the gods?"

Hederick risked an upward glance. Tarscenian's gray eyes were direct; the friendliness was back. And yet . . . "What do you take me for, a fool?" Hederick exclaimed suddenly. "I'm no part of a plan. . . ." He crawled out from under the canvas. Tarscenian surprised him by letting him go.

Rain lashed at the boy, and in moments he was soaked. A few steps away, the campfire still flickered under a scrap of suspended canvas, but Hederick was determined not to return to Tarscenian's sanctuary. Lightning erupted. Thunder crashed through the trees.

"Where will you go, lad?"

"Home!" Hederick said desperately. "My . . . my mother will be worrying about me in this storm."

Tarscenian said nothing for a few moments. Hederick's words hung between them. "From the sounds of it, lad, your mother worries about no one but herself," the Seeker priest finally said. "She'll not take you back if you return to Garlund so soon, you know. She wants you to suffer. You're being made an example. She craves the power, and you're a threat to her. None of the other villagers has the spunk to take her on, is my guess."

"She's my mother," Hederick whispered. "You've never met her. What would you know?"

The priest laughed. "I've met hundreds like your mother, Hederick—men as well as women. I'm a priest. I run into all sorts of troubled souls who think they've reinvented the gods." He sighed, then failed to suppress a yawn. "I'll take you home in the morning, Hederick. I believe I can make things right with your mother. Why not trust me, at least for now? I'd hardly snatch you from a lynx's jaws to devour you myself, son."

Still Hederick hesitated. "You'll take me back?" He imagined the villagers' faces when he strode back into Garlund with this sword-wielding, towering heretic. "Tomorrow?"

"If you wish."

Hederick crouched to peer under the wide canopy. The rain streamed down his back. "Early?"

"At dawn, if you want." A smile creased Tarscenian's

face. "Lad, I'm bone-weary. I walked many miles today. I did battle with a giant cat and, what's far more daunting, locked horns with a stubborn twelve-year-old. The New Gods will watch over us tonight, Hederick. I must sleep now, son, and I won't be able to if I must worry about you wandering off in the rain. You'll be prey to every creature and lung ailment on the prairie." He yawned hugely. "Make your choice, lad. Truce?"

"All right," Hederick finally said. "But I'll listen to nothing more about New Gods."

"For the night, anyway. Good enough."

Hederick crawled back into the shelter, dribbling rainwater like a sodden kitten. Stripping off his wet clothes, he accepted Tarscenian's spare shirt, so huge that the sleeves fell past his fingertips. Dry again, Hederick curled up in his blanket. The priest, already snoring, exuded heat like a hearth even though he'd relinquished both blankets.

Hederick was asleep in seconds.

* * * * *

The boy saw Garlund as though through Tarscenian's eyes as they approached it early the next day, Hederick perched on the big man's shoulders. The village rose from the lush prairie like an abscess. Hungry-looking people stared from windows and doorways.

Venessi appeared in the square and halted, struck as dumb by this towering visitor as the common villagers were. She made a gesture for the stranger to halt, and Hederick suddenly realized how short his mother was. Of course, he told himself, wouldn't fate enjoy the joke of him, the son, taking after tiny Venessi, whereas Ancilla had inherited Con's height, strength, and good looks?

Venessi's faded blond hair, cropped just below her ears, waved in uncertain curls around her round face. Her eyes, which appeared green in some light, were frigid blue in the early morning. Hederick saw in Venessi's face the same round nose and protruding eyes that he bore.

"That's your mother?" the priest asked beneath his breath. "The round one with the nervous hands?"

"That's her."

"*I'd* certainly not take her on unarmed," Tarscenian said *sotto voce*.

Hederick waited for Venessi to order the attack. Could even a man such as Tarscenian stand long against the united villagers? The priest had spent a few moments earlier in special prayer, muttering rhymes and tracing figures on the ground with colored sand. He seemed to think that would evoke his Seeker gods to protect him. But Hederick pulled at the stranger's hair. "Tarscenian, maybe we should . . ."

"Hush, lad. I'm well-armed, and with more than a sword."

Tarscenian's pack was too small to hold more than food, bedroll, and perhaps a small hand weapon or two. "A knife?"

"Ah, you disappoint me. I am a priest; I have my gods at my back. Follow my lead." Tarscenian's head swung to the left. "That's the building where the precious icons are stored? The stone-and-daub hovel?"

"The prayer house."

"It is locked?"

"Only from the inside, when someone is within. It's for the use of the common folk. Mother prays in her own house."

The priest grunted. Then the convivial Tarscenian of the night before was back.

"Greetings, people of Garlund!" he boomed. "I bring you joyous news! I am Tarscenian, Seeker priest. I have news of wondrous gods who can ease your lives of strife and trouble and promise you immortality!

"What a splendid community, and what pious residents. I am fortunate to have the opportunity to visit with you and bring you the word of the New Gods."

"Stranger," Venessi said coldly, "you are not welcome here. Nor is this *boy*."

Tarscenian stepped back as if slapped. Anger colored his face. "You are Venessi—the one who dared to banish this brave lad? This boy who last evening helped me beat off a deadly predator thrice his size? Truly he walks in the grace of the New Gods—yet you reward him with banishment? Don't you care about your soul, Venessi?"

Tarscenian stood taller. His voice was so deep that it growled like thunder. "Have you no idea how much you—and these poor folk who have followed you in innocent trust—have sinned in the eyes of the New Gods? Do you intend to make that sin even greater?"

"*Kill them*," Venessi snarled to the villagers.

Hederick closed his eyes. Certainly Tarscenian could not hold off so many armed villagers. No doubt the priest was afraid—he was mumbling distractedly. The villagers had formed a ring around Tarscenian, Hederick, and Venessi, but they had not yet made their move. Hesitantly, Hederick opened his eyes again.

"Kill them!" Venessi screamed. "Tiolanthe orders it!"

The men and women shuffled their feet. They exchanged nervous looks, yet none dared act. When the Seeker priest finally spoke, his voice was gentle. "Good people of Garlund, has Venessi ever shown you a sign from this supposed god, Tiolanthe?"

No answer came from the villagers, but Venessi shouted, "I order you to slay them!"

Tarscenian ignored her. "Has this Tiolanthe appeared to any of you? Has he given you a personal sign of his regard? Have you any evidence that he is more than this deluded woman's imagination?"

Furtive looks passed between husbands and wives. Venessi's face grew livid in her rage. "Begone, stranger!"

she shrieked. "And take that sinner of a boy with you."

"I challenge you, heretic," Tarscenian said, facing her anger with calm confidence. "My Seeker gods demand a duel. You speak for this Tiolanthe. Do you consent to a duel?"

Venessi, the paleness of her face giving way to mottled pink and red, gawked around the circle of villagers. "Garlunders, you are ensorceled!" she cried. "He is a witch! You have pledged your lives to me and my god!"

"I'm no witch, and no mage, either, Venessi," Tarscenian responded. "I am only a priest for the *real* gods. Do you accept my challenge? My gods will act through me, yours through you. Or would you prefer to concede defeat now and allow these poor folk to begin working immediately to save their tarnished souls?"

"Tiolanthe, destroy him!" Venessi raised her fleshy arms, then gestured toward Tarscenian with a flourish. *"Destroy them both!"*

The observers took in a breath and held it—all but Tarscenian. He cocked his head like a bird viewing the curious movements of an insect. After a time, Venessi lowered her arms and smoothed her dress. She looked flushed but stubborn. "My god speaks when he chooses, not when heretics demand," she said primly.

Tarscenian set Hederick upon the ground without comment. The priest held his hands skyward and shouted, "Omalthea the Motherlord! Sauvay of the blessed revenge! Cadithal, Ferae, Zeshun! Bring hope to this village! The people here long to know you, to feel your approbation. If you are loving gods, give them the sign they so desperately need!" He swung his hands down and out to the sides.

Fire danced around him in a ring, leaping between him and the watchers. "Show them your power!" Tarscenian demanded. "Show them that you, *unlike their false god*, are not afraid to demonstrate your force to those who would believe." The fire ebbed and surged. Then it vaulted over the heads of the people and encircled them. Flame crackled.

Tarscenian gestured, and the blaze died. "The Seeker gods are prepared to accept you, people of Garlund. Renounce this false deity."

"No!" Sweat beaded Venessi's red face as she hurled a desperate warning at the villagers. "This is a test, you fools! Can't you see that as soon as you accept this cheat's words, you are through? Has my work been for naught? Have you learned nothing?"

The people seemed barely to hear her. Tarscenian said quietly, "My New Gods have provided further proof, Garlunders. Open your storehouses. At my words, they are full."

"But they are empty," one man faltered. "We've been rationing. . . ."

"No longer. Seeker gods provide for *their* faithful. Open your storehouses, people of Garlund. Behold your new riches."

Venessi's eyes bulged, and she made a choking sound. As always when she was having a vision, she fell to her knees and groveled in the dust. "Tiolanthe, help me!" she cried.

But this time, the villagers paid her no heed. They plucked the keys from her waist, unlocked the swinging doors of the storehouses, and gaped at enough food to feed the village ten times over.

"Praise the New Gods!" cried one scrawny woman. The crowd cheered and surged forward, filling their arms, aprons, and pockets with much-needed foodstuffs.

Tarscenian directed his next words to Venessi. His gray eyes were sympathetic. "You may keep your house, Venessi. I will take up residence in the prayer house. My duty is to tutor the villagers in the true religion. Especially brave, wise Hederick." He patted the boy's shoulder.

"Hederick will be released from field work. He is too frail for coarse labor, anyway. His talents are more cerebral. He will be my assistant."

Venessi watched with eyes like stones. Silently swearing retribution on the evil child who had brought about her downfall, she returned to her house. She remained there, closeted behind locked doors, for four days, while the grateful Garlunders feasted and celebrated.

* * * * *

". . . and Sauvay, Zeshun, Cadithal, Ferae, and Omalthea," Hederick finished, anxiously watching Tarscenian's face for sign of approval.

The priest nodded. "You're a quick learner, son—you know both pantheons and their histories by heart, and your prayers are wonders of rhetoric. Your gift of words will stand you in good stead, should you ever consider joining the priestly orders." Tarscenian reached for a wooden tray that held a half-eaten loaf of bread and a porcelain tub filled with soft butter. "Another portion of this blessed bread?" he asked.

Hederick nodded eagerly, grateful for the words of praise and the attention he received from Tarscenian. The boy, who had seldom known kindness before the arrival of the Seeker priest, had become the man's near-constant attendant, caring for his quarters and assisting him at the services the villagers willingly attended.

The priest had transformed the dilapidated prayer house into a home. A braided rug concealed the dirt floor, and long, flat cushions lay on the pair of benches. A tile-topped table held the tray and bread. A brazier heated the room, for the temperature grew brisk at night, although the days were still stifling. Tarscenian led daily worship just outside the prayer house, much as Con had years ago, but Tarscenian's performances lacked Con's wrath and threats of doom, holding instead the promise of full bellies and better times.

If Tarscenian were the messenger of gods, he was the most genial messenger the village had seen. Certainly, he lectured on sin and redemption, but he also instructed the villagers on how to brew ale and urged them to drink it with each meal. It was a gift from the New Gods to aid the digestion, he said. He sang songs until the shutters rattled. And he drew children to him with the enthusiasm of his embraces and the freedom with which he dispensed sweets from the deep pockets of his brown robe.

In addition, he ordered one of the villagers, Jeniv Synd, to make Hederick some new leggings and a loose overshirt with decorations of embroidery and shiny stones, endearing himself even further to the impressionable boy.

And Tarscenian performed miracles daily—innocent-looking tricks that ended in a scarlet explosion or in a rabbit appearing in his cupped hands. He told villagers these miracles were signs that the Seeker gods approved of the Garlunders.

One way to impress the Seeker gods, Tarscenian reminded everyone, was to be generous with the religion's holy men and women. As gifts began to pile up in the prayer house, Hederick grew worried. He had nothing to give of his own but his new clothes.

Tarscenian ordered feasts held regularly to fete the New Gods. For the first time, the people of the village began to lose their gaunt appearance. Yet not all the villagers, it seemed, were happy. Those who had been favorites of Venessi would grumble whenever Tarscenian was out of earshot.

"It's not right," Jeniv Synd told her friend, Kel'ta, as they watched Tarscenian lead evening services one night. Hederick, leaning against the side of his mother's house, out of sight of the two women, caught the words.

Kel'ta nodded at Jeniv. "Lady Venessi kneels in prayer

from dawn to dusk. She never wavers in her faith. She is a true holy woman."

"This Tarscenian says she is a fake, but he suffers her to remain in Garlund," Jeniv muttered. "Were she seer of a false god, wouldn't he expel her? Her holiness rebukes his tricks and lies."

Hederick started to speak out in indignation, then thought better of it. There were other ways to deal with those who spoke against Tarscenian and the New Gods. That night at midnight, when even Venessi had left off praying and retired, he sneaked out of the village and, by the light of the moons, dug in the prairie soil. Even after ten years, Hederick could remember Ancilla's voice as she held a bulb before his face and warned, "Never, *never* eat this, Hederick. It looks like an onion, but it is poison. It's the macaba bulb. Don't even touch it!" Her injunction had lingered all these years. Now Hederick had need of this poison bulb.

He made little sound as he crept into the Synd house, keeping to the deepest shadows. He went to the pantry and selected a jar of spice—a common one, but not too common. There was no hurry. It would be eaten eventually. It would be easier to maintain an air of innocence if Hederick did not know exactly when death would strike.

The next day, Tarscenian ordered two huge wagons built. Four men headed west a week later to sell the best of Garlund's wares in Caergoth. "The harvest is fast upon us," the priest said over the protests of Venessi's dwindling band of supporters. "We'll refill the storehouses. Garlund needs money, and it is time that the village gave to the Seeker church. I ordered the men to present half the proceeds to the church in Caergoth."

The dust from the pair of wagons had no sooner settled on the horizon than a scream came from the central village. Jeniv's friend, Kel'ta, stood in the doorway of the Synd house and bellowed until her face was ruddy. "Jeniv is dead!"

Jeniv's husband, Santrev, pushed past Kel'ta and rushed to his wife's side. Jeniv's body was contorted, her face twisted beneath tangled blond hair. The skin about her mouth was discolored, as though flames had touched her lips. Venessi shoved past them all, fell to her knees, and began to pray to Tiolanthe. Half the crowd joined her; the other half gawked and exclaimed.

Tarscenian touched Kel'ta's shoulder. "What happened?" he asked.

"I don't know," she wailed, and pulled away. "We spent the morning at my house, gardening. Then Jeniv went home to prepare lunch. I came to borrow eggs and found her like this." Kel'ta broke into fresh tears.

Tarscenian cleared everyone away but Venessi, Santrev Synd, and Hederick. He intoned the Seekers' Prayer of the Passing Spirit. "Great Omalthea, accept the commitment of this guiltless soul. Gather her to your breast and comfort her. Jeniv Synd is free of the pain of this world. Comfort her loved ones, and help us remember that we, too, await this fate. Gather this soul and make ready for all others to follow. *For there ever will be more.*"

Hederick sat frozen as he contemplated Tarscenian's words. What could the prayer be but a secret command to him to do more?

The Seeker priest must be aware of the sacrifice Hederick had made—knew he had taken the life of one of the enemies of the New Gods—and clearly approved! What could the last lines of his prayer be but an order to continue to silence those who would oppose the priest?

"I hear," Hederick whispered. "I shall prevail."

Tarscenian looked penetratingly at him but said nothing.

Santrev Synd died in twisted agony that very night. The villagers gathered in the central square as Tarscenian laid a torch to the double funeral pyre the next afternoon. At the same time, Hederick made his way surreptitiously into the Synd home, retrieved the spice containing the poison, and moved it to the pantry of Jeniv's friend Kel'ta, next door. Then he went back and tipped over the remembrance lamp that burned upon the Synds' kitchen table.

"Fire purifies," Hederick whispered, watching the growing flames as though hypnotized. "So says the *Praxis*." Smoke from the new blaze rose into the skies to mingle with that of the pyre, so no one noticed the flames for some time.

No one saw or suspected Hederick. "Thus the New Gods protect their own," he told himself righteously.

After the funeral, life continued almost as it had since Tarscenian's arrival. The priest—when he wasn't eating and drinking or leading worship sessions—told stories and sang loud songs about redemption and glory and freedom from sin. He continued to lead Hederick in study several hours a day, praising the boy for his diligence and encouraging him in his labors.

A week after the Synd funeral, he and Hederick sat alone on the thick rug of the prayer house. Tarscenian regarded the boy with thoughtful gray eyes. "Have you considered taking priestly orders, son?"

For the past weeks, the boy had thought of little else. The magnificent Tarscenian was only ten years older than Hederick. He'd been a wandering priest since he was fifteen, and Hederick was nearly thirteen.

The priest offered a piece of bread to the boy, a dollop of butter plopping onto the braided rug. "It's a good life. There are no ties but those to your gods. You wander freely, bringing words of joy to people who need them. The people feed and house you. There's much to recommend this life."

The priest stroked the steel candlesticks. "As a Seeker priest, you bring them hope and a chance for a future. Do you realize the people of Krynn are worshiping hundreds of 'gods' now that the Old Gods are gone? And all these new ones are fakes, lad! All but the Seeker gods." He wiped his mouth and continued. "Imagine: I, a mere cooper's son, could bring thousands of souls to Omalthea and her pantheons!"

The great Tarscenian, son of a barrel-maker? Certainly Hederick, son of visionaries, could do much better.

Tarscenian leaned closer until Hederick could see flecks of dark green in his eyes. "You could lead people, Hederick. You have the insight needed for the Seeker priesthood. Imagine it, lad!"

Hederick saw himself robed like Tarscenian—only more richly—standing before scores of people, looking down upon them as he bestowed a blessing. "You would show me the secrets of the miracles?" Hederick asked. "The explosions? The fire?"

Tarscenian caught the boy's astute stare. "You know that they are my work? And you still believe?"

"Your 'miracles' help the people believe in the New Gods," Hederick whispered reverently. "The New Gods *are* the truth. Therefore, anything done to further their cause cannot be a lie." Fervor warmed him. "How we compel people to turn to the New Gods doesn't matter, I think. What does matter is that they *do* turn. It is their ultimate salvation. I would commit any number of crimes to ensure that!"

The priest put a hand on Hederick's shoulder. "You speak like a much older and wiser man," he said. "There are miracles that only Seeker priests can perform, and the demonstrations with the red and yellow fire are of that sort. I will show you all these things, and more. You will do the priesthood proud, Hederick."

"I'm invited?"

Tarscenian nodded.

Hederick cleared his throat. "I have no wealth to give," he stammered.

Tarscenian shrugged. "You have considerable talents. I have seen you use them."

He knew, then, about the poison? "And . . . that is acceptable?"

Tarscenian's brow wrinkled. His voice grew curt. "Of course, Hederick. Not everyone has material wealth to share with us. Some people's gifts must take other forms."

"I *have* begun to use these talents," Hederick admitted. "You approve of my . . . gifts to the faith, then?"

A bushy eyebrow curved upward. "Of course, Hederick."

Hederick raised a silent prayer of thanks to Omalthea, Sauvay, and the rest.

At that moment, a cry went up outside.

The villagers had found Kel'ta's body.

* * * * *

Upon Tarscenian's orders, the villagers dined in the square to honor Kel'ta's passing. Once again roast prairie pheasant, stuffed with sage, disappeared from fired-clay platters as though it had taken flight. With it went golden squash dotted with honey, thick bread slathered with butter, and streams of fresh milk. Despite the funereal aspect of the adults, some of the children chattered and played.

Seated at the table in their cleanest work clothes, the men paused often to gaze reverently at Tarscenian. He occupied a grand chair at the head of tables that were spread with cloths newly embroidered with Seeker symbols. He'd given up his travel-stained brown robe for a new one of fine linen, lovingly stitched by one of the women.

Venessi had been coaxed from her house for the funeral and dinner. Tarscenian sat next to her but paid scant attention to her. The rest of the villagers did the same. Venessi's champions had been silenced. Hederick's mother looked so forlorn that the boy went over next to her, taking a free chair on the side away from Tarscenian. She didn't look at him, even when Hederick touched her hand. Her gaze seemed never to leave her lap. She picked at her cold pheasant and sipped a glass of wine without seeming to care.

"Mother?" Hederick whispered.

"Leave me alone," she answered vehemently. "This is all your fault. You and your evil nature."

"Mother, you are just being stubborn."

"You have abandoned Tiolanthe. You brought this infidel here."

Hederick patted her hand and imitated Tarscenian's tone. "You were mistaken about Tiolanthe, Mother. But you have another chance, thanks to Tarscenian. Surely Omalthea will forgive you if you beg her understanding."

Her head came up. "Forgive me? *Forgive me?* I should seek forgiveness from a goddess who does not exist?"

Hederick's breath caught. Her eyes held horror and hate. "Heathen boy!" she whispered, and caught his arm with a clawlike hand.

Just then a sound came from the far end of the table. A ripple of started exclamations made its way through the villagers. One man stood up, knocking his chair over, and froze. "You—" he choked out.

Hederick's gaze went to Tarscenian's face. The priest's expression flashed from thoughtful to surprised to panic-stricken, then to awestruck. It's like he's seen a real god, Hederick thought. The boy swiveled toward the foot of the table.

Tarscenian was right. A goddess had appeared in Garlund.

Her grass-green eyes glittered like the wings of a dragonfly. Her hair, the hue of ripe wheat, curled and swirled around her head like a mass of golden snakes. She wore a robe, but not of the indigo or gray homespun type favored by the Garlund women. This was pure white, made of some slippery-looking material that Hederick later learned was silk. Turquoise and green stitching glittered at the neck and wrists. A twisted silken rope the color of a summer cloud cinched the robe at her slender waist and fell to tassels at her ankles.

Then Hederick knew her.

It was Ancilla.

Chapter 2

Hederick's sister was nearly thirty, but she looked young and ravishing. Slender fingers curved around the gnarled head of a worn wooden staff.

Struck dumb, the villagers studied her.

" 'Cilla?" Hederick finally whispered. The murmur resounded like a shout.

She closed her eyes, moved her lips in soundless words, then turned and looked at him. Her wide mouth parted in a familiar smile.

"I told you I'd come back for you, Hederick," she said softly. "I surely had not expected that my little brother would become a man while I was gone."

As Ancilla glided toward him, Venessi's nails dug into his arm. Hederick sat motionless and did not move to grasp Ancilla's proffered hand.

Tarscenian cleared his throat, half stood up, and spoke rustily. "You're Ancilla, I gather." He spoke his own name. "I am a Seeker priest."

Hederick's sister turned cold green eyes his way, but she had no time to reply. Venessi found her voice at that moment. Some of the old imperiousness returned as she snapped, "She's a witch, Tarscenian! I condemned her years ago. Send her away. She's evil."

Annoyance crossed Tarscenian's handsome face. He towered over Venessi. "Madam, this woman is your daughter. You seem to make a bad habit of casting off your children."

Venessi gestured excitedly. "She uses magic. Look at her! Is that the garb of a righteous woman?"

Tarscenian stared at Ancilla like a thirsting man gazing at a spring. "Perhaps," he finally said. The rumble returned to his voice. "Venessi, you are tolerated here solely because you are Hederick's mother. Be silent."

Venessi cast Ancilla a glance of pure hate and drove her nails deeper into Hederick's arm.

Ancilla had been watching Tarscenian all the while. "I could destroy you easily, you know," she said to him. "Your powers are nothing next to mine."

Tarscenian appeared unimpressed. "Your white robe tells me you're aligned with good. From what I've studied, such a one would not kill blindly. And I *do* have my gods to protect me, Ancilla."

They locked stares for what seemed an eternity. "The Seekers are misguided," she said.

"There's always that possibility, with humans."

"The Seeker gods are myths."

"Plenty of people believe in them, Ancilla."

"I have seen many like you," she said quietly. "You offer poor folk hope, and then you abandon them. You glean them of everything of worldly value. They never realize it until you are gone. You are a charlatan."

"People with hope are not poor."

"But the hope is vacant!" Ancilla cried. Her green eyes flashed. "There are no Seeker gods!"

"*I* believe in them," Tarscenian repeated.

"Of course," Ancilla shot back. "They're making you rich, 'priest.' "

The villagers watched, fascinated, their common minds comprehending little of the argument. They knew, though, that a condemned witch challenged their holy man, and it ought to be only a matter of moments before Omalthea herself would rise and slaughter the sorceress.

"And *your* gods, Ancilla?" Tarscenian demanded. "Where are they while the world's spirit starves? Your Old Gods are the ultimate cause of this misery." Ancilla said nothing. Tarscenian added, softly, "Are you a mage?"

"I am." Her chin was high and proud. "I studied for ten years and have at long last passed the Test."

"The Test!" a woman whispered. Villagers gasped.

"Kill her!" another woman shouted, and others, encouraged by Venessi, took up the call.

Tarscenian silenced them with an imperious gesture. "This woman is under my protection—at the moment." He ignored Ancilla's faint laugh.

"Ancilla," he went on, "you wear the white robe openly. Such an outfit would cost you your life in most towns these days. Like the Knights of Solamnia, the mages of Krynn broke their promise to save the world from the Cataclysm. The people have plenty of reason to avenge that betrayal. Most mages are more circumspect nowadays."

Ancilla's pale brows rose over green eyes. "Your point?"

"Why are you here, Ancilla?"

"I might as well ask you that."

Gray eyes locked with green. Venessi's hand was so tight on Hederick's arm that blood trickled from half-moon cuts where her nails had broken the skin. He noticed it dimly, as though it were the blood of someone else.

Ancilla stretched out her right hand; a mixture of blue dust and herbs lay in a small pile on her palm. *"Bhazam illorian, sa oth od setherat,"* she whispered. She closed her hand, then reopened it. The powder was gone. Instead, a perfect dragon sat immobile, the slender shaft of a lance seeming to grow right out of its body. Speckles of light glittered from colorless gemstones that covered its back. At first Hederick thought the ruby-eyed figure was a statue, but then it shifted position, unfolded papery wings, and looked around.

Ancilla whispered and repeated the movements with her left hand. A tiny replica of Tarscenian, half the size of the dragon, appeared on her palm. It drew a sword the size of a sliver—far shorter than the dragon's lance. The little dragon glimpsed the figure, screeched, and leaped into the air, hurtling toward the Tarscenian figure with talons outstretched.

"No, Ancilla!" Hederick cried out.

"Bhazak cirik," Ancilla said immediately. Both figures vanished. She gazed at him. Compassion shone in her eyes, but thwarted power was apparent, too. "You protect this 'priest,' Hederick? What has happened to change you?"

Hederick wrenched his arm away from Venessi. "Tarscenian saved my life." Briefly he told her of the lynx and all that had happened since Tarscenian had come to Garlund. "He's been teaching us about the Seeker gods. I . . . I *want* to learn from him, 'Cilla."

"But I came back for you, Hederick," Ancilla reminded him. "I've dreamed of this day. I will instruct you in the true ways. My gods, unlike this phony priest's, are real. Get your things, Hederick."

The temptation to escape Garlund was strong, especially when Hederick felt Venessi's hand clamp down on his arm again. But Ancilla had been away too long. Hederick had found a new champion, and Ancilla had maligned that champion. "I want to study with Tarscenian," he said stubbornly. Hederick heard the Seeker priest expel a long sigh. Again Hederick shook off Venessi's grip. "He has much to teach me."

Ancilla stayed silent for a moment. Her gaze flicked from her brother to Tarscenian. She ignored Venessi. "No doubt he does," his sister whispered at last. "This warrants some prayer. I'll be in the copse, Hederick, if you change your mind."

Ancilla turned. Her robe swirled like white wings. "People of Garlund, heed me," she cried. "Know that I will set wards around the copse. Do not attempt to interfere with me if you value your safety."

"Witch!" one man exploded. He hurled a beer-filled mug at her head. She raised a hand. "*Esherat!*" The flagon crashed into an invisible barrier and shattered. Shards of glass clattered around her but never touched her.

Then Ancilla shrugged. "Mage, witch, whatever. I use magic. But I use it for good."

"Good as *you* see it, witch!" the man shouted.

Ancilla looked surprised. "Certainly. What on Krynn did you expect?" She clapped her hands and, with a whispered command, vanished in a swirl of silver snow. At the same moment, a puff of glitter appeared in the air above the copse, then drifted into the trees.

The villagers were quiet for a moment. Then chatter and oaths filled the air. "Shall we go after her, priest?" shouted the man who'd thrown the mug. "Surely if we all . . ."

Venessi cried, "Kill the witch!" She half stood, hands clenched in fists, leaning over the table like a fat hen.

"Ancilla has harmed no one," Tarscenian stated firmly. "And don't forget that she is of this village, too. She is still your kinswoman."

"But the dragon! The figure of you!"

Tarscenian snorted, but his face was unusually pale. "Illusion. Any sleight-of-hand artist could do it. *Sedelon talimen overart calo.*" The priest opened his hand. A tiny dragon and miniature Tarscenian lounged together in his palm. They were statues, not moving figures. The priest closed his hand and reopened it, and they were gone.

* * * * *

Nothing more was heard of Ancilla, although none of the villagers could forebear occasional worried glances toward the copse in the distance. Two days later, in the depths of the night, Hederick went to Tarscenian's prayer house to speak with him and found the Seeker shrine empty. The same occurred the next night, and the next, and several more nights after that. Perhaps, the boy conjectured, Tarscenian went onto the prairie to pray at night. He was back in Garlund each day, however.

To silence his growing disquiet about the man he'd grown to idolize, and to appease the gods he'd grown to revere, Hederick doubled his efforts to ferret out blasphemy. He'd become experienced in entering houses without making a sound. Since the deaths of Kel'ta and the Synds, some Garlunders had developed the caution of locking their doors at night. But Hederick was small enough to wriggle through windows and openings that they never thought to block.

He mixed the macaba poison with ordinary basil or lemonwort stores. The stuff was nearly tasteless. The afflicted sinner would not detect it until it was too late, when he or she would suddenly go into violent paroxysms that allowed only a moment's conscious thought, spent most often on a desperate denial of death. Just a small amount of macaba would kill a victim, and the poison extinguished life so quickly that the sinner had no time to voice alarm.

It was perfect.

Four more people died that week. The villagers laid the blame on the witch, unseen since her arrival nearly a week before. For the moment, though, they feared her too much to assault her sanctuary.

Hederick continued his campaign of righteousness every night, sleeping only a few hours before each dawn. During the day, with Tarscenian, he studied Seeker creed and old Seeker parchments such as the *Praxis*. Each day thus found him newly aware of some fresh sin that the New Gods had as much as ordered him to stamp out. The villagers blithely violated divine laws—*laws*—as though they were mere suggestions on the part of jovial, indulgent gods.

Hederick asserted as much to Tarscenian one day. "Look at Frideline Bacque," the boy said. "Just yesterday I saw her mix up a paste of oatmeal, cornmeal, and milk and apply it to her face to lighten her freckles. This she does although the *Praxis*, right here, declares bodily vanity a sin."

He waited for the priest to leap to his feet and rush to confront the village woman, but Tarscenian only shrugged. "Hederick, she's nearly forty. She's only trying to win the heart of Peren Volen. If it's a sin, it's a harmless one. Anyway, I doubt Frideline has even heard of this particular passage in the *Praxis*. Few in this village can read, and I've not gotten to that passage yet in evening devotions."

"That's an excuse?" Hederick raised his voice. "She's violating Seeker law! And isn't Peren Volen also to be chastised for enjoying the lengths to which Frideline goes to draw his attention? The whole village is laughing about it. Isn't *every* holy rule important? And what is a 'harmless sin,' anyway, Tarscenian?" Hederick was so overwrought that he had to pause for breath. His reddish brown hair was damp with sweat.

The skin beneath the priest's eyes was translucent and creased, his eyes bloodshot. Tarscenian sighed and took a sip of the mead that had been his near-constant companion since Ancilla had arrived.

"Hederick," the Seeker priest said sadly, "it occurs to me that all the words of the *Praxis* cannot be equally important—or equally true. The document is hundreds of years old, lad. It's been copied many times by clerics of varying skill. How easy it would be for errors or misconceptions to creep in!"

"Errors? In the *Praxis*?" Hederick's voice cracked. "You dare say that?"

Tarscenian's eyelids drooped. "I'm tired, lad. You always were one for rattling on unabated. Leave me."

Hederick pressed on, pulse racing. "But how could the New Gods permit errors to form in the *Praxis*, Tarscenian? Are you saying the gods are fallible? If the Seeker gods don't guard each word of their holy parchments, how am I, a beginner, to know if a particular phrase is correct or not? You *must* be wrong."

Hederick sat bolt upright and reached for the priest's sleeve. "Is this a trial of my faith? You're testing me, aren't you?" Hederick gazed hopefully at Tarscenian. It would be just like the priest to see how angry he could make Hederick, to measure his devotion to the Seekers. Hederick waited for Tarscenian to grin and slap him on the back.

But the priest only drained the rest of his mug.

"Tarscenian?"

"Leave me!" The priest refilled his mug, splashing mead on the rug. Tarscenian ignored the stain, although Seeker law clearly declared that one should maintain discipline in one's surroundings as strictly as in one's thoughts and emotions.

"The *Praxis* advises caution in the use of spirits," Hederick remonstrated.

"That's for those of lesser standing," Tarscenian snapped. "The *Praxis* also orders us not to wear certain types of wool in certain seasons, which strikes me as something the New Gods, *if* they ever existed, shouldn't be wasting their precious time worrying about."

"*If* the New Gods existed—?" Hederick's heart pounded until he thought he'd expire on the spot.

Tarscenian drained the mug nonchalantly. "Take the damned parchment and go elsewhere to study it, lad. Your yammering is giving me a headache of ogrelike proportions." He limped to a chair and slumped into it, his back to Hederick, facing the wall.

Feeling betrayed and hurt, Hederick blindly did as ordered. He spent the rest of the day behind the paddock, huddled over the parchment. He examined each word, seeking holy guidance, wanting any error to be his, not Tarscenian's. So deeply was he absorbed in his studies, he even ignored the call to supper.

Hederick found the passage about the wearing of wool, and rejoiced that the New Gods cared about each small detail of their devotees' lives. He reviewed the parts about glorification of the body over the mind, and concluded that Frideline and Peren—and most of the occupants of Garlund—had committed far more sins than he'd previously thought. He had great work before him.

Hederick probed the centuries-old, hand-lettered words of the *Praxis* until they swam before his eyes. Finally, just as the setting sun withdrew the last bit of light, he found a passage that both inspired and frightened him.

Allow not a caster of spells to live, the *Praxis* read. *Magic corrupts and infects. Magic derives from the old, betrayer gods. Magic defiles even the most faithful, if suffered to continue. Magic, and belief in its use, is evil. Those who seek the New Gods have no need for magic.*

Tarscenian had been different since Ancilla had arrived,

the boy thought as he remembered the priest's heavy drinking and irreverent words. Had Hederick's sister enchanted him from the very first? Hadn't she lured the priest, that first day, into using spellcasting, in the show of the dragon and human figurines? And didn't the witch hover like a rapacious bird within sight of Garlund even now? She'd spent ten years studying the arts of magic, ten years that should have been spent caring for him!

As though the thought came directly from Omalthea, Hederick suddenly knew where Tarscenian was spending his nights. Ancilla had tainted the priest. That meant Hederick was now the only true believer in a town of sinners. But what to do? Hederick vowed to pray until his gods sent him a sign of what course to take next.

And they did. A wondrous, holy, terrible sign.

* * * * *

It was past midnight in Garlund. For hours Hederick had been secreted in the grass on the prairie west of the village, praying to the New Gods and staring at the red moon until he could see it with his eyes closed.

At first he'd been conscious of every night whisper of the greenery around him. Prairie spiders, while only the size of his fist, built webs so strong and sticky that creatures as large as a dwarf had little chance of escape. Southlund ticks, while only the size of his thumb, could drain the blood from a grown deer in half a day, and they were fearfully difficult to dislodge. Earth elementals, disguised as hummocks, had been known to burst through the prairie soil and engulf whatever lay on the surface.

But some time passed, until all but one lamp in Garlund was extinguished. Hederick felt as though he were alone with the New Gods. The prairie still whispered, but no footfalls broke the night.

Then the last lamp—the one in Tarscenian's dwelling—

went out. A door creaked, and a tall figure staggered from the prayer house. Tarscenian paused and carefully surveyed the prairie in the direction of Ancilla's Copse, gazed upward briefly at the moon Lunitari, then headed north.

The boy watched him go, his heart numb with disillusionment. With the aid of magic, the witch had destroyed a devout priest in less than a week. Certainly the Seekers could not rise to any position of power in the world until they eradicated magic.

Perhaps Tarscenian's only purpose in life had been to bring Hederick to Seekerism. Now that purpose was fulfilled, and the Seeker gods had no more use for the priest. Perhaps he was like a dumb beast now, conscious only of hunger and thirst—and whatever base urge drove him toward the witch Ancilla in the dead of night.

Hederick marked the priest's passage across the prairie, and a voice within—straight from the pantheons, he knew—urged, *Follow.* There was no refusing. At times Hederick drew close to Tarscenian, but the once-alert swordsman suspected nothing. His hand never went to his blade. The tall, broad body moved like a dead man brought to life. Tarscenian's gaze had but one object now: the copse.

While they were still some distance from the trees, the inner voice advised Hederick, *Pause. Keep back from the witch. She has set wards. Pray.* Hederick sank to his knees.

Tarscenian went on alone.

"Omalthea," Hederick entreated, "send me a sign to tell me what you desire. In all of Garlund, I am the only one who is truly devout. Your priest has lost his faith. I know it is my destiny to continue without him. Please make me worthy, Divine One. Send me a sign."

Hederick's body ached down to his soul. He clenched his hands, pressed his teary eyelids shut, and bowed his head. He begged for Omalthea's grace and wisdom.

At that moment, the boy became aware of light. "By the New Gods!" he whispered.

This was more than mere illumination from Solinari and Lunitari: neither red nor silver-white moon was full enough to account for this growing brilliance. The luminescence, diffuse at first, soon concentrated on a rise directly in front of him. The light became a glowing column. Sparks of seafoam green, blue, and purple danced within. Roaring wind filled his ears. "Omalthea, be merciful!" he shrieked.

Was this a sign from the New Gods? Or had Ancilla detected him and brought down the force of her magic?

The smell of a forge assailed him. It brought more tears to his eyes, and Hederick fancied he could taste the tang of metal, heated nearly to liquid. His hair whipped in the gale. He could not see for sobbing. He threw himself facedown on the grass.

The wind changed to keening—banshees? The light, the sounds, the smell engulfed him, and Hederick could not stop shaking. "Ferae, daughter of the gods, come to my aid," Hederick begged. "Cadithal. Zeshun. Sauvay. Omalthea, please! I desire only to serve you. Don't slay—"

Then the roaring, the keening, the cries in the wind—all stopped.

Hederick lay, muscles jerking, in a circle of brilliance, bathed in heatless fire. His heart quavered in his chest. All warmth had fled his hands and feet.

Heddderrrick.

He could not open his eyes.

Heddderrrick.

He whimpered, sure he would be struck blind or mad if he lifted his head. He prayed that this was proof that he'd been ordained to greatness. But fear so paralyzed him that he could not raise himself from the crushed grass—not even to accept the mantle of exaltation.

Heddderrrick. I orrrder you to rrrise.

"I will die," Hederick whispered.

I hhhave plans for you. Yyyou mmmust be my priessst, Hed-ddderrrick. I hhhave need of you. Rrrise.

Hederick inhaled, then let out the breath slowly, trying to expel his fear. The gods were calling him, or were they? Was this what Venessi had felt when she experienced visions of Tiolanthe? It could not be the same; his mother was insane, prey to fertile imaginings.

This was certainly real.

He drew himself together, then stood in the circle of brightness.

Opennn your eyyyes.

Hederick obeyed.

At first the boy could make out only a rough shape before him. Then he saw a muscular torso that appeared to flow right from the prairie soil. Corded shoulders, draped with a gauze shirt, bore a proud head with flowing yellow hair. The jaw was broad, the mouth severe. A braided circlet of iridescent threads banded the god's forehead. Tiny bolts of gold and purple lightning radiated from the crown. Sparks rained down on Hederick, but still he felt only coldness.

Below the glittering crown, the eyes beamed fire. They looked straight at him.

Heddderrrick.

"My lord?" Hederick forced his voice low and steady. This being would not tolerate weakness; Hederick must not show any.

Yyyou knnnow mmme, thennn? That is good. Sssay mmmy nnname, Heddderrrick of Garlund. Greet me as I deservvve.

Warmth coursed through the boy. This magnificent being *approved* of him! "I honor and welcome you. You are Sauvay, supreme god of power and vengeance and Fatherlord of all the Lesser Pantheons."

Annnd ... ?

"Once consort to Omalthea, Motherlord of the Pantheons.

41

And father of the goddess Ferae."

Annnd nnnow demmmoted beneath mmmy own daughterrr, Heddderrrick. The fire in the heartless eyes burned brighter.

Hederick measured his words. "That is so."

Yyyou wwwill be my chief mmminion, Heddderrrick. You will ssserve me. For I ammm Sauvay, God of Vvvengeance, and yyyou have mmmuch to avenge, young Heddderrrick of Garlund.

"I?"

Mmmuch evvvil hhhas been done here in the nnname of fffalse rrrighteousness, Heddderrrick. Yyyou have begunnn to rrright those wrongs. I sssee and approve. You must continue. Escalate this hhholy wwwar. Dessstroy all sinners, if it takes until yyyour dying day.

"I will do as you order."

Yyyou mmmust destroy the witch in the treesss.

Hederick nodded readily. "And Tarscenian?"

The stench of molten metal thickened. Hederick's eyes watered. The wind sighed.

Hhhe wwwas a Seeker priessst, Heddderrrick. He hasss sinned the greatest sin. If Tarscenian were ssstrong in faith, Heddderrrick, magic wwwould have no hold on himmm. He hasss made hhhis choice. Know, Heddderrrick, that if yyyou are faithful, I will be at yyyour side alwaysss.

Hederick bowed. "I will do what you ask, my lord."

The being vanished.

* * * * *

Hederick plunged through the grass like an antelope, and within moments he was crouched by the copse. Birds chirped sleepily, though sunrise was still hours away. The boy's clothes grew uncomfortably damp with dew as he waited.

Hederick knew Sauvay was watching. He knew that when the time came to annihilate his sister and her traitorous lover, Sauvay would show himself in all his brilliance, and for a few moments, Sauvay's power would be Hederick's power.

Ancilla and Tarscenian would die.

There was no need for stealth. Hederick had Sauvay's protection.

"Ancilla! Tarscenian!" Hederick shouted into the leafy blackness.

Silence swallowed his words. No magical carnivorous being, no emissary of the undead, reached for him. Had the witch and the blasphemer sense enough to be frightened? Were they hiding? Hederick longed to stalk them as the lynx had pursued him months before, when he was only a boy of twelve. Now he was thirteen, practically a man, and a servant of the Seeker god of vengeance.

Something sparked before his eyes. A globe, scarlet and silver, the size of a forest puffball, hovered and sputtered, moving away, then back. It repeated the motion, the message clear: Hederick was to follow.

Either Sauvay or Ancilla could have sent the globe, but to Hederick it didn't matter. One was on his side, the other helpless before him.

Within moments, Hederick stood before a stone cottage—magically created, for there had been no building in the copse before—and the globe disappeared. The door stood open beneath the thatched roof, and lights gleamed within. "Ancilla!" Hederick shouted. "Tarscenian! Your wards are powerless before me!"

Ancilla's warm voice flowed from the doorway. "Did you think I would set wards against my little brother? After I worked so long to come back to free him?" She appeared in the doorway, silhouetted in the orange light from the fireplace. "The wards were for the people of the village."

"But not Tarscenian?" Hederick's voice filled with contempt.

"Tarscenian did not come to the copse to do me harm. He came to learn." She stood aside. The firelight glinted on the embroidery of her white robe and on her curly cascades of pale hair. "Come inside, Brother. We have much to discuss, the three of us."

Tarscenian sat cross-legged on the floor before the fireplace. He didn't look up as Hederick entered. Instead, the priest's gaze seemed riveted on a tiny, glittering object. Hederick thought at first that it was a smaller version of the sparkling globe that had led him here, but as he drew nearer he recognized the steel and diamond dragon that Ancilla had displayed in her palm in the village. It had appeared to move then; now it was still once again, only a statue.

It was pretty, but Hederick could see no reason for it to fascinate Tarscenian so—none but witchcraft. That Ancilla had the priest in her power was painfully clear.

Hederick remained standing before the fire, while Ancilla arranged herself in a comfortable sitting position on the floor. "Hederick is here," Ancilla said soothingly to Tarscenian.

The priest lifted his head slowly, as if the Diamond Dragon released him from its spell grudgingly. Recognition dawned in the gray eyes. "You have come at last," he said, his voice hoarse. "I have done great wrong, son. I am grateful that you are here. We must atone, you and I."

Ancilla spoke gently. "I've been instructing Tarscenian in the ways of the Old Gods."

"The betrayers," Hederick spat out.

Tarscenian quickly shook his head. "No, Hederick," he said. "I was wrong. The Seekers are wrong. The Old Gods did not betray us with the Cataclysm. We humans brought it on ourselves. We sought to become gods, nearly three centuries ago." His voice grew more excited, and he reached out to clasp the boy's small hands in his. "There are no Seeker gods, Hederick," he said. "Omalthea, Sauvay, and the rest—they are illusions, no more real than

Venessi's god, Tiolanthe. Believe me, lad!"

He tugged, and Hederick knelt down next to him. Ancilla wordlessly watched the two. The fire crackled in the background.

"No!" the boy denied vehemently, pulling back. "The Seeker gods are the true gods. I have proof."

"What kind of proof can you have that the nonexistent exists?" Tarscenian asked.

Triumph rose within Hederick. "Sauvay showed himself to me tonight," he declared. Excitement choked his voice. "He spoke to me, Tarscenian! Sauvay, god of power and vengeance! *To me!* He has been waiting for me to follow the Seekers. It is my lot to punish the sinners! I have been especially chosen."

Tarscenian stared dumbly at Hederick, and the boy redoubled his efforts to convince the priest. "To bring *me* to the Seekers—this was your mission in life, Tarscenian. That's why you were drawn to Garlund. Perhaps Sauvay even sent the giant lynx to bring us together. You've fulfilled your purpose."

Hederick felt the power of oratory fill him. "Don't compound your sin by denying your faith and betraying the pantheons. Pray with me! If you prostrate yourself, you may die forgiven!"

Ancilla watched silently, her face devoid of emotion. Her unblinking gaze flicked between her brother and Tarscenian.

The false priest came to himself with a start. "You . . . saw . . . Sauvay," he said, shaking his head in disbelief. "A god . . . showed himself to *you?*"

Hederick clasped Tarscenian's hands tighter. "Yes," he replied eagerly. "Outside the copse. I . . ."

"Did his voice rumble? Venessi always said the voice of her god rumbled like thunder."

"No, it was more like the wind speaking—like a loud whisper. I . . ."

"Were there explosions? Did he wear a robe? Or did he come to you like Tiolanthe did to Venessi—half naked and built like a Caergothi blacksmith?"

"I could see only half of him, Tarscenian. He flowed up out of the ground. His torso was covered with a loose shirt. It could have been a robe, I suppose . . ."

Hederick's voice trailed off, and he felt the strength drain from him. The fallen priest was laughing! Mirth so filled Tarscenian that tears streamed from his eyes. He fell backward against the rug, chortling.

"By the True Gods!" Tarscenian roared. "He's as crazy as his mother!"

Ancilla reached across and placed her hand comfortingly on Hederick's arm. "You could not have seen a god that doesn't exist, little brother," she murmured. "You are hysterical. Forgive Tarscenian; he's had no sleep in a week. Calm yourself. Perhaps when you have rested, you will come to see, as Tarscenian has . . ."

Hederick snatched up the dragon figurine and leaped to his feet. Ancilla grabbed for the charm, but Hederick held it away from her, eyes flashing.

"I saw Sauvay, I tell you!" he roared. "He warned me about you, witch. It *was* Sauvay, and he spoke only to me. He praised me, Ancilla. He *praised* me! Whether you accept it or not, the Old Gods are gone. I will lead the followers of the New Gods, and together we will annihilate magic and cleanse the world. *It is ordained!*"

Alarmed by the boy's words, Tarscenian stopped laughing and sat up.

Hederick, clutching the dragon in his left hand, launched himself at his former mentor. Hederick heard Ancilla chanting, and out of the corner of his eye, saw her fling dried herbs in the fire and move her hands in a spell. Sauvay guided his blow; Hederick's punch knocked the priest back on his elbows.

Blood dripped from one corner of Tarscenian's mouth,

but he seemed not to notice. "The magic?" Tarscenian asked Ancilla apprehensively as he stood and pulled her to her feet.

Hederick's sister was noticeably upset. "I tried, my love," she replied disconsolately. "Nothing . . ."

"Magic will not work against a true believer, you fools!" Hederick thundered. They fell back a step, surprised at his vehemence.

"What shall we do, Ancilla?" Tarscenian pressed.

"Hederick has the dragon," she whispered back. "We must get it!"

"Sauvay!" Hederick bellowed to the skies. "Kill them both!" He yanked the cloth from a table and whisked it toward the fireplace. The fringe touched the flames, and soon Hederick was whirling the blazing cloth like a flag. The curtains caught fire, and likewise the sleeve of Tarscenian's robe, but Ancilla's silk robe seemed impervious. "Fire purifies!" Hederick shouted.

The roof thatch seeped smoke. "We must leave, Tarscenian!" Ancilla cried. "I'm bound by my vow to him. I can't hurt my brother. I am powerless!"

"Of course you are, witch," Hederick snarled. Now it was his turn to laugh. "*I* am the righteous one. You have seduced Tarscenian away from virtue. You have doomed both of you. You are . . ."

Ancilla hurled more of the herbs into the fire. "*Ranay nansensharn*," she chanted desperately. Again her fingers danced wicked figures. "*Ranay nansensharn*."

Hederick threw himself at Tarscenian and Ancilla.

One moment the two traitors stood together, arms entwined, surrounded by flame. The next moment they were gone. Hederick found himself sprawled on the smoldering rug before the mantel. He escaped from the evil dwelling just as the roof began to collapse.

*　*　*　*　*

It seemed as if no time at all had passed when Hederick returned to the sleeping village of Garlund. The glow from the flames that were eagerly devouring Ancilla's cottage and the copse around it lit up the sky. The moons had set. Hederick lit a lantern and set it on the back of a wagon in the courtyard.

"People of Garlund, arise!" he shouted. Sauvay was watching over him; his voice had never been so deep and confident. The boy crawled up onto the back of the wagon so that he was gazing down upon the sleepy Garlunders when they spilled out of their houses and into the village courtyard.

"A great moment has arrived!" Hederick called. "The New Gods are about to present us with a precious gift!"

In every face, from the youngest to the eldest, Hederick detected godlessness. How could he have been so blind, creeping into houses one by one to find evidence of individual crimes? It would have been better to search for those who *hadn't* sinned.

"A gift!" Hederick shouted again.

Voices churned around him. "What's the boy doing, waking us at such an hour?" "What's wrong?" "Is someone hurt?" "It's Venessi's boy, causing trouble again." "Where's the priest? The lad answers to him now." "Tarscenian is gone. The prayer house is empty. His things are missing."

Hederick raised his hands. "The false priest has abandoned us. He's betrayed us and joined the witch, Ancilla."

"What's the idiot talking about?" "Tarscenian was as devout as I." "Send the boy back to bed." "Where's his mother?" "Let Venessi deal with him." "But where *is* the priest?" "Has Hederick hurt him?" "That weasel, hurt anyone?" The voices surrounded Hederick, firming his resolve.

At last the boy's mother pushed through the crowd, angrily shoving the villagers out of her way. "What are you doing, Hederick?" Venessi snapped, scowling. "Haven't you sinned enough? Must I banish you permanently? See where your willfulness has gotten us! Tiolanthe will punish you!" She reached into the wagon, but Hederick easily slipped away from her grasp.

"Venessi"—Hederick would call her "mother" no more, for the Seeker gods were his parents now—"Tiolanthe is a myth." He sneered down at her, glad that at last the tables were turned. She was beneath him, and powerless to hurt him now. "You *imagined* him—to lead these people into sin and satisfy your greed. But Tiolanthe does not exist, and never did."

"Hederick, get down!" Venessi ordered. "You are a mere boy. That heathen priest has filled you with grandiose ideas. Get down, I say!"

"No."

"Tarscenian has fled like a cheat and a thief," she continued, satisfaction ripe in her tones. "I knew he would. Tiolanthe will forgive you, Hederick, if you stop this now. Even *I* will forgive you. Recant at once."

Again he refused.

"Then you will die," she announced with smug satisfaction. "I'll not permit such viciousness, not when I can so easily prevent it." Venessi pointed to three of the largest men in the crowd of villagers. "Peren Volen. Willad Oberl. Jerad Oberl. Fetch my worthless son!"

The men hurried to do Venessi's bidding. "Sauvay, god of vengeance, stand for me," Hederick prayed. He expected Sauvay to strike the three dead, but they advanced up onto the wagon, towering over him with balled fists. All looked delighted with their mission. "Sauvay, your servant awaits," he whispered. "Come to me now."

There was no rushing wind, no circle of brilliance. Sauvay had said he'd be with Hederick as long as the boy was faithful, but now there was no sign of the god. Had Hederick weakened? Was Sauvay angry with him for some reason? Perhaps this was a test of his resolve. "I will show myself worthy, Sauvay," he murmured.

Hederick searched his pockets for some weapon. There was nothing but the glittering dragon he'd taken from the witch. Garlunders were simple people, he thought, perhaps the gaudy thing would distract them like crows, just long enough for him to escape.

He cradled the dragon in his bare hand. It felt warm to the touch. "Stop!" he cried. He raised one arm to throw the dragon—then halted, stunned.

All the villagers, Venessi included, looked at him as though entranced. The bauble was bathed in an eerie glow. A miracle!

"The sign!" Hederick breathed. "Sauvay *is* with me! Blessed be the Seeker gods," he intoned, raising his voice. "People of Garlund!"

They gaped. Some actually beamed inanely. "Look," said a woman who'd berated him earlier, "it's young Hederick. Hasn't he grown! Venessi must be proud."

Venessi emitted a beatific smile. "Certainly, Marta. Hederick is the joy of my life. All my trials become nothing when I see his triumph. Everything I have done, I have done for him. I am blessed."

Now all were speaking, smiling, pointing. "What a pious young man!" "Aren't we lucky to have a saint among us." "He is destined for great acts." "I always saw promise in the lad." "He has been set apart for a higher calling." "Blessed be the Seeker gods!"

They cheered, and the boy who stood above them felt the power of their acclamation. Sauvay had been bountiful beyond Hederick's imagining. He stroked the dragon and sighed a prayer of thanks.

"People of Garlund," he repeated, purposely pitching his voice low. The villagers had to fall silent to hear his every word. "We are at a holy crossroads tonight. Venessi has led us down a false path. For a long time we followed her fraudulent gods, but the real gods, the gods of the Seekers, cry out for justice. Venessi deserves punishment. She cares nothing for us."

Frowns fell across their dull faces like flickering lamplight, and they began to mutter. "Lad's right." "Venessi would see us damned before she'd admit to being only a common woman." "She's too proud." "She murdered her own husband!" "See her fine house—so much nicer than ours." "We fed her, served her, and for what?" "She must think we are fools." "Cast her out! Banish her!"

"People!" Hederick interjected forcefully when their emotions had been raised to fever pitch. All heads turned his way. Venessi backed away from the wagon, but two women caught her arms and prevented further retreat.

"This woman tricked you into duplicity and sin!" Hederick cried, pointing at the woman who had been his tormentor for thirteen years.

"That's true," one man shouted. "Listen to Hederick."

"This woman used your piety against you!"

"That's so," another man responded.

"This woman stole from you!"

"Yes."

"She starved you and your families!"

"Vile witch."

"This woman endangered your souls by leading you to a deity she knew to be false—and by spurning the very gods who could redeem you!"

Peren Volen spoke from behind him. "She is evil," he said.

"This woman led her own daughter to witchcraft, sent her away to study the black arts!"

"She is evil." Jerad Oberl added his voice.

"This woman slew her own husband!"

"She is evil," Willad Oberl agreed.

"And you would do no more than *banish* her?" Hederick's eyes blazed, and he raised his hands before the crowd.

"Kill her!" Peren and the Oberls howled.

"You would leave her alive to lead others into blasphemy?"

"Kill her!"

"The Seeker gods watch you now, people of Garlund, to see if you will prove your faith. Do you love the New Gods, villagers of Garlund? Do you fear them, adore them?"

The people screamed and shouted. They danced, leaping into the night air as though ecstacy forced them to take vigorous action or die.

"Kill the sinner!" Hederick shouted. He swept his hand toward Venessi. She struggled against the women who held her, then cowered as strong, determined hands twisted her arms and vicious fingers pinched and pulled at her.

"Let not such an evildoer remain alive to infect you and your children. Kill her!"

With a roar, the crowd fell upon Venessi, drowning out her screams with their cries of righteous rage. Hederick caught one last glimpse of his mother's terrified face, then she was swept under clawlike hands and booted feet like a leaf in a whirlwind.

At length, the people drew back. Some looked bewildered, as though they had awakened only that moment to find Venessi inexplicably trampled and beaten to death on the ground before them.

"People of Garlund." Hederick held the dragon aloft and offered another silent prayer to Sauvay. "See what you have done," he remonstrated quietly. "This dear woman lived only for you. She risked her life bringing you out of the decay of Caergoth to the richness of these plains. Venessi gave up her beloved husband for you because he had sinned and no longer could set the example she knew you needed. She sent her daughter away for the same reason: *to keep you safe*. It was through her actions that you, the people of Garlund, came to the altar of the New Gods. She tried her utmost to warn you about the false priest, yet you have so little love in your hearts that you . . ."

Hederick sighed, gesturing at the body. He clasped the dragon so tightly that the diamonds cut his hand; tears welled in his eyes. He let a few drops spill onto his cheeks. "She was my mother, never forget." He forced more tears to flow, and several villagers began to cry. All avoided looking at Venessi's dead body.

"This is murder," Hederick whispered, so piercingly that all could hear him. "You have sinned, people of Garlund. You know such a heinous act cannot be expiated by prayer and fasting, or by sacrifices and gifts to the gods and their priests. There is only one punishment for such a crime.

"Willad, Jerad, Peren, attend me." The three men straightened as if hypnotized. "I order you, in the name of Sauvay, god of power and vengeance, to execute the sinners of this village." To the villagers, Hederick said, "I order you, in the name of Sauvay and the Seeker pantheons, to accept your just punishment."

The villagers stood, sheeplike, awaiting their fate. Hederick rejoiced inwardly to Sauvay.

The three men set silently to work. Not one villager ran or struggled. The Oberl brothers and Peren Volen strangled the life's breath out of each. Frideline Bacque, who'd worked so hard to attract Peren Volen, did not even blink when he killed her.

When there were but the three men left, Hederick ordered Peren to slay the Oberls. Then, at Hederick's command, Peren Volen walked obediently down to the river and drowned himself, and the people of Garlund were no more.

Soon Hederick had the Oberls' best horse harnessed to

the wagon. A short time later, the back of the vehicle was piled with items for his travels. Then he set fire to Garlund.

"Fire purifies," he murmured, reveling in the heat and cleansing power of the blaze. Once again flames lit Hederick's way as he left a place of sin. Soon he and the horse and wagon were miles away, and the sun had begun to rise.

"Think of the converts I can bring to the Seekers, and to Sauvay!" he whispered to himself. He wrapped the dragon figurine in a scrap of leather, tied a thong to it, and slipped it around his neck, inside his shirt.

Hederick faced the world alone, but he knew a god watched over him.

* * * * *

For more than three decades Hederick traveled the lands, a wandering Seeker priest, bringing the words of the New Gods to the people. The *Praxis*, his constant companion, served as both inspiration and confirmation that his purpose was preordained by the gods themselves. As he grew older and more experienced in the ways of the world and its peoples, his gift of oratory grew accordingly. Soon he was able to assess a crowd in moments and know how best to handle it. Some needed fire and brimstone, some only gentle persuasion.

And just as he made good use of his gift for speaking, he made use, also, of the sleight-of-hand tricks that Tarscenian had taught him so many years ago.

Fame followed him. Hederick, the holy man of the north, converted hundreds of thousands of people to the New Gods.

The devout cheered as Hederick entered their towns. He always took care to hold the Diamond Dragon against his palm as he entered a village. Time and again, townspeople vied to offer him lodging for as long as he wanted it, presented him with fine clothes, and fed him the very best their tables had to offer. He lived well—as was proper for a prophet of the gods. He was the favored of Sauvay, after all.

Always, upon arrival in a new location, Hederick was careful to ferret out the irretrievable sinners. The Diamond Dragon, macaba root, and Sauvay helped him ease them out of this world. They were poor and rich, of low status and high, men and women, young and old.

No one stood above Seeker doctrine.

Finally, when Hederick was well into middle age, Sauvay sent the Highseeker Elistan to persuade him to come to Haven to join the main body of Seekers. Elistan seemed to have no awareness of Sauvay's hand in his mission—a sign, to Hederick, that much of the recognition Elistan had received was undeserved. Elistan told Hederick what the wandering priest already knew—that the Highseekers Council in Haven had need of his powers of oratory.

The pious and crafty Hederick rose quickly in the Seeker hierarchy. He knew Seeker law well. It was a simple matter for him to have superiors removed for transgressions that few others had detected. Those few who were impervious to slander or blackmail succumbed readily to the poison of the macaba root.

Through all of this, Hederick basked in the approval of Sauvay.

* * * * *

"There," Eban said, dumping the huge scroll on the desk in the Great Library. Olven sat at the desk, quill pen in hand, before an empty piece of parchment. "I've done my part, and in only half a day! Hederick's background"—Eban lovingly patted the curl of paper—"all set down here in black and white. I could

have gone on twice as long as I did. Oh, you should see the scrolls back there, you two! And the bound parchments. By the gods!" Eban whistled. "More books than I've seen in my life, all together in one room. It's absolutely amaz . . . Why, what's the matter?"

Olven was looking sourly at the red-haired youth. Marya, leaning against a bookshelf, also scowled.

"Your youthful enthusiasm is wonderful, child," she said sarcastically, "but we seem to have a problem."

"We?" Eban echoed. "Me, too?"

"We're in this together," she reminded him in a surly tone. "Look."

Eban followed her gesture and finally took in the empty parchment before the luckless Olven. "Nothing?" Eban cried, prompting a duet of "shhhh" from his fellow apprentices. He dropped his voice to a whisper. "You two have been here for four hours, and you haven't written a thing? Not a word? What have you been doing?"

"Well, I sharpened all the quills," Olven muttered.

"And I went for an extra supply of ink," Marya added mulishly. "We didn't have the luxury of writing down things that are already well in the past and skillfully recorded. We three have all done countless research papers, Eban; anyone can do that. Olven and I were in charge of writing the present—and the present as it occurs nowhere near Palanthas. That's considerably harder, I'd say." She sniffed.

"And . . . ?" Eban shot back. "What's happening?"

"Nothing's happening," Olven mourned. He rested his forehead on the parchment and tore a piece of white fluff from the quill pen. "Astinus said to sit here. The history would come to us, Astinus said. But it hasn't. I thought it was magic. Now I don't think so. It's just a test, and I've failed."

Eban shot a blue-eyed glance toward Marya. "How about you?"

Marya shook her head. "Same as him. Nothing. Something's not working."

"Maybe the desk is broken," Olven theorized despondently. "Or the chair."

"And you concentrated on Hederick, both of you?" Eban demanded. "The whole time?"

"Yes, on Hederick, and only Hederick," Olven and Marya said together.

Eban looked down at the parchment and then at the long crane's feather drooping from Olven's sweating hand. Most of the feathery portions had been stripped away from the quill in Olven's agitation. "Maybe that's it," Eban said. He patted Olven's shoulder, as though the red-haired youth were the elder of the two. "Let me try."

Marya snorted. "He and I have years of experience beyond yours. You're practically still a child. What could you possibly try that we haven't thought of?"

Olven groaned. "Give it up, Eban. Your willingness to help is laudable, but we're doomed." He rubbed his eyes and continued his lament. "I'm going to end up back home, selling hot potatoes and sausage from a pushcart. I just know it."

"And I'll have to go back and marry the butcher," Marya added. "He has six kids." She went white and closed her eyes for a moment. "By the gods, I'll never have time to read a book again!" She slid down the end of the bookshelf until she was seated despondently on the stone floor.

Eban ignored them both. He pulled at Olven's arm until the elder man heaved himself out of the chair and made way for the youth. One pair of black eyes and one pair of brown watched hopelessly as the youth settled against the chair's cushions, took a deep breath, let his head fall back, and appeared to go into an open-eyed trance. Eban's voice startled them then, for there was nothing dreamy about it. "Perhaps you were concentrating too narrowly," he said, "in thinking only of Hederick. History— even the story of just one person—consists of more than events that happen directly to one man. Maybe we should widen our thoughts."

As the other two watched pessimistically, the youngest

member of the trio reached forward and grasped a new quill. Eban dipped the tip into a ceramic pot of black ink, placed it just above the paper, and waited. He made no sound. Olven and Marya held their breath.

Soon the pen began scratching on the parchment.

Chapter 3

Two score men and women stood motionless in the fog, their white robes clinging in the dampness. The setting could have been day or night, north or south, pinnacle or plain. The mist muted everything to colorlessness.

At the center of the circle stood the only figure wearing other than the robe of a mage. He was also the only one carrying a sword. Homespun shirt, dark shift, patched leggings, and dusty boots covered his tall frame. The man appeared to be in his seventies. Unbent and powerful despite his age, he held in his arms a woman so slender and weak that a casual observer might wonder whether she still breathed.

She was at least eighty. Yet even in her sleeping frailty, it was apparent that once she had been a great beauty. The woman, too, wore the white robes of a mage of Good.

Tarscenian held Ancilla and quietly surveyed the circle of mages around him. When he finally spoke, the fog muffled his voice.

"Ancilla argued for three days before the Conclave of Wizards," Tarscenian said, "and when they still refused to help her, she collapsed. She is weak." He paused, unwilling to say the words that would put voice to his worst fear. "She is dying."

The other mages knew Ancilla had spent decades trying to stop the fanatic Hederick from realizing his ambition to lead the Seeker religion—and, ultimately, all of Krynn. He had installed himself as High Theocrat of Solace. Now Hederick was hoping to so impress his gods that they would admit him into their pantheon as a deity. He called himself The Chosen One and considered himself the special favorite of the Seeker god Sauvay.

"Hederick has the Diamond Dragon of the White Robes," Tarscenian said.

The men and women inclined their heads. Ancilla had received the Diamond Dragon when she passed the Test that made her a white-robed mage. Hederick had taken it from her. It was a sad irony that the artifact of the White Robes now protected one such as Hederick from their magic.

"Doubtless you have tried stealing the artifact back," the elven mage Calcidon said.

Tarscenian nodded assent. "To no avail. That is why Ancilla wanted to enlist the help of the Conclave of Wizards, including all Neutral and Evil mages."

"And the Conclave of Wizards refused her," Calcidon mused. "Even those mages allied with good."

"The White Robes were somewhat willing," Tarscenian said. "The neutral Red Robes were unsure, and the Black Robes of evil were absolutely set against any action."

Strands of mist coalesced and whirled around Tarscenian and the others as though the fog expressed some of their agitation.

"What interest could the Black Robes have in supporting a man who would gladly see them all burned?" Calcidon asked. "They *are* mages, after all. Like us, they favor the Old Gods."

The mage Benthis spoke next. "Refugees have been arriving from the far north with tales of strange armies, mercenaries, and nefarious creatures," he said. "Minotaurs. Hobgoblins, goblins, and worse. There's no logic to the rumors, unless a source of unheard-of evil is behind such a military undertaking." Benthis looked Calcidon straight in the eyes. "An evil on the scale of a deity."

The elf frowned. "You are suggesting . . ."

"Takhisis herself."

"The Dark Queen!" Calcidon laughed. "Oh, surely one of the Old Gods would not intercede on Krynn . . ." The elf halted, taken aback by the intent looks of the other mages. The last time the Old Gods had interceded on Krynn, the resulting debacle practically destroyed the world. Three centuries earlier, the Cataclysm had drained seas, created oceans and deserts where none had been before, and killed hundreds of thousands of humans, elves, dwarves, kender, and other beings. All because a human, the kingpriest of a faraway city, had aspired to godhood.

Calcidon, wearing a mask of elven calm, turned to Tarscenian. "The Conclave has refused to help you, but two score white-robed mages hear your tale now. What do you seek of us?"

"Hederick is slaughtering scores of mages," Tarscenian replied. "All of you have lost someone dear to Hederick's Inquisition."

Indeed, it was true, the mages agreed, nodding to each

other. In the past three months, Hederick had leveled dozens of vallenwoods. The Solace trees were sacred to the followers of the Old Gods but merely another source of firewood to the Seekers. Hederick was employing goblins and hobgoblins as spies and assassins. The goblins in turn had enlisted other evil creatures to assist them.

On the land cleared of vallenwoods, just north of Solace on the shores of Crystalmir Lake, Hederick had built an opulent temple. The High Theocrat called the temple Erolydon, which meant "scourge of heresy" in Old Abanasinian. There Hederick had set up the headquarters of his Inquisition. Anyone caught using magic was deemed a heretic, according to the Seeker faith, and thus was subject to execution, which came both swiftly and mercilessly.

Benthis, surveying the assembled White Robes, noted the melancholy expression on the face of the elven mage. "Even you, Calcidon?" he murmured. "I thought you and yours never ventured forth from your cozy elven nest in Qualinost. Who have you lost to Hederick's Inquisition?"

"A cousin," came the tight-lipped answer. "And you, Benthis?"

The hawklike visage softened. "My sister."

Other mages chimed in. "Hederick executed my brother." "My friend of twenty years." "My partner."

"What do you want of us, Tarscenian?" Calcidon repeated.

"Ancilla gave me instructions before she addressed the Conclave," Tarscenian said. "She feared she would fail—once more—to persuade them. And she worried she would be too frail afterward to summon you herself."

Tarscenian chose his next words carefully. "Ancilla discovered a way to collect the powers of willing mages, and channel them through her own willpower. She thought that with such unusual strength at her disposal, she could at last wrest the Diamond Dragon away from Hederick. In turn, she planned to use the artifact to defeat him."

"Take our powers?" Benthis cried. "That's unacceptable. Where would that leave us? Devoid of magic at a time when Hederick is sending spies and kidnappers all over Krynn to capture spellcasters! You'd leave us unprotected against this tyrant?"

"Ancilla found a means to shelter you," Tarscenian explained. "If you will transfer your powers to her, the vallenwoods will shelter your bodies and nurture you until the Diamond Dragon releases you."

A flurry of protest, led by Benthis, rippled through the gathering. But as Calcidon and the rest of the wizards intoned the names of the loved ones lost to the Inquisition, one by one the opponents backed down.

Benthis tried one last argument. "If Ancilla fails, what happens to us? What if she dies despite our combined powers?"

"I cannot say for certain," Tarscenian said. "You will be part of the vallenwoods, but whether you will die or stay in the trees for years—or forever—Ancilla could not foretell."

Benthis gazed around the circle. His look met only obdurate stares. "And we *all* must be part of this?" he asked.

"All who are present now," Tarscenian replied. "Or the spell will not work."

Benthis closed his eyes. At last he opened them and attempted a weak smile. "If it comes down to dying at Hederick's command or perishing inside a vallenwood, I suppose it ultimately makes no difference," he conceded. He wiped the damp from his forehead with his sleeve. "I loved my sister. I'm with you."

For the rest of the day, Tarscenian led them through the steps Ancilla had forced him to commit to memory. When all had learned the spells and movements, he spread his cloak on the ground in the middle of the circle and laid Ancilla upon it. Then, because Tarscenian was but a minor spellcaster, he backed out of the circle, leaving the wizards to do their work.

Calcidon led the spell. "*Shiriff intoann ejjitt,*" he intoned.

"*Borumtalcon,*" the mages replied.

They raised their hands and lowered them in the prescribed movements. Each wizard inscribed upon the fog a different portion of the magical traceries. The gestures of their fingers left blue, green, and red lines on the mist. Ancilla had stressed that each segment of the total was crucial, but to Tarscenian, each mage's work appeared to be nothing but errant scribbling.

The fog began to glow. The white robes gleamed like burnished silver.

"*Bilum merit ayhannti,*" Calcidon sang in his elven tenor.

"*Achet shiral pescumi. Relaquay,*" came the chanted reply of the group. The men's voices rumbled. The women's tones floated like feathers.

Suddenly the forty robes glittered like diamonds. They scattered light until tears streamed from the mages' eyes. Ancilla had been adamant: the mages' eyes must remain open, whatever their inclination to close them against the brilliance.

"*Ayhannti, shiral livvix xhalot.*" Calcidon sang on. "*Polopeque.*"

The shine that had transformed the robes now leaped out of the cloth as though it had life of its own. The glitter shone silver and white. Ice blue appeared in the swirling fog. The lines that the mages had traced formed into figures—a tree, a dragon, a lance, a crown.

Then they muted to nothingness.

The mist evaporated around the ring of mages and intensified above Ancilla's still form. The air filled with the clattering and chiming of bells.

"*Shiral livvix trassdiv dhelli!*" Calcidon shrieked the words. Yet the other mages could barely hear him over the noise from the twisting tendrils of fog.

"*Reveese rou ripow nad borrah rou carpeh,*" the mages shouted in unison. "*Reveese rou ripow nad borrah rou carpeh!*"

The fog enveloped all the mages. The light from a thousand stars exploded within the circle. Wooden bells, silver chimes, steel cymbals could be heard. Some of the mages began to bleed from the ears. Others cried out with pain and made as if to clap their hands over their eyes.

Then all disappeared. The fog vanished with them, revealing a late-afternoon mountaintop without tree or living beast.

All was silent.

At that moment, Ancilla shivered and awakened. Her green eyes stared blankly at Tarscenian for a moment. "I am alive?" she finally whispered. "They agreed to help us?" At Tarscenian's nod, the old woman accepted his hand and stood. She wobbled at first, then supported herself without aid. Ancilla waved away Tarscenian's arm.

"By the Old Gods, Tarscenian, the power!" she whispered. "I have the might of two score mages inside of me."

Her companion waited while Ancilla composed herself. She closed her eyes, and her lips moved, but Tarscenian could not divine whether she spoke spell or prayer. After a few moments, Ancilla seemed to gain some control over the magical forces raging within her.

"This is our last chance, Tarscenian," Ancilla said resolutely, looking up at her longtime friend and companion. "We go now to Erolydon—to challenge my brother."

Chapter 4

Pounding and shouting at the front door of their treetop mansion in Solace shook the Vakon family from their beds just after midnight. Jeffers, the manservant, was the first to the door, but Ceci Vakon, mistress of the home, followed a short distance behind.

"Is the master home?" Jeffers whispered to Ceci. He clutched a small axe of the variety normally used to chop kindling.

She shook her head. "Mendis isn't home yet. Perhaps something has happened to him."

A resonant voice boomed through the locked door. "Death to heretics!" Ceci recognized the booming bass voice as that of the high priest of the Seeker temple in Solace.

"High Priest Dahos!" she whispered. "And Hederick's

goblins. What are they doing here?"

Jeffers's face was young, pale, and defiant. "I'm the only man in the house," he said staunchly. "I will protect you."

"No. This must be a mistake," Ceci replied. "The High Theocrat promised us protection. Open the door. I'll speak to them."

The young servant followed her orders but kept the small axe in view and stood stubbornly in the doorway next to his mistress. Clutching her lacy nightrobe at her throat with one hand, she surveyed the tall, robed Plainsman and the half-dozen goblins who ranged on the walkway just outside the door. Behind them was nothing but the forty-foot drop from the walkway to the forest floor. The Vakon home, like most in Solace, was built in the branches of a vallenwood tree, linked to the other treetop buildings by snakelike wood-and-rope walkways.

"What do you want?" Ceci demanded. "It's the middle of the night, Dahos. You've frightened my servants and my children."

Dahos inclined his head, and replied. "The High Court of the Seekers of the New Gods in Solace has convicted you and your family of heresy, Mistress Vakon." The formal tone could not mask the gleeful triumph in his dark eyes. "We are here to take you into church custody. Come outside."

"I will not!" Ceci Vakon retorted. "There's been a mistake. We are under the protection of the High Theocrat of Solace. My husband will take care of this misunderstanding in the morning. Now go!" She turned on the ball of one foot, dismissing the dark-robed priest with a toss of her head.

Thus it was that she missed the signal that passed from Dahos to the six goblins. A half-dozen maces and spears came up to the ready.

But Jeffers saw. He drove his shoulder into Ceci's side

and sent her sprawling onto the walkway. He lifted his axe.

He never got a chance to use it.

Out of the darkness flashed a spear—hurtling sideways, like a long-handled sword, not point forward like an ordinary spear or lance. It was a movement peculiar to the Plainsman tribe from which Dahos hailed. The weapon slashed above the maces of several chattering goblins and cut through the manservant's neck like a cleaver through a round of cheese. Mendis Vakon's young sons piled into the room in time to see the loyal servant's head spin over the railing of the aerial walkway. His body crashed to the doorstep. Ceci Vakon and her children screamed in terror.

Several months ago, the cacophony would have brought dozens of neighbors running to their aid, but no one appeared now. All of Solace cowered under the boot heel of Hederick, the new High Theocrat of the treetop village.

"Yellow Eyes, take two goblins and empty the house," Dahos snapped at one of the goblins, whose broad nose twitched at the smell of Jeffers's blood. "There may be other servants within. If they resist, kill them. If not, bring them along. They'll bring more money to Erolydon's coffers. Find the daughter. Assemble them on the walkway, next to the railing, with their backs to the drop."

It was a complicated command for a goblin, but the one called Yellow Eyes was smart for that species. The leader of sorts, he scurried to obey. The high priest turned toward the far walkway.

"People of Solace!" he shouted into the darkness. "Bear this in mind! This is how Hederick, High Theocrat of Solace, rewards heretics and other sinners!"

Ceci Vakon, her young sons, teen-age daughter, and serving maids lined up on the walkway. The goblins scrambled through the dwelling, gathering platinum candlesticks, jeweled chalices, polished steel serving plates, and anything else that seemed valuable. The rest of the furnishings they destroyed.

"These precious objects will be better used in the holy setting of the temple Erolydon than in the lair of heretics," Dahos proclaimed. "We will consecrate them first, of course."

"My husband will avenge this!" Ceci snapped. "What are you going to do with us—pitch a woman and children off the walkway, pious coward that you are?" Ceci's daughter burst into tears, but her mother continued her brave but foolhardy speech. "My husband will have your head for this, High Priest. He'll go to the Highseekers Council in Haven! We are under Hederick's protection, I tell you!"

"Silence!" Dahos thundered.

Yellow Eyes flourished a short-handled sword before Ceci's face. Discomfited as much by his rancid breath as by the violent gesture, she clamped her mouth shut and glared at the smelly creature. Her children swarmed around her, but the goblins forced them back into line.

Then Ceci heard the screams in the distance. Loons, she thought at first. But the only loons in Solace would be nesting out at northern Crystalmir Lake, out of earshot. Along with the screeches came the unmistakable thrumming of wings. The strange sound grew nearer.

Defiance drained from Ceci Vakon. Her youngest son spun around.

"Mama!" he cried. "Huge bats!"

She whirled. "Night hunter bats!" she breathed. Ceci lunged forward to drag her children into the house. But Yellow Eyes and the others easily pinioned their captives.

There were eight giant bats—each one seven feet long. Their eyes, some red, some violet like their fur, glowed in the night. They could kill easily with the claws that glittered at the end of their papery wings. They could kill just as deftly with their rapier-sharp, triangular tails. And, of course, like any Krynnish bat, the night hunters had fangs that were deadly.

"Death to heretics!" Dahos bellowed again at the silent houses of Solace. "Gather by your windows and watch, sinful people. Witness the fate of those who reject lives of holiness offered in the sanctity of the New Gods!"

Each bat plucked up a human in its claws. Holding their captives by the scruff of their nightclothes, the bats fluted and screeched as they bore away their screaming victims.

"Take them to the slave trader Arabat!" Dahos shouted over the noise. "He waits on the southern edge of town."

Mindless of the consequences if the bat dropped her, Ceci twisted back toward the high priest, her nightrobe swirling in the humid air.

"My husband . . ." she shouted.

". . . is dead, Madam," Dahos finished for her. "Or soon will be."

* * * * *

Mendis Vakon heard faint screams as he crouched in the darkness before Erolydon's wrought-iron gate. He was north of Solace, and whatever emitted that caterwauling was headed in the other direction. Small blessing, he thought; the screeching gave him gooseflesh. He scrambled to his feet and stood before the long, solid, white walls of the temple.

Avoiding the bustle of Solace, Hederick had chosen to build his blessed temple on the shores of peaceful Crystalmir Lake less than a league north of the city. Hederick hated dirt, and cities, even treetop communities like Solace, had a lot of dirt. Hederick also loathed noise— unless he himself was making it, Mendis Vakon thought sourly. Solace had plenty of pandemonium, too. Especially now, with refugees arriving every day, telling their unbelievable tales.

This wooded place, however, was as quiet as a crypt. Unfortunate thought. Mendis tried to pretend his heart was not hammering like that of a terrified mouse.

The silver and scarlet moons of Krynn provided some light but little comfort. The humidity, even at midnight, pressed against Vakon, and he caught the scent of his own body heat. As usual for midsummer, the mosquitoes were aggressive. Their droning added to Vakon's tension. He swatted at the insects and looked nervously from side to side. Where was Hederick? The marble of the temple glowed faintly in the darkness.

The stout wooden inner doors, just behind the ornamental iron outer gate, were shut to the night. There was no sign of guards. All was as Hederick had promised.

From inside the compound, the scrape of a footstep on cobblestone sent Vakon jumping, and he cursed inwardly. In a short time I will be well away from here, he said to himself. I'll have money to last to the end of my days. And I'll not deal with this madman, or any of his Seekers, again.

The inner doors swung slowly open. Then the outer gates, the ones of wrought iron, opened. Vakon could not see the hand that controlled the mechanism. He slipped inside. The metal gate locked behind him.

"Over here, idiot!" came a whisper. "Do you want someone to see you?"

Mendis Vakon peered toward the shadow of the wall and spied the short, lumpy man whom all Solace had come to fear. Despite the languid heat, the High Theocrat wore a heavy dark cape over his brown and gold-braid robe. His gray hair was unaccountably dark and thick, and Valcon realized Hederick was wearing the ludicrous wig he sometimes donned for state occasions. As always, Mendis marveled that such an unassuming figure could inspire such terror in people. Hederick was in his sixties, as near as anyone could guess, with bulging blue eyes that had faded long ago, a spongy, bulbous nose, thin hair, and the mottled complexion that came from imbibing too much mead for too many years.

Vakon held himself with his most military bearing and strode toward the High Theocrat. He was taller than the religious leader, and he relished the fact that it annoyed the diminutive man.

"You took your time opening the gate," Vakon complained. "Anyone could have seen me out there."

"At midnight?" Hederick retorted. "I opened it at the promised time, no sooner and no later." He motioned for Vakon to follow him. They headed between the outer wall and a lower, inner one that ran parallel to it. This was the corridor within which people gathered to witness the executions of heretics and other enemies of the faith.

Mendis hesitated, then spoke warily. "I want my money. Where are you taking me?"

"To get it, fool. Did you think I would just open the gate and throw it through?"

"Where is it, then?" Just to be safe, Vakon lingered a few paces back.

Hederick stepped from the outer corridor, opened a door into Erolydon's central courtyard. Keys jangling, he unlocked a plain wooden portal that was off to one side of the temple's huge main entrance. He stepped into a pitch-black hallway. Vakon stopped just outside the door. "Why aren't we using the main doors, Hederick?"

The High Theocrat's carefully modulated voice, which had lulled thousands of Seeker converts over the past decades, echoed out of the tunnel. "Mendis Vakon, you have the sense of a mole. Why not just pick up your reward at noon in the center of the temple courtyard, with hundreds of people around? We must be circumspect, you blockhead. Come on."

Vakon grunted in protest, but still he followed Hederick

into the dark tunnel. "Didn't you order everyone to remain in their cells?" he complained. "The priests and the guards? Who else would be about?"

The floor was slick, scored with deep striations. Vakon could feel the ruts through the thin soles of his dress slippers. The tunnel seemed to lead gradually downward.

"Of course, lunatic," Hederick snapped back. "I declared a night of prayer and fasting for priests and novitiates alike. I have ordered all to remain in their quarters tonight."

"So? We're safe then."

"That means they'll be confined—but awake—you fool. Now be silent."

Vakon started to retort, then he reminded himself of the wealth that soon would be his, and held his tongue.

Mendis Vakon believed in no gods—Old Gods, Seeker gods, or otherwise. The Seekers, true, were manipulative, cunning, and greedy, but so were the leaders of most of the religious movements that flourished on Krynn these days. What interested Vakon was that the Seekers were the biggest group—and the richest.

And the meanest, he added to himself. He was glad he'd slipped a dagger into a pocket in his leggings when he'd dressed earlier that night.

Suddenly, Vakon bumped into Hederick and cursed. He stretched a hand to each side and felt only dank air. "Where are we?" he asked apprehensively.

"Right outside the treasury. Be still." Hederick's keys clanked.

Just a few more moments, Vakon thought. It's so damned dark. Why doesn't Hederick light a torch while he opens the lock? We're below the temple. Everyone is in their cells above us. No one will see. No one . . .

Mendis Vakon turned and ran back the way he had come.

His slippers skidded on the incline. Hands caught at

the back of the knotted cord that belted his shirt. The
hands jerked upward, and Vakon crashed onto his knees.
He tipped forward. His head hit slimy stone, and he cried
out. Then another stone crashed into his temple. Vakon
rolled over and felt for his dagger.

Hederick laughed knowingly. "I already have it, Vakon.
I had to learn some such skills in my years on the road,
after all."

The priest was surprisingly strong. Vakon felt himself
being rolled across a slight rise. Suddenly the air was not
merely stale, but fetid. Vakon sprawled on uneven slabs of
rock as a lock clicked behind and above him, then he
heard Hederick wheeze, as if from beyond a door.

Something stirred in the blackness within the chamber.
Rats? "The dungeon!" Vakon protested. "You can't keep
me in a dungeon! I am Mayor of Solace!"

A breathy chuckle came from the darkness. "No longer.
I lead Solace now—thanks in part to you, Vakon." Another
chortle. "Ironic, considering that you refused to embrace
the Seeker faith, isn't it?"

Vakon scrambled to his feet and pounded at the steel-
clad door. Dimly, he saw a small, barred window and
sensed the High Theocrat peering through. Then a torch
flared from Hederick's side of the door, and Mendis
Vakon found himself eye to eye with the Seeker.

"Seekerism is claptrap," Vakon hissed. "False miracles
and phony revelations. Your Seekerism is a farce, Hederick!"

"I knew you'd feel that way, Mendis Vakon," Hederick
replied. "In fact, I have several witnesses who heard you
speak in just such a fashion last night in the Inn of the Last
Home."

"I was in no tavern last night, the Inn or otherwise!"

"My witnesses say you were. It's blasphemy, you know,
to criticize the Seeker gods, Vakon. The *Praxis* says so.
And the *Praxis* guides my life, as it does that of all truly

pious people."

A snarl broke the silence in the chamber behind Mendis Vakon, and Hederick laughed. Vakon flung himself around as the rumbling—halfway between a growl and thunder—reverberated within the stone walls. Whatever lurked in the shadows was dreadfully near.

"You're a heretic, Vakon," Hederick hissed through the door. "Heretics deserve to die."

"Then bring me to trial," Vakon spat out, terrified. What stalked him? He heard a rustling sound and felt cautiously around the straw that littered the floor, seeking something—anything—he could use as a weapon. "I have friends in Solace, Hederick," he spat out. "If I disappear, people will wonder."

"Friends? No longer, *ex*-Mayor," the High Theocrat rejoined. "Some of your friends are the very ones who were with you when you made those sacrilegious statements in the Inn."

"I tell you, I wasn't there!" Vakon insisted. "You can't prove that I was. I demand a trial!"

"As a matter of fact, *I* am judge and jury in Solace."

The growling came closer.

Hederick continued speaking as though he and Vakon were carrying on a normal conversation. "I found you guilty of heresy a few hours ago," he said, "just before I had your dear family carted off to a slave camp." There was a pause, then soft laughter from the High Theocrat. "I can tell that the sentence pleases my god Sauvay and the Motherlord Omalthea. Just listen to the happy rumblings of Sauvay's pet."

"No!" Vakon shouted. Nearby, something roared, and fire belched through the dungeon. Sparks ignited clods of damp hay near the door. Vakon's cloak began to burn, and he thrust it away from him.

Then Mendis saw what awaited him—a lion of sorts, but two or three times the size of that beast. It had enormous eyes and a thick tongue that curved out as though in anticipation toward the terrified mayor. The lion's huge front claws emerged and retracted as it watched its prey.

"A materbill?" Vakon said in disbelief. "But they don't exist!"

"They do now," Hederick whispered through the door. "Sauvay sent me one. A birthday present of sorts. Did you know my birthday was in midsummer, Vakon?"

The flames smoldered and failed in the dampness. Darkness returned, leaving only a fearful afterimage of the materbill burning in Vakon's brain. Then claws clattered on the stones. Another roar split the silence.

The creature belched more fire as it leaped upon Mendis Vakon. The former mayor of Solace didn't even have time to scream.

Once Hederick was sure his former co-conspirator was dead, the High Theocrat made his way to a nearby stone column. He held his torch higher and examined a row of marks. Drawing the dagger he'd filched from Vakon, Hederick used the rapierlike point to scratch one more line at the top of a row of similar scrapes. Then he counted the lines.

"Fifty-six, fifty-seven, fifty-eight," Hederick murmured with a self-satisfied air. "What a ferocious appetite the materbill has." He smirked as he remembered the terror on Mendis Vakon's unrepentant face. "How fortunate that there are heretics aplenty in Solace to feed him."

Chapter 5

At first glance, Crealora Senternal didn't look like a woman who had slain an entire family with evil magic at fifty paces. But these days you couldn't tell about someone by merely looking.

In Solace, only High Theocrat Hederick seemed to know for a certainty.

As men and women filed into Erolydon's gleaming vallenwood-paneled Great Chamber, they stole glances at the tiny woman who stood awaiting sentencing. Her head was bowed, and her hands were clasped so tightly that her fingertips were white.

At least a dozen guards, swords sheathed but unbuckled, stood at the edges of the room. Six novitiates tended incense burners in a ring around the woman accused of being a witch. A veil of flower-scented smoke hung in the air around Crealora. Few people in the room gazed long at her, but all stole cautious glimpses.

"Be careful, Gilles," a pregnant matron whispered to her husband as they edged through the crowd to a vacant spot. She plucked at his sleeve. "Don't meet her gaze, Gilles. They say the witch of Zaygoth can ensorcel a man with but a look!"

Gilles tut-tutted her but kept his voice low nonetheless. "That dried-up old stick? She's nothing but huge eyes and brittle bones, Susta. I've faced far worse monsters than Crealora Senternal, though it's a wonder her poor husband stood her oddities for so long. I've nothing to fear from such as her. You merely grow fanciful because of your expectant condition. I wanted to leave you home, but you'd have had my head if I suggested it."

"Gilles Domroy!" his wife exclaimed, forgetting to whisper. "If you think I'll miss the biggest spectacle in Solace since the Cataclysm, you're . . ."

Susta Domroy's shrill voice drew the attention of the prisoner. Crealora lanced the mother-to-be with a penetrating stare. The prisoner's sapphire-blue eyes glittered, and her colorless lips began to move silently. Her hands shook despite the heavy chains at her wrists.

"A spell!" Susta gasped and snatched forward the kerchief she wore over her hair, hiding her face. Her right hand shielded her belly, and she raised her left in the gesture that peasants believed averted witchcraft. She dragged the now stone-faced Gilles down onto the bench with her. People on each side quickly slid aside to give them more than enough room.

Crealora Senternal smiled grimly at the pair, then returned her gaze to the front of the room and the doors beneath the towering pulpit. "If I had magic for spells, would I be standing here now?" she muttered to herself. "Pah! I'd be winging my way across the forests of Ansalon." She looked around the room. "All these 'converts.'

Converted Seekers, indeed! Converted by Hederick's threats and goblins."

Let the Domroys believe that the long-despised witch of Zaygoth had laid a curse on their precious unborn heir. Crealora no longer cared what the people of Solace thought of her. She knew she had no more witchcraft in her than did the hammered iron links that bound her, supposedly to prevent her from completing the gestures necessary for spells.

"If one wet hair is out of place on the head of the Domroys' newborn babe, they'll place the blame at my door," she whispered. "Fools! I'll be at the side of my lord Paladine before long, and well beyond this farce." Still, she shivered.

The witch of Zaygoth waited on the subterranean floor of the semicircular room. Behind and above her stretched the packed benches of Erolydon's Great Chamber. Erolydon's builders had constructed the Chamber in a pit dug deep into the sandy soil at the eastern edge of Crystalmir Lake. The top tier of seats, like Hederick's pulpit, was actually at ground level.

The burnished vallenwood glowed with a beauty richer than oak. Vallenwoods were sacred trees, and at one time the residents of Solace would never have dared to lay an axe blade to the great trees. No one knew how ancient the towering vallenwoods were, only that some people thought they'd existed on Krynn before any living beings.

Hederick had overridden that reverence in short shrift. He'd wanted vallenwood for his temple, and that was that.

Crealora coughed in the incense-choked air. Today was the last day of her inquisition. Today Hederick would pass sentence. There was no doubt about the verdict: Hederick had never acquitted anyone. The form of the sentence was the only mystery. Despite her fear, Crealora felt a kind of relief.

Hundreds of voices rose and fell. They throbbed and ebbed behind her like the roar of the ocean waves that pounded the shore east of her native land of Zaygoth, which had been her home for her first twenty years. Then a handsome but godless trader, Kleven Senternal, traveling through Southern Ergoth selling his wares, had glimpsed her and fallen instantly in love. As smitten as he—and bolstered by his oath that he'd not interfere with her worship of the Old Gods—Crealora had left her tiny village of fishers and netcrafters for the trader's home in Solace.

With her abrupt manner of speaking and her foreign ways, Crealora was always an outsider in Solace, but she'd lived there happily enough with her Kleven for fifteen years. In the early years, before the Seekers had spread their new religion over the land like a poison, she'd been tolerated well enough.

Then only a few weeks ago, her mate had met the slashing claws and fiery breath of a mysterious beast after a trading run to the east. The creature, by some reports a materbill, had seared Kleven's horse with flames from its gullet and then ate the mount. It scattered Kleven's belongings and left Crealora's husband to bleed to death on the forest path.

One of the novitiates, a man of about thirty years, approached the witch and waved a curl of incense in her direction, his gaze carefully averted.

"Idiot!" Crealora snapped. "What can smoke do against sorcery? Were I a witch, could I not snuff a tiny ember, a mere arm's length away? Were I a witch, could I not snuff *you* just as easily?"

The man took a quick step backward, but made no response. None but Hederick dared speak to the witch.

Another yellow-robed novitiate cleared his throat. "All rise to honor Hederick, most reverend High Theocrat of Solace and judge of this holy court," he called. Hearing the shuffling of many feet as the spectators rose behind her, Crealora forced herself to breathe evenly. The High Theocrat would not see her quail.

"Hederick the Heretic, you do not frighten me," she whispered. She forced an insolent smile to her face as she studied the Chamber's portal. No sound came from the oiled hinges as two more novitiates pulled the double doors apart. The door beneath the pulpit was reserved for Seeker priests and novitiates; lay persons entered the Chamber for worship services through doors at each end of the topmost tier of seats.

The High Theocrat of Solace entered, regally dipped his head to the assembled crowd, and solemnly mounted the steps to the pulpit that doubled as judgment seat. The flickering light from ceremonial candles glinted off the gold threads interwoven with the mink-brown silk of the High Theocrat's robe. Dahos, Hederick's high priest, remained standing by the entrance.

Crealora marked the despised Theocrat's progress with bitter eyes and despairing heart. That Solace had fallen into the hands of such a wretch!

Hederick moved into the pulpit and began a prayer. Crealora craned her neck to look up at him. The angle gave her a splendid view of his pouchy chin and the bottom of his fleshy nose.

"Who'd think such arrogance and evil could fit in so small and lumpy a package?" she murmured.

Hederick was decidedly round in girth and not very tall. Thin, lank hair framed protruding blue eyes. At times during the witch's trial he had donned a ridiculous dark brown wig and a midnight-blue robe of velvet, but he'd eschewed those trappings today in favor of the traditional Seeker colors of brown and gold.

"Pious hypocrite," Crealora said softly, then added, more loudly, "Hederick, you are a heretic to the religion of the True Gods, and a hypocrite to boot!"

When Hederick ended his prayer, he gazed down at her without a word. Silence hung as heavily as the incense.

She burst out, "Everyone knows you destroy your opponents by any means. These people merely fear to say it!" She gestured as best she could under the weight of the heavy chains. "They know they'll be the next to face this court if they speak out against you, heretic! I ask you, Hederick—what threat am I, a poor widow, to one so great and powerful as you?"

Hederick pointed dramatically down at Crealora. Despite the murmuring of the crowd, his words filled the huge room. "You accuse *me* of impure motives? Of violating Seeker laws? You—an unholy witch, spawn of the dark gods?"

Crealora kept her face impassive. That voice, she thought. It had held countless audiences in thrall. Hederick's fame for oratory stretched from Solamnia to the shores of New Sea. He spun sentences like a spider threw a web, lingering over words as though he savored each syllable. If oratory were sorcery, Hederick would head the magical orders, Crealora thought.

"I'm no witch," she said flatly. "The charges against me are false."

Hederick stepped back and threw up his hands in exaggerated surprise. "Witch of Zaygoth!" he exclaimed. A few spectators chuckled. "Do you not recall the testimony of our own trial? The *sworn* testimony of dozens of your long-time neighbors who attest that they have personal knowledge of your witchery?"

Crealora turned to fling a withering glance at the assembly. As one, hundreds of people also twisted—to look anywhere but at the prisoner. Crealora grimaced and turned back.

"They lie to win your favor, Hederick," she said gently. "They lie to protect themselves. They are afraid, as all wise and thoughtful people in Solace are afraid in these troubled times."

Hederick, not normally one to allow prisoners to address him directly, seemed in uncommonly good humor today. He feigned great incredulity at Crealora's words.

"Surely the righteous don't fear *me!*" he retorted. "I am the protector of all who follow the true gods—the Seeker gods. Your neighbors—do they lie? Does Dugan Detmarr deceive us when he says he dreamed that he saw you hurl bolts of magical lightning at the Bayard family, killing them as they lay sleeping innocently in their beds?"

"The Bayards were slain by arrows, not lightning, Hederick." Crealora's voice filled the space between them. "How could I, a solitary woman, slaughter them all with no help, without any of the Bayards awaking to leave their beds and cry a warning? How could they be killed by lightning and not have a trace of a burn on their bodies?"

"The evil power of witches is great indeed," Hederick replied unctuously, "as must be the power of good that hopes to uproot it."

Crealora held up her chin defiantly. "Again I say, heretic, that it was not me. I was at home asleep."

"The location of your body is immaterial, witch. If it was not your actual physical being, then it was your spiritual likeness. Both are incriminating."

"My spiritual likeness? What Seeker pap!" Crealora laughed bitterly. "My likeness, taken flight to do mischief at the behest of evil gods? If I have such a likeness, Hederick, it surely was asleep at home beside me that night."

Dozens of onlookers gasped. Several men snickered. Hederick looked over the crowd, noted the overly merry ones, and used a quill to scrawl on a parchment. He dropped the paper from the pulpit. Dahos hurried forward, retrieved the fragment, bowed to Hederick, and conveyed the note to two guards near the double doors. The snickerers sank back into the press of bodies, cowering; no hands reached to comfort them.

"And why would I slay my neighbors?" Crealora demanded.

"Marka Uth Kondas and others witnessed your ire when the Bayard pigs trampled your garden early this summer."

"For a parcel of ruined flax, you think I would *kill?*"

"The logic of witches is not the logic of the pure and holy." Hederick gazed piously upward. "And why else would little Elia Bayard, a child of only five years, cry out your name as she lay dying, if you were not the guilty party?"

"I'd often taken herbs to the child when she had minor ailments. If anyone could help her that night, it would have been me. Elia knew that. It was only natural—"

"What? You claim to be a healer now?" Hederick exclaimed as though outraged. "Many have said that except for the miracles wrought by the Seekers, there has been no true 'healing' since the Old Gods abandoned Krynn at the time of the Cataclysm. Clearly you are no follower of the Seekers, yet you claim now to be able to heal. What new sin is this?"

Crealora knew she was doomed, but perhaps there was a reasonable person here who would recall her words later. "That's no sorcery, heretic Hederick," she said loudly. "Nor is it a miracle. Certain plants are able to effect certain cures—of minor complaints. And the only gods who can claim responsibility for that are the old, ancient gods, who created the plants and their wonderful properties in the first place."

Hederick snorted, inspiring another flicker of titters from the crowd. "Those gods are long gone, Dame Senternal. There are only the Seeker gods now. And if you claim to heal and are no Seeker, the only possibility left is that you are a witch."

"You killed the Bayards, Hederick!"

Onlookers cried out as Crealora let the accusation burst forth. "Sethin Bayard had complained loudly because you cut down the vallenwoods he treasured. You had plenty of reasons to want him dead. I say *you* sent the bowmen who slew the Bayards in the night. *You* are responsible for the arrows that pierced the hearts of five-year-old Elia Bayard and her parents. And because I, too, have criticized you, you use this farce of a trial to rid yourself of me as well! Who's to say that you didn't have a hand in the slaying of my husband, as well? Kleven's low opinion of you was well-known in Solace."

Hederick went white, then red. He clutched the railing so tightly his nails bit into his palms. "You dare to speak thus to one of the Seeker high ministry? Surely this is proof of your heresy!"

Crealora turned to face the crowd. She tried vainly to raise her chained hands as she addressed the mass of people. "Why would I want the Bayards dead?" she cried. "They were my neighbors. As most of you are!" Her voice rang out over the rising noise of the assembly. "Can you truly believe that I would hurt you?"

A pall fell over the crowd. No one met her gaze. Too late, Crealora recalled the exchange with the Domroys. A moment of frightened vengefulness on her part, and look at them now. Of course they feared her—they'd "seen" her put the evil eye on an unborn baby! By the time the child was born, strong and healthy, she would be dead, and it would no longer matter what they believed or thought they'd seen. Tears in her eyes, she turned back toward Hederick, her chin high.

"It has been proved to this court's satisfaction that you, Crealora Senternal, killed the Bayards with magic lightning. The penalty is death." Hederick smirked as he leaned over the railing and motioned to the guards.

At his signal, one of the men tied a gag over her mouth. Hederick triumphantly went on declaiming, but Crealora barely heard him. "Bind her to the vallenwood stump . . . the courtyard . . . until dead." She was hustled roughly from the room to the sun-splashed courtyard, the eager crowd pushing and shoving behind her.

Four guards clambered up onto a small platform in front of the vallenwood stump. They bound the woman's feet to two pegs jutting out four feet above the ground and her hands to iron rings placed in the stump almost seven feet above that. She was so short that her feet barely reached the pegs. Crealora looked for tinder, for dry sticks, at her feet, but there was none. How did Hederick propose to burn her without tinder?

Only a handful of spectators remained in the central courtyard. The rest had been shoved back behind a stone wall nearly as tall as the stump, with risers behind it so people could watch the show.

When the temple guards finished guiding the onlookers to their places, five men remained in the courtyard with Crealora. They were the five who had tittered when she'd ridiculed the High Theocrat.

Metal creaked. Crealora and the men turned their eyes toward the temple. Hederick, on a viewing stand behind the barricade, gave directions to some novitiates. The priests-in-training pulled the chains that opened a portal near the side of the temple doors. Something large slid into the courtyard, and the gate banged shut behind it.

"By the Greater Pantheon! What is it?" cried one of the trapped men.

Crealora could have told them. She'd heard Kleven describe materbills; he'd thought he spied one only a week before his death. Two or three times the size of a lion, he'd said. Retractable claws the length of her arm. A leonine mane in the colors of flame—orange and gold and red and black. And when the materbill roared, real flames burst from its mouth.

Reason denied that there could be two such rare creatures suddenly near Solace. This beast, Crealora knew suddenly, was the one that had slain Kleven; it would now likewise slay her. She tried to scream, but the gag almost choked her. The five men who shouted and ran to the wall, imploring friends on the other side to rescue them.

The monster paused just inside the courtyard gate. It stopped and, catlike, gazed around in a bored manner. It licked one huge front paw, then the other. Then it licked its chops.

The trapped men doubled their entreaties.

Hederick, brown-and-gold robe fluttering in the afternoon breeze, stood confidently on the viewing stand high above the crowd. The rest of the viewers shrank back from the inner wall. Several people tried to force their way through the main gates to the outside path, but armed guards and goblins prevented them from leaving.

"People of Solace!" Hederick cried, his voice rebounding off the stone walls. He slowed the tempo of his words, adjusting to the echoes. "A lesson." The High Theocrat pointed at the monster. "This is a materbill." Several people cried out in surprise. "Yes, a creature of legend, delivered out of myth by the New Gods, the Seeker gods, to help us find the way to truth."

He waited for the commotion to subside and continued. "Sauvay, god of power and vengeance, has presented me with this gift, this proof of his approval of my mission in Solace. I will weed out all who waver in their allegiance to the Seekers. I will keep the community safe for those who are pure of heart and true to the New Gods!"

His hand went to his chest, and he patted something under the front of his robe. Not a whisper rose from the crowd. Even the five men at the opposite end of the courtyard seemed mesmerized. Crealora felt her willpower drain from her as though the beast—or more likely Hederick himself—had deftly absorbed it.

The materbill broke the spell. It bounded across the courtyard in three leaps, pouncing on the men. Two escaped, screaming. The other three lay pinned under the beast's massive front paws. One of the three appeared to have died instantly, but the remaining two writhed in pain and fear. Then the materbill slowly extended its front claws. They were as long as a man's arm and came to wicked points, as Kleven had said. The creature pierced the men's bodies, and their blood flowed freely onto the ground. Crealora heard a wail from between the inner and outer walls—a new widow, no doubt.

The materbill picked up one man's body and shook it in its teeth. Another carcass the creature nuzzled almost lovingly, licking it from breastbone to head. The third corpse it ignored.

Then the materbill looked around again, focusing on Crealora this time. Her mouth went dry; sweat drenched her skin and clothes. She almost fainted from the pounding in her heart and the fear in her mind. But she met the materbill's unblinking gaze steadily as she intoned a silent prayer:

Dear Paladine, I am willing to die for you and the Old Gods, but I beg that if you have any power left on Krynn, any mercy remaining for your few devout followers, you will make my passing as swift and painless as possible. Don't let me show my fear to the heretic and humiliate myself and the others who still pray to you.

Abandoning the three dead bodies and ignoring the pair of survivors cowering behind the stump, the materbill padded purposefully across the bricks and cobblestones toward Crealora. Its eyes were sea green, the huge vertical pupils obsidian black. The creature halted, long tail twitching, bloodied tips of its foreclaws etching lines in the stones of the courtyard. It stank of blood and death.

Crealora closed her eyes, then reopened them. This would be her last glimpse of life in this world. Frightened people were crammed between inner and outer walls, but only a few curious heads could be seen, their expressions alternately horrified and fascinated.

All except one man and a woman.

The couple stood in plain sight near the main gate. The woman was nearly as tall as the man and, like him, wore the plain cloak of a traveler. Refugees, perhaps. Both were apparently of great age. The woman, whose curly gray hair extended unbound past her waist, held a fringed silver scarf, which concealed her hands and part of her body. Her eyes were closed, her lips moving. Under the plain cloak flowed a long white garment.

The man's gaze caught Crealora's eyes.

He was ordinary-looking, with a salt-and-pepper beard and nearly bald head. He carried an unexceptional wooden staff. The man wore a plain traveling shift of rough green cotton over patched leggings, and his boots were scuffed. He and his elderly companion must have arrived just as the gates were barricaded; Crealora had not seen them in the Great Chamber. The man's arms were folded across his chest, his stance sturdy, although Crealora could tell even from this distance that he was not young—and perhaps was even older than Hederick.

Do not fear, the old man's eyes seemed to say. *You are not alone.*

"Crealora Senternal, you stand condemned of witchcraft and heresy," intoned Hederick. Crealora started at the sound, so riveting had been the other man's stare. Even now she felt herself unwilling to look away from the two people at the gate.

Hederick droned on. "Let the death of this evil woman, O goddess Omalthea, show you that our hearts and our souls are only with you. Let the death of this sorry soul, Omalthea, steel the resolve of those wavering against sin. Let the death of this unrepentant heathen, O Motherlord, serve as a warning to all who risk the ire of the New Gods by disregarding the *Praxis*.

"The Old Gods are gone, and you, Omalthea, have come with your blessings in their stead," Hederick finished. "So be it."

Crealora glanced back toward the couple by the gate. The old woman had doffed the worn cloak and dropped the scarf. Her white robe drew all eyes. "A mage!" one of the novitiates shouted.

The woman stretched her arms above her. Wind swirled around her slender figure. She displayed the strength of a much younger person—a woman a third her age. "Hederick!" the old woman shouted. "Cease this charade!"

The High Theocrat's head shot around. Hederick gazed at the woman. His lips moved, but no sound issued forth. The Seeker priest caught the edge of the lectern, his blue eyes staring from his face like the orbs of a heathen stone idol. "Ancilla," he said softly. "Ancilla. In the flesh, at last."

"Cease this sin, Hederick."

"I should have known you'd not give up, Ancilla," Hederick whispered. "All these years you've hounded me, ever since I defeated you at Garlund. You've sent countless magical creatures to harry me, but never have you appeared yourself." The High Theocrat actually bowed, a mocking smile on his lips. "I always knew it was you behind the harassment, Ancilla. I suppose I should be honored that you come in person to pay court to me at last, witch." His tone was thick with derision.

"I will stop you this time, Hederick," Ancilla said. "I have the power now."

Hederick laughed, then he struck a commanding pose

and pointed at the old woman. "Fellow Seekers!" he cried, his voice thundering across the intervening space as though he could strike the old woman down with words alone, "you see before you another witch! Let her die here with the witch of Zaygoth. Sauvay demands her death. Guards!"

At Hederick's words, Ancilla turned slightly toward Tarscenian. The High Theocrat seemed to realize for the first time that Ancilla was not alone. He gazed for a moment in puzzlement at the tall, bearded man. "Tarscenian?" he said wonderingly. Then his voice rose above the noise of the crowd once again. "False priest! Guards! Arrest them!"

The materbill growled. Tarscenian looked away from the woman whom Hederick had called Ancilla. His gaze locked into Crealora's eyes, far across the courtyard. The materbill roared rage and fire, and Crealora smelled her own hair burning. Flames flickered at the fringe of her shawl; the hem of her skirt caught fire. Crealora sensed all this as though it were happening to someone else, at a great distance. She pointed her face skyward, where a curl of smoke rose into the sky. Soon her essence would rise within that spiral toward the plane of the Old Gods.

The materbill roared again. The fire doubled, but Crealora felt little pain. She peered through the smoke with watering eyes and spied Tarscenian and Ancilla.

The old woman was chanting and gesticulating. Lightning had erupted from her fingers and was roaring around the courtyard. A ring of temple guards had circled the spellcasting pair but appeared frozen in the act of trying to capture them. What was going on?

The materbill snarled. Dimly, Crealora heard screams from the two men still seeking to secret themselves behind the vallenwood trunk. Then the man called Tarscenian caught Crealora's gaze again, and continued to hold it. He was chanting, too. He hurled a handful of powder to the ground.

New calm spread through Crealora. This was the end, then.

The materbill roared once more.

The witch of Zaygoth closed her eyes and died.

Chapter 6

"Your Worship!" Dahos called. "The woman has turned the guards to stone!"

"I see that, you idiot!" Hederick raged. A dozen noviciates huddled underneath the platform, but Hederick refused to show any panic. "Send more guards against her, fool!"

The high priest didn't move right away. Instead he stared in awe at the elderly mage. "What power!" he murmured. Then Dahos raised his voice to a level that could be heard by Hederick. "Your Worship, the woman has stopped two dozen guards. She hurls bolts of lightning around the courtyard like so many twigs. Yet she has harmed no one. Why should this be?"

"She wants only me," Hederick shouted. "She would kill me if she could, but I am too strong for her! Double the forces, high priest!"

Dahos looked from the bolt-hurling enchantress to the High Theocrat. Then he gestured curtly to the captain of Erolydon's guards. The chief guard put a horn to his lips and blew.

The front entrance of the temple building crashed open, and six goblins, clad in leather armor and wielding maces and spears, hurtled through. Blinking against the painful light, they shoved the panic-stricken people aside, injuring more than one person in the process. Yellow Eyes dashed toward Ancilla and Tarscenian, his five comrades at his heels. "Endit the ladywitch!" Yellow Eyes thundered. "Kill 'em!"

The goblins did no better than the guards. Twenty paces from Ancilla and Tarscenian, they crashed into an invisible wall of magical origin and slid, senseless, to the cobblestones.

"By Sauvay!" Hederick swore. The witch had never challenged him so directly before. He shoved his hand into the front of his robe and drew forth an object. Then Hederick thrust his hand toward Ancilla. Suddenly he and Dahos were bathed in glittery light. The device shone too brightly for any but Hederick to discern its subtle details. To most, it was a glowing ball, no more.

"Leave off, witch!" Hederick bellowed. "My gods protect me, here as everywhere."

"You must stop this evil, Hederick." Ancilla spoke in a normal tone, but her voice seemed to echo from the marble walls, the stones of the courtyard, and the iron of the gates. Lightning continued to ricochet around the area. The materbill, smeared with ashes and blood, snarled and dashed back to the door through which it had emerged. Responding to Hederick's command, a frightened novitiate frantically hauled on the rope, and the leonine creature disappeared safely into Erolydon's lower reaches.

"*Norvir tonwek.*" Ancilla's gravelly voice insinuated

itself around Hederick like a noose.

"You can't stop me, Ancilla," Hederick said.

"Centinbil chuffhing, adon."

"I'm well aware of your pathetic attempts to impede me," Hederick shouted. "You cannot harm me—not while I have the Diamond Dragon of my lord Sauvay." He held it aloft, exulting in the control it gave him. Let the masses see the power that their High Theocrat wielded!

"Gatefil antogys adon."

"What will it be this time, Ancilla? Will you again use magic to try to usurp my followers, my closest aides? They will not forsake me, witch. They cannot harm me, either, despite your wishes. My lord Sauvay made the Diamond Dragon too strong for simple subterfuge."

Hederick taunted her, suddenly conscious of the stares of hundreds of awestruck Seeker converts. He could imagine their thoughts: The High Theocrat was single-handedly taking on a mage of the highest order—and clearly winning—*without magic!*

"Surrender now, Ancilla," he coaxed. "I will make sure you and Tarscenian die quickly. I will not draw out the time of your deaths, even though you do not deserve my mercy. A mage and a false Seeker priest! Sauvay and Omalthea will rejoice at your deaths. They will rain their benefactions upon me and my followers." He turned to face the crowd, once again holding forth the Diamond Dragon, and cried, "Hear me, people of Solace!"

Ancilla's hands could barely be seen, so quickly did they whirl in the air. Her eyes gleamed. *"Gatefil antogys adon. Shiral."* Magical powders gyrated around her, joining and separating to create rainbows of color. The High Theocrat had never seen such a display of magical power.

But there was nothing here that the Diamond Dragon of Sauvay could not stop, Hederick was sure of that. He held the artifact higher, shifting it so that it threw off multitudinous sparkles in the midday sun. As always, the people appeared mesmerized—all but Ancilla and her unholy mate. Hederick's sister appeared to have thrown some sort of protective spell around Tarscenian, sheltering him from the effect of Sauvay's Diamond Dragon.

Ancilla spoke. "If you will not cease this activity, Hederick, I will remove you from your beloved Erolydon."

Hederick smiled disdainfully, confident that with the support of Sauvay he would prevail. The High Theocrat had nothing to fear.

Ancilla's seamed face was implacable as she continued her warning. "Oh, I'll not send you too far away, Hederick," she said. "I would not deprive you of your temple. But you will be someplace where you can no longer harm the innocent."

He laughed malevolently and once again displayed the Diamond Dragon.

"*Ghezhit.*"

Hederick saw a purple cloud speed toward him. The front of the magical creation opened like a dragon's maw. The nimbus expanded, the vapor reforming until a purple lizard seemed to tower over him, nearly as large as the courtyard. Claws reached hungrily for the High Theocrat.

Ancilla continued to chant, triumph apparent in her stance and in every syllable she uttered. Where had she accumulated such power? Hederick wondered.

"*Centinbil chuffhing, adon. Ghezhit. Gatefil antogys adon. Ghezhit.*"

The lizard's nebulous mouth opened farther. The magical creature lunged.

And Hederick turned the Diamond Dragon to face the magical wyrm it so closely resembled.

A flash, and roiling smoke. Then the lizard recoiled in the sky above Erolydon, tail churning the air, front legs pawing at a slash in its vaporous belly. It wheeled about in midair.

And charged back toward Ancilla and Tarscenian.

"Sederai donitan!" Ancilla chanted. She shoved Tarscenian aside and stood alone against the monster's charge.

The cloud creature swallowed her whole. Where Hederick's sister had stood only moments ago, now there was . . . nothing.

Chaos prevailed for a few moments before the temple guards and Hederick's goblins regained their senses. By the time the High Theocrat's minions recovered and could begin forcing their way through the panicked people, Tarscenian was out the gate and racing toward the vallenwoods.

Chapter 7

The temple guards had no chance against Tarscenian's advantage of surprise, and his magic gave him even better odds of eluding them.

The leather-clad goblins and the blue-and-yellow-arrayed guards raced after the sound of running feet that seemed to be pounding toward Solace. Thanks to an effective illusion on Tarscenian's part, the guards followed only sounds. His pursuers were certain they would catch up with their elusive quarry around each bend in the Solace road, only to find when they rounded a corner that he was still beyond their line of sight.

Meanwhile, Tarscenian lay in an outcropping of ferns near the temple.

Ancilla was dead.

After five decades fighting Seekerism together, they had

ultimately failed. Hederick was High Theocrat, and was fully convinced of his own divine destiny. He was stronger and more powerful than ever, seemingly invincible. Forty white-robed mages were doomed to slow deaths within the bark of as many vallenwoods. Worse, the people of Krynn now stood helpless against the evil of Hederick and his Seekers.

"Farewell, my dear Ancilla," Tarscenian whispered. "I will never forget—"

I am here, my love.

Tarscenian leaped to his feet, drew his sword, and dropped into ready position. Then the realization came over him that he recognized the faint voice. He forced himself to take a deep breath.

After more than fifty years with the female mage, one would think nothing could surprise him anymore.

Tarscenian peered through the trees. "I feared the worst, Ancilla," he murmured. "I feared you were—" He stopped talking, surveyed the scene again curiously.

There was no sign of anyone. And especially no sign of an eighty-year-old, white-robed wizard.

The voice whispered again, and Tarscenian realized he heard it inside his head.

Even with the powers of two score mages, I could not defeat him. The Diamond Dragon is stronger than I'd ever thought possible, Tarscenian. By Paladine! I thought forty mages would be enough. Now—

"Ancilla," Tarscenian snapped impatiently, interrupting her. "Where in the reaches of the endless Abyss *are* you, woman?"

I tried to place a binding spell on Hederick. I had the power of forty mages, after all. Have you heard of a binding spell, Tarscenian?

Of course he had, although casting such a spell was far beyond his carnival-level powers. A binding spell could pluck something or someone out of one reality to be dropped at the whim of the spellcaster into another one.

So now I'm right where I'd hoped to put Hederick. And the spell has left me too weak to reverse it myself. Not without the Diamond Dragon. I . . .

"Where *are* you?" Tarscenian repeated. "I can barely hear you, Ancilla."

Within the vallenwood trunk, back in the courtyard of the temple. I am trapped!

The old man sat back down in the ferns and contemplated this news. "Be calm, my love," he said at last. "At least you are alive. Thank Paladine for that."

I will do what I can to help you from here, Tarscenian, but the battle, I fear, belongs to you now.

"Must we use only magic?"

What other means do you suggest we use? The Seeker "gods" have corrupted my brother's mind and confuse his thoughts; you know he will not listen—

Tarscenian interrupted angrily. "Couldn't we simply wait until Hederick leaves the temple and waylay him? Let me do it, Ancilla. I am old but still strong. I assure you I would enjoy the task."

We have argued about this before, Tarscenian.

"Please. I can easily kill him if the opportunity presents itself. One quick thrust . . . I promise you he will not suffer."

Stop! I will not have Hederick harmed. I made an oath—I swore never to physically hurt him. If I cannot halt him here and now, his own greed and ambition will eventually take care of him—but I must stop him from doing irreparable harm to the world. Tarscenian, I am afraid.

"He's dangerous. Let me . . ."

He is dangerous because he is weak but believes himself strong. It is not his fault, Tarscenian; his wrongheadedness is born of pain. It could play powerfully into the wrong hands.

"Ancilla . . ."

I fear the evil goddess will make much use of Hederick.

Nonetheless, Tarscenian, I swore an oath to my brother.

"Hederick despises you, Ancilla. I could dispatch him with a quick thrust of steel. He'd not hesitate to do the same to you, you know that. For your sake, I'd make sure it was instantaneous, which is more than he'd grant you."

No, Tarscenian. I cannot renege on such an oath.

"Let me follow him, at least, and divine where he keeps the Diamond Dragon. I will try to steal it back for you."

We have tried that. You are a crafty illusionist, my love, but you have no skills as a thief. And Hederick knows what you look like now.

"I could hire a thief."

We have tried that, too. Many times. But perhaps Solace thieves are more adept than those we have engaged in the past. Do that—hire one. It is something, anyway.

Tarscenian's thoughts shifted. "We were not able to save the woman Crealora."

We eased her passage to the next world. She felt little pain.

"But she died!"

The woman is with Paladine, my friend. She is away from the pain of this world. It is not our place to wish her back.

Tarscenian did not reply. This time it was Ancilla's turn to offer comfort.

Don't despair, my love. Lie low until the guards stop looking for you, and then find us a ring of thieves. I will do what I can from here. I still have a few ways to annoy my brother, never fear. Perhaps I cannot stop him permanently, but surely I can make his life miserable . . . as he has made mine.

Chapter 8

The High Theocrat changed into a fresh robe after the execution and turned his sullied garment over to a novitiate for burning. Then Hederick headed straight for the Great Chamber. He sent Dahos and the others away, then closeted himself to prepare for the evening revelations.

He may have defeated one of the greatest mages ever, but routine was sacred. Seeker gods did not tolerate sloppiness.

Everything in the Great Chamber was out of place today, of course. It always was this way, despite repeated punishment of his terrified aides. The incense holders, the ceremonial crystals, the holy parchments—all were only a hairsbreadth awry, but wrong nonetheless. Had no one else read the *Praxis*?

Hederick resolved to speak once more with his high

priest. Perhaps he would have to make an example of one of the novitiates before the rest applied themselves more dutifully. But now he busied himself setting things to rights in the pulpit. It wouldn't do to have the Greater and Lesser Pantheons gaze down on untidiness when he summoned them before hundreds of devout Seekers.

Setting out the ritual implements according to intricate, century-old patterns was an exacting task, but Hederick had a passion for detail. He routinely caught lapses in Seeker protocol that far younger men missed.

I may be well past sixty, but I have sharper faculties than most priests, he told himself. That's why I'm High Theocrat. The New Gods have blessed me. After all, they helped me defeat Ancilla.

He stood a little straighter despite the cramp that had creased his back since the tussle with Mendis Vakon. Hederick frowned and moved the goblet of holy mead an inch to the right.

Then he froze. Cold fire gripped the pit of his stomach. Sweat drenched him.

He swept the room with a stare.

Undeniably, Hederick was alone. But *not* alone.

The High Theocrat stood quietly for a moment. Then he reached into the front of his robe and pulled out the Diamond Dragon. He removed the leather covering and shook the artifact onto his palm.

The Diamond Dragon, as always, was warm to the touch and all aglitter. Hederick squinted and stared directly at it, even though that always made his head ache. If he concentrated enough, he could see the artifact's outline: jagged scales, wicked tail, and toothy maw of a tiny dragon. A lance grew from its midsection like some misplaced egg tooth.

Crafted in precious steel, with ruby eyes and encrusted with diamonds all down its back, the thing was worth a fortune. Early in his Seeker career, when he had been poor enough to fear starvation, he was tempted to pawn it.

But Sauvay, his god, had invested it with his blessing. The Diamond Dragon had protected Hederick more than once. The High Theocrat stroked the figurine, replaced it in the bag, and dropped the pendant inside his robe once more. The knot in his stomach eased.

Then the fear hit full-force. He *was* being observed, and the observer was malevolent. Hederick maintained his emotionless mien and, as though it were an afternoon like any other, poured sanctified mead from a silver vase into a stemmed goblet of crystal, its tiny bowl barely larger than a thimble.

Hederick had performed this rite many times in his decades as a Seeker. So practiced were his actions that even now, with his pulse hammering, none of the sweet fluid dripped onto the altar cloth. The High Theocrat felt the hair prickle at the back of his neck. He carefully replaced the vase on the altar, then raised the chalice and quaffed the honey-colored beverage.

"To you, Great Ones, I offer my fealty," he murmured. "I greet another evening with hope and passion, and I beseech you to punish this sacrilege of your holy chamber . . . for something threatens the peace of this place." He quickly poured another glass of mead and downed that one, too.

As always with the potent beverage, Hederick's vision swirled, then snapped into focus. But unlike the other times, on this occasion he suddenly felt exposed and vulnerable, so high above the floor of the Great Chamber. Vertigo assailed him, then faded away.

Because of Hederick's lack of physical stature, he'd derived peculiar joy in ordering the builders of the temple Erolydon to construct the holy altar and pulpit at the top of four narrow flights of stairs. Each sunset, when Hederick passed on the revelations of the New Gods, he spoke down—*down*, he rejoiced—to the hushed worshipers that jammed the tiers of wooden benches. Special windows and mirrors allowed the blushing sunsets over Crystalmir Lake to pour into the room, bathing the priestly figure at the top of the chamber in glorious purples, pinks, and scarlets.

Then, as now, the pulpit gave him an unobstructed view of everything within the Great Chamber.

Hederick raised his head, gaze shifting around the cavernous amphitheater. There was no sign of an intruder, but he had the distinct feeling that somebody's eyes were upon him. Slowly the feeling grew, until he felt seared by what was happening, as if his skin was blistered and peeling away in charred strips. His free hand found its way back to his neck and again grasped the leather-swaddled dragon figurine.

Face me.

The unheard words filled Hederick. The priest felt his mind expand and contract dizzyingly. His body remained motionless, arrested in the act of lowering the sacred chalice to the altar. But in his mind, Hederick saw himself bleeding on the marble floor below, at the bottom of the vallenwood stairs. The broken Hederick of his imagination lay naked to whatever torture the Presence that shared this chamber chose to inflict.

Face me.

"Unholy thing!" the religious leader shrieked. Tremors shook him. "Sorcery's bastard! Show yourself!"

I am Ancilla. Face me, dear one.

"You are dead!"

Alas, my little brother, you are mistaken.

Hederick shook a tightly clenched fist in the air and shouted again into the vast and seemingly empty chamber. "For decades I walked the roads of northern Ansalon, witch, spreading the word of the deliverance to come," he shouted. "I am—I was—the Holy Wanderer of the Seekers. Entire villages joined the Seekers upon my inspiration. I worked miracles in the name of the New Gods!" His voice dropped to a piercing whisper. "Always you have followed me, dear sister. And *never* have you defeated me. Nor will you. I proved that this afternoon. You had never been stronger—but I was stronger still." Hederick placed the crystal chalice on the altar and shook his fist again. "This is *my* temple. You cannot hurt me here!"

There was no answer.

After a moment, Hederick's hands weakened and fell to his sides. He damply fingered the folds of his robe. The ache grew behind his eyes, and sweat trickled through his hair. His heart lurched.

I'm getting old, he thought suddenly. How many more years of this can I stand?

Accept me.

"Never! You are a demon, Ancilla."

Hederick found himself peering over the low railing that protected those at the altar from the sixty-foot drop to the floor. He saw movement in the depths below. Smoke rose through the solid marble floor of the Great Chamber. It clung to the stone, a purple-gray miasma of evil.

"Begone!" he boomed. Exultation grew in the High Theocrat. His was the voice that had ensnared more Seeker souls than any other priest over the decades. His was the name that countless followers breathed aloud reverently as they worshiped, believing him the soul of the new church. He had dispelled the witch in the courtyard; he could dispel her here. Hederick's forceful baritone voice shook with indignation. "Erolydon is a holy place! Leave it at once!"

The words echoed off the gleaming wooden walls. "Erolydon . . . Erolydon . . . holy . . . at once . . . once."

The echoes stopped, swallowed by the smoke.

You must accept me as part of you, if you hope to achieve what you wish.

The smoke thickened, roiling over the floor.

"You do not frighten me," Hederick lied, eyeing the four tiers of steps. Perhaps he could race down and leap through the smoke before Ancilla's Presence grew stronger. But he grimaced at the vision of himself bounding down the stairs to escape fog that he was quite sure no one else would be able to see. Dahos could enter at any moment. It wouldn't do to have the priest witness the highest Seeker in Solace leaping and running away from . . . nothing.

"You cannot stop me," he said. "You are the dying breath of the Old Gods. You are magic . . . and you fear me." He forced a laugh. "*You* fear *me!* I will end your gods' reign upon this world. I am Chosen. Few believe in the Ancient Ones. Now is the time of the New Gods. We grow stronger with every passing moment." Spittle leaped from Hederick's mouth as he spoke.

Hederick, you are old, and I . . . in this form, I am ageless. Welcome me. Turn away from these false gods.

The fog now covered the first two tiers of stairs. It deepened and grew more purple; streaks of black oozed through.

Hederick backpedaled to put the altar between him and the Presence. He once again drew out the Diamond Dragon.

The artifact is useless against me in this form, Hederick. Will you spend your few remaining years with your eyes still closed to the truth? Your lauded Seeker gods are only pathetic wishful thinking. Remember Venessi? Remember our mother's false god?

"I will lead all the Seekers!" the High Theocrat shouted. "And not just those in Solace! We will destroy all who follow the Ancient Ones. Only the fool Knights of Solamnia, a handful of mages, and a few deluded losers still believe in the Old Gods. Move aside for the new order. Admit your defeat!"

You cannot defeat such as I. You must accept me, love me as I love you, little brother. I came once to bring you to the true gods and you turned me away. Let me help you now.

Stair after stair gave way before the rising fog. Hederick detected flashes of lightning. He waved the Diamond Dragon at the smoke, but the artifact seemed to have lost its power.

Hederick's rich baritone was gone now, his mouth dry. He rallied, though his voice cracked. "Magic," he spat out. "The magic of the Old Gods wanes daily. Wizards have hidden themselves in covens and towers, they so fear the new Seeker order." Hederick felt a surge of religious fervor. "Magic is leaving Krynn! But call it by its true names, Ancilla: Witchcraft! Sorcery! Sin!"

You have but a short time left, Hederick. In this form, I have forever.

He heard a hiss, as though of fog dissolving. The smell of rotting meat filled his nostrils. The High Theocrat swallowed a mouthful of bile and closed his eyes. Hederick leaned back against the railing and held out the Diamond Dragon again. The altar cloth slipped unseen to his feet.

His voice still rang with bravado, but the fog deadened the words, stealing their edge. "I will end magic, end witchcraft, and Krynn shall praise only the New Gods. I have slain mages from Haven to Solace and beyond. My spies . . . The Old Gods have abandoned Krynn. Only fools refuse to abandon them in turn!"

Carried away by his own rhetoric, Hederick opened his eyes. Purple and black smoke boiled around him, extending to the rafters. Hederick smelled death. His spine convulsed. He pitched forward.

Crouching unsteadily at the base of the altar, Hederick screamed, "What are you? What evil do you hide?" He scrabbled to the railing, grasped it with a pudgy hand, and hauled himself to his feet. "I will fight you! I *am* the Seekers! Show yourself!"

The fog wavered for a heartbeat. Something like a sigh sounded. Then the smoke thinned. One hand on the rail and one on the altar, Hederick stood, bracing himself, and looked downward where he could make out what might have been the silhouette of a woman—or an ogre—or a lizard. It hung in the air, standing on nothing, suspended over the open expanse of the Great Chamber. Clots of fog and smoke obscured its true form. It took a step toward him and seemed to beckon.

Ah, Hederick. Face me, my brother.

Hederick's nails carved half-moons in the wood. The scent of magic was everywhere. He sank back into the dimness under the altar.

"No!" he screamed. "Go back!" Sobbing like a child, Hederick buried his face in the crumpled altar cloth. "I don't want to look. Go away. Go away, please. I'll be good, I promise." He waited, shaking. "Please?"

He waited a bit longer, then lifted his head. The foul odors were gone. Gouges from his fingernails marred the red-gold vallenwood railing. The altar cloth was tear-stained and ruined. But the fog had vanished.

Hederick heard a voice, quite an ordinary one.

"Your Worship?" A slender woman, light hair braided into a coronet, stood in shadow at the bottom of the steps. She held a basket topped by a pink cloth. Shakily, Hederick rose and, gripping the railing, staggered down the steps toward her.

Had the woman witnessed his humiliation?

From a distance, she had appeared young. But as Hederick drew nearer, he could see that the hair was white, not blond. The face was wrinkled.

"Did you see anything?" he demanded.

"Your Worship?" The old woman gazed up at him in awe. Her words tripped over themselves. "I come now with a gift for the priests. I seen you tending something under the altar, and I waited until I think you was done, on the off-chance you was doin' something religious. Your Worship." She nodded rapidly, twice.

Hederick, standing on the landing, inspected the hag. She was just like the multitude of other peasant converts who had been drawn to the Seeker religion for comfort in the troubled years since the Cataclysm. They came in droves but brought little money.

"What is your name, old woman?" he demanded. "How did you get in here?" He suddenly realized that the sun was about to set. Soon the crowds would converge upon the Great Chamber for the nightly revelations.

"Norah, Your Worship." She smiled tentatively at him and ventured stiffly up the stairs, still holding out the basket. She favored one knee, and her knuckles were swollen. "Your man, the high priest, said as it was all right for me to come in here. He said you was probably near done with your religious duties. So I come in here to wait."

"And you saw nothing?" Hederick pressed. "Heard nothing?"

Norah looked around in bewilderment. "Are you all right, Your Worship? Can I help you?" She came closer, hand outstretched, until she stood two steps below him.

Hederick hesitated. Sympathy glowed in the old woman's bright blue eyes. For a fearful moment, he wanted nothing more than to lay his head on her shoulder. Once again his hands shook, and he hid them in his robe.

Norah continued to reach a knobby hand toward the High Theocrat. "You look awful, Your Worship, if you don't mind my sayin'. I could make up an herb charm for you, a tea or poultice, say a few special words over't. My mother used to make 'em, and my grandmam afore her. It'll fix you right up, sure." She smiled reassuringly. "A bit of harmless family magic, y'see." Her hand picked at his sleeve.

"Magic! Witch!" Hederick cried out, recoiling. "You are Ancilla! You are the witch in mortal form."

"Ancilla?" Bewilderment crossed the woman's features. "Who? But I told you, m'name is . . ."

The flat of Hederick's hand struck the side of Norah's startled face. Her basket soared over the stair railing. A dish shattered. She pitched backward and careened headlong down a flight of stairs to the temple floor. There were a few groans, a luckless attempt to rise, then . . . nothing.

Hederick waited on the stairs.

The double doors banged open under the pulpit. Dahos hurried into the room and stopped short. Two temple guards, arrayed in their ceremonial blue and gold, followed. "What has happened?" the high priest asked, alarmed. "Your Worship, you are harmed?"

"No, Dahos," Hederick said.

The tall priest knelt over the crumpled figure. Large hands moved deftly. Dahos loosened the woman's clothing and chafed her hands. He gently tapped her face, then bent close to see if she still breathed. Finally he sat back and sighed. Blood stained his face and robe. "She is dead." Dahos bowed his head and began the Prayer of the Passing Spirit. "Great Omalthea, accept the commitment of this guiltless soul . . ."

"Stop," Hederick snapped. "The hag was evil. She deserves no final blessing."

Dahos's head shot up. "Your Worship?"

Hederick made his way past the high priest, moving toward the door. "She was a witch, Dahos," he spat over his shoulder.

"A witch?" Horror showed on Dahos's face. He edged away from the corpse. "This is Norah Ap Orat," he said. "She baked bread and blended special teas to sell in the marketplace. We were one of her customers, Your Worship!"

"Be quiet." Hederick replied. "Have the guards remove her. Burn her—no, better yet, have her fed to the materbill; the creature likes carrion." Hederick watched the high priest as a pair of guards hefted the woman's slight body and bore it out of the room. The High Theocrat felt the strength of leadership rekindle within him.

"Personally oversee the destruction of any of this witch's wares in our stores," he commanded. "And order all who have partaken of her wares to undergo immediate emetics and begin two days of prayer and fasting." A thought occurred to him. "Was her tea served at my table, Dahos?"

The priest shook his head. "To the novitiates, mostly."

"A week of prayer and fasting, then. Tell them immediately, Dahos." As the high priest rose, Hederick stopped him. "Wait. Bathe first. And change your robe. It disgusts me."

Dahos nodded mutely.

"You are dismissed," Hederick finally said, and the high priest hurriedly left the chamber through the doors beneath the pulpit.

Alone again, Hederick glanced upward and around the Great Chamber. Statues of Omalthea and the pantheons stood behind the top tier of benches. There was no sound, no sign of Ancilla. The sun was sinking low. It was the sweetest, holiest time of the day. Usually.

Hederick.

With no warning, the thing stood before him. Part lizard, part dragon, part woman, part smoke, its shape shifted ceaselessly. Whatever Hederick tried to focus on melted and was no longer there, or became something else. The only way to see it, apparently, was out of the corner of one's eye. He did not doubt that if he reached out to touch Ancilla's apparition, his hand would pass right through.

The shadow Ancilla held in its filmy claw a lance the length of a man. The lance was real enough, and the monster seemed to have strength enough to wield it.

The lance began as green and purple mist and solidified

to terrifying sharpness just under the High Theocrat's breastbone. The tip of the lance severed the fibers of his robe, but stopped short of pricking him. If Hederick moved at all, if he shouted for help, he knew the projectile would pierce him through his heart before anyone could rescue him.

Before, the Presence had appeared as smoke; this was a more solid emanation. "You are forbidden here," he whispered. "I blessed this chamber in the name of Sauvay and Omalthea themselves." Sauvay's Diamond Dragon has failed to protect me here, he thought in panic. What have I done to offend the New Gods?

Do you remember the Garnet Mountains, Hederick?

He dared not move. The creature's whispery voice continued.

They stood to the east of our village. Sunrises in Garlund village were nothing to boast of, but we had sunsets to inspire the gods. I see you continue that tradition here.

When Hederick again refused to answer, the sibilant voice resumed.

Remember, little brother? We were refugees. Con, our father. Venessi, our mother. A handful of lost souls from Caergoth who believed that a new god had spoken to our parents. Do you remember the tales of that time, Hederick?

"I forget nothing," Hederick muttered. "Ever."

Alas, I have watched you for years, and I believe you have forgotten much that matters.

Hederick realized the numbing terror that the Presence originally inspired in him had lessened. "It is time for my evening revelations, lizard." He turned his back on the Presence and made his way toward the pulpit stairs.

Will she kill me? he thought. He risked a glance back.

The Presence was gone.

Dahos stood at the double doors. He had donned a fresh robe, as ordered, and waited for Hederick. Novitiates were making their way up the aisles. The audience would be seated before the Seekers began the nightly procession. Hederick hurried to join his high priest.

Tonight, as always, he would prophesy for the New Gods.

Chapter 9

People crammed the benches, knelt in the aisles, and squatted on the floor of the Great Chamber. Children sat on parents' laps, but did not chatter or fuss. Everyone watched the High Theocrat as he busied himself in the pulpit above.

Hederick sipped yet another chalice of mead and examined the sinners below him. The crowd sat mesmerized, like fat blueberries, ready for plucking in late summer.

The High Theocrat imagined himself harvesting souls— a handful for Omalthea, a bucketful for Sauvay, a basketful for Hederick. . . . He resisted the urge to giggle. Truly the mead was working miracles tonight. Hederick swayed in the pulpit, lightly touching the Diamond Dragon. All was going well.

The High Theocrat had delivered the greeting, encouraging Omalthea and Sauvay and those of the pantheons to enter the hallowed ground of the Great Chamber. He had already downed two goblets of mead . . . or was it more? His head was swimming devoutly.

He'd gone on to exhort the crowd to abandon sin, to reject magic and spellcasters, to ferret out and punish all who continued to show fealty to the Old Gods. And, especially, to report the sins of their neighbors.

The crowd had followed the novitiates' lead admirably, nodding when they did, weeping when two neophytes burst into noisy tears of repentance, and surging forward when Hederick issued the call to the converted: "Come to the altar. Receive the blessings of the New Gods. Join with them, O Faithful Ones."

"Join with them." The priests, led by Dahos, echoed the response.

Converts moved their lips: "We come to the altar of the Seekers, O New Gods, to receive the blessings and to mingle our wealth with yours."

They presented their offerings—coins or precious stones wrapped in parchment and purchased at exorbitant prices from the Seeker peddlers who roamed Solace and the rest of Krynn. The peddlers, in turn, handed over most of the proceeds to the Seeker organization.

As always, High Priest Dahos handled his offices with aplomb. He looked each convert in the eye, and remembered to follow the sipping of the mead with the welcoming handshake. "The eyes of the New Gods smile upon you," Dahos intoned to each penitent, directing them toward the two priests who would retrieve the chalice, take down each individual's name, and receive the pledge of further money and goods for the holy cause.

Hederick looked down upon the winding line of would-be Seekers and swallowed more mead, always tilting the glass first toward the marble-and-gilt statues of the members of the pantheons that stood by the slit windows at the upper back of the chamber: Omalthea—tall and forbidding, with an unsheathed broadsword in one hand; Sauvay—broad-chested, with flowing hair and implacable visage; Ferae—pale and womanly, one hand stroking a doe and the other cradling a basket of grain; Cadithal—the laughing god, hands on hips and head thrown back; and Zeshun—earthy and sensuous.

Excited signs from the two priests told Hederick that people were far exceeding the usual gifts this evening. There was a sense of tension and excitement in the air. "Nothing like an execution to increase the pledges," he murmured.

All of this was for the glory of the New Gods, of course. The Highseekers Council be damned, Hederick thought, momentarily considering the Seekers council in Haven that, theoretically at least, ran the holy order. I have more wisdom and holiness than that whole lot combined, he thought.

Now the people had returned to the benches and were watching the High Theocrat intently. They knew what came next: the revelations. The priests doubled the incense and began to drone.

As always, Hederick's first words were barely above a murmur, a private conversation between supplicant and gods. "Omalthea, be with us, who adore you," Hederick whispered. "Likewise Sauvay. Bring with you the Greater and Lesser Pantheons. May all New Gods know that I, Hederick, am here to serve as your dutiful voice. Devoted am I to you, to the order, and to your work in this world. I join my will to yours, O New Gods, secure in the knowledge that you will never betray us as the Old Gods did."

His voice grew in strength as he repeated the invocation. His eyes closed. The divine ones approved of him. He, Hederick, was their chosen vessel on Krynn. All eyes were upon him.

Hederick infused his voice with throbbing passion. "Omalthea of the Greater Pantheon and mother of us all, be with us, these who adore and exalt you."

"So be it," Dahos replied.

"Likewise Sauvay, Fatherlord of the Lesser Pantheon. Bring with you tonight your hierarchy."

"So be it." Dahos's voice gained power.

Hederick felt the strength of the New Gods surge through him. His head began to drum. Exultation rose, and his voice thundered. "May all New Gods know that I, Hederick, High Theocrat of Solace, builder and leader of Erolydon, am here to serve as your voice on Krynn."

"So be it."

"Devoted am I—to you, to the order, and to your sacred work on this world."

"So be it."

"I give up my will to further yours, O New Gods," Hederick intoned. "I, and all those in this temple blessed by you, stand secure in the knowledge that the New Gods will never betray us."

"So be it."

"The New Gods plan no Cataclysm, no vile abandonment of their children on Krynn!" the High Theocrat shouted. "They are true parents! We, your Seekers, are secure in you, our gods!"

"So be it!"

Hederick opened his eyes slightly, peering around the Great Chamber. Several novitiates were rolling on the floor and crying out. Others had begun to dance cautiously in the crowded aisles, arms above their heads. The novitiates were singing an old Seeker hymn:

"We are the Seekers.
We seek the New Gods.
We give our souls to the true gods,
Who will not abandon us."

One priest pounded a large wooden drum trimmed with steel and silver. Hederick's heart seemed to beat in time with the pounding. He felt young and powerful, tall

119

and vital as a vallenwood. The priests joined in. The Great Chamber rang with a chorus at least two centuries old:

"Centuris shirak nex des.

Centuris shirak nex des.

Centuris shirak nex des.

We seek the truth of the New Gods."

"I invoke you, Omalthea," Hederick shouted over the voices. "I invoke you, Sauvay, once her consort!"

"Centuris shirak nex des."

"I call to your daughter, Ferae, issue of Omalthea and Sauvay!"

The converts had joined in. Some of the newcomers couldn't keep from sobbing, Hederick noted through slitted eyelids.

"Centuris shirak nex des."

"I cry out to you, Cadithal, consort of Ferae! Share your gifts. Offer us wealth!"

"Centuris shirak nex des."

"Come to us, Zeshun, queen of the night!"

"We seek the truth of the New Gods."

"Be with us now, New Gods, true gods! Speak to the faithful! I, Hederick, High Theocrat of Solace, await your healing wisdom!"

The crowd sang the hymn again and again. Finally the room was still, its occupants waiting in an expectant, breathless hush. Hederick pressed his hand to his chest until the diamond figure cut into his flesh. Be with me now, Sauvay, he prayed.

Hederick took his time. He stared pointedly at one convert after another, holding each one's gaze until he felt the person grow frightened, then he frowned and moving on to the next victim. When the tension was at the breaking point, the New Gods would speak through him. The revelations would commence. This had never failed.

Hederick beheld a young woman. She flushed deeply but dared not look away. He felt himself draw power from her. Then suddenly Omalthea, not Sauvay, was upon him, the first of the divine visitors tonight, filling him with her strength. Hederick closed his eyes. He sensed, without seeing, the woman collapse against the young man at her side as the High Theocrat's eyelids fluttered shut.

"Omalthea, arbiter of all virtue, is with us." To begin with the Motherlord of the Pantheons—what promise that held for the night! Hederick rocked back on his heels, smiling up at the ceiling. An auspicious beginning. Then he frowned again. "Omalthea is displeased. For some of you talk of virtue—but talk more than you care to practice."

Hederick suddenly looked again at the young woman. She was pretty, with a face and form that surely attracted the attentions of many men. Now her face was colorless, lips parted. Seeing Hederick's gaze, her husband looked at her with horror.

"Some of you sin greatly . . . and regularly . . . and happily," Hederick intoned. "To sin against virtue is to blaspheme Omalthea herself. Truly the Motherlord is angered."

Hederick touched his chin: the signal. Dahos, out of sight, touched a flame to a hair-thin line of string. The flame coursed on its track beneath the aisle stairs, turned at the highest step, and shot toward the statue of Omalthea that graced the top of the amphitheater. "Omalthea, be with us!"

At that instant, an explosion rocked the room. Red smoke billowed from the base of Omalthea's statue. Smelling of burned metal, the cloud spread over the room.

The young woman gave a cry and fainted. Her husband let her slip unchecked to the marble floor.

Smoke and noise did wonders for increasing people's faith, Hederick thought. It was all perfectly acceptable in the service of the New Gods. The people demanded the spectacular.

The explosion over, he let his gaze rove toward a man in the first row whose face wore a decidedly self-satisfied expression. The man, probably a merchant, wore silk hose, billowing silk shirt, and a fine leather doublet tooled with griffins; the splendor of his outfit matched the arrogance of his expression. Hederick pressed the dragon to his breast and waited for another spirit to inspire him—Cadithal's, this time.

"Cadithal, God of Wealth, is with us. He is pleased at our generosity this evening." Hederick's voice was practically a whisper, yet the room was so still that every word was audible, even to the last row, he knew. The smug-looking man was smiling and nodding, chin outthrust. "And yet . . ." Hederick drew out the words as he stared at the sinner. The man's smile faded.

"And yet . . . Cadithal, consort of Ferae, Goddess of Growing Things, is unhappy tonight. For there are some here . . ." Hederick let the suggestion trail off meaningfully. He stood in the gods' stead now; he was imposing and terrifying—and godlike. "There are *some* tonight who remain miserly, who think the New Gods can be fooled by a 'considerable' gift measured in mere steel coins, but a gift that in reality amounts to a pittance of what ought to be contributed."

The well-dressed man whom Hederick had targeted slouched as if trying to make himself smaller. "What a cruel, cruel joke to play upon the gods—and upon one's own soul," Hederick said softly, "and upon the souls of one's family."

Suddenly the man was back before the pair of priests at the side table, speaking urgently and emptying his pockets.

Hederick looked around, even more pleased than before. Which god would guide him next? Which onlooker would he draw power from?

Then he spied her.

Ancilla's Presence occupied an aisle seat in the top row.

No one but Hederick appeared aware of her. The High Theocrat lost confidence momentarily, and the Diamond Dragon slipped from his grasp. He heard the artifact clang to the floor.

The lizard-woman in the Great Chamber sat up immediately, eyes wide. In an instant, she vanished from the bench and reappeared on the pulpit next to Hederick, apparently visible only to him. She reached for the glittering artifact.

And her clawed hand went right through it.

Ancilla tried again, with the same result. For a moment, sister and brother locked gazes. Hers brimmed with frustration, his with drunken joy.

Then the High Theocrat reached out to reclaim the Diamond Dragon. Unfortunately, the mead made his brain swim, and he inadvertently knocked the artifact down the stairs.

Hederick took a step toward the staircase. But at the moment his outstretched hand brushed against the mist of a scaly body, panic assailed him.

The Presence was chanting softly.

Despite the terror, Hederick fought to get control of himself. "Sauvay, come to me," he pleaded softly. Sauvay, once Omalthea's consort, now god of vengeance, surely would dash this lizard-woman to bits on the floor of the chamber. "Sauvay, attend me."

Hederick forced his thoughts away from Ancilla's Presence. "Sauvay, stand with me!" he cried. He prayed desperately. His mind's eye still saw the green orbs of the Presence. The red smoke had dissipated, but the metallic odor remained. The thing chanted monotonously.

Then, at last, Hederick felt the reassuring touch of the gods. Sauvay had arrived at Hederick's behest and now demanded his turn to speak. It *must* be Sauvay. The High Theocrat forced himself to stop thinking about Ancilla. The revelation was everything now. Ancilla could not harm him during the revelation.

"I dreamed last night," Hederick whispered. Each word fell shimmering into the amphitheater like a glass bead dropping into a lake.

But something was wrong.

Always before, Hederick had known that deep down, on some level, he controlled his words—even though the gods provided guidance from some distance. But this time he lost control. He stood atop his vaulted pulpit like a gasping carp, words erupting out of the depths of his belly. Was this, then, what a true revelation felt like? Were the New Gods physically directing him?

"I had a dream last night," he blurted. "I dreamed I was in my parents' house in Garlund." He'd never—*never*—revealed his roots. Garlund didn't even exist anymore.

"I was in the root cellar. It was damp. We lived near the river, and the cellar was always damp." Someone giggled; Hederick looked around the room, mouth agape. He could almost hear the priests wondering aloud. The High Theocrat in a root cellar? And where was this Garlund?

Indeed, Hederick *had* had such a dream, between the executions of Mendis Vakon and Crealora Senternal. But what purpose could the New Gods have in exposing him to ridicule like this?

The High Theocrat prayed to Sauvay, but no relief came. Just the voice, so much like Hederick's own, spilling forth, babbling.

"I was alone in the cellar," the voice boomed. "It was dark, but I could see a crack of light. There was a door somewhere. There'd always been a door, but now I couldn't find it. They'd moved it! Venessi and Con, my parents, had hidden the door. On the opposite side of the cellar, they'd opened a crack to provide air."

People in the audience glanced at each other nervously, but no one said anything. Several priests looked curious, but none dared interrupt the High Theocrat during a holy revelation. That would be tantamount to challenging the gods themselves. Dahos was standing at the bottom of the pulpit steps, his face pale and worried, duties obviously forgotten.

Hederick's voice rose suddenly to a piercing shriek. "Don't you *see* people? Are you blind—or merely stupid? They'd locked me in! I could hear them piling dirt where the door had been. Con and Venessi, my own parents! I heard them pounding nails into the doorjamb, sealing the basement shut! *And I was sealed inside!*"

The words came in spurts now, like vomited blood. "And then I saw . . . another light . . . a wider crack . . . as wide as my hand. . . . And I knew . . . that if I were careful . . . and held my breath . . . I could turn sideways . . . and escape through the crack. I could become that thin, as thin as that crack. I could! I moved . . . toward the light . . . in my dream I turned sideways. . . ."

Sweat poured down Hederick's forehead. A breeze from the open doors caressed his damp hair, and he shivered. His tongue was dry; his throat hurt. He yearned to swallow.

The blessed mead. If only the High Theocrat could reach it, wet his mouth, soothe his throat. His hands groped for his goblet.

The voice, this visitation from Ancilla's Presence, had to be quelled. Hederick tried to speak, but only dry whimpers emerged. Then the voice returned in full force.

"I turned to slide through the crack . . . I was going to escape . . . and then I saw them. Dozens of them—no, hundreds! Hundreds of spiders! Black and evil. Insatiable."

Hederick could see that the earlier mood of holiness had left the people. No longer were they converts awaiting the truths of the Seekers, but children listening to a good bedtime story. Novitiates, who had sunk to their knees on marble stairs, were also listening raptly. Brown-robed priests in various stages of shock stood around motionless.

The voice spoke again, hurriedly, breathlessly. "And then . . . and then I remembered something. . . . I cried out to my father. 'Con!' I screamed. 'Feed the spiders! Feed the spiders!' I moved toward the voracious insects, drawn as if by a web. I couldn't stop; I drew closer. The spiders reared back to receive me, to devour me . . . and Con didn't hear me! My own father didn't hear me! Don't you see? Don't any of you idiots *understand?*"

Hederick's right hand, unseen under the lectern, touched the mead goblet. He tried to force his rigid fingers to grasp the stem. The High Theocrat looked wildly around the room. Why did none of his priests step in? And why wouldn't his fingers do his bidding, by the accursed Pantheons?

He felt the goblet tip, heard it break. The pitcher from which he'd filled the goblet was under the altar, behind him. Hederick made himself turn and stretch toward it. His left hand found the mead pitcher and hefted it. It was empty.

Still the voice continued. Even with his back turned, the false voice sounded as clear as the evening gong that called believers to revelations. Ancilla's Presence, only an arm's length away, cocked its ghostly head to one side.

"Don't you see?" Hederick shouted. "It was *his* duty to feed the spiders—Con's duty, my father's! Don't you see?" The voice rose to a wail. "If he didn't feed them, the spiders would find food somewhere else. And the only thing down there to eat . . . *was me!*"

A scream rocked the Great Chamber. To the onlookers, it seemed as though the sound came from Hederick, but the High Theocrat knew it had burst forth from the Presence.

As suddenly as the spell had taken Hederick, it left. He slumped over the altar, ill with vertigo, nearly retching. The sounds of the rabble soared around him.

"Did you hear?" "What was that all about?" "That's not

like the other revelations." "What does it mean?" "Is the Theocrat growing senile?" "Perhaps he's a prophet." "Do the gods really speak through Hederick?" "What do we do now?" "Is it over?" "Can we leave?"

Babies cried. A few older children whined.

Hederick forced himself upright. Instead of the Presence, Dahos stood at the top of the stairs. The Plainsman held out a clean cloth in one hand and a spare chalice filled with mead in the other.

The crowd stilled amid a chorus of "Hush!" and "There's more!"

Hederick took the tiny goblet, dragged himself to the pulpit, tried to speak, and broke into a paroxysm of coughing. He rolled the blessed beverage around his mouth, but it was as though his tongue itself absorbed the liquid. There was little left to swallow.

"Tonight . . ." Hederick, relieved to hear his own voice again, coughed and tried to speak. "Tonight . . . "

Dahos was at his side once more, holding out a small object. The Diamond Dragon! Hederick snatched the artifact. "Tonight, we have been in the presence of something . . ." How to describe it? If he said it were evil, would that suggest that Solace's own High Theocrat was vulnerable to diabolical forces? ". . . in the presence of something stronger than us, something holy. It is yet to be explained, but rest assured that the answer will come. The New Gods will explain all in the end."

The High Theocrat paused to gather his strength and look around the Great Chamber. Ancilla the lizardwoman was gone.

The crowd remained. All those staring eyes—wanting something, demanding something. Why was it always Hederick's lot to provide? His mind was as empty as a wind-scoured desert.

He clutched the Diamond Dragon to his chest. "So be it," he rasped out. "Tonight's revelation is over."

Hederick, High Theocrat of Solace, bolted past Dahos, down the steps and out the double doors.

* * * * *

Marya put down the quill and rubbed her eyes. Olven stood in the shadows next to the door of the Great Library, waiting to take his turn at the desk. He was unsure whether Marya had heard him enter, she was so still.

At this hour of the night, only a few scribes, all of them apprentices, remained in the Palanthas library. Those few sat as silently as Marya did, on stools and chairs before desks that held numerous quills and pieces of parchment. Each desk was illuminated by a single candle, which cast a small circle of yellow light. The rest of the library was pitch-black. At night in the Great Library of Palanthas, there was no gray—only light and dark. Astinus was in his private study down the hall, not to be disturbed.

"Isn't there something we can do?" Marya finally asked, not seeming to expect an answer.

So she was aware of him. Olven had not read the latest passage, the one that Marya had recorded. But he remembered his own feelings of helplessness after inscribing his most recent segment of Hederick's current schemes.

"We are doing something, Marya," he said, affecting a confidence he certainly didn't feel. "We're recording the actions of a madman. The world will judge him, even if we can't. Remember our oath of neutrality."

"Yet you've read Eban's work on Hederick's childhood," Marya returned. "Hederick wasn't always evil. Look at the things that happened to him when he was still an innocent child. He was just . . . adapting."

Olven shrugged. He remembered something his mother used to tell him when he was railing against the world's injustices. "Bad things happen to a lot of people," he quoted now. "The choice between good and evil is still a personal decision."

"But can't we stop him, Olven?"

The dark-skinned scribe was well aware that Marya knew the answer to that question as well as he did, but he spoke anyway, partly to remind himself. "We can't influence history. We can only record it. We are scribes. We must remain neutral. Remember the oath, Marya."

"But someone has to stop him, Olven!"

"If the gods mean for Hederick to be stopped, someone will stop him."

Marya was silent for a few moments. "Someone tried for years—his sister. Yet Ancilla seems to be no more effective against Hederick than . . . than we are, Olven. By the gods, I wish I were there in Solace!"

Olven watched her steadily but said nothing. At last Marya sighed and rose from the chair. Without another word, she handed him the quill and left the Great Library.

Chapter 10

Tarscenian!

The wispy voice jolted Tarscenian out of a doze. He'd found himself a new hiding place among the ferns and trees, and was waiting for nightfall. "What is it, Ancilla?"

Hederick dropped the Diamond Dragon.

Tarscenian sat up. "You have it?"

I could not lift it!

The whisper was thick with disappointment. The voice, which had never been potent, faded even more.

I am constrained. I can call up a formidable Presence, but no corporeal body. With a simple panic spell, I was able to stop Hederick from immediately retrieving the Dragon himself and was also able to control him enough to help him make a fool of himself. But . . .

Tarscenian missed the next few words, so quiet had the

voice become. Then it returned, slightly revived.

But then that high priest of his rushed up the stairs and straight through me—with the artifact! It broke my spell, Tarscenian. I am weaker than ever, by Paladine's love. I had the power of forty mages, and what good did it do me?

Tarscenian heard nothing but the sighing of wind for a long time, then another whisper.

What will I do, Tarscenian?

"Rest, my dear," Tarscenian whispered. "Leave Hederick alone. Gather your strength. Leave this to me for now." He rose and belted on his sword. "It is time for me to explore Solace. Rest, Ancilla."

I suppose I . . .

Then nothing.

"Ancilla?"

An agitated Tarscenian waited for nearly an hour, until the moon Solinari was rising in the sky, red Lunitari slightly behind. There was no further word from Ancilla, and Tarscenian's worry and impatience grew at last to unbearable bounds.

Finally he pulled up the hood of his cloak and set out for Solace.

Chapter 11

Most of the treetop village had settled into the stillness of night-time, but one section of Solace never slept. This was the part of Solace where the northern refugees congregated with talk and activity, day and night.

Solace's lodgings for travelers had long since filled. Nearly every resident had found sleeping space on the floor for one or two visitors—for a hefty price, of course. Refugees who had arrived more recently had been forced to set up camp on the damp forest floor, bereft of the protection that a vallenwood perch would afford.

Hood up, Tarscenian stalked unnoticed through arguing humans, dwarves, and elves. Even a few centaurs walked the paths, although none of the hoofed creatures ventured up onto the bridge-walkways, of course. The presence of the solitude-loving centaurs in a population center was a sure sign that something was gravely amiss on Krynn.

Tarscenian stepped carefully around puddles and mud and muck. The light of the moons did not penetrate through the vallenwood canopy to the forest floor; torchlight was the rule in the refugee section. The torch smoke burned his eyes, which were already strained from piercing the darkness. The smell was unbearable—the refugees dumped their wash water and garbage wherever they cared to.

The refugee area combined homes with marketplace. As always in the Seeker lands, there were the sellers of the holy offerings, those overpriced paper packets that pilgrims could purchase then deposit with Seeker priests to protect their immortal souls. Tarscenian gave these entrepreneurs a wide berth.

Despite the late hour, some refugees still sat on the ground behind cloths spread with items they hoped to sell or barter. Some swayed as they kept vigil, half asleep but with a sixth sense that brought them to full awareness whenever a potential buyer ventured by.

Tarscenian stepped over a pool of black water and stooped before one such seller. The woman, whose wares were displayed on a greasy blanket, hefted a double-bladed dagger for him to examine.

He spoke softly to the woman as she watched him with glittering eyes. "A fine piece of work," he said. "It looks like the product of Garnet dwarves."

" 'Tis," she rejoined. "I'll sell it for steel or trade it for provisions as will get me farther south."

"Where did you obtain such a fine dagger?"

She grabbed the weapon away from him, scratching his hand with her jagged nails in the process. "You're implyin' I stole it, is that it? You're a spy for Hederick, aren't you?"

Tarscenian hurriedly shook his head and backed off, but the woman ranted on. "You can tell your master as I am the most devout Seeker here. I buy my offerings, same as everyone here, and gives 'em to the church, even as it means taking food from my own self—an' it frequently has."

She brandished the dagger about wildly. "The knife, *Seeker spy*, was my husband's, him that died on the road when we fled Throtl. I be sellin' my belongings now to get the necessary food to keep from dyin', and to buy a donkey to carry this body as far from the North as I can. And I be doin' it legal, scum, so just you leave me be!" She waved the dagger at him again.

"I never . . ." Tarscenian protested, then broke off arguing. Other refugees stared at the hooded traveler with open hostility. Several temple guards and an equal number of goblins began to circle around Tarscenian.

"Tense times, indeed," he whispered to himself.

He pulled his cloak farther over his face and, one eye on the guards, unfastened the band that held his sword in its scabbard, swathed under the long cloak. At the same time, he loosened one of the spellcasting pouches at his belt and, from the depths of his hood, studied the guards and leather-clad goblins. He didn't see the goblin he'd heard called Yellow Eyes; these beasts seemed to be lower both in rank and intelligence.

A scuffle suddenly resounded nearby, interrupting his thoughts and distracting the guards.

"Be off, kender! I am not a carnival pony, here for thy amusement! If thou wishes to steal a ride, find thyself someone other than a centaur. Be off, embezzler!"

This was followed by the muffled sound of hooves striking something soft. The refugees' laughter nearly drowned out the outraged protests, high-pitched and copious, that came from a small figure.

"I wasn't stealing anything!" an offended kender screeched. The short-legged creature managed to cling to the centaur despite the man-horse's kicks and gyrations.

Mud daubed the centaur's silver-white haunches, evidence of its attempts to dislodge the kender.

The kender's brown topknot was bouncing up and down, and his words came out in bunches. "I just wanted to"—kick—"check your back"—scrape against a vallenwood trunk—"for ticks," the kender gasped. "They've been plentiful"—another kick—"hereabouts"—sidestep—"this summer"—buck—"and I thought to do you"—succession of kicks—"a favor!"

The centaur bucked once more, then reached back and tried to pummel the kender, but by this time the kender's hands were fastened around the creature's human torso. "I meant to be your friend, horse," the kender wailed.

More laughter erupted from the refugees. This time the guards joined in; even the goblins poked one another and grinned.

The centaur fumed. Its head, torso, and arms resembled those of a male human between twenty and thirty years old. "I am no *horse*, and certainly no friend of a kender, thou half-pint larcenist! Now get thee off my back before I roll myself over and squash thee flatter than a Haven bedbug!"

Glad of the distraction, Tarscenian picked that moment to sidestep up a stairway that curled around the massive trunk of a nearby vallenwood. The wooden steps would take him to the upper walkways in the vallenwood branches, and out of the guards' view.

Only someone was blocking his way.

The young woman's back was toward Tarscenian. She gazed downward, intent on the altercation between kender and centaur. Much as she studied the goings-on below, Tarscenian in turn studied her—or as much of her as he could see from his dubious vantage point behind her.

The woman's garb was in disarray, and in a manner that suggested grooming was customarily low in her priorities.

Her ankle-length skirt, of some dark material, was ripped in several places, and the loose blouse she'd tucked into it had gone too long without a wash. Her dark brown hair had been sawed off at shoulder length, and Tarscenian suspected she'd done the job herself with a short sword or axe—which was very likely, since she also boasted the musculature and sturdy stance of one whose livelihood depended on strength and quickness.

The woman turned her head, and Tarscenian saw unkempt bangs, dark eyes, a rounded chin and nose, and a lone silver-and-lapis earring that dangled from her right earlobe nearly to her soiled gauze collar. Her face bespoke youth and an innocence that was almost gaminlike, but Tarscenian suspected she was nearer forty than twenty.

"If you want to keep your entrails tucked into your belly, you'd best step into the light, stranger. I've no patience with spies."

It took Tarscenian a moment to realize that the woman was speaking to him. "I'd just as soon not put myself on display to the temple guards, friend," he answered. "I'll stay back here, near the trunk, if you don't mind. I'm no rabbit offering itself up for the fox's dinner."

"Some might say you already have."

Tarscenian saw that she held a dagger in her hand, and he knew that she could flick the weapon before he had a chance to draw his sword. She kept her face toward the commotion below, however, giving no outward sign to guards and goblins that she was anything but alone on the stairs. "They are distracted," she said suddenly. "Come around now."

Tarscenian obeyed her without question, his cloak snagging on the tree bark as he slipped behind the woman. She continued watching the centaur. The man-horse had dislodged the kender and now was accusing it of thievery. "What did the kender take?" Tarscenian asked.

"The centaur's silver neck-chain." The woman murmured without appearing to move her lips. "Short-stuff says he borrowed it, of course."

"Of course." Tarscenian decided it was time for introductions. "I am . . ."

". . . Tarscenian, of course," she finished. "I'm called Mynx. Hederick has all of Solace looking for you, stranger. You're a fool to have come here. With the description of you that Hederick's priests have posted all over the city, anyone with sense could identify you, even in that cloak." She laughed softly and ran her hand through her hair, increasing its disarray. "Fortunately for you, Tarscenian, I'm the only one here with any sense right now."

"I'm looking for some people."

"Their names?"

"No names. I want to find a thieves' ring."

Mynx gasped, then laughed outright. "I hope you don't plan a career in picking pockets, Tarscenian. It strikes me that your talent as a thief might be somewhat limited. Men over six feet tall are rare in Solace. It would be difficult for you to blend into a crowd, don't you think? How old are you, anyway?"

"My talents are greater than you think." Tarscenian murmured a magical chant and released a pinch of herbs from a pouch. Then he held out his hand. The double-bladed dagger owned by the Throtl woman gleamed in his palm. It was an illusion, not the real item, but as long as Mynx didn't touch it, she might not guess. Her eyes widened at the sight of the dagger, but she said nothing.

Tarscenian whispered another chant. At that moment, a screech sounded from below, and then the Throtl woman screamed, "The kender! He took my dagger! Guards! Did you see? It must've been him!"

The real dagger was still firmly in place on the woman's blanket—although Tarscenian's spell kept most people from realizing this.

Together, Mynx and Tarscenian watched the guards corral the kender and search the scrawny creature. The search of the kender's four pockets and seven pouches revealed three pieces of rose quartz, a silver ring, two money pouches, one crochet hook, three coins, six maps, a fragment of red leather, seven balls of twine, a chunk of yellow cheese, one child's leather sandal decorated with fake gems of colored glass, half a loaf of brown bread, some metal implements that Tarscenian recognized as lock-picking tools, and a quill pen. But no double-bladed dagger.

A dwarf and two humans, uttering terrible oaths, lunged forward to retrieve the ring and money pouches.

"Oh, are you the owners?" the kender asked, brown eyes wide under his bobbing topknot. "I'm so glad I found you! You should keep better watch on your valuables, you know. Solace is full of thieves. The next person who finds your belongings might not be as honest as I am."

Despite the protests of the humans and dwarf, the temple guards gave the kender only a shake and, laughing, turned him loose. "Not likely the High Theocrat would want a thieving kender anywhere in his temple—even in the dungeons!" one guard called to another. They guffawed loudly and moved away.

Mynx was smiling, too, but sadly.

"What's wrong?" Tarscenian asked.

She turned and took Tarscenian's measure. "The kender reminds me of someone I knew once," she finally said.

"Once?"

"Hederick killed him."

Tarscenian opened his mouth to speak, but Mynx frowned. "So you want to find a thieves' ring," she said.

He inclined his head.

"With half of Erolydon on your trail, a thieves' ring would be crazy to help you."

Tarscenian remained silent.

"Still, it's clear you're no man of Hederick's," Mynx continued. "That's something in your favor. Perhaps I can introduce you to someone who could help you—for a price. But first you must show me more of this vaunted thieving skill of yours."

Tarscenian could only hope his modest magic would see him through whatever it was she had in mind. "What would you like me to steal?"

Mynx's brown eyes swept the crowd below. Then she pointed. "There. Take his badge of office—the death's-head ring."

Tarscenian followed her gaze, groaning inwardly. The man she had pointed at was Hederick's high priest. "Dahos will recognize me immediately," Tarscenian said.

"All the more challenge. Take it, or leave me alone."

Tarscenian was already on his way down the steps when he felt Mynx's gaze on his back. Remembering her warning, he slouched within his dark cloak. He might pass unnoticed, at least in this dim light. His mind raced to concoct a plan.

He bent forward and affected a confused, trembling walk, mumbling as he made his way through the crowd. He found the kender first. "Sweet creature, can you assist me?" he quavered. "I am weak and need help walking. Would you lend me your staff?" He pointed stiffly at the weaponlike, forked stick that the kender held.

The small creature gazed up. "It's not a staff, it's my hoopak. It's a weapon. And I can't lend it, but you can make me an offer anyway. My, what a huge hood! I can't even see in there. Are you human? You're certainly tall. Twice as tall as me. More than that, even. What do you—"

The kender reached up in an attempt to pull back Tarscenian's hood. The small creature's voice trailed off in a squeak a moment later as Tarscenian grasped his wrist in an iron grip. "Ouch! You're hurting . . ."

Tarscenian leaned over. "My back pains me, small one," he said loudly. "I need to lean upon your shoulders." Tarscenian bent closer and whispered, "Would you like to see something marvelous, kender?"

Curious, the creature stopped struggling. "What?" His brown eyes attempted to probe the depths of Tarscenian's hood.

Tarscenian spoke so softly that the kender had to strain to catch his words. "The high priest's ring is enchanted. The being who holds it can see things that ordinary mortals cannot."

"See what things?" the kender whispered.

"Into people's dwellings. Through walls, if you desire. If you stole . . . rather, if you 'borrowed' the ring, you could watch people, unseen. For example, you could view them as they empty their pockets at night. Think of the treasures you could behold!"

The kender's face glowed. "How exciting!"

"What is your name?"

"Kifflewit Burrthistle."

"Come with me, Kifflewit. And be still." They made their way around the periphery of the torchlight, Tarscenian leaning heavily on the kender. As they sidestepped blankets of trade goods, Tarscenian kept a strong grip on Kifflewit's right wrist, but he couldn't be certain the small creature wasn't filling his pockets with his other hand. Nevertheless, Tarscenian moved on, behind a goblin, around a pair of arguing dwarves, over a rivulet of scummy water, until he reached the young white centaur.

"Sir?" the centaur said. "Thou needest something?" He was a Crystalmir centaur, Tarscenian could see—leaner than Abanasinian centaurs, with an angular face and tilted violet eyes that appeared otherworldly beneath his shock of silver-white hair. No great intelligence shone in those eyes, but they were gentle. His face and torso were deeply tanned and muscular.

Tarscenian kept the kender behind him and made his voice tremble as much as his walk. "Please, noble creature, have you alms for an old soul? I have had no food since yesterday. I am quite weak."

Tarscenian tilted his head. He peeked out from beneath the fabric of the voluminous hood. The centaur already had opened a pouch at its waist—the point at which the human torso became horse withers—and was holding out a coin.

"Here, old man," the centaur said. "Thou needest this more than I. I can sleep anywhere, and I am surely young and strong enough to forage for my meals."

"Bless you, noble creature."

"The name is Phytos, old sir. And thou art welcome." The centaur's voice lost its gentleness. "Just thou keepest that embezzling kender away from me."

Tarscenian nodded and moved on, again leaning on Kifflewit Burrthistle, who was beginning to wobble beneath the weight. None of the guards paid them any attention; in these times, one more limping beggar was nothing of note. And High Priest Dahos had ensnared the bystanders' attention by haranguing the unfortunate Throtl woman.

"Your holy offering contained nothing but a bit of granite, hag!" the high priest shouted. "Is this evidence of your devotion—to hold back from the religion that sustains you? This, you think, will gain you everlasting life? A worthless offering? Perhaps an extended visit with the slave traders would improve your generosity. Perhaps the materbill . . . "

The woman, pale with fear, was stammering, "B-but I p-paid a g-g-great amount . . . t-to your own agent . . . it c-could n-not have b-been worthless . . . I l-looked ins—"

"Alms!" Tarscenian shouted, interrupting. "Alms! Alms for the poor!" He lurched toward Dahos, and blankets suddenly were gathered up, sleeping places vacated. The crowd edged away.

Dahos stared at the old, bent figure leaning on—of all things—a perspiring kender. "You dare interrupt me, old man?"

Tarscenian invested his voice with all the misery he could muster. "Holy man of Solace, I am destitute! Have you something for an old, crippled man, a devout Seeker all these many years? I have need of you, brother of the new faith! I reach out to you!" He stretched forth a hand.

Dahos looked at the quivering limb with undisguised distaste. "Have you tithed? Have you provided the church with its due portion of your money all these years, old man? And have you proof of this? Only then may we consider your case."

"But how could I tithe when I never had money, my lord?" Tarscenian maintained a plaintive tone, though he felt a bolt of anger surge through his body.

Dahos sneered. "The truly devout find a way. Now leave me and find yourself employment. Your laziness deprives the church and angers the gods."

With great difficulty, Tarscenian controlled his desire to slide his sword from beneath his cloak and rearrange the man's entrails. "Your blessing, at least," he whined instead. "To protect me on my way, Your Worship." He knelt, dragging Kifflewit down with him. Dahos unwillingly proffered his ring. Tarscenian kissed the air over the death's-head, murmured something appropriately pious, then motioned Kifflewit Burrthistle forward. "Look, my little friend," he whispered. "The magical ring."

Kifflewit reached forth, pointed ears atwitch and brown eyes glistening. At that moment, Dahos jerked his hand back. "Seekers give no blessings to kender!" he roared. "What blasphemy do you ask of me, old man?" The high priest launched a foot into Kifflewit Burrthistle's face, knocking the air from the kender as he fell over backward. Dahos shouted for the guards.

Tarscenian rose to his full height and tossed two temple guards behind him like discarded rags. "Leave the kender be, coward!" he yelled. His hood fell back from his face as he drew his sword, and in a mere moment, temple guards and goblins were swarming toward Tarscenian and Kifflewit Burrthistle—with more on the way.

The kender protested noisily despite the blood that oozed from the corner of his mouth. Kifflewit swung his hoopak and slammed one of the goblins flat in the midsection. The toothy creature, barely taller than a kender but thrice its weight, went down heavily.

"Guards! The man from the courtyard!" Dahos bellowed. "*Guards!*" He turned to scream commands at the handful of refugees who remained standing about. "I *order* the faithful to assist in this man's capture. Failure constitutes blasphemy!"

The Throtl woman was first to throw in her lot with the guards. Another dozen people soon gathered in a threatening knot. Tarscenian, sword in hand, stood within the thickening circle of enemies with the furiously cursing, hoopak-swinging kender at his back.

Clearly, Kifflewit was having a marvelous time. Kender knew no fear.

There was no sign of Mynx. There was also, Tarscenian saw with satisfaction, no sign of the high priest's ring on his left hand. Dahos, however, was so preoccupied with capturing them that he had noticed nothing amiss.

Suddenly a rope dropped out of a tree, dangling above Tarscenian. A whistle pierced through the tumult. "Burrthistle! Up here!" It was a woman's voice. In an eyeblink, the nimble kender was up the rope and out of sight.

Tarscenian parried a thrust from the nearest guard and wound his left hand around the rope. He was not as agile as the kender, and fumbled his attempt to pull himself up. His attackers were on the verge of overwhelming him.

Then Tarscenian's feet left the ground. And not through

his own doing.

He glanced upward. Far above him in the shadows, he dimly perceived a woman pulling at the rope, which she'd wisely slipped over a vallenwood branch before letting it drop down.

Meanwhile, Kifflewit had materialized in a new position near the bottom of the stairs. Blood smeared his childlike face, but he was grinning happily and his hoopak was poised for mayhem. Any guards who thought to storm the upper walkway and grab Mynx would have to battle their way through him first. Not to worry—their foes appeared sorely confused by prey that rose through the air like a soap bubble.

Then a goblin broke the trance, roaring as he charged, mace whirling. The goblin managed to snag the rope, and dumped Tarscenian to the ground. In a moment, Tarscenian was up and moving, but his attackers were close behind.

Three goblins stood between him and the way to the treetop walkways. Kifflewit, behind them, rained hoopak blows upon their heads and shoulders, but the blows glanced like raindrops off the foul creatures' thick leather armor.

Tarscenian wheeled.

A dozen temple guards, flanking Dahos, stood before him. "And so do heretics come to their end," the high priest said with a smile.

"Take me to Hederick, High Priest," Tarscenian demanded.

"Of course," Dahos said. "I would not deprive His Worship of the joy of dispatching you himself. He's wanted your head for years, Tarscenian."

"You know something of me, then?" Tarscenian asked, slipping his sword back into his scabbard. In the same motion, he surreptitiously retrieved a pinch of herbs from one pouch and, beneath the cover of his cloak, began to weave his fingers in a discreet spell. His eyes swept the scene and noted a large puddle of stagnant water near Dahos.

"Of course, Tarscenian," Dahos said with mock politeness. "You were the priest who brought Hederick into the Seekers, years ago. I know, too, that you betrayed him and the New Gods by deserting the Seekers for the lust of a woman."

"Ah," Tarscenian said. "And do you know who that woman was?"

"Some whore, long dead now, I suppose," the Plainsman said offhandedly.

"It was Hederick's sister, Ancilla, the mage who accompanied me in the courtyard today."

Dahos appeared startled. "Hederick, brother of a mage?" he murmured. Then the high priest recovered his composure. "Lies! Had I not promised Hederick otherwise, I'd slay you myself this instant for your blasphemy."

"Ask Hederick about her, High Priest. Unless you fear the response."

"I would not bother . . ."

"*Falt recoblock!*" Tarscenian shouted. "*Jerientom benjinchar!*"

Before the guards and Dahos could catch on, Tarscenian leaped high into the air. He bent in midair and dove straight into the pool of stagnant water at Dahos's feet.

And disappeared.

* * * * *

An instant later, high above Dahos and the rest, Tarscenian leaned over the railing and watched the confusion below. Though too exhausted to speak, he gave Mynx a wink. Kifflewit Burrthistle raced up the steps, barely winded.

"That was great, Tarscenian!" the kender burbled.

"How did you do that? Dive into that puddle, I mean. And you're not even wet! Sweating a lot, of course—but not *wet*. Could you teach me? Or is it more magic? Not that I couldn't learn a simple little puddle spell!"

"Not real magic. It's pure illusion," Tarscenian corrected. "I never disappeared because I wasn't trapped by Dahos in the first place. I never left this staircase."

"But I saw you!"

"Be still, little one, lest you bring all the guards upon us," Tarscenian cautioned. "They're not on to us yet. From all appearances, they're going to spend quite a lot of time staring into that puddle."

"What a trick! Can you . . ."

"Ahem." Tarscenian narrowed stern gray eyes at Kifflewit. "The ring, little friend."

"Mmm?"

"Dahos's death's-head ring. The one you placed in your red pouch, right there on your belt, after you 'borrowed' it from the high priest."

The kender's face fell. "Oh. That." He rallied. "What a good thing I picked it up! He might have lost it. I might have . . ."

"The *ring*, Kifflewit."

The kender produced the jewelry reluctantly, and Tarscenian handed it gravely to Mynx. "Present that to your chief as a token of my sincerity. Now it's time for us to talk, Mynx. I want you to take me to meet your fellow thieves."

Her dark eyebrows rose. "How did you know I . . . ?"

He laughed, shortly. "Oh," he said, winking at the kender, "I've known a few thieves in my time."

"I've known some, too!" chimed in Kifflewit, not wanting to be left out.

With somber brown eyes, Mynx regarded the balding, gray-bearded stranger. Then she nodded, her long, lone earring tangling in her unkempt brown hair. She gestured

146

for him to follow her.

She didn't know what Gaveley, the head of the thieves' ring, had in mind for Tarscenian. The tall stranger seemed a decent enough sort, but appearances were nothing to count on these days. Her own role in the scheme was simple: She was to carry out Gaveley's orders, and Gaveley would pay her accordingly. It had gone off almost too easily, she mused.

What a piece of luck, she thought, that the selfsame Tarscenian who was seeking a ring of thieves was, himself, being sought by just such a group.

Chapter 12

For some time, the three traveled southwest on the wooden walkways, making as little noise as possible as they passed dark dwelling after dark dwelling. The tumult from the refugee part of town receded behind them. They passed the Inn of the Last Home, a tavern that—before Hederick's installation—would have rung with song and drink even this late at night, but now the Inn was still.

Even the kender managed to stay mostly silent. Single file, they wound down a circular vallenwood stairway to reach the ground, and there they paused. The forest stood thick around them.

"We meet just outside Solace," Mynx explained.

"Odd place for a thieves' ring," Tarscenian commented.

She snorted. "Everything's odd, now that Hederick's in charge. Gaveley thought we'd be safer out here. The temple is north of Solace. This place is as far southwest as you can be and still find quick access into the city. Gaveley wanted to keep out of Hederick's way, I guess. My chief is not one to offer explanations, and it's a wise thief that doesn't look for them."

"This Gaveley, he's the leader?"

Mynx nodded. Then she stopped and addressed Kifflewit. "You needn't attend us any longer, kender. Go back to your family, wherever they are."

"But . . ."

Mynx cut him short. "Gaveley's ring of thieves has no use for another kender. Go away."

Another kender? Tarscenian thought. Mynx's kender friend had been a member of the ring?

Kifflewit protested loudly. "But we're a team! Didn't you notice how we were working together back there? Could Tarscenian have pulled it off without me? Could he?"

"It won't seem so wonderful when Hederick's guards find you," Mynx snapped.

"Mynx had a kender friend who died because of the High Theocrat," Tarscenian told the kender.

Mynx swung on him angrily. "He was *killed*, Tarscenian. Executed by one of Hederick's bowmen. I was an arm's length away when it happened."

"All the same, my dear, I doubt you'll be able to lose a kender who doesn't want to be lost," Tarscenian said.

"Ha. You just wait."

A footstep sounded before them in the trees, and the three darted into the shadows. This time, Tarscenian's was the hand firmly planted over Kifflewit's mouth. There were more footsteps, then muted voices, and finally a pair of figures hove into view. Mynx relaxed. "Gaveley," she mouthed soundlessly to Tarscenian.

A half-elf of medium height, his arm slung casually across the shoulder of an equally well-dressed human, strolled past without any sign that he'd noticed them—if indeed he had. He was speaking so softly to his companion that the three in the shadows couldn't make out a word.

After he had passed, Mynx let out a sigh. "Lesson one: Never interrupt Gaveley while he's on a job," she whispered to Tarscenian. "Lesson two: Never admit to knowing him outside the den." She turned toward the kender. "And lesson three: Keep kender away from him. *Far* away." She pointed south. "Out, Kifflewit Burrthistle. Our paths part now."

At that, the little creature shrugged his shoulders and skipped off without so much as a protest or backward glance.

Odd, Tarscenian thought. He could see that Mynx, too, was surprised by such unaccustomed obedience from a kender. But after Kifflewit Burrthistle was out of sight, she too shrugged and led Tarscenian away.

Soon they stopped, and she left him waiting before a huge boulder while she disappeared into the underbrush. Tarscenian heard a click; the boulder shifted aside. Mynx returned, leaned over the rock, and triggered a mechanism behind it. She put her shoulder to the granite chunk and easily pushed it aside.

"Gaveley's invention," she muttered. She disappeared into a hole; Tarscenian felt her grasp his hand and tow him behind her. He felt something else slip past him in the dark but, guessing what it was, said nothing.

There was the scrape of the boulder returning to its place. Light flared from an oil lamp.

"Gaveley won't be back for a while," Mynx said as she adjusted the wick. "We may as well make ourselves comfortable while we . . ." She spotted the kender, and her jaw dropped. Tarscenian, stifling a laugh, tried to look disapproving.

"This is terrific!" Kifflewit burst out. "What a superb

locking mechanism! A three-way Ergoli trip with a sideways catch—I've never seen one of those. And look at this place! All the jewels! Are they real? What . . . "

Mynx collared the talkative creature. "Out, kender!" she repeated vehemently. "Gaveley would kill you for intruding. You're lucky I have a soft spot." Still holding Kifflewit by his skinny neck, she reached toward a shelf and moved a bejeweled statue of a harpist a few inches to the left. Just in time—Kifflewit grabbed at air. Then there was the sound of something sliding aside. Mynx tossed the kender up the entryway and into the night.

"Ouch! But . . . !" Kifflewit protested.

"Be gone by the time Gaveley returns, or kiss your topknot good-bye," Mynx growled. "And don't let me hear you try fiddling with the lock, either."

The slamming of the door drowned out the kender's reply.

Mynx turned toward Tarscenian again. "Gaveley himself designed this place," she said calmly, as though she were used to ejecting kender from the den. Perhaps she was, he thought.

Tarscenian gazed around. The half-elf certainly had a taste for the ornate, he thought. He examined the thick, imported rug with its border of pegasi and unicorns. Tapestries hung all around. He drew his sword and went around the room, lifting the panels. Nothing lurked behind them but plastered rock. Mynx, still holding the lamp, stood watching with a faint smile. "Nobody here but us, stranger," she said. "But it gives me hope for you."

Mynx placed the oil lamp behind a thin slab of translucent peach-colored quartz, studded with rubies. With her movement, the room's light went from yellow to pale pink. She proceeded around the room, in succession lighting three other such lamps, and the illumination in the den deepened to rose. She halted before the last quartzshaded lamp. The slab of rock held three rubies—and one empty setting.

"I know there were four jewels when we got here," she muttered.

"I suspect the fourth ruby is traveling through the woods with Kifflewit Burrthistle right now," Tarscenian commented.

Mynx grimaced, then directed Tarscenian to a seat on a green brocade divan, handing him a crystal goblet filled with sweet elven wine.

"Where are the rest of the thieves?" he asked.

"Some are working. Others are sleeping elsewhere. This is a meeting place, not a boarding house." She regarded him with direct brown eyes. "Gaveley's unlikely to be back for some time. In the meantime, there are things I'd like to know."

"Such as?"

"The high priest said you were a Seeker priest once."

"True."

"Yet no longer."

"Also true. I follow the Old Gods now."

Mynx's expression revealed what she thought of fools who followed any gods at all. "You know much of Hederick," she said. "Tell me about him."

"Why?"

"I want to know everything I can about the High Theocrat."

"Again, why?"

"It may help me kill him."

Tarscenian ventured a guess. "Because of your friend?"

"He was only a kender, I know, but honor is honor."

Interesting to hear a thief talk about honor, Tarscenian thought as he watched her, but he held his tongue. He had promised Ancilla not to slay Hederick himself, but he'd never pledged to stop anyone else from doing so. Still . . .

"We have at least an hour," Mynx said, urging him to tell her more.

"Not now," he said. "I prefer to rest while we wait for this Gaveley." He drained the rest of his wine, leaned against the back of the settee, and pretended to close his eyes. He watched Mynx through slitted lids.

Mynx frowned, but made no further effort to coerce him. She ranged around the room for a while, sipping her wine and studying Gaveley's collections of statues, jewels, and tapestries. Then she sank onto a stool, drained her goblet, and leaned over a table. Her chin on her hands, she stared into one of the rubies in the pink quartz lamp screen.

Tarscenian closed his eyes. He could tell her plenty about Hederick, but not right away. No point giving anything away to a thief for free.

Chapter 13

Several leagues away, Hederick was having trouble falling asleep. Dahos had reported Tarscenian's escape to the High Theocrat immediately, of course, and the thought that the former Seeker priest was out there in the darkness, no doubt laughing at him, kept Hederick wide awake.

He shoved himself upright in his silk-sheeted bed and made his way to the window, where he opened the shutters and lit a candle. Holding the light in the window, he described a circle, and then another, and finally a third. Then he waited.

A stench from outdoors sent his stomach heaving, and he battled back the nausea. Hederick's nose always told him of the goblins' approach before his eyes could confirm it. A combination of rotten eggs and stale fish, the odor was enough to turn the strongest stomach. The creatures were too stupid even to know they stank.

Still, they served a purpose now. Goblins operated mostly at night, obeyed orders without question, loved to kill, weren't bright enough to be any threat to Hederick, and worked cheaply. Hederick had imported a half-dozen of the beasts shortly after he'd first occupied Erolydon, and lately had added a few dozen more. Already the troop of spies and bloodletters had more than paid for their keep. He had been adding some hob-goblins to his guard force as well, but these were more difficult to control.

The goblins all boasted broad noses, small fangs, pointed ears, sloping foreheads, dull eyes, and short stature. Although goblins came in a variety of colors— generally shades of yellow and orange and red—most of the beasts that lived in a knoll just north of Erolydon were all dirty orange, indicating they hailed from the same tribe.

Hederick could tell the beasts apart solely by their eyes. Yellow Eyes had eyes that were lemon-colored. He was one of the more intelligent goblins—which wasn't saying much.

"You want I?" Gradually the beasts had learned that this new employer comprehended them only when they spoke slowly and plainly, which was how most of them spoke anyway.

Hederick took a step back from the creature's rancid breath. "I have a task for you," he whispered, trying not to breathe.

"Extra meat? Yes?" The beast's lemony eyes gleamed brighter. Were these stupid creatures always hungry?

Hederick fought the urge to barter. After all, the goblins earned little enough as it was. "Yes, extra meat." He was growing faint, affected by the goblin's odor in the oppressive heat.

"Kill 'em someone?" The wide-eyed goblin asked.

Hederick nodded again. "Tarscenian, the tall man in the courtyard yesterday. Remember?"

"Tall man? Beard with cloak? Mage lady next to? Him that run-run out door when boom take ladymage?"

Hederick grimaced. "Yes."

"Not kill 'em, no. Just capture. Bring 'em back temple. Not kill 'em, never, no, never. Not!"

"That's what Dahos told you, I know," Hederick said. "I'm changing his order."

The yellow eyes narrowed. "Change 'em orders?"

"Kill him," Hederick repeated.

"Kill 'em?"

"Yes, kill Tarscenian, the tall man in the cloak."

"No!" Yellow Eyes chanted again. "Not kill 'em, no. Just capture. Bring 'em back temple. Not kill 'em, never, no, never. Not!"

Hederick heaved a sigh. He should have imported hobgoblins first. Certainly they were more vicious and harder to manage, but at least they had brains larger than pebbles. Some even spoke passable Abanasinian. "By the sword of Sauvay! You idiot, listen. Kill Tarscenian. Yes, kill. *Kill him!*"

After repeating the new instructions five times, Yellow Eyes seemed to catch their drift. "Kill him dead?"

Hederick nodded.

"Eat 'em, yes?"

Suddenly Hederick was sweating a river. Nausea thickened his throat again; his hands shook. But he struggled to maintain control and nodded. "Yes, eat him . . . No, wait!"

Yellow Eyes looked even more confused. Hederick took a deep breath. "Kill Tarscenian, yes. Do whatever you want with the body. But . . ."

"But?"

"But bring me the head." Hederick would not trust the goblins to have followed his orders until he had some proof of Tarscenian's death.

He made Yellow Eyes repeat the orders several more times, then he dismissed the goblin. The High Theocrat made his way back to his bed and stretched out. The steamy predawn heralded another sultry day in Solace.

Hederick felt like vomiting.

Discipline, he told himself. Breathe slowly. Loosen your fists. Steady yourself, you fool! "Order is the greatest good," he whispered to steel himself. "The Seekers will rule the world." The thought of all those waiting, needy souls braced Hederick, as it always did. "I will lead them all," he murmured.

Solace had had a modest Seeker church in the center of the city long before Hederick had arrived. When Solace had chosen to join Gateway and Haven in the Seeker theocracy, and the Council of Highseekers had gone on to appoint Hederick as High Theocrat, he had persuaded the high council that a trading center of Solace's stature needed a marvelous monument to the Seeker gods.

"Let us fulfill the prophecies of the *Praxis* and show the world the glory and strength of Omalthea and the pantheons!" he had argued. One by one, the Highseekers had come around. Only that perpetual troublemaker, young Elistan, had seemed unconvinced. But even Elistan had ultimately gone along with Hederick's plans for Erolydon.

Hederick forced himself to focus his thoughts. The trouble with Tarscenian was all but solved, and it was entirely possible that for the first time in decades, Hederick might be free of his sister.

The High Theocrat forced his thoughts through the duties of the coming day. He would join Dahos in the dawn devotions. There were many Seeker rites of devotion; each god and goddess in the two pantheons demanded a separate rite of adoration. But there were also novitiates to instruct, priests to meet with, and workers to be supervised as they put the finishing touches on Eroly-don. Hederick also planned to step up his inquisitions, and later, during the evening revelations, he would again welcome converts to the cause.

The silk oversheet clung damply to Hederick's skin, and he wadded it up and tossed it in a corner. Later in the day, a pair of Seeker novitiates would spend hours in the airless laundry room beneath the women's quarters. Glorying in the heat and discomfort, they would reverently steam out each crease in the precious fabrics that enhanced the private quarters of the new High Theocrat.

The bedclothes and Hederick's garments were cleaned daily, whether worn or not. The frescoed walls, vallen-wood ceiling, and tile floor were swabbed daily with a solution of herbs and spring water. The room was kept thick with the scent of valley-lily incense night and day to cleanse away impurities in the air. Hederick, in his advancing age, was taking no chances with his health.

His rooms faced Crystalmir Lake, and at this time of day, the surroundings were quiet enough that the slightest sound carried. Somewhere, a horse-drawn wagon rattled over the cobblestones of the eastern courtyard. The scents of daytime began to assail Hederick; the smell of a roasting side of beef—a gift from a follower—brought saliva to the Theocrat's mouth. Two gnomes argued somewhere. Diverting creatures, Hederick conceded—much like otters. But unclean. They must be outside the gates; Hederick allowed only humans inside the temple.

"Impure," he muttered, "unblessed by the New Gods."

He felt a familiar wave of piety swell into prayer. "Oh, Motherlord, I will prove myself worthy. In the name of the New Gods, I will rid Krynn of the unclean. Of elves and half-elves and dwarves and gnomes. Of weavers of heretical charms. Of witches—of anyone who dares gather the waning powers of the Old Gods to cast their spells! This again I vow!" He sat up and pounded one fist into an open hand.

When the New Gods eventually spoke and named him, Hederick, their chief emissary on Krynn, he would have his revenge—on Highseeker Elistan, on the Old Gods, on Ancilla if she still lived, on everyone. His advanced years would not matter; no doubt the New Gods would reward him with eternal life.

A burst of laughter floated up from the kitchens—coarse female laughter. Women from the poor sections of Solace were allowed inside portions of Erolydon late at night to empty chamber pots and perform the basest cleaning.

Hederick saw the disgusting scullery wenches in his mind's eye—tall, lustful women with knowing eyes, tawdry clothing barely covering breasts and buttocks, legs bare, sandaled feet permanently rimed with dirt. They would be joking as they worked, raising their voices in filthy insinuations as though they hoped to provoke Hederick, back in the sanctity of his rooms. He could hear them; he could always hear them, even when they were far away.

Sometimes, piqued by a particularly vile exchange, he ordered the entire lot whipped by Erolydon's guards. The guards knew their trade well, but the women would return, apparently undaunted, the next night to scrub the day's dirt from Erolydon and collect their meager wages. In these times, a paying job was not to be abandoned for a mere beating.

The darkness in Hederick's room gave way to gray, although the sun had not yet risen. He heard guards ushering the women out through the gates. Cursing beneath his breath, Hederick stood and rearranged his damp robe around his thick body. He padded barefoot across the tile floor to his prayer table and sat stiffly on the carved granite block that served as a bench. Closing his eyes, grasping each wrist with the opposite hand, and folding his arms in his lap in the manner decreed by the *Praxis*, Hederick bowed his head and began his morning devotions.

"O New Gods who inhabit the skies above us, hear my prayer," he intoned. "The day begins, and the first thoughts of this faithful follower are of you."

He raised his voice, aware that priests and novitiates would pass his door, hear him, and know that the High Theocrat was communing with the gods. "You are the true gods, ascending at last to your rightful position over the false gods of the past, whose speciousness was revealed by the devastation of the Cataclysm more than three centuries ago.

"Cadithal, God of Wealth, may we receive your loving glance today. Zeshun, Goddess of Material Things, may you shower your benefits upon those of piety who deserve them. Ferae, Goddess of Beasts and Flying Things, may you make the land bountiful so that we may praise your munificence by our enjoyment of your gifts.

"Sauvay, Supreme God of Power and Vengeance and Fatherlord of All the Lesser Pantheon, may you accept the loving attentions of your Krynn-bound disciple, Hederick, and declare him as worthy as a son."

The High Theocrat halted. Had he implied that the blood of the New Gods flowed in his own mortal veins? Did he, Hederick, dare to believe that he was a god? Surely that was blasphemy of the deepest conceit. And certainly it would not sit well with the Motherlord.

He had departed from the ritual words. Hederick vowed to do an act of penance today. "Order is the greatest good," he reminded himself. "And self-control is the first step toward order."

Where had he left off in the prayers? And when had the incense gone out?

He exclaimed, pulled a perfumed stick from a porcelain container, and hurried to the fireplace, where he lit the scented twig upon an ember. Such was the discipline of the High Theocrat that even on the hottest days of summer, the fire was not allowed to go out.

Hederick closed his eyes. "Sauvay, Supreme God of Power and Vengeance and Fatherlord of the Lesser Pantheon, may you accept the sadly inadequate attentions of your High Theocrat, Hederick, and declare his pitiful gifts worthy of you, Great One."

Was that better? The Theocrat clutched his silk robe to his chest and plunged on. " . . . Father of the Lesser Pantheon, may you accept . . ."

Had he repeated himself?

Where was Dahos, by the New Gods? Certainly someone must have told him by now that Hederick was awake.

Where *was* he in the devotion?

Hederick's palms were slick, and a trickle of perspiration caused his robe to cling more tightly around him. He'd gone unbathed for nearly a day. Nausea tightened its grip. There'd be no swallowing his breakfast until he was sure he'd scrubbed every pore. And if Erolydon's occupants—those not already fasting in the wake of the witch Norah's death—had to wait until midmorning to break their fast today, such was the price of a disciplined religious life.

No one, priest or novitiate, broke their fast until the High Theocrat did. Hunger brought holy thoughts.

Yet the thought of food made his stomach rumble. Perhaps it would not be necessary to offer praise to the *entire* host of Seeker gods this morning, he thought.

He couldn't remember having opened his eyes—another departure from routine—but his gaze was fixed now on the items that lined his prayer table: his incense pallet, a flat piece of blue-glazed tile the size and shape of a maple leaf, with a hole that held the twig steady; a shallow bowl in which he laid the most precious of consecrated gifts before consigning them to the treasury; and a sky-blue velvet cloth.

"Blessed be the New Gods," he murmured.

He'd lost track of the litany again. Hederick closed his eyes. " . . . Father of the Lesser Pantheon, may you accept . . ." No—he'd finished with Sauvay. The High Theocrat gratefully moved into the traditional closing. "In the name of the mightiest of gods, whose ascendancy is surely close at hand, and who will restore order to this chaotic world and ensure salvation in the next, I, your lowest of servants . . ."

Omalthea. The Motherlord, the unbending one who could not, according to lore, be placated by anything less than a soul. He'd forgotten her!

In Hederick's darkest terrors, he'd imagined that the creatures who'd tracked him through numberless nightmares bore, not Ancilla's likeness, but the visage of Omalthea.

"Your servant has transgressed deeply and humbly begs your patience." Sweat poured down Hederick's face. The heat in the room seemed to triple with the rising sun.

His robe stuck to him like mucilage. His fingers clenched the incense stick. Hederick closed his eyes tightly and inhaled a whiff of lily of the valley. In his agitation, the words of the prayer ran into each other. "Omalthea Supreme Motherlord of the Pantheons praise be always to you and know that I your abject servant will always hold you in the highest reverence joyfully offering even my pitiful life and paltry position in the afterlife to you if they please you."

He waited. Would she strike him dead? His thoughts fluttered like the wings of a moth, darted to his beloved Erolydon. He'd designed every engraved stone, every vallenwood-paneled hall, every drainage canal and secret passageway.

Hederick bowed his head lower until his forehead touched the blue cloth on the prayer table. "Omalthea's will be done," he whispered. "I am hers to destroy."

Hederick's muscles twitched with tension. Eventually he lifted his head from the velvet and the cool stone. He still lived. The ceiling was intact. No claws had torn into his flesh.

He opened his eyes. Several novitiates began a Seeker hymn as they worked on the lawn outside his quarters. The sun was barely visible.

"We greet the day
In praise of the New Gods.
We labor in their honor.
We praise the new day.
All praise, all praise
The glory of the New Gods."

Ancilla had sung a version of that tune as she cleared the dishes from the table in the morning, back in Garlund. How old had he been—barely two? Hederick closed his eyes. The past, like always, threatened to sweep over him like a wave washing him out to sea.

Then, with an oath, he started. The past was behind him.

Dawn services, he thought. Discipline.

Dahos would be lost without him.

Hederick hurried from the chamber.

Chapter 14

The sound of the rock scraping back from the entrance startled Tarscenian into wakefulness. He was alert and standing by the time the half-elf Gaveley entered the den. Mynx sat at the table, her expression unreadable.

Gaveley was dressed in the fashion of a pampered noble—snowy white silk shirt, tight green leather leggings, and fawn-colored kidskin boots. He stopped dead in his tracks when he spotted Tarscenian. His almond-shaped, hazel eyes flicked to Mynx, then back to the tall traveler.

Two humans, both men, stood behind Gaveley. Their manner and guise contrasted sharply with that of the more elegantly attired half-elf. One man was nearly as tall as Tarscenian, but far huskier; he had the crushed ear and flattened nose of someone who was no stranger to tavern brawls. The other man was small and slight and so ordinary-looking as to be overlooked in almost any crowd—which was probably to his advantage, Tarscenian thought.

"What is this?" Gaveley said in a hostile voice, almost a hoarse whisper. "What is a stranger doing here? Mynx . . ." His hand went to the ornate sword at his waist.

Mynx stood to introduce Tarscenian. She sketched in the events of the afternoon and evening. "He wishes to join us. To my mind, he has some promise. He fooled the high priest and the temple guards handily in the refugees' quarter, Gaveley. You should have been there. Look."

She dug Dahos's ring out of a pocket and handed it to Gaveley, who accepted it with a half-smile.

"Still," he rasped, "you overstepped yourself in bringing him here of your own volition."

Mynx muttered an apology, but Gaveley was already circling Tarscenian. The older man turned with him, hand on the hilt of his sword, warily noting the position of the other thieves.

Suddenly, Gaveley's sword was out and poised at Tarscenian's throat. "You're rather old to take up our company, stranger," Gaveley whispered. "Are you certain you're not a spy for the High Theocrat? He'd love to get his pudgy hands in our coffers, I'll warrant." He nodded toward the two men. "Xam, Snoop—check the area for Hederick's henchmen."

The two left without remark. The hulk of a man, Xam, cut through the den and disappeared through a back portal. Snoop wheeled and vanished back in the direction from which he had come.

"You understand that I cannot be too careful, old man," Gaveley whispered.

"Tarscenian."

There was the sound of the rock again. In that instant, Gaveley's concentration wavered, and Tarscenian acted. His sword, held in a firm grip, swept up and clanged against Gaveley's. An instant later, Gaveley's weapon lay discarded on the floor, and it was the half-elf who was staring down a blade.

Tarscenian's voice was edged with anger. "I may be old, Gaveley, but I have learned much in my time."

Xam and Snoop, entering, froze. Gaveley, held at the point of Tarscenian's sword, flicked his gaze toward the smaller man. Snoop said simply, "All clear." Xam nodded as well. At that, Gaveley released a breath, stepped back from the swordpoint, and casually retrieved and sheathed his own weapon. In the light of the lantern that illuminated the hideout, he regarded Tarscenian with a cold half-smile.

Gaveley's more relaxed attitude signaled something to Xam, Snoop, and Mynx. All three helped themselves to the carafe of wine and took up comfortable positions around the room, waiting for what would happen next.

"We will see, Tarscenian," was all Gaveley said to the older man.

Mynx brought Gaveley a goblet of wine and poured another for Tarscenian. The older man refused with a shake of the head. Unlike the human thieves, who gulped the wine as though it were water, Gaveley sipped his drink elegantly. He leaned against a stool, glaring down at Xam and Snoop. "Report, you two," he rasped.

"I know where to find Von Falden," Xam said. "I expect to bring him in tomorrow."

This meant something to Gaveley, for he gave a satisfied nod. "Splendid. Pantrev upped the bounty to two hundred steel yesterday," he said in his hoarse voice. "That was a tough assignment. Good work, Xam."

The bounty hunter grunted. "Years o' practice," he said and proceeded to down the rest of his wine.

Gaveley turned to the small, nondescript man. "Snoop?"

The spy shrugged. "Still looking. I know there's something up between the young lady in question and the head of the weavers' guild, but proving it . . ." He shrugged again.

"Keep at it," Gaveley said. "It could mean hundreds of steel in blackmail—from each of them. If you can't come up with something solid, we can always bluff our way along, but blackmail always has more teeth when you can offer a bit of irrefutable evidence."

Gaveley's gaze fell on Mynx. "And you?"

She smiled lazily at him. There was a casualness between the two that suggested to Tarscenian that they'd once been much more than colleagues.

"I fulfilled my assignment, Gav," she said archly, "as you well know. And . . . " She unfastened a pouch from her waistband and spilled its contents onto the shelf. "And I have two purses, a copper bracelet decorated with what seem to be amethysts, three rings—including the high priest's, but I suppose I really can't take credit for that—and a hair clasp made of polished steel. Very pretty." She fondled the last-named item. "Can I keep it, Gav?"

"And risk running into the owner?" Gaveley laughed gruffly and extended his goblet for a refill. "Besides, Mynx, nothing could tame that lion's mane of yours."

"Coupla hours with a comb wouldn't hurt," the spy Snoop cracked. Mynx socked him in the arm with her fist, then turned back to Gaveley, who shook his head.

"You know the rules, Mynx. Everything to the fence. We can't risk having our goods surface in Solace. Better Haven or Gateway or Caergoth."

She accepted Gaveley's mandate without protest, and Tarscenian realized the banter between the two was a longstanding routine.

Then the leader was addressing Tarscenian. "And you, old man? Now is your turn. Why are you here?"

"I want help stealing something," was Tarscenian's curt reply.

The half-elf leaned forward. The movement parted his dark hair, revealing the pointed ears that proclaimed that his mother or father was a Qualinesti. Gaveley licked his lips like a man about to set upon a fine supper. "Something valuable?" he asked

"Quite." Tarscenian spoke tersely. He had no money to offer the group. They'd not help him unless they knew the artifact was worth something, but he had no intention of revealing just how valuable the Diamond Dragon was magically. He described the artifact in more mundane, but financially attractive, terms.

"Steel, you say," Gaveley murmured.

"With dozens of diamonds," Tarscenian added. "And ruby eyes."

"Too distinctive," Mynx said.

The half-elf nodded. "It would have to be melted down. The diamonds alone would be worth a fortune, though."

Tarscenian said nothing. He would have to find some way to prevent the thieves from keeping the dragon artifact, but at this point he was better off pretending his motive was the same as theirs—pure greed.

"What do you want out of this, Tarscenian?"

"My share of the take."

Gaveley regarded him dubiously. "And where is this marvelous piece of jewelry?" he asked.

"Around Hederick's neck." Tarscenian held his breath, expecting some explosive reaction.

He was wrong. Gaveley, Xam, and Snoop continued to sit stoically. Only Mynx perked up, her eyes sparkling. "What a chance to get even with the old goat!" she crowed. "You say this piece of jewelry is especially important to the High Theocrat?"

Perhaps revenge, rather than greed, was the tack to take, Tarscenian thought. "Tremendously so," he said. "He's had the Diamond Dragon with him for decades. He believes it's a gift from his gods."

Mynx turned to the others. "Here's our chance to avenge the kender," she said excitedly.

"But to steal something the High Theocrat always keeps on his person?" Snoop protested. "With all those guards and goblins around? Mynx, you've got talent enough to do it, but . . ."

"Let me try, Gav," Mynx pleaded.

"Well . . ." Gaveley paused. Several emotions seemed to be warring in his contorted expression. Finally, a bland mask dropped over his features. "I need time to consider this. Mynx, escort the old man to his lodgings."

Mynx looked at Tarscenian. He shrugged. "I just arrived in Solace. I have no lodgings. I'll sleep in the woods."

"You can't do that," Mynx objected. "The goblins can espy things in the dark. And they'll be looking all over for you. I know where to hide you."

* * * * *

Kifflewit Burrthistle leaned away from the back door of the thieves' den and considered. First the kender had had to evade the huge man and the tiny, ferretlike one when they'd come out in search of spies—as if Kifflewit would allow any spies nearby! Then he'd had to pick a lock specially created by thieves to keep out other thieves. They'd set it up with a latch-pin keyed to a needle, daubed with poison that the kender was sure was fast and deadly.

But kender grew up learning how to pick locks. One of the first sayings a young kender learned was: "The most interesting things are behind locked doors. So get moving." If one thing set off kender from the rest of Krynn's creatures, it was their overwhelming curiosity. That and a total absence of fear.

So there was never any question that Kifflewit Burrthistle would do a little eavesdropping on the thieves.

But Mynx and Tarscenian were coming out now. Kifflewit was torn between staying at the den and hearing some more tantalizing talk or dogging the steps of his earlier acquaintances. Excitement had followed Mynx and Tarscenian once before, and it might again. He'd not had as much fun in a long time as he'd had shinnying up that rope in the refugee section.

Besides, Tarscenian might spill a little more information about that Diamond Dragon. The desirable object certainly seemed as though it would be worth a closer look!

He decided, and let the door swing shut. Absolutely silently, of course.

Few creatures can be as stealthy as a kender.

* * * * *

"So why don't we grab the old man now? And turn him right over to Hederick?" Snoop demanded as soon as Mynx and Tarscenian were out of sight. "Five hundred steel for a bounty! That's not someone I'd like to leave walking around loose. Not with plenty of other people willing to collect that kind of money."

"Mynx'll hide him well enough."

Snoop rolled his eyes. "But when do we turn him over and collect, Gaveley?"

The half-elf didn't answer right away. "Maybe we won't," he finally said.

"What?" Xam and Snoop erupted at the same time.

Gaveley swirled his wine in his goblet, watching the

pattern form on the chalice in the rosy light. "Not right away, at least," he whispered. "I want to learn more about this Diamond Dragon."

"But . . ."

He cut them off. "We've got to be flexible to get by. You know that."

Xam and Snoop exchanged glances. Then they shrugged. "You're the leader," Snoop said, and smiled ingratiatingly. "And what's more, you're usually right."

"What about Mynx?" Xam asked. "Are you still going to hand her over, too? She's a good thief, one of the best we've had."

"She made her choice," Gaveley shot back. "She could have accepted Hederick's offer, but she turned him down flat."

"She can't forgive him for killing the kender," Xam said softly.

Gaveley fixed a hard glare on the big man. "He was a *kender*. And Hederick caught him sneaking into his temple, remember. If Hederick thinks kender don't belong in Erolydon, I'm not one to argue. The High Theocrat offered us a lot of steel to bring in Tarscenian." He placed his wine glass on the shelf next to the little statue that operated the door mechanism. "Mynx refused to help out of stupid sentiment. There's no room for emotion in this business."

Snoop spoke up. "But she's been with us for a long time. . . ."

"She opted out," Gaveley said stubbornly. "We can't trust her. She's got to go."

Snoop frowned, then nodded. But Xam kept on staring at Gaveley. "But . . ." Xam shook his head.

Gaveley cut him off angrily. "That's enough. We'll turn them both over—*after* they steal this Diamond Dragon for us. If you don't want to go along . . . Well, wouldn't it be ironic if a bounty hunter ended up with a bounty on his *own* head?"

They locked stares. Then Xam lifted his huge shoulders and let them fall. "Oh, well," he said with a sigh. "I'll miss her."

* * * * *

Saying nothing, Mynx passed stairway after deserted stairway in the darkness. Tarscenian glanced upward at the web of walkways crisscrossing overhead.

Mynx answered the unasked question. "I prefer to keep my feet on the ground when I can. Too easy to get ambushed on the bridges." She halted and ran her fingers back through her hair without speaking. Her eyes were troubled. "Tarscenian, all that you said about that dragon artifact—it was all true? It's that valuable to Hederick?"

Tarscenian nodded. Everything he'd said was true; he merely had left a few things out.

"I could help you," Mynx said. "If Gav says it's all right."

"Thank you."

"Don't thank me," she snapped. "I wouldn't do it for *you*. I'd do it for the money . . . and the kender."

They continued on for quite some time without speaking. The vallenwood canopy admitted no light from moons or stars. Tarscenian could tell when they were passing beneath a home in the treetops only by the slight thickening of the darkness.

"Tell me about Gaveley," he finally said.

Mynx snorted. "You saw him. He loves fine clothes, and he goes about dressed like a nobleman—as if 'nobleman' means anything since the Cataclysm! But his mother was the daughter of a rich man here in Solace, closest thing Solace has to nobility. She got in trouble with an elven trader who was passing through, and her family cast her out."

She tried to untangle the lapis-and-silver earring from her hair as she walked, but only succeeded in making the snarl worse. "You know how most people treat half-elves—as not quite human, not quite elf," she continued. "And Gav's mother raised him to despise the rich. He loves nothing as much as stealing from the wealthy. Not that many people in Solace fit into *that* category any-more." The thief fell silent.

"And you?"

Mynx gave him a hard look. "For all that it's none of your business, stranger, I've been a thief for as long as I can remember. Joined Gav's ring when I was ten. Before that, I was on my own. Gav took care of me and taught me my trade. That's something to appreciate when you've got no family—or at least none that wants to admit knowing you."

A faint snarl, quickly muffled, reached Tarscenian's ears. He and Mynx halted at the same time. Within an eyeblink, his sword was ready, as was Mynx's dagger. They proceeded carefully, taking as wide a berth as pos-sible around shadowed vallenwoods and stairways.

They covered some ground without incident, and Mynx relaxed. "Maybe we were just imagin—"

"Look out!" Tarscenian shouted. He whirled—and dove to the ground as a mace hurtled over his head. He heard Mynx curse and hit the ground next to him.

She rolled and was up on her feet in an instant. They were being attacked by something, but in the dark it was hard to tell what.

"What is it?" Mynx panted, peering into the darkness, "A bear, in Solace? And with a mace?"

"A bugbear," Tarscenian replied, moving cautiously to put the monster between him and Mynx. "Not a bear, really, although it looks like it. More like a goblin. Smarter than it looks, but not too bright. Sees in the dark—at least, a little."

"Magic?"

"None that I know of."

"Good."

The monster suddenly materialized in front of them, towering over them, a warhammer hanging from one paw and a spear balanced in the other. Its eyes were pale, its fur coarse and dark. Wedge-shaped ears rose from the top of its head, and lips wrinkled back from long fangs. It grunted and snarled as it jabbed at them with the spear.

Suddenly, the monster roared and swung its hammer at Mynx. She took advantage of the beast's outflung paw to leap forward and slice its forearm from elbow to wrist. It squealed and thrust the limb under one of the hides that protected it. Its mismatched armor clanked and jangled in the still night. It whirled, forcing them back to avoid the needle-sharp edge of its spear. And all the while it kept shrieking.

"It'll soon bring the guards down on us, if it doesn't kill us first," Tarscenian hissed.

"We'll have to kill *it*, then," Mynx said calmly. Without hesitation, she ducked and dove under the whirling spear. Then she leaped again, burying her dagger to the hilt in the bugbear's side. The bugbear moved quickly, though, and caught the thief in the abdomen with a clawed paw, flinging her high over Tarscenian's head.

The movement left the creature exposed. In an instant, Tarscenian thrust his sword into the bugbear's belly and wrenched the weapon to one side. The creature stood for a moment, entrails spilling onto the ground, then it pitched forward with a horrible scream.

Tarscenian whirled. Mynx was just sitting up behind him, rubbing her head and rearranging her skirt and blouse. "Come on!" Tarscenian shouted. "Before any guards get here!" He pulled her to her feet, mindless of any injuries she might have suffered.

Mynx shook her head to clear it. "Next time I go hunting bugbears, I won't wear a skirt," she muttered. Then she raced over to the dead creature, pulled her dagger from its ribs, and sprinted into the trees. Tarscenian followed a few paces behind. He could hear the cries of an approaching phalanx of guards.

They ran through the underbrush beneath the vallenwoods until their sides ached, then dove behind the huge trees to conceal themselves until blue-and-gold-clad guards pounded past. Despite the noise, the walkways remained deserted above them; no one ventured forth from the safety of the tree-homes.

Tarscenian paused at a fork in the path. Mynx skidded to a stop. "What is it?" she hissed.

Tarscenian pointed to the left. "They're coming from that way. And the other way, too. And from behind us as well." He bounded off the path into the underbrush, burrowing beneath thick ferns. He hoped she had the sense to follow and hide herself.

The three groups of guards almost collided where the paths met. The air filled with oaths as each contingent accused the other of missing the quarry. Finally an authoritative voice cut through the rest. "They could be hiding anywhere around here." The leader ordered the guards—two dozen or so, as near as Tarscenian could guess—to fan out. "Beat the underbrush," the leader ordered.

"Who are we looking for?"

"Whoever killed the bugbear, you idiot."

"Fine, but who's that?"

The captain answered with curses. Tarscenian heard him muttering as he and his partners began to wade through the ferns and bracken. It would be only a matter of moments before one of the guards stumbled over Tarscenian or Mynx. They'd have to make a stand.

The guards were nearing, and Tarscenian was gathering himself to leap up and confront them when a whistling sound brought him up short. He'd heard that sound somewhere. A hoopak?

"Hey, you hopeless pack of overdecorated ninnies!" The voice was high-pitched and sarcastic. "Did you lose something?"

"It's the kender!" one of the guards cried.

"Forget the kender," the captain shouted. "We're looking for whoever killed . . ."

". . . the bugbear!" Kifflewit interrupted. "That's me. Up here."

Tarscenian raised his head slowly until only a few inches of ferns covered him. He looked up.

There was Kifflewit, leaning far over the edge of a walkway, brown topknot bobbing, waving gaily to the guards. His hand held a familiar-looking dagger, the one the woman from Throtl had wanted to sell. No doubt the kender had "found" it during their adventure in the refugee market earlier in the evening. Tarscenian heard a muffled snort off to his left, and realized Mynx had spied the kender, too.

The captain ordered his men to ignore Kifflewit's taunts. "No kender could kill a bugbear," he scoffed.

"Except this kender had a magic dagger," Kifflewit rejoined. "It was terrific! I didn't even have to hold on to it. It knew the bugbear wanted to hurt me, so it flew across the clearing, smack into the creature! Then it flew right back to me! Isn't that splendid? Want to see it?"

"It's possible," a guard ventured. "We found no weapon."

Kifflewit giggled, leaning even farther over the walkway. "You overpaid losers!" he taunted. "What? Did Hederick get you at a group discount? Cheaper by the dozen? Or do *you* pay *him*, so you can pretend you have a job?"

The men began to grumble. This same kender had caused them a bundle of trouble earlier in the night. He'd gotten away before, purely by luck. He dared to ridicule them now?

"Come down here, kender," the captain commanded.

"Ah, no," Kifflewit said, snickering. "I do believe I have an appointment elsewhere. I can't wait to tell my friends how one little kender outwitted two dozen Seeker guards. My, what a good story that will be! Bye-bye, ladies! Don't muss your petticoats during your search!" He waved again happily and scooted off down the walkway.

"*Ladies?*" the captain exploded.

In an instant, the guards went howling after the kender. Moments later, Tarscenian and Mynx were alone amid the silent ferns. The old man rose stiffly to his feet and found Mynx already upright. "That kender," she said, shaking her head. "I owe him one."

"He's a tough little rascal," Tarscenian concluded softly. "Maybe you and Gaveley ought to recruit him."

Mynx took Tarscenian's hand. "Come on," she said. "We still have a way to go."

Tarscenian started to protest, then found himself pulled down the path. Although the night's activities had left him virtually exhausted, he did his best to keep up with the agile thief.

At long last Mynx stopped. She swung under the low-hanging branches of a thick pine tree and disappeared. Tarscenian dropped to his knees and followed, cursing when a pine needle drove into his shin like a porcupine quill.

There was no sign of the thief.

Then a hand grasped his in the dark. Tarscenian pitched into nothingness, dropped a short distance, and landed with a bone-jarring thump on packed earth. "What in—" he complained. "Now what?"

"I have to say, physical grace is not one of your talents, Tarscenian."

He bit off his reply.

"Follow me, old man."

"Where—?"

"Don't ask questions." A strong hand grasped his again. "Crawl."

He did as Mynx ordered. He was in a tunnel, that much was certain. Every few moments his back grazed a rock or root overhead. Then suddenly he sensed that the space had opened up around him. Mynx whispered, "You may be able to get to your feet now. But be careful."

He *could* stand up—as long as he bent at the waist. But after creeping along on his hands and knees for so long, half-standing didn't feel half-bad. Mynx hurried him along the tunnel, which curved every few paces. "Who dug this tunnel?" he muttered. "A bunch of drunken dwarves?"

"Not a bad guess," Mynx whispered, chuckling. "It was abandoned when I found it. I cleaned it out and shored it up."

"Where are—?"

Mynx pulled him forward and placed his hand on the rung of a ladder. He could tell by the air that they weren't exactly underground anymore, but where were they? Tarscenian took a deep breath. "Wood?"

His fingers grazed something rough and crumbly. He broke off a piece and sniffed. "Oak?" he murmured. He stood cautiously and began to climb. The ladder curved to the right as it led upward. "We're inside a tree?"

"Of course. This is Solace, remember?" Mynx muttered, climbing ahead of him in the dark. "Or near enough."

She had halted and seemed to be fumbling with something. A moment later a trapdoor swung open before them. Enough moonlight seeped through a lone

178

curtained window that Tarscenian could make out a chair with a skirt and shirt flung across the back, a mattress, and a small table with a lantern, three dirty plates, and a half-dozen tiny ceramic vials strewn on it. The furniture occupied most of the floor space in the tiny hollowed-out tree-home.

Mynx kicked her sandals off, nudging them under the table. "Sit," she ordered, removing the clothing from the chair and dropping it on the floor. "I'll be right back. Don't light the lantern." She ducked under a curtain in a second doorway.

Tarscenian ignored the proffered chair and stepped across rough-hewn floorboards littered with pine needles. He peeped through the curtained window. Mynx's minuscule home perched in the branches of a burr oak. Thick pines dotted the landscape. Whether he and Mynx were south, north, or east of Solace, he could not have said. By the Old Gods, I need some rest, he thought.

"May I help you?"

Startled, Tarscenian let the curtain drop and faced the lilting new voice. A blond woman stood in the doorway. She wore chain mail leggings, patched leather armor, and knee-high boots with steel cladding up the front. A tight helm framed her face; the visor was up. He saw ashen hair, high cheekbones, dark eyes, full lips.

"Excuse me," he stammered. "Mynx brought me . . ." He paused. "Rather . . ." He stopped again. He realized he'd rather be facing the bugbear again than be in this situation. "It's not what you . . ."

"Mynx?" the woman asked. "Who is Mynx?" She regarded him with a bewildered look. "And what are you doing in my house?"

What trick had Mynx played on him? Obviously she'd abandoned him, but what was her objective? The blond woman wore warrior's garb—was he being held prisoner, then? Never trust a thief, he thought.

He drew his sword.

The woman laughed, pulling off her helmet. Straight blond hair spilled to her shoulders. "Whoever you are, I'm glad you're here," she said merrily. "It's been an age since I've had a man here." She ran her fingers through her ashen hair and smiled.

That gesture.

"Mynx!" Tarscenian shouted. "May the Old Gods damn you to fourteen kinds of Abyss!"

Mynx chuckled. The chuckle became snorts, then helpless guffaws. She dropped into the chair, eyes streaming with tears, while the old man raged.

"Put your sword away, Tarscenian," she finally managed to say between chortles. "You might decapitate me, and what good would I be to you then?"

He regained control with difficulty. "I see now how you maintained such a tight friendship with a kender," he snapped.

The laughter died away, Tarscenian instantly regretting his words. But after Mynx wiped away the last tears, she assumed a businesslike tone. "You're under a death sentence," she told him. "You need a disguise, and if I'm going to spend any time with you, so do I. Obviously, this one will do for me, but you . . . ."

She plucked a wooden box from under the table, opening it. Inside Tarscenian found more vials of the type that littered the table, plus a straight-edge razor, a brush, a chunk of brown soap, and dozens of items Tarscenian couldn't identify. She stood and motioned Tarscenian into the chair.

His joints cried out as he sat down despite his better judgment. "What do you propose?" he snapped. "How do you plan to hide a six-foot-tall bald man with a beard?"

She smiled at his mulish tone. "First of all, the beard has to go."

He tried to jump to his feet, but Mynx's hands were firm on his shoulders. "Never!" he shouted. "I've had this beard for fifty . . ."

"Then it's high time for a change. Besides," she added with a wicked grin, "where else will we get the hair for your wig? Now sit still."

"Pushy as a . . . as a bugbear," he muttered. "You remind me of Ancilla at times."

"Who?"

Tarscenian didn't answer.

Mynx shrugged and wet the soap from a dish of water. She rubbed the brush in it until lather festooned the bristles. Then, brush in one hand, long-handled razor in the other, she bent over Tarscenian and set to work.

Chapter 15

"Leave this place! These trees are sacred!"

Halfway between Solace and Erolydon, five centaurs milled agitatedly around ten burly men wielding axes. The men continued to laugh and joke as they chopped away at the base of a vallenwood, which shaded them from the heartless midday sun.

"Horse," one of the men yelled, "if we doesn't cut this tree, Hederick don't pay us none. An' we got families to feed."

"As do I, humans," countered one of the centaurs, the violet-eyed, white one named Phytos. "But thou dost not find me slaying nature's children to feed *my* young."

The man waved him away. "Don't you love the way they talk?" the woodcutter said to a comrade. They shared a derisive laugh and continued their hacking efforts.

"Stop!" Although the centaurs, two females and three males, held clubs and bows, they did not use them. Shouldering their way into the circle of woodcutters, they shoved three of the men aside, knocking them off their feet.

"These vallenwoods have flourished here since the days of the Old Gods," shouted Phytos as the trio of humans rose slowly to their feet, retrieving their axes. "We warn thee, wrong-headed humans. Dare not to harm them, lest thou wish to feel our wrath!"

"How about *our* wrath, horse?" one of the humans cried. All ten, swinging their axes, waded into the centaurs.

Too late the horse-men brought their clubs into play. A male centaur, hit squarely between the eyes with the dull side of an axehead, collapsed without a sound and did not rise. One of the two female centaurs had just nocked an arrow and fitted it to her bow when a woodcutter's axe blade bit into her neck. She went down screaming, blood spurting, flailing hooves catching a comrade in the leg, arrow wedged uselessly in the vallenwood's bark.

"Retreat!" Phytos called. The centaurs withdrew to the shade of another vallenwood.

The woodcutters did not pursue them, but simply returned to work. "Damned tree lovers," one of the men spat out, hewing at the vallenwood with renewed energy. "If the High Theocrat says we're supposed to chop a tree for his new pavilion, then we does it. What are we supposed to do?"

The wounded female centaur kicked feebly, gave a sobbing cry, and lay still.

"Phytos, please thou let me slay the bastards with arrows," cried the remaining female centaur, who from her lilac eyes and silvery hair looked to be a close relative of the centaur leader. "I can do it easily from here. They have naught but those axes. It would be quick work."

Phytos shook his head. "Nay, Feelding. The Seekers

have long sought reasons to send their minions against the centaur community. We have harmed none of Hederick's people yet, given them no real reason to badger us. Let things remain that way for now."

"But they killed two of our own!" Feelding protested.

Phytos closed his eyes, nodded, and bowed his head in mute prayer. After a moment the two other centaurs followed suit. When they lifted their heads, their angular faces were wet but resolute. "We will go directly to Hederick of the Seekers," Phytos said. "Perhaps he does not know what his men do in his name."

"He knows, all right," the female centaur said venomously. "And he encourages it."

Phytos regarded her with sad violet eyes. "Perhaps. But we will not provoke war if we can avoid it. I would fear to see our small community in the woods take on an entire city of humans. Feelding, Salomar," he said, addressing his companions, "I cannot order thee about like servants. Wilt thou, friends, go with me to this Erolydon to petition the High Theocrat, or wilt thou wait here or, perhaps, proceed home?"

"Go with thee, of course," both replied. Phytos and the others turned as one to go.

Just then, the axes bit a crucial portion from the trunk of the vallenwood. The men scattered, shouting. The huge tree teetered and creaked, and for an instant those on the ground could not tell which way the behemoth would fall. There was a moment of breathless suspense, then the enormous tree fell—hesitantly at first, then gaining speed—toward the east.

Suddenly the clearing that had been shaded was flooded with the jarring light of noonday. The three centaurs looked on, faces pained, their lips moving in silent prayer. The ten humans, however, cheered as they tossed their sweat-drenched handkerchiefs into the air in jubilation.

As the trunk of the vallenwood smashed into the ground, a wailing split the air. The woodcutters ceased their celebration and stood stunned.

"What is it?" the centaur Salomar cried.

"The tree, I believe," Phytos replied with a frown. "It does not die easily."

At that instant, as men and centaurs stared, a mist arose from the form of the dying tree. A pale image of the tree, the fog hovered ghostlike above the vallenwood. The woodcutters dropped their axes and backed away, fear in their faces.

Then a misty figure rose from the vaporous tree, like a corpse sitting up in a coffin. The men cried out and ran, but the centaurs continued to stand where they had, bowing their heads. "We honor thee, o specter of the wood," Phytos murmured. "We witness thy pain and feel it."

The figure's face was contorted, its limbs drawn up against its torso as if it were in agony. Suddenly it reached trembling hands toward the sky, as if to beseech some unseen force. A moan reverberated through the clearing. *Feliton kay* . . . The wraith faltered, pressed a hand to its brow, and tried again. *I, Calcidon . . . Feliton kay . . .*

Then the apparition clenched its fists and slumped forward. Both it and the mist above the fallen vallenwood dissipated.

"Phytos, what was that?" Salomar repeated.

Phytos shook his head.

"Its face was elven," Feelding said softly, "and it wore a robe. A mage? But what was a wizard doing in a . . . ?" She fell silent. The three exchanged uneasy looks before she spoke again. "Friends, I am newly frightened."

The others said nothing, but all three pivoted on swift hooves, then broke into a canter. They headed north, toward Erolydon.

* * * * *

Kifflewit Burrthistle stood in the shadows of a vallen-wood, across from the gate of Erolydon, and pondered what to do. He wasn't exactly in the good graces of the temple guards anymore. He'd led them in a delightful chase all around Solace for an hour last night before tiring of the game and losing them with ease.

Tarscenian had spoken so feelingly of the Diamond Dragon. Kifflewit just had to see it. Just one look, he promised himself, and then he would put it back where he'd found it. Honest.

Unless, of course, where he'd found it wasn't handy or safe anymore. In some cases such an artifact would be safer with someone who would guard it zealously. Someone like Kifflewit Burrthistle.

But how to get into the temple? He was still musing about the problem and absentmindedly running his fingers through his brown topknot when three centaurs cantered up to the gate. His brown eyes narrowed. He tipped his head and pricked up his ears.

"We are here to see Hederick," Phytos called firmly to the guard. "I am Phytos, chieftain of the Fyr-Kenti centaurs, and these are my ministers. Thou wilt admit us and announce our presence to the High Theocrat directly."

The guard didn't move. "Hederick's holding his witches' court. He's busy. And I never heard of no Fyr-Kenti nothin', anyway."

" 'Tis our home glade, north of here," Feelding put in.

"No one but humans passes through these gates," the guard snapped. "Temple Erolydon is a holy place."

"We have news that Hederick must hear," Salomar added.

"What news could a trio of *ponies* have for the High Theocrat of Solace? Although, truly, I could find good use for the female, there." The guard motioned lewdly at Feelding, who, like most centaurs, saw no more point in clothing her human torso than in donning garments for her horselike body. The centaurs wore only the wide bands that held their quivers of arrows and leather bags that contained goods from the Solace markets.

The guard gestured at Feelding again and roared with coarse laughter. Two compatriots, who'd remained by the gate, joined in.

Phytos, Salomar, and Feelding took a quiet step toward the gate at the same instant, slipped arrows in their bows, and raised their weapons. Mirth dropped from the guards like a cloak. One guard drew his sword. The two nearer the gate hoisted spears.

A crowd of pilgrims waiting near the gate drew back, blocking Kifflewit Burrthistle's view. The kender crept from his hiding place behind the tree, slunk unnoticed through the pilgrims, and poked his head around the voluminous skirts of a traveler.

High Priest Dahos had arrived at the gate, Kifflewit saw. Hederick's lieutenant gestured the centaurs away. "Heathen creatures!" he cried. "You don't belong here, centaurs. Get back to your forest meadows with your pagan offspring and your primitive, bestial rites, lest you find yourself on trial for heresy!"

"We have important information for the High Theocrat," Phytos said obdurately. "News he will require if he hopes to avoid a war."

The guards laughed, but Dahos gave the centaurs his attention. The high priest appeared unfazed by gazing directly into a centaur arrow. "Perhaps His Worship *would* be interested," the brown-robed priest said calculatingly. "Give me your news, and I will give it to him when he is through passing sentence this afternoon."

"We will present our news in person," Phytos said. "We wish to see him now. Call High Theocrat Hederick from this court of his."

Dahos refused.

Phytos, Feelding, and Salomar released their arrows at

the same time. They'd gauged their aim to miss the three guards—but just barely. Each man leaped aside, swore and clapped a hand to an ear, an arm, or the side of his neck. They started toward the centaurs.

Dahos held them back. He gazed blandly at the centaurs as though he was unimpressed by their little stunt. Then, to the guards' disgust, he bowed slightly, said, "Come with me," and strode back through the gate. He drew an incense-holder from his pocket; incense would cleanse the air, lessen the sacrilege of allowing nonhumans into Erolydon. He stopped once to speak to a yellow-robed novitiate, who rushed ahead of him to spread the word.

Kifflewit saw his chance at that moment. He darted through the confused crowd and leaped into the leather pouch on Phytos's back. None too soon, either; the centaur had already launched into movement.

The kender squatted among three thick carafes of wine, as many rounds of milk-white cheese, and a handful of smooth stones. He searched along the seam of the pack until he found a loose stitch and used his fingers to widen the seam until he had a passable view of his surroundings.

The hole also admitted some much-needed fresh air; the cheese was of the fragrant sort. "Smells like old boots," the kender muttered. He wondered if Phytos would notice if he jettisoned a couple of cheese rounds, and decided the centaur probably would.

Kifflewit had heard about Erolydon's splendors, of course, but seeing the temple up close and in person was a different experience. Although he'd viewed all this in his mind's eye countless times, now he actually *saw* the blackened vallenwood trunk, which they passed in the courtyard, and the double wall that allowed spectators to observe the daily executions. He saw, too, the scratched portal through which the materbill entered.

And then they were inside Erolydon itself. Kifflewit blinked. The tapestries! The jeweled statues! Precious gems were inlaid into the marble floor. Crystals suspended at the doors caught the light and fractured it into a dozen colors, and the visitors' movements sent the prisms whirling. Rainbows darted into every corner. And the colors! The kender's jaw dropped in amazement, and he gasped—taking in a lungful of cheesy air.

Kifflewit stifled a cough, then put his eye back to the hole.

More tapestries. They stretched from floor to ceiling, about the height of four tall men, and each depicted high points in Seeker history. A muscular-looking god leered at a seductive-looking goddess. A fearsome goddess beamed fire from her eyes as she pointed an accusing finger at a quivering soul. An emaciated god stood in a mountain of coins and jewels, valuables dropping from his outspread fingers. An innocent-looking goddess, deer and wildlife surrounding her, stared adoringly at the emaciated god and stretched her hand toward the man's steel coins.

"How terrific!" Kifflewit whispered. If Tarscenian was right, the Diamond Dragon would be even greater a sight than all this. Perhaps he'd take a closer look at these things on his way out, though.

Thick incense from Dahos's holder found its way into the pack and mingled unpleasantly with the odor of the cheese. That, combined with the centaur's swaying stride, gave rise to a distinct feeling of queasiness on the part of the kender. He swallowed and gulped to sip fresh air through the inadequate hole in the pouch. All he took in was a belt of smoke redolent with gardenias and valley lily. He cautiously lifted the top of the pack to see if there was any opportunity for escape.

They had passed through double doors and entered a long, tilted hallway, illuminated by torches set in sconces on the walls, and were picking their way downward.

Dahos pointed. "The Great Chamber is down here. I will send a messenger into the room to request His Worship's presence."

Kifflewit frowned. He thought about the layout of the temple that he'd worked out in his head, piecing together stories and scraps of overheard conversation.

"Meet in a *hallway*?" Phytos snorted. "High Priest, we will be received in ceremonial fashion, just as human emissaries."

"I'm afraid that won't be possible," Dahos said, smiling.

Phytos, Feelding, and Salomar pushed past the high priest. Salomar and Feelding reached for the heavy oak doors at the same time. Dahos was retreating up the ramp toward the temple's main entrance even as Kifflewit sprang from Phytos's pack.

"Stop them!" the kender shouted into the centaur leader's ear. "That's the door to the materbill's dungeon! See?" A slamming of the door confirmed that Dahos had run away. Kifflewit heard a bolt being drawn, then another.

The doors were cracked open. A huge golden paw snaked around the portal and raked Salomar across the torso. As Phytos backpedaled frantically, fire spewed through the doorway. The flames caught Feelding full in the face. Both centaurs dropped their clubs and their bows. Phytos, the kender clinging to his back, lunged toward his wounded friends, his bow ready.

"No! Run, Phytos!" Salomar gasped. "We two are lost. Go back to Fyr-Kenti glade. Tell the others. Prepare for war."

Phytos hesitated. Another gout of fire belched through the door, downing Feelding and Salomar. The materbill roared and leaped through. He tore into the two centaurs with claws and fangs.

Phytos whirled and pounded back up the hallway. A

short distance from the double doors, he reared and struck the portal with both forelegs. The centaur pounded at the door with his club, then whirled and loosed a volley of blows with both hind legs.

Kifflewit fell from Phytos's back.

Then the centaur crashed through. He shook off shards of wood and splinters, then clattered through the opulent entryway past the tapestries, crashing out through the main entrance into the sunshine.

Kifflewit, hiding behind the broken door, saw the centaur bound to the top of the inner wall, teeter for a moment on top, then vault over the outer wall to freedom.

A snarl brought the kender's attention back to his own precarious circumstances. The materbill, gorging on centaur, lifted its head and gazed up the hallway. As it chewed, it surveyed the kender and the route to freedom. It took a step toward the door.

Then a phalanx of temple guards, armed with spears and shields, entered the hallway. The materbill seemed to gauge this new enemy. The guards edged down the hallway, holding up huge shields. The materbill retreated to the opposite side, behind the carcasses of the centaurs. The guards came closer. The leonine creature crouched. Then the first row of guards, shields before them, reached with their spears, nudging the dead centaurs toward the materbill. The materbill backed up slowly until it had moved back beyond the doorway. Then the guards slammed the doors to the materbill's quarters and barricaded them.

Kifflewit Burrthistle dove out of sight behind the wreckage of the doors just as the High Theocrat appeared at the top of the hallway, flanked by Dahos. A dozen lesser priests crowded behind them. "What is this?" Hederick bellowed. "Unholy creatures in my Erolydon? By my own high priest's orders? Dahos, have you lost your mind?"

"I thought to rid us of the centaurs, Your Worship," Dahos replied. "I know that you . . ."

"By committing sacrilege?" Hederick screeched. "We'll have to reconsecrate the entire building! By the New Gods, Dahos, I should . . ."

Dahos waited, his face ashen. "But I used incense. . . ." he ventured, then swallowed hard. The guards grew silent and watchful.

Hederick drew in a shuddering breath. "No," he whispered. "I have need of you, High Priest. You are valuable to me—at the present, at least." He chewed his lower lip and raised his voice. "We will see if you can atone."

"I will try, Your Worship," Dahos murmured.

"You will oversee the reconsecration. Get to work immediately."

Dahos bowed and, at a trot, left the High Theocrat.

Hederick surveyed his priests. Kifflewit peeked, unnoticed, from the pile of boards. "The temple is defiled," the High Theocrat announced. "We will not return to the Great Chamber. We will reconvene on the shores of the lake immediately. Priests, move the spectators onto the back grounds. Guards, bring the prisoner to me there."

The guards marched past. The priests' robes swirled busily as the priests hurried to do Hederick's bidding.

In the confusion of robes and uniforms, one small kender went unnoticed. Soon Kifflewit Burrthistle was standing in the sunshine outside on the grass. Marble walls extended westward from the building to the lake. Beyond the walls to the north and south, vallenwoods and pines stood like sentinels. The gentle wind buffeted leaves and needles, creating a sound like a thousand people whispering.

Hundreds of people milled around Kifflewit. Although some spied him and clapped their hands over their coin pouches, no one cried out at the presence of a kender. They were outside the temple proper, after all, and Seeker rules forbidding kender and other unclean creatures applied only to the building itself.

Kifflewit Burrthistle slipped through a crowd to get a better view. Along the way, he picked up three coins, a copper bracelet, and a hand-mirror—putting them in his pockets for safekeeping. In the process, he realized he also carried several of the stones that Phytos had secreted in his pouch.

"They can't have been very important, for him to have gone off and left them like that," he said to himself. "Good thing I found them. If I ever run into him again . . ."

Hederick mounted a small stile. He had changed into a new ceremonial robe; the brown one had been sullied by the presence of the centaurs. He now wore deep blue velvet, with carmine and silver edging at the neck.

"What a pretty robe," Kifflewit whispered. "But it seems a bit hot for summer." Other topics were of greater consequence. For example, where was the Diamond Dragon? Tarscenian had said Hederick wore it around his neck, but no pendant swung against the blue velvet. "Must be inside," Kifflewit mumbled, leaning forward near a portly man in black. Yes, the kender decided, there might just be the faintest V of a thong beneath the material, with a swelling at the point of the V.

"Blessed Seekers," Hederick intoned, "I encourage you to enjoy the goddess Ferae's sunshine while I make several announcements and pass judgment on an unrepentant sinner."

The crowd waited expectantly.

"First," Hederick said, "you may know that the ground you are standing on will soon be the site of Erolydon's Ceremonial Pavilion, a splendid new structure created for worshipping the New Gods outdoors."

The crowd murmured. Hederick raised one hand and waited until the noise had diminished. "With that holy object in mind, my followers, I know you will rejoice at the opportunity to help provide the steel coins to raise the structure."

"What does that mean?" a woman whispered to her husband.

"He's raising our taxes again," the man whispered back.

Murmuring rose again from the crowd and this time did not die out when Hederick raised his hands. "The wood for the blessed pavilion will be the finest vallenwood, of course."

"*More* of the sacred trees?" a man exploded from the center of the crowd. Two guards immediately pinioned him and hustled him back into the temple. Several marked his passage with haunted eyes.

The High Theocrat smiled. "I rejoice that you are now unanimous in your love for the New Gods. Surely the pantheons will bless you doubly for your latest gifts."

"All the pantheons have blessed *my* family with so far is great poverty," came a woman's voice. This time, when the guards pushed to the vicinity, they could not identify the detractor, and the unhelpful crowd gave no hint.

"Who spoke?" demanded the captain of the guards. He swept his glance over a group of four huddled women. They glared at him from beneath gaily colored kerchiefs but said nothing. "Who spoke?" the captain repeated.

After a few moments had passed, Hederick snapped, "That's enough, Captain. Take them *all* into custody."

"It was me!" cried an exhausted-looking woman in an embroidered skirt and plain black blouse. "Leave the others alone!"

The captain and his guards looked irresolutely from the women to the High Theocrat. "I said take them all," Hederick ordered. "Now do it, unless you want to find yourselves included with them."

The women were dragged, screaming, into Erolydon.

Hederick leveled an angry stare at the crowd. Kifflewit

retreated behind the portly man. "Does anyone else yearn to blaspheme the New Gods?" the High Theocrat demanded.

Briefly the people parted, and Kifflewit glimpsed two figures who looked strangely familiar. The blond woman was clothed as a warrior. The man, a seeming beggar, was festooned with clumps of hair atop his head, and his cheeks and chin were bright with new cuts. The crowd closed again, and Kifflewit couldn't see what happened next.

At that moment, a new disturbance broke out from the direction of Erolydon. The guards hauled a man, gagged and bound, through the crowd and threw him down at the base of Hederick's stile.

"A mage of evil!" the portly man above Kifflewit breathed. Entranced, the kender made his way past a few people to get a better look. A black-robed mage! You didn't see too many avowed mages these days, with feelings running high against them and all. And an evil mage was even rarer.

Hederick gazed serenely down at the black-robed mage. "Your hands are bound, your mouth stopped, to prevent you from unleashing a heinous spell amid these believers. I prefer to allow my prisoners last words before I pronounce a sentence of death, but I'm sure you would agree that that would be a mistake in your case." He chuckled.

The man, whose severe features and gimlet stare hinted at his alignment with Evil, managed to look disdainful.

"That's not fair, High Theocrat!" Kifflewit said. "He should get a chance to talk, like everyone else." In a twinkling, the kender had drawn out a knife and skipped over to the captive mage. A moment later, and he had slit both gag and ropes. The mage sat up, rubbing his wrists.

Hederick and his guards stood stunned for a moment. The crowd edged back as speedily as possible.

"Repent, mage," the High Theocrat finally choked out.

"Commend your soul to the grace of the New Gods."

The wizard laughed. Suddenly he was standing.

Hederick's guards leaped toward the mage.

The black-robed wizard sprinkled powder retrieved from a packet hidden in his boot and swept one hand around him in a huge circle. "*Anelor armida na refinej!*" The guards doubled over as if they'd been poleaxed.

The High Theocrat fumbled inside his robe and pulled out a leather-wrapped bundle. The Diamond Dragon! It had to be! Kifflewit rejoiced.

"Hederick!" the mage shouted. "You call me evil, yet you cannot see the same in yourself! *Centriep ystendalet trewykyl.* See, then, what you have brought upon yourself. *Gantendestin milsivantid!*"

Hederick untied the leather. The Diamond Dragon glittered on his palm.

"There it is! The Diamond Dragon! Let me get a closer look!" Kifflewit cried and bounded up the stile.

"*Cariax povokiet wrekanenet res,*" the mage shouted at that precise moment.

The kender reached for the dragon and found it in his grasp. Suddenly, an explosion sent him crashing to the earth. He heard screams, smelled burning grass and something worse, and rolled sideways under the stile as people stampeded, seeking escape. The kender raised his head. The back gate was locked. There were only two getaways: over the wall to the lake, for those few who could swim, and back through the temple Erolydon. The crowd ebbed and surged, unsure which way led to safety.

There was no sign of the mage.

Kifflewit crawled out from under the stile, clutching the Diamond Dragon. "Wasn't that exciting?" he said to no one in particular. "Where'd the mage go? Did he disappear? Turn into a bird? Fly away? What—"

He turned and saw the body on the stile. The outflung hand still clasped the thong and empty leather cover that had masked the Diamond Dragon. The puffy face had relaxed. The blue robe was blackened and tattered.

In the center of the High Theocrat's chest was a scorched hole the size of a fist. Hederick's heart was gone.

It was enough to silence even a kender. Kifflewit crawled up on the stile. "Gee, I'm sorry," he said to the corpse. "You were really fond of this." He held out the Diamond Dragon. "You probably would have wanted to have it with you when you died." The kender sighed. "Well, you can have it back now, if you like." He held his hand, the one with the Diamond Dragon in it, above the High Theocrat's lifeless palm.

"No, Kifflewit!" came a shout.

That voice. Tarscenian? The kender looked over his shoulder just as he dropped the artifact into Hederick's hand. But this wasn't Tarscenian; this was that beggar. And what a mess he was!

At that moment, Hederick's hand grasped the kender's wrist.

Kifflewit gave a squawk. Hederick held his wrist firmly. The kender could only stare in fascination as color returned to Hederick's flaccid cheeks. Then the pale blue eyes opened—and the wound closed in the High Theocrat's chest.

"But you can't live without a heart!" Kifflewit protested as he yanked his wrist away.

Hederick sat up, his face devoid of expression. Kifflewit held out the thong and rewrapped leather. "I think you lost these," the kender said apologetically. Wordless, Hederick accepted the gift.

And then Kifflewit was off through the crowd, scrambling over the rocks and up the wall, and diving into the lake. He swam underwater until a change in the light told him he'd passed beyond Erolydon's walls. Then he surfaced, turned south, and paddled in that direction until the Seeker temple had vanished behind the trees.

At last Kifflewit Burrthistle climbed up on a boulder. The sun was warm, the sky cloudless. A warm breeze promised to dry his clothes in short order. A perfect day, really.

Perfect for examining the Diamond Dragon at leisure, he thought, pulling the artifact from his pocket.

Kifflewit hoped idly that Hederick didn't have the same goal in mind. If he did, the High Theocrat would find nothing in his precious leather packet but one of Phytos's stones.

* * * * *

Astinus, historian of the Great Library of Palanthas, gazed at the words he had written. The ink had not even dried yet.

The sentence had come to him in the middle of a routine history of the doings in the northern kingdom of Kern. The leader of that kingdom was showing disturbing signs of following in the footsteps of his late uncle, whose campaign to conquer the world had been narrowly stopped only a short time before.

And then Astinus's hand had written the words that stood out from the page now as though etched in flame: "And at that moment, two apprentice scribes in the library at Palanthas attempted to alter the course of history."

Although Astinus's expression of alert concentration didn't change, an assistant gasped as he looked over the chief historian's shoulder and saw the latest notation. Astinus gave no sign that he'd heard the aide.

The historian merely gazed at the sentence and waited patiently.

* * * * *

"This has to be illegal," Olven hissed from his seat at the desk. "Or maybe it's even a sin. No, I won't move from this chair and let you in. I know what you have in mind. Are you crazy, Marya?"

"So just leave," the woman rejoined. "Say you left as I entered and that you assumed I, not Eban, was replacing you. Say I lied to you, told you he was sick. I don't care, Olven. Someone has to do something about Hederick." Her face brightened as she looked down at her fellow apprentice. "Just think!" she exclaimed in a near-whisper. "What good could be done if someone were able and willing to battle evil from here—from the very core of history!"

"But Astinus . . ." Olven held up an arm and warded off Marya's attempts to grab his quill away from him.

"Listen," she insisted, "if I write something down here, it becomes history, doesn't it? And when something actually happens as I wrote it, who will know it wasn't meant to be that way? It's not really a lie, then, is it?" Another thought occurred to her. "And what if you and I were actually meant to do this— to change this? What if we're part of the gods' plans? You believe in the gods, don't you, Olven?"

"Of course. I work here, don't I? Some say the Old Gods themselves created this library. Some even say Astinus himself is . . ." Olven decided he was getting off the track. "Anyway, I haven't decided to do anything yet, Marya," he continued. The apprentice looked uneasily around the library. No one had taken notice of their heated, although circumspect, discussion. The other scribes were deep in their work, as usual.

Eban wasn't due to relieve Olven for at least an hour, the scribe thought. It could be done as Marya said.

"Olven, think!" Marya persisted, unaware of the battle raging within him. "All we have to do is write one simple line: At that moment, Hederick died. No one will know. The black-robed mage burned out the man's heart this afternoon, for the gods' sake! Who would be surprised if the High Theocrat died? We can even make it a peaceful death, if you want. Hederick can die in his sleep. It's better than he deserves, but if you're squeamish . . ."

"But the Diamond Dragon cured him."

"We only know that the hole in his chest closed," Marya said quickly. "Perhaps Hederick is meant to die now, Olven. And perhaps we are the ones who are meant to cause it to happen. We could do the gods' work. We could save Krynn!"

Olven gazed up at Marya. As she watched the younger apprentice's face, the middle-aged woman saw his indecision give way to resolve and then soften again to uncertainty almost immediately.

"Olven, we have to hurry," she insisted. "You know that Eban wouldn't even consider doing something like this—and who knows what could happen in Solace while Eban is recording events? He won't step in to help; you know that!"

The scribe met Marya's stare with sudden calm. "Eban isn't due for some time yet. Be quiet, and let me think."

For a moment, Marya seemed disposed to argue further. Then she nodded and climbed up on a nearby stool. When Olven resumed writing, she leaned over in sudden excitement. He was merely recording more of Hederick's history in the making, however. She returned to the stool and waited, watching intently.

Chapter 16

Tarscenian fumed as he and Mynx stomped along the walkways toward Gaveley's den. "The kender had the Diamond Dragon, and he gave it back. By the Old Gods, Mynx, *he gave it back!*"

"It was stolen once, it can be stolen again," Mynx countered stoically. "Limp a bit more. You're not a very convincing beggar when you stride along like a king returning to the palace, old man."

"And that's another thing," Tarscenian snapped. He did slow his pace and hunch forward, however, earning him an odd stare from a woman selling silk scarves at the junction of two walkways. "Did you have to fasten the hair to my head in tufts? By the gods, I look like I'm in the throes of some noxious disease!"

"How many beggars do you think are in perfect

health?"

That silenced Tarscenian for a time, but after a while, he began to mutter again. "I almost had it. By Paladine's helm, I almost had it! Now Hederick's going to be more careful than ever. That's *twice* he almost lost it."

The vallenwoods were beginning to change color. It looked to be an early autumn, Mynx thought. They stepped past the deserted home of Solace's former mayor, Mendis Vakon.

"You've got to admit that disguise is convincing. No one has recognized you yet," Mynx said, "not even in that crowd at the temple." Tarscenian grunted grudgingly. "I'll be glad when we get to Gav's den," Mynx went on. "I'm guessing the goblins we've passed aren't out in the sunshine for their health. Goblins hate daylight. There must be quite a price on your head, old man."

"Hederick hates me."

"No kidding. Want to tell me why?"

Tarscenian glared at her. "I abandoned his religion, eloped with his mage sister, and have spent the past five decades with her trying to steal his most prized possession."

Mynx raised her eyebrows as she edged around two goblins, squinting and chattering on the walkway. "That'd do it, I guess."

They went on in silence. Tarscenian limped, pausing periodically to wave his begging bowl halfheartedly at a passer-by. Mynx walked confidently in her armor and helm, periodically halting to allow Tarscenian to catch up. She rather enjoyed the deference people gave to warriors. They didn't step aside quite so easily for thieves.

"If there's such a huge price on my head, why haven't you turned me in?" Tarscenian asked after the sixth person had given him and his begging bowl as wide a berth as possible on a four-foot suspended bridge fifty feet above the ground.

"Gaveley'd have *my* head," Mynx said matter-of-factly. "I'd be undercutting him. I'm not in a mood to start my own ring of thieves—or find legitimate work. I stay in line."

"What if Gaveley ordered you to turn me over?"

Mynx glowered at another pair of goblins. They appeared not to notice the ferocity of her stare. "He won't," she said. "Gaveley allowed you to remain in his den last night. That means he's honor-bound to treat you as a friend. Gaveley places a high value on honor; he says it comes from his noble blood." She snorted. "Anyway, Gav hates Hederick. He hates everyone with money, but especially religious fanatics with money." She grunted. "Not that I blame him."

Having reached the southeastern edge of Solace, they made their way to the ground by one of the stairways that circled the vallenwood. A disquieting noise now disturbed the whispering of the vallenwood leaves and pine needles. The sounds of grief and fear halted their steps halfway down the staircase, but they could see nothing untoward.

"Good gods," Mynx whispered. "What is that?"

This was more than a lone soul facing heartache—more, even, than a dozen souls. Mynx and Tarscenian exchanged uneasy looks. Her dagger was already in her hand. Her palms were sweaty. Tarscenian's hand had gone to the hilt of his sword under the filthy cloak.

"We should investigate," Tarscenian whispered.

"It's none of our concern, old man," Mynx snapped. The vehemence of her remark was surprising.

"Someone needs help," Tarscenian insisted.

Mynx shook her head. She could barely speak, her teeth were chattering so hard. "No one's ever helped *me*, old man. And I don't help anyone. Unless they pay me."

"You helped me."

"Gaveley told me to," she snapped. "Don't give me credit for that."

Then Tarscenian was gone, bounding down the stairs. He raced across a clearing, through an opening in the underbrush, and down a wide, packed-earth pathway lined by pines.

Mynx stood irresolutely. Then a crow squawked overhead, and she rushed after Tarscenian.

She caught up with Tarscenian at the edge of a clearing, bounded in slender logs like a corral. But inside milled, not horses, but fifty or so people. Mynx recognized some of them—including the mayor's wife and her four children.

It was from this crowd of captives that the chorus of muffled sobs, entreaties, and shouts arose. A dozen hobgoblins stood guard outside the fence, and another dozen goblins patrolled the inside of the corral, helping to keep the people packed in a tight circle.

Mynx and Tarscenian hid in the underbrush of honeysuckle vines and maple saplings, observing the scene.

Unlike their goblin cousins, who rarely exceeded four feet in height, hobgoblins reached six feet and higher. These beasts were dark gray, with red faces and yellow eyes and teeth. They carried swords, spears, whips, and shields. Mismatched metal armor protected their shoulders, arms, and shins. Leather armor covered their torsos.

Most of the hobgoblins called to each other in gibberish. However, two spoke to each other and to their captives in a rough form of Abanasinian. Both carried bows.

"Sergeant," one said. "We ready move."

"We go when I say," the leader snapped back. "Not enough yet. Wait for more."

"But gets late," the first protested. "Won't get far 'fore sun downs, set camp."

The leader responded without a word by pulling a

dagger and pointing it at the other. The reluctant one slunk away, mumbling, around to the other side of the corral.

One of the captives, a young man, broke loose from the knot of humans and goblins and tried to vault over the log fence. The sergeant calmly lifted his bow and shot the youth in the chest.

"Shoulda paid taxes, fool," the sergeant remarked. "Wouldn' be here then." He gestured to the goblins, who swarmed over the body.

Mynx hid her face in her hands, and Tarscenian put a gentle arm around her shoulder. "We must help them, Mynx," he whispered.

She lifted her head. "The two of us against two dozen goblins and hobgoblins? Are you crazy?"

"All these people did was refuse to pay Hederick's taxes," Tarscenian replied, voice low.

"What do I care? Thieves don't pay taxes."

"Don't you see what's happening? They're being sold into slavery, Mynx!"

"Not one would lift a finger for me. We're outnumbered, old man."

"There are fifty people in that ring, at least thirty of them strong men and women. Plus we're armed. That's not being outnumbered."

"And you think those two-legged sheep will stand with you against hobgoblins?" Mynx laughed out loud. The nearest monster looked over its shoulder into the greenery, frowning, pointed ears atwitch.

"There's only one way to find out." Tarscenian rushed out of the underbrush, sword at the ready. Without warning, the old man slipped the blade under the hobgoblin's arm and sank it into its rib cage. The creature bellowed and went down, arms and legs churning.

"Hejami, Tycom, Gret!" the sergeant called to three of his men. "Attack!" The rest of the force remained around the slaves. In a moment, Tarscenian was surrounded by three spear-wielding hobgoblins. Mynx watched from the underbrush, barely breathing. She'd stay right here; she didn't owe the stupid old man anything.

The blue-nosed one called Hejami closed first with Tarscenian. The others held back, poking each other and smiling. They didn't seem to think it would be much of a battle—a full-grown hobgoblin against a tuft-haired beggar—although the beggar did wield that sword with some assurance. The hobgoblin Hejami jabbed at the man with his spear.

Tarscenian dodged, feinting, and the hobgoblin leaped after him. Tarscenian doubled back and struck. Hejami fell, lifeless, to the ground, blood from his nearly severed neck soaking the ground.

The other two launched themselves at Tarscenian at the same instant. Tarscenian parried and whirled. As he held off the hobgoblins, he called out to the captives. "Join with me! We can outfight them."

None of the prisoners moved. If anything, they huddled even closer together. "They might hurt us!" one of the women called.

"Don't listen to him," a man counseled his fellow slaves. "He's a beggar. We're worth more to the hobgoblins if we're healthy. They won't hurt us as long as we cooperate with them."

Another woman called, "It's easy for you to order us to help, old man, but we have children to think about!"

Although Tarscenian brandished the sword as though the weapon were part of him, horror grew on his face.

"You old fool," Mynx whispered from the honeysuckle vines. "I told y—"

Then she was dangling in the air, grabbed around the middle by the largest hobgoblin she'd ever seen. Its laughing grimace exposed yellow teeth and a slimy red tongue. The monster jabbered something, then hoisted her over one shoulder, all the while howling with glee.

"You big overgrown . . . "

She kicked wildly, hoping to catch the beast in the face. Hanging head-downward over his back, she had an excellent view of the dagger she'd dropped, but not much room to maneuver.

The creature swaggered over to the other hobgoblins. "New slave!" the creature crowed.

The arms around Mynx's waist tightened suddenly, and she heard a screech from her captor. Then she was falling. In her years as a thief, Mynx had dived out of many windows—most often with enraged homeowners close behind her—and knew how to land on her feet. She caught herself lightly with her hands, then threw herself over into a somersault and rolled away from the dying, gabbling hobgoblin.

Tarscenian pulled his sword from the creature's middle. He grabbed Mynx by the arm, hauled her to her feet. Then they were off and running, dodging around the other hobgoblin corpses and leaving the slave market behind.

A pair of hobgoblins and three goblins pursued them along the path. As Mynx and Tarscenian swept around a curve, Tarscenian shouldered her to one side and began to chant. "What are you doing?" Mynx cried, trying to break free.

"Be still!" Tarscenian snapped. "*Yessupot siagod idae.*" His hands fluttered. He sketched an outline around Mynx from foot to head and back down again to the forest floor. Then he pushed the thief into a bush, crushed a silver aspen leaf between the fingers of his left hand, and shouted, "*Nilad ur'sht, yjod wraren, sar ytakreryt.*" He dived after the real Mynx. A lifelike version of the thief raced down the path just as the pursuers hove into view.

"You take it the female!" one of the hobgoblins hollered, pointing to the magic-induced Mynx vanishing down the trail. The other hobgoblin and one of the goblins raced after her. That left one hobgoblin and two goblins beating the underbrush in the immediate vicinity.

Tarscenian shoved the hilt of his dagger into Mynx's hand. "This time," he whispered, "try not to drop it."

Then he was gone, attacking with an intensity that far belied his years. He dispatched one of the goblins before the creature could raise a squeak, but the other goblin managed a cry.

"Go get it, more fool!" the hobgoblin yelled at the goblin. "Is order, verminstink!"

The last goblin hurtled at Tarscenian without pause. It found itself facing two weapons—Tarscenian's sword and Mynx's dagger. Yellow-orange eyes blinking spasmodically, it glanced at Mynx, then at the corpse of its comrade and, frantically, down the path where the other, magical Mynx had gone.

Then it raced away, abandoning the field to the hobgoblin chief.

The monster clutched a sword in its right hand, a spear in its left. Tarscenian saw immediately that he and Mynx faced a creature well versed in combat.

"How close are we to the ring's den?" he hissed to Mynx. Tarscenian slurred his words, hoping the hobgoblin wouldn't understand him. He and Mynx circled the creature.

"Short run," Mynx answered, mimicking his mumbling. "Want to make a dash for it?"

Tarscenian shook his head. "There'll be no outrunning this thing. Get your fellow thieves, bring help back here. That Xam fellow is big enough to—"

"No luck, old man. They'll never come."

Tarscenian growled. "What's a gods-blasted thieves' ring *good* for, then, if they won't help you when you need it?" His face was pale with exertion.

"Gav calls the moves," Mynx panted. "We're the players. And I don't think he'd risk the others for a new man—someone who isn't even one of us, yet."

"What about for you?"

Mynx sidestepped a tree root. "*I* can leave here at any time, Tarscenian. Can't you tell the beast's after you?"

Tarscenian looked the hobgoblin in its tiny yellow eyes. The creature waved its sword tauntingly and leered. "Big money," the hobgoblin said. "Bounty fat on ol' funny-looking guy. Hederick plenty mad you, human."

It was still leering when Mynx landed on its back, looped her arms around its neck, and butted its helmet forward, obstructing its sight. She sliced at its shoulders and neck. The blinded creature howled but continued to slash at Tarscenian with its sword hand, thrusting its spear at him with the other. The double blades formed a whirlwind of steel. Tarscenian tried to sidle to one side, but the creature's hearing must have been acute; even without sight, it followed whichever way Tarscenian moved.

Then Mynx and her dagger found a crucial artery in the beast's neck.

"For the Old Gods!" Tarscenian bellowed, and struck at the same time.

In an instant, the hobgoblin lay on the ground. Its lifeblood pumped out of twin gashes in its neck and side.

A short time later, Tarscenian and Mynx raced into the thieves' den. Mynx threw herself, gasping, onto the green settee. "By the gods, Gav, Solace is crawling with hobgoblins!" she croaked.

The half-elf widened his eyes at their disguises, but merely rasped, "Yet you came through all right, I see."

"Sure, but we had to kill . . . how many beasts, Tarscenian? Half-dozen goblins and hobgoblins?"

"About that," Tarscenian said offhandedly. Even though his knees were trembling from the strain he'd been through, he forced himself to breathe slowly and deeply. He stood there, pretending he was no more winded than a young man would be, and shrugged casually.

"It's over now," Tarscenian said. "I want Gaveley's answer. "Will you and your ring help me steal the Diamond Dragon from Hederick?"

The half-elf looked at Tarscenian across the crystal rim of a wine goblet. Gaveley was dressed with his usual flair, this time in scarlet leather breeches and black silk shirt, a white silk scarf knotted at his slender throat. He was smiling, but his tilted hazel eyes hinted danger. "I've reviewed your request, old man," he whispered. "I believe we will pass it by."

There was a short pause before Mynx exploded in protest. "Why, Gav? Stealing the thing would be a great way to get Hederick's goat! You hate him; we all do. He's killing our business. With taxes so high, no one has anything worthwhile to steal. Why not go along with Tarscenian? I'd help him steal it, and you all know I'm the best thief here. This dragon thing's worth a fortune!" She looked at each of the three thieves in turn. "We all could practically retire," she finished, trying to make a joke.

Gaveley snarled. "It's my decision, Mynx. Accept it or leave." Xam and Snoop nodded in tandem. Tarscenian frowned, his gray gaze flicking from Gaveley to Mynx.

Mynx looked startled. "Leave? But I grew up in this ring, Gav."

"And I taught you from the start that in Gaveley's ring . . ."

". . . Gaveley's word is law," she finished. She pulled her helm from her head, and pushed her hand back through her newly blond hair. She looked at Tarscenian. "I'm sorry," she said simply. "I won't go against the group. I don't dare."

Tarscenian's expression didn't change. "Like the

slaves," he whispered. "What did you call them, Mynx—sheep?"

"That's not fair," she flared. "It's not the same thing at all!"

"Isn't it?" Wordless, Tarscenian bowed slightly to Gaveley, then moved the statue of the harpist as he'd seen the others do, and left. He managed to look dignified despite his angry feelings and beggarly disguise.

"Go out the back," Gaveley rasped at Snoop. "Keep him in sight but don't let him see you. If the temple guards accost him within Erolydon, make as if you're delivering him to Hederick. Then at least we'll get the bounty, if not the Diamond Dragon. We can always steal that later."

"And if he gets the Diamond Dragon?"

"Steal it from him," Gaveley whispered. "Then kill him. Present the old man's head to Hederick. Then we'll *still* get the bounty."

Mynx leaped up. "*Gaveley!*" She tore at his arm. "What happened to honor? You were always so proud that you were more honorable than the rich people. Remember, Gav?"

He shoved her away. "I'm a *thief*, Mynx. And I'm not human. What use to me is a human idea like honor?"

"But . . . but elves have honor, too," she stammered.

"Neither elves nor humans recognize my noble lineage," he spat. "Better to throw in my lot with someone who at least will give me some money, if not respect."

She stared at him, then at Xam, who was watching the exchange from the back doorway. Her gaze, now disgusted, went back to the half-elf. "You've gone in with Hederick, Gav? Is that it? After we decided not to?"

"*You* decided not to, Mynx," Gaveley whispered. "The rest of us . . ."

Mynx turned to Xam. The bounty-hunter shrugged. "It's a job," he said. "Hederick's no worse than anyone else we've worked for, Mynx." The big man's eyes took on a pleading look, like a dog's. "Honest, Mynx. It's better to go in with us on this."

"But Hederick is crazy," she whispered. "Tarscenian is . . . is *good*."

"Since when do thieves care about good?" Gaveley whispered. He motioned to Xam, who lumbered across the room toward Mynx.

"I'm sorry, Mynx," the large man said. "There's a reward for you, too. A small one, but every bit counts these days."

"A reward?" Her voice cracked. She took a step backward and found herself pinioned by the half-elf.

"Hederick doesn't like it when people refuse his offers," Gaveley snapped in her ear. "Xam, we have work to do. Take care of her."

Her mind screamed for her to struggle, to run, but her body refused to obey. She merely watched, stunned, as Xam raised a meaty hand. He was a bounty-hunter, skilled at subduing his quarry. The blow struck the side of her neck. Her knees buckled, and she fell unconscious to the floor.

* * * * *

A short time later, Kifflewit crept through the back entrance of the thieves' den, busy hands replacing his lockpicking tools in one of his pouches. "Certainly dark in here," he whispered to himself. "Maybe Mynx is sleeping."

He'd seen Gaveley, then Xam and Snoop, and finally Mynx and Tarscenian enter the den. All but Mynx had emerged. Kifflewit wanted one last look at the splendors of Gaveley's den before he left Solace. The temple guards, still failing to show any sign of humor, had been dogging his steps. He'd managed to keep away from them, but even a kender grows tired of some games.

Mynx had been adamant about keeping him out of the thieves' den, the kender remembered. But if she were sleeping . . . Kifflewit brightened. Perhaps he could sneak a peek without waking her up.

"Surely one small light won't disturb her sleep," he reassured himself. Still standing in the doorway, he felt in his pockets for steel and flint, and scraped some lint from the bottom of a pocket. The first time he struck stone and steel together, he heard an immediate groan in the darkness before him and jumped. The steel went clattering away into the darkness. Another groan. Had he awakened Mynx?

Kifflewit felt in his pockets, one by one, for more steel. His slender fingers found nothing helpful until he reached into one particular pocket. Light streamed from the pocket—sparkly, swirling light. "How pretty!" he breathed. His restless fingers drew out the Diamond Dragon. It was just the size of his hand. He'd never seen it in the dark before, and the artifact was all aglow. He could barely see the outline of the dragon, the diamonds glittered so brightly.

"It must be magical!" he said softly.

Another groan resounded through the den. Kifflewit raised the Diamond Dragon above his head and stepped carefully inside. The artifact's glow bathed him in light.

"Perhaps it's not Mynx," he whispered. "Perhaps it's a really interesting monster." He'd heard about plenty of beasts that lived underground. Some cave crawlers were even poisonous. He wondered what it would feel like to be eaten alive. If the thing ate the Diamond Dragon along with him, would he be able to see the crawler's insides? That would be something!

Mmmmmmmnnfff?

"You! Are you a cave crawler?" he shouted.

Mmmmmmmnnfff?

"Mynx?"

Mmmmmmmnnfff!

If one muffled *Mmmmmmmnnfff!* could convey rage, frustration, and fear, this one did. It was sounding less and less like a cave crawler, Kifflewit Burrthistle thought. He shuffled forward in the darkness, holding the Diamond Dragon higher in order to cast the largest possible circle of light.

Then a tousled head of blond hair, angry brown eyes, and a gagged mouth came into view.

"Mynx? Why do you look like that? Why's your hair yellow? I liked it dark. And why are you wearing armor? Aren't you a thief anymore? Are you a mercenary now?"

Mmmmmmmnnfff!

He held the Diamond Dragon close to her furious face. "See? I found this in the temple. Isn't it pretty?"

Mynx stared daggers at him. The kender's eyes were wide and innocent. "What's the matter?" he asked.

MMMunnnpie mmmmmmeeee, mooooo mbiddllle pfoool! came through the gag.

"You're awfully hard to understand with that rag . . ." Kifflewit set to work loosening the restraint, while Mynx continued to gnash at the cloth with her teeth. The kender chattered merrily on. "The High Theocrat mustn't care much for this dragon thing or he wouldn't have let it lie around. I think I'm doing him a favor by taking care of it, don't you?"

The gag was gone. "You idiot!" Mynx cried. "That's the Diamond Dragon!"

The kender blinked. "Well, sure."

"Tarscenian thinks Hederick still has it!"

"Oh. Well, there's nothing to worry about. It's safe with me."

"Untie me, you little fool," she snapped.

"You don't have to be rude. After all . . ." He reached over Mynx to her hip, plucked Tarscenian's dagger from

her sheath, and, still talking animatedly, severed the cord
that bound her wrists and ankles.

Mynx's mind raced. Tarscenian had no clue that the
thieves were after him. And of course he had no idea
that the kender possessed the Diamond Dragon.

Kifflewit Burrthistle prattled on, dangling the Diamond Dragon in front of Mynx's face as though it were
some mere bauble. The glow caught her attention. For a
moment Mynx forgot everything but the radiance that
came from within the precious stones. Suddenly everything made sense. Tarscenian wasn't after this thing in
order to sell it, she realized. He was going to use its magical powers against Hederick.

She had to take the artifact to him before he tried to
get inside the temple. Only then would he have a chance
against the High Theocrat's forces and Gav's thieves.

"Give me that, kender!" she shouted, lunging for the
artifact.

Kifflewit squealed, "It's *mine!* I found it!"

Kender and human hands fought for possession of the
Diamond Dragon.

"Tarscenian needs it!"

"But I found it!" the kender howled.

"He could defeat Hederick!"

"No fair! It's mine!"

They tussled on the carpet. The Diamond Dragon see-
sawed back and forth. The artifact spat tiny bolts of
lightning around the den, burning holes in the tapestries.
It began to hum. Neither woman nor kender realized
what was happening; the object they were fighting over
had become a glowing ball of steel-cold fire.

"Tarscenian needs it!"

"I found it!"

"It could stop the Seekers!"

"It's mine!"

Szzzzezmetoffff algolorum!

The loud, strange sound came from the Diamond Dragon itself. The kender let go and fell back, brown eyes agog. Mynx crowed triumphantly, cradling the trophy to her breast. She stroked it, exulting in its possession. She would find Tarscenian . . .

Szzzzezmetoffff algolorum!

The second burst of sound and light penetrated Mynx's triumph. Magic—from the thing itself? Sudden terror drenched her. She tried to throw the Diamond Dragon away from her.

It refused to let go.

The Diamond Dragon clung to her hands, humming louder. There was no pain—only a coldness that extended from her hands up through her elbows.

And then she realized that her hands were inside the artifact. Even as she watched, the Diamond Dragon absorbed more of her. She could see her hands, then her wrists and forearms, moving frantically inside the thing. She still could control her movements, but her hands were shrinking. She placed one booted foot and then the other against the thing, to brace herself and wrench her arms free.

Then her feet were sucked in, too.

"Kifflewit!" Mynx shouted. "Help me!"

But the kender could only gape at her, wide-eyed.

The coldness shot like a catapult up her arms and legs. It froze her torso and reached her head.

And then she was *inside* the Diamond Dragon.

Smooth crystal curved around her, impervious to her pounding and kicking. Mynx raged within the dragon as the kender stared at the thing from without. She was miniature enough now, within the artifact, to stand in Kifflewit's hand. Clearly he could see her tiny figure dancing inside the Diamond Dragon. Couldn't he?

She could hear the kender. Could he hear her?

Mynx cried out, but Kifflewit merely gazed at the Diamond Dragon from every angle. He picked it up, shook it—throwing Mynx to her knees—and put it down again.

"I wonder where she went?" the kender said softly. "What a terrific trick!" He glanced around, as though he might find Mynx peering out from under a table or settee.

Inevitably, the kender's attention wandered, and he abandoned the artifact on the carpet as he poked through the den. Gaveley's den had numerous gems and objects of special interest to a glitter-loving kender. All went into his pouches and pockets.

Then Mynx and the artifact that imprisoned her were snatched up and tucked back in a bulging kender pocket, too. She could sense movement; Kifflewit was scampering off somewhere. Mynx sat down on the curved crystal floor of the Diamond Dragon to avoid falling again.

She rested her head on her arms. "Oh, Tarscenian," she whispered. "You're heading into danger for nothing." Here she was, trapped within the only object that could help him, and she couldn't do a thing.

She rode for some time in Kifflewit's pocket, hearing only the muffled sounds of the market and occasional yelps from angry guards. Twice the kender began to run and continued until the shouting died away.

Then a new voice spoke, quite near. "Ah, 'tis thee, small one. What dost thou want of me? I am in haste. I have no time to stop and natter with thee, yet thou saved my life back at the temple. What dost thou want, kender?"

It was the centaur she'd seen in the refugee section, Mynx realized.

"The guards are after me," came Kifflewit's stifled reply. "I need to hitch a ride out of Solace."

"Small one, that I can grant thee, in gratitude for thy service. I am bound for my home glade, to apprise my people of the coming danger."

Mynx braced herself against the insides of the Diamond Dragon as Kifflewit Burrthistle clambered up onto the centaur's back. The man-horse settled into the rocking gait that could cover many leagues, seemingly without great effort.

The centaur and Kifflewit soon left Solace far behind.

Chapter 17

As Tarscenian worked his way back through Solace, he regularly stooped and held out his bowl to passers-by.

"Alms?" he would quaver from the depths of his hood, detesting the pitiable tone he had to adopt. The slow pace galled him, too. He wanted nothing more than to throw off his beggar's cloak, yank the tufts of hair from their glued moorings, and race into Erolydon with sword drawn to challenge Hederick directly. "Directly and honestly," he muttered.

Solace's residents sidestepped the surly beggar with neither word nor offer of aid.

Tarscenian's disguise was holding up well. Hederick's goblins and guards didn't give him a second look. He slunk past a few more sword-carrying hobgoblins and caught enough of their garbled words to realize that the slave caravan had left Solace without further incident. Tarscenian forced himself to focus on the task at hand—to find Hederick, who rarely left Erolydon, and steal the Diamond Dragon or die in the effort. But how to enter the temple?

Twice Tarscenian felt suddenly uneasy, as though he were being observed. Each time, he paused to fumble in his cloak, mumbling and weaving as though he were daft or physically ill. The gray eyes hidden in the shadowed cloak missed little, but Tarscenian saw no evidence that guards, goblins, or anyone else scrutinized him. There were only the usual late-afternoon refugees and excited pilgrims, brown-robed priests and the sellers of temple offerings, and dozens of common people. Down below he saw farmers unloading barrels from wagons, and a half-dozen fishermen and women hawking Crystalmir bass and perch from tub-laden carts with huge wooden wheels.

He paused to catch his breath. He was showing signs of increasing fatigue. Sometimes it seemed as though his mind were whirling in circles. He'd had no time to study the little magic he knew, and the spells he'd used in the previous days were long gone from his memory.

Then Tarscenian raised his eyebrows and forced his brain to clear. He had no difficulty making himself sag into an even more beggarly stance.

There was one stairway within sight. And at the bottom of the steps that twined around the nearest vallenwood, Dahos, Hederick's high priest, stood behind the fishmongers. The high priest surveyed the scene with an air of proprietorship. It wasn't only the tall priest who caught Tarscenian's eye, but the ring on his right hand. Tarscenian squinted, leaning over the railing of the walkway.

Dahos wore the death's-head ring.

I stole it. Mynx gave Dahos's ring to Gaveley last

night, he thought. And now Dahos has it back.

That meant one thing: the half-elf had done more than turn down Tarscenian's proposal.

Gaveley had sold him out to Hederick's forces.

Tarscenian glanced behind him, starting to edge backward as Dahos, with a jerk of his head, summoned a blue-uniformed captain. The high priest bent down to speak quietly to the man. The captain nodded, saluting crisply. The captain hustled over to a pair of goblins.

Tarscenian paused. Then he sank to his knees and pretended to look for something on the walkway. His hands plunged into his cloak to search through his pouches.

"Hurry, hurry," he whispered to himself. Soon he was using blood-red sand to outline a fish on the boards of the walkway. Another fish, the size of his hand, joined the first, and then another. "*Pesqi d'armotage, oberit getere*," he murmured. A shout rang out below. Tarscenian hurried to finish. "*Getilin ornest gadillio dehist.*"

"There he is! Up there!" a man's voice shouted from below.

"*Pesqi d'armotage, oberit getere. Getilin ornest gadillio dehist!*" Tarscenian finished the chant, then used both hands to whirl the sand figures into oblivion. The guards' shouts below turned into oaths as Tarscenian's spell overturned six carts full of slippery fish and water between the guards and their prey.

Most of Dahos's men lost their footing amid the flopping fish and cursed loudly. A few goblins, unhampered by hard footwear, made it to the steps. But Tarscenian was already on his feet and racing away to the north.

After several months of Seeker reign, Solace residents were used to fugitives fleeing along the wooden walks in front of their treetop homes. They stayed invisible behind their doors, assisting no one.

This walkway connected with another. Tarscenian chose the path that would take him northwest toward the lake. This area contained only homes, no shops or open markets. It was deserted now. Ropes were laced from branch to branch, many of them draped with drying clothes.

Tarscenian glanced back. A hobgoblin was thirty paces behind him, two goblins following.

Three temple guards stood fifty paces ahead, pikes set on the wooden boards of the walkway, smiles broad under their helms. His pursuers had him cornered, fifty feet above the ground.

Tarscenian could see the lowering sun glittering on Crystalmir Lake behind the guards. The lake was but a short distance away, yet it might as well have been leagues distant for all the good it did him now.

To add annoyance, some Solace housewife had stretched her laundry across the walkway. Tarscenian was forced to slap aside dripping shirts, socks, and bedding as he watched the guards and goblins edge forward. The sheets flapped like huge wings.

"Wings!" Tarscenian said suddenly. Did he know a flying spell? He drew his sword to worry the approaching foes. "A flying spell," he hissed. "Think, Tarscenian! By the Old Gods, if only Ancilla were here!"

He focused intensely on the memory of the white-robed mage. Had she been a goddess, his call would have been a prayer. "Ancilla!" An answering murmur rose within Tarscenian's mind, teased him, and died.

"Ancilla!" If she could hear him, could she dispatch a spell?

Again the teasing sensation, as though a hibernating animal stirred within his mind. "Ancilla!"

My . . . My love?

"Ancilla, I'm trapped. They will capture me unless . . ."

The guards and goblins were short paces away. The hobgoblin pounded one of the goblins on the head with a mailed fist as though they shared an obvious joke.

"See! Old man crazyfool," the hobgoblin chortled. "Talk-talk self. Stuck now. Bounty bounty." The goblin, rearranging its helmet, continued its approach, crouching behind its bigger cousin.

"Ancilla . . ."

Tarscenian . . . I . . . The voice died away, then returned as though communicating drained almost every iota of the mage's energy. *I have . . . no . . . I cannot . . .*

The hobgoblin leaped.

Tarscenian sliced through the air with his sword. The weapon severed, not the hobgoblin's neck, but the laundry rope between them. Tarscenian lunged for the rope, caught it with his left hand, and swung over the railing.

"Pray Paladine it's well tied at the other end," the man gasped on the way down.

Tarscenian arced through the open space that separated Solace's border from a few scrub pines at the edge of the lake. Sheets, pillowcovers, and knit socks cascaded through the air.

The captain of the guard was waiting for him on the ground, flanked by six men. Each flourished swords and spears.

"For the Old Gods!" Tarscenian bellowed, swinging his sword wildly. The guards threw themselves to the dirt as Tarscenian hurtled directly toward them, but they were not quick enough. Tarscenian managed to sever the arm of one and the hand of another. A third guard fell unconscious when he was clouted in the head by Tarscenian's boots.

Then Tarscenian was heading up again, higher and higher, until it seemed he could almost touch the lake. He remembered, as a child, leaping off a swing at the highest point of its curve, soaring through the air like the panther he'd been pretending to be. He remembered, too, the broken ankle that had kept him in bed for weeks after that escapade.

"Paladine," he prayed, "let this work."

He was coming back down again. The hobgoblin stood on the ground now, urging the others toward the sword-wielding human pendulum. Tarscenian hit one of the goblins, a reddish-orange creature with bright lemon-yellow eyes. The goblin staggered into another one. They both careened into the hobgoblin, who tossed them aside like rags.

Then up . . . and up. Tarscenian hastily stuffed his sword in its scabbard—no easy task while curled around a rope. His right hand, now free, unclasped the cloak, loosely holding the garment in place.

The hobgoblin swept the other guards aside, and waited alone in Tarscenian's path. The butt of its spear rested on the ground, the point glinting toward the human.

Tarscenian could see victory and consternation mingled in the creature's tiny red eyes. He could almost hear the beast's thoughts: Why did this daft human sheathe his sword?

Then, just as Tarscenian was about to collide with the hobgoblin, the man whipped off his cloak and snagged the spear. The force of Tarscenian's charge whipped the weapon into the neck of the monster that had held it. A bellow rocked the clearing behind the old man as he swung toward the lake.

And then he jumped free of the rope, soaring over two pines toward the water. Tarscenian curled himself into a ball. The landing would either save or kill him.

Water, deep blue and icy even in summer, closed around him. His sword dragged him down, but he dared not jettison it. He kicked his way to the surface, then he made himself relax, lie back, and breathe regularly. He kicked forcefully, away from shore.

The captain of the guard ordered the goblins and hob-goblins into the lake after their quarry. Tarscenian heard the goblin's shrill refusals, and the hobgoblin's deep shout, "Water. Hobgoblin. No. Lake hobgoblin. Wait, see, masterguard."

Tarscenian's sword dragged him down. At this rate, he would tire and drown long before he reached the western shore. "Paladine, please," he prayed, gasping for air. "Ancilla still lives. Let me save . . . Let us save . . . We have to . . ." Then he halted in wonderment.

A spell, long-forgotten, floated into his mind. Tarscenian gulped air and raised his arms. With his fingers, he pounded a tattoo on the water surface until the muscles in his forearms threatened to cramp. All the while, he repeated the chant that played through his mind.

"Fotatol aerifon hexicadi pfeatherlit. Fotatol aerifon hexicadi pfeatherlit. Fotatol aerifon hexicadi pfeatherlit."

He paused to breathe and drew in a lungful of water. He coughed and sputtered, but chanted on.

"Fotatol aerifon hexicadi pfeatherlit."

He felt his wig disguise wash loose from his scalp. A cramp began to hurt his side. He speeded up his chanting.

Suddenly his muscles eased. He was borne up in the water as though the giant hand of a god had scooped him up. The heavy sword weighed nothing. His sodden garments ceased to hamper him. He glanced back toward Solace. There was no sign of his pursuers.

Suddenly, a craft floated before him.

"A canoe?" Tarscenian muttered. "I don't recall this part of the spell."

He paddled over to it. The canoe appeared to be birchbark. It glided easily on the water. A plain plank seat spanned the widest section of the canoe. The other seat, at the stern, was marked with a red star.

Tarscenian treaded water while he unbuckled the belt that held his scabbard and sword, and slung the weapon and holder into the craft. Then he grasped the side of the canoe and hauled himself up.

Suddenly the canoe went askew. Tarscenian hurriedly released the craft, treading water again while it bobbed back into position. Clearly, this business of climbing into a canoe from the water was no simple task. He was a landsman, mystified by most things aquatic.

Tarscenian took a deep breath, let himself sink below the surface, and kicked as hard as he could. He shot up through the water and lunged enough above the surface to clutch the plank seat itself.

For an instant, the technique seemed to work. Then Tarscenian, cursing, felt himself sliding back toward the water as the canoe tipped slowly toward him. Once more he let himself slip back into the lake.

Once again he tried. This time he placed more and more of his weight upon the canoe until the waters of Crystalmir Lake lapped into the boat. The boat sank in the water. When the craft was half-full, it floated low enough in the lake for Tarscenian to slip over the side.

Soon he was seated on the middle plank, shin-deep in cold water. He had nothing to bail with, and his pursuers would soon be after him. He decided to try paddling despite the heavy load of water, then reached toward the craft's floor—and swore. "No paddles, by the Old Gods?"

Tarscenian dug deep into his pouches. Everything in his pockets was sodden. Marjoram, thyme, pepper, and pine—he had them all still, despite his dunking. He spread the items on the other seat, the plank with the star insignia, then passed his hands over them, chanting. *"Elvi nahana teta, d'a min bidyang. Bidyang d'a mina."* He turned his hands over and raised them slowly. He'd not performed a levitation spell in a long time, but the boat began to lift off the water.

The boat rose, but only a few inches. The craft bulged at the center. For a moment Tarscenian feared that the heavy burden of man and water would cause the canoe to burst. He grabbed his sword from the bottom of the canoe and plunged the weapon into the craft's side.

The water gushed from the canoe back into the lake, and the craft rose higher until it reached a foot above the surface. "Good," he murmured. "Now if I can manage to put the craft in motion . . ."

Tarscenian gazed north toward Erolydon. The sun was almost down. He had a hunch how to get into the temple, but he'd need some light to find his way. Every moment was important. *"Ebal gi entoknoken ty wrent."* The boat did not move. *"Ebal gi entoknoken ty wrent."* Still the craft remained motionless.

"All right," he muttered to himself. "Fine." He clapped his hands. *"Quantenol sina fit."*

The sun touched the horizon. Rays of pink and red immediately shot into the sky. Tarscenian pondered. What could he be doing wrong? He gazed around. His stare fell on the starred plank. A quizzical look came over his face, then he shrugged. "It's worth a try," he said.

He moved to the other seat, the one marked with the star, and sat squarely upon the decoration. Tarscenian closed his eyes and concentrated. *"Ebal gi entoknoken ty wrent. Ebal gi entoknoken ty wrent. Quantenol sina fit."* Again he clapped. The boat raised itself slightly higher above the water.

Tarscenian imagined the craft speeding across the water, heading northward. He imagined the breeze across his bare head, felt the spray wash over him when the craft struck an upflung wave. He imagined Erolydon coming into view, and in his mind he saw the canoe, coming to a stop just outside the walls that extended into the sea. He saw the grounds of Erolydon devoid of people, the temple empty after the evening's revelations.

Tarscenian opened his eyes to find the white marble wall rising smoothly before him. All was as he'd imagined it. The sun was only a fraction lower in the sky, but he had arrived at Erolydon. "The magic worked," he whispered, smiling.

But where should he search? Tarscenian remembered the *Praxis*, and recalled how Hederick had taken particular passages to heart. "Moral purity is impossible without physical cleanliness," the *Praxis* taught.

There must be discharge tunnels, then, to guide waste from the temple. And what was the most logical place to deposit the filth? Tarscenian knew Hederick would want the refuse emptied as far away from his own quarters as possible.

Tarscenian considered the expanse of wall before him. He leaned over to lower himself into the water and take a look.

Suddenly something burst up out of the water beneath the boat, which shattered, dumping Tarscenian in the water. As he swam to the surface, he saw his sheathed sword disappear into the muck far below him. His spellcasting components floated on the surface.

A shadow warned him that he was no longer alone, and he lurched backward. A lance, barbed like a harpoon, whisked past his face.

At first Tarscenian thought the hobgoblin from Solace had caught up with him, but this creature circling him now had gills. Webbed fingers held the barbed lance and a small shield. Tarscenian realized the creature's toes were webbed, too.

He searched his memory. *Koalinth*, that was it. An aquatic hobgoblin. Of course Hederick would have no compunctions about employing the entire goblin race.

The koalinth stabbed its lance efficiently through the water. Tarscenian had given his dagger to Mynx and now he had no sword, either. He would have to surface to breathe. Each gulp of air would leave him vulnerable to the gill-breather.

I didn't come this far to be stopped by an overgrown fish, Tarscenian thought.

Then the creature stopped circling and came at him.

Chapter 18

The rocking of the centaur's gait nearly lulled Mynx to sleep, especially curled up as she was inside the Diamond Dragon.

When the centaur halted, however, the thief awoke and made herself sit up. The walls of the Diamond Dragon glowed violet around her. Beyond them, even though she knew the Diamond Dragon was made of something impermeable, she could make out the contents of Kifflewit's pocket—a few buttons, three coins, a stub of chalky stone, and an apple. Even the ruby the kender had stolen from Gaveley's den was there.

The artifact seemed to hum, and soon Mynx's head pounded from the beelike drone. Despite the small space she occupied, the air was cool.

She listened.

" 'Tis time to halt and gather our strength, little one. Slide down from my back. We shall share wine and fine cheese from my pack."

"Nothing for me, thank you. Oh, just some wine, please," Kifflewit's lilting voice rejoined. "And, oh, maybe a little cheese. Don't you have any bread, Phytos?"

The centaur must have had some, for Mynx heard a muffled, "Mmmm, thanks," that told her the kender had found something that suited his tastes. She could have used a chunk of bread herself, not to mention wine and cheese. If she remained in the dragon very long, would she starve?

"Hey!" she shouted. "Hey, out there! Kifflewit! Phytos! Help!"

She waited in vain; nobody heard her words.

"Wouldst thou like some more cheese, kender? 'Tis quite a good variety, Qualinesti, full of elven vigor. I traded a full bag of fine-quality grain for it."

"Mmmm . . . Thank you." Kifflewit coughed.

Mynx, annoyed, struck the flat of her hand against the Diamond Dragon. The blow aggravated the drone into a bell-like tolling that set Mynx's teeth on edge. "Hey, you two!" she shouted. "Help!"

She tried screaming as loud as she could. The artifact took her scream and returned it tenfold, until Mynx thought she would shout her lungs out from sheer frustration.

All right, so they couldn't hear her. Maybe Mynx could make her presence known some other way. The kender must realize she was here, but he couldn't be relied upon. Mynx pinned her hopes on the centaur.

She braced her hands on the sides of the dragon and rocked to one side. The artifact wobbled slightly. Encouraged, Mynx pushed even harder the other way, and the Diamond Dragon tipped so far in that direction that Mynx lost her balance on the slippery bottom and tumbled to her knees.

"Blast this thing to the Abyss!" she shrieked, then had to cover her ears again from the resulting reverberations.

Then a huge hand—did that monstrous palm, those fat fingers, those imposing nails really belong to a little kender?—crashed into the pocket, swept under the Diamond Dragon, and carried it and its occupant out of the pouch and into the light. Mynx leaped to her feet and rocked back and forth again, harder than before. The centaur had to notice something odd—the artifact was moving of its own volition.

"See what I have, Phytos?" the kender chirped. He wrapped his fingers around it securely. Mynx fumed, but kept up her strenuous efforts.

Phytos did not look up from arranging the items in his pack. " 'Tis time we continued, little one. We're not even out of the vallenwoods. We have many leagues . . . By the gods!" The centaur's head was up now, violet eyes staring. "What is that thou holds, kender? It glows like lightning! 'Tis magic! Is it evil?"

"It was Hederick's, Phytos. He gave it to me, back at the temple."

Phytos clucked. "Did he, kender? And could it be that the High Theocrat is unaware that he gave thee such a precious bauble?"

Kifflewit faltered. "I . . . I don't remember." He brightened. "Anyway, I'm keeping it for him. Until he needs it again."

"Let me see it."

The kender opened his hand. Mynx held her breath. New fingers, slender and strong, cradled the artifact. The centaur's angular face, with those piercing eyes, came into view. Mynx jumped and waved, rocked the Diamond Dragon, and shouted Phytos's name until she was hoarse. The slim fingers closed firmly around the quivering artifact.

"By the gods, kender, the bauble glows so that I am

nearly blinded! It seems to tremble with magic. Put the thing back in thy pocket and keep it safe. If 'tis Hederick's, it may prove useful to us in the coming war."

"War?" Kifflewit's voice held new interest. He replaced the Diamond Dragon in his pocket. Mynx slumped to the artifact's bottom, disconsolate.

"Hederick's forces committed an atrocity against my race," Phytos told the kender. "His minions slew four of my companions. It is highly likely that my tribe will choose to retaliate, little one."

Kifflewit's voice went even more shrill with excitement. "Centaurs, go to war with humans? Wow! Has that ever happened before, Phytos? Is that . . ."

"I neither know nor care, little one." The curt reply was followed by a soft, "Come, Kifflewit Burrthistle. 'Tis time we left. My glade lies outside the vallenwoods, and we've a way to go."

Inside the Diamond Dragon, which remained inside the kender's pocket, Mynx beat her fists against her knees and howled.

* * * * *

"The revelations went well tonight, Your Worship," Dahos said.

Hederick grunted noncommittally as he arranged his scrolls in the room of his quarters. He had summoned the high priest, then refused to speak to him or dismiss him. He'd learned an important lesson from Venessi, his mother—that silence is the worst prison imaginable.

Hederick half-smiled. Let the priest suffer for fear of losing his neck, he thought. The Plainsman had erred twice in the preceding day. First with the centaurs. Then he'd allowed Tarscenian to escape once more. Did Hederick have to oversee *everything* to make sure things were always done correctly?

233

The High Theocrat had no doubt that if he, Hederick, had been leading the guards against Tarscenian this afternoon, the old fool would have been executed and out of the way by now.

Still, the half-elf Gaveley had had some valuable information for the High Theocrat. Tarscenian was planning vengeance against Hederick, Gaveley informed him, although exactly what form that vengeance would take the half-elf had professed not to know. Hederick had paid him well for the warning.

"As if there were any doubt that Tarscenian continues to stalk me," Hederick muttered. "Tarscenian won't rest until he sees me dead. He's supremely jealous of me."

"Your Worship?" Dahos's voice held a spark of hope.

Hederick said nothing in reply. After a suspenseful wait, the high priest sagged.

The High Theocrat stifled a chuckle. Suddenly he felt a twinge in his upper torso. He clasped a hand against his breastbone, moved his beloved leather-swaddled pendant aside, and gingerly probed a tender spot. He'd felt odd intermittently since this afternoon, when he'd ordered the black-robed mage executed.

The mage had injured him, but the god Sauvay had healed him before hundreds of people. Hederick wished he could remember exactly what happened, but his memory seemed impaired. Still, he had seen and noted witnesses of his miraculous revival. There could be no greater sign of Hederick's favor in the eyes of the Seeker gods.

For a moment the High Theocrat considered unwrapping the leather covering and admiring the Diamond Dragon. But, no, he'd nearly lost it once—then a second time this afternoon, his aides told him. No telling when Tarscenian would attempt his evil-doing. Hederick would keep the treasure under cover, close to him.

"Sauvay smiled upon me today," Hederick said

suddenly, momentarily abandoning his oath to shun the high priest.

"Yes, Your Worship," Dahos returned quickly. "It is truly . . ."

"How are your plans coming for the reconsecration ceremony, Dahos?" Hederick cut in.

"They are . . . going well," Dahos replied carefully. "We should be able to conduct the ceremony in three or four days. I have sent word to the Highseekers Council that . . ."

"Hang the damned Highseekers Council, you dolt!" Hederick snapped. "This is *my* temple. I don't need that batch of old women and sinners snooping around Erolydon. I can conduct my own ceremony, myself."

"But the *Praxis* says . . ."

Hederick's voice took on a new edge. "*I* am the judge here of what the *Praxis* says, Dahos. Don't overstep yourself. It could be a fatal mistake."

"I . . ."

"Yes, High Priest?"

Dahos swallowed and stood taller. "Nothing, Your Worship."

* * * * *

Snoop cursed his luck as he crept along the shoreline, spyglass in his left hand, dirk in his right. It was growing dark, and he knew pitifully little about the area where the land met Crystalmir Lake.

Snoop hated the outdoors—all bugs and poison ivy and fanged creatures with no sense of civilization. The bucolic folks who frequented the area outside Solace actually *enjoyed* stalking animals and birds and killing them—and for food, not even for a meaningful bounty! And as for fishing, well, the day that Snoop would be found trying to lure a slimy fish onto a hook so that he could skin it and cut out its entrails and cook and eat it would be the day he'd . . . well, the day he'd eat dirt.

No, give Snoop city life any day. True, Solace was a bit small for Snoop's liking, but Gaveley had made it worth his while—for these last few years, at least. Snoop had chafed lately.

With the Diamond Dragon, though, Snoop hoped to set up his own thieves' ring. Someplace far from Gaveley, it was certain, but that was fine. He'd heard tales of many cities stuffed with riches that beckoned a clever thieves' ring such as the one Snoop longed to run.

He'd be cursed if he'd settle for his measly cut of Tarscenian's bounty. Not when he could have that Diamond Dragon free and clear, all his own.

Snoop tripped over a stone in the gathering dusk, and swore aloud. There was no sense to Gaveley's latest plan. Why order Snoop to follow Tarscenian when everyone in the ring knew the stranger was bound to head straight for Hederick? The question rankled in Snoop's mind, eating away at him until he thought he'd go mad. It was an unfamiliar feeling. He'd never questioned Gaveley's methods before.

"I could be lounging in the grass behind some tree right now, watching the infernal temple through my glass," Snoop grumbled. "Instead, I'm being eaten alive by mosquitos, I'm soaked up to my knees trying to keep one eye on some fool who's drifting around the lake in a leaky boat. Damn the luck!" There was no point lowering his voice, not this far out in the woods. "No one out here but the bugs and the rabbits to hear me, anyway."

He swung up his spyglass . . . and there was Tarscenian, sitting calmly in the blasted canoe. "Not even rowing, for the gods' sake!" Snoop mumbled. "And he isn't swatting bugs, that I can see. It isn't fair. Gods, how can that canoe be making such speed? And Gaveley and Xam both know where he's going, so why tell me to follow—?"

He broke off his harangue. There was one excellent

reason, it occurred to him, why Gaveley would have sent Snoop on this particular wild-goose chase.

The half-elf hoped to get to Hederick first and steal the Diamond Dragon for himself.

The thief-turned-spy sorted out his thoughts. "Not that the guards'd let a half-elf into the temple, of course. Gaveley couldn't get in himself unless . . ." Snoop thought harder. Example after example came to his mind, instances in which Gaveley had had no trouble at all gaining entrance where he'd been expressly barred. And Gaveley had a hulking man like Xam to back him up. Snoop had no one.

No one but the man he'd been ordered to trail, that was. The man who knew more than anyone else about the Diamond Dragon—including, no doubt, where Hederick kept it.

Snoop started to run toward Erolydon. He'd be blasted to the depths of the Sirrion Sea before he'd let Gaveley get the best of him.

He arrived, sweating and panting, and crouched near some trees just south of the temple. The last worshipers were being let out through a gate in the southern wall. A priest slammed the door behind the chattering people. Snoop heard three bolts being thrown, then nothing. The thief leaned, wheezing, against a tree, and trained his glass on the western horizon.

There—*there* was Tarscenian, just arriving at the seaward wall of the temple. Snoop squinted through his lens. The old man was just staring into the water as though he was thinking. Why didn't he hurry, for the gods' sake? Didn't the idiot know the sky would soon be dark? Snoop swore anew.

He watched, aghast, as the water churned around the small canoe and exploded around Tarscenian, who disappeared into the boiling water—Tarscenian, the only one who could lead Snoop to the Diamond Dragon!

The thief found himself racing along the shoreline, heedless, for the first time in his career, of who might see him. Tarscenian *had* to survive to lead him to the artifact, Snoop raged. After that, he planned to end the old man's life with a thrust of his dirk, but until then . . .

Snoop drew out a grapnel and rope and tossed the barbed hook atop the wall. He pulled himself up hand over hand until he reached the top. A quick glance showed no one inside the compound—no eyes to see him. There was hope, after all. Snoop retrieved his grapnel and hurried along the wall. He adroitly sidestepped the slivers of sharp metal and chunks of jagged glass that Hederick had ordered set into the top of the marble to discourage intruders.

Snoop came to the end of the southern wall and turned north. A short dash, and then he was on the wall above Tarscenian—or, at least, above the roiling water where Tarscenian was probably drowning. Snoop squinted in the dying light and saw what appeared to be a huge froglike thing poking at the man over and over. A fish with a harpoon?

Snoop snugged the rope around a chunk of glass. Then he dropped the grapnel so that it rested just at the surface of the water. Tarscenian saw the hook and made a break for it, the fishlike creature following.

This wasn't all that different from garroting someone in an alley in Haven, Snoop reflected. He snagged the koalinth just under the gills. The aquatic hobgoblin jerked back in sudden pain, setting the hook. Then it leaped above the water, panic-stricken. Snoop wrapped the rope once more around the wall outcropping.

There was a jerk, then the koalinth was left shrieking and struggling, its bloody gills dangling just above the waterline.

Snoop climbed partway down the rope to where Tarscenian was treading water. Both waited until the beast suffocated.

Tarscenian caught the dead creature's dropped lance and spoke. "I thought Gaveley wasn't in on this."

"He's not," Snoop replied. "I'm working on my own now. Going solo, you might say. And I'm throwing in with you, stranger."

Tarscenian regarded him, an impassive look on his face. Finally he said, "As you wish."

Snoop nodded.

"Come on, then. I know how to get into the temple."

Chapter 19

Snoop dove toward the place Tarscenian had indicated. Twice his own height in depth, the old man had said. The marble wall became some other kind of rock below the surface of the water, and Hederick's workers had not paid as much attention to attaining a smooth surface. Holding his breath, Snoop swam, forcing himself downward, pulling his body deeper by grabbing handholds in the rough wall.

A good swimmer, Tarscenian caught up with the thief and passed him. They would have to hurry, however, to find an air pocket before they ran out of breath. It was growing increasingly dim in the water. Tarscenian nearly collided with Snoop as they groped along the wall's base.

Snoop grasped something, then, with a horrified look, drew his hand back. He thrust something soft and squishy behind him. It scuttled away, emitting a cloud of ink.

And then they saw the tunnel—a thick circle smooth with algae and black as night within. Tarscenian felt for Snoop's arm, pointed with the lance they had taken from the koalinth, and shoved the smaller man toward the hole. Snoop broke away, shaking his head violently. All right, I'll go first, Tarscenian thought. But if I get wedged in front of you, you're done for, my friend. On the other hand, if another koalinth was waiting in the tunnel, Snoop might have made a wise choice.

Tarscenian fastened the lance to his waist, dove toward the tunnel, grasped the slippery edge with difficulty, and forced himself inside.

It was a tight fit. Tarscenian made progress only by keeping his arms outstretched before him and his legs tight together. He could swim through the water and the growing muck, but barely. He closed his eyes and scissored his legs feverishly.

Tarscenian felt Snoop's hand bump against his foot and draw back. The thief followed him closely, then. At least Tarscenian hoped it was Snoop.

Soon his lungs burned, and Tarscenian lost track of direction. Were they traveling horizontally or upward? Did it matter? He kicked weakly now, at times resting his legs and using his arms to pull himself along. A voice shrieked in his mind: *Need air need air need air.* He tried to focus on the Diamond Dragon, on his hatred of Hederick. On Ancilla. This would be worth it if somehow she could be saved.

Then his hands broke water. He came to rest on an incline, his cheek cradled in soft mud—above the surface. Tarscenian allowed himself to fill his lungs again and again; it didn't matter that the air was fetid, the mud foul in his nostrils, the light dim. It was air. Somewhere, water dripped. That and his gasping were the only sounds.

Then frantic scrabbling at his feet reminded him of Snoop's presence. Tarscenian pulled himself farther out of the muck and heard the thief emerge behind him. Snoop coughed, retched, and swore.

"By all that's holy . . . old man . . . I've been in some spots before . . . but this . . ." Tarscenian heard more retching, then still more cursing. "Where do we . . . go from here?"

"Be quiet," Tarscenian ordered. "Let me think." They needed to let their eyes adjust. He stood guardedly and unfastened the lance from his waist. Warily, he used the koalinth's weapon to probe the space around him.

"Ouch! By whatever gods there are, man, watch out!"

Tarscenian grunted an apology. They seemed to be in a second tunnel, this one much larger than the first—tall enough for Tarscenian to stand in. He was ankle-deep in muck.

His lance poked something soft but solid. He pulled it free and felt again, a bit to the right, with the same result. Then to the left. His lance met a similar obstruction. It was too soft for stone or wood, too hard for mud.

Tarscenian felt in the pocket that carried his steel and flint. "I don't suppose you have a supply of dry tinder on you, do you, spy?" he whispered.

"Certainly," Snoop snapped. "In the same pocket with my emerald collection."

It would have to be magic, then, although Tarscenian had barely any strength left. Each spell had drained him, and he'd had precious little time to rest, these last few days. "*Shirak*," he whispered, and molded his hands around the point of the lance. The tip glowed like a torch. Tarscenian gazed around him, half-expecting what now met his eyes. Snoop, unwarned, inhaled suddenly and drew his dirk.

There were four of them—four bodies, facedown—and when Tarscenian lifted the lance-light, he could make out other, similar mounds farther up the tunnel. He lowered the light again. Pale blue slime coated the four corpses from head to foot.

Tarscenian used a booted toe gently to turn over one of the four. Snoop gagged.

"The man from this afternoon," Tarscenian said quietly. "He dared to question Hederick. The guards hauled him away."

He remembered that Snoop had not been at the sentencing of the black-robed mage. Tarscenian overturned another corpse. This belonged to a middle-aged woman; a kerchief was still in place on her head. "One of the women the guards arrested. Also this afternoon." His stare went to the other bodies. Two more kerchiefs. "Her friends."

Snoop looked like a wild-eyed ferret, partly terrified and wholly nauseated. Tarscenian, on the other hand, merely felt tired and old.

"I suppose the materbill was sated, so they put the bodies in here," he said. "Eventually the remains will wash out into the lake."

Snoop burst out, "But what *happened* to them? What's that coating? There are no wounds, nothing but this blue ..." He stooped and reached toward one of the still forms.

Tarscenian shouted a warning, but too late. Snoop touched the blue substance with his forefinger and, screaming, jumped up. Tarscenian grabbed the thief's hand and used the light of the lance to burn away the ooze. The man's finger turned blistered and red.

"What is the stuff?" Snoop cried.

"It's digesting the bodies," Tarscenian replied tensely. "Now be still."

Snoop controlled himself with an effort. "Why?" he finally whispered. "Who will hear us in here?"

"Whatever spread this stuff."

Horror increased tenfold on Snoop's face.

"I don't know what the monster is called. The man who told me about it years ago referred to it as a slime creature."

"Where is it?"

"Somewhere in this tunnel, I'd guess. If it had been in the first tunnel, we'd be dead by now. The creatures spread their ooze on living or dead things, then retire to a cave to wait until the ooze does its job and the prey is soft enough to absorb."

"Did that man tell you how to fight such a creature?"

Tarscenian grimaced. There was something he half-remembered, but he couldn't quite put the words together. It had been a long time ago.

Snoop gasped in the foul air. "I can handle human enemies, maybe even a hobgoblin or two. But this . . . I don't know if I can stand this, Tarscenian."

"You made your decision when you entered the tunnel."

"But I . . ."

"Be quiet," Tarscenian repeated. "Listen."

Water splashed somewhere, and a sound, as of something slithering through the tunnel, came to them. "Maybe you should turn out that light," Snoop whispered.

"The creature can see in the dark. Can you?"

Not waiting for an answer, Tarscenian stepped over the slimy bodies and moved toward the sound. He thrust his lance-light before him.

Ten feet in front of them, a waist-high mound of pale blue ooze glistened.

Snoop halted, dumbfounded, then sneered. "That unimpressive thing?" he asked. "That's it? I can probably take care of that beast all by myself, old man." He raised his arm. In an instant the spy's dirk was hurtling through the air toward the creature. Tarscenian's shout came too late.

The weapon sliced through the slime monster's covering of ooze, then bounced off the creature's hide and landed back in the water at their feet. Snoop slowly bent to pick it up, then halted. He used his foot to nudge the weapon out of the water. The doused weapon was clean and free of ooze.

Tarscenian frowned. Something still tickled at his memory.

The monster slithered forward, slow and sluglike, as though it had all the time in the world. "How do we stop it?" Snoop whispered, less cocksure now. He took a step backward.

"Stay back. It catches live victims by interfering with their thoughts. At this distance, you may be safe. If it gets closer, that won't be so. It will offer you what you most desire. Ultimately you will actually urge it to devour you."

Snoop shook his head. "That thing? Not a chance."

"It has overcome stronger men than us."

The thief doggedly shook his head. "It has to have a weak spot, Tarscenian—someplace where my dirk is welcome." Snoop moved forward. Tarscenian tried to grab him, but the thief shook him off and continued. "It's moving this way," Snoop said. "There must be eyes or something where there's no hide to pro . . ."

Snoop's voice trailed off into silence. He stared at the creature, an arm's length away. A whisper hissed through the tunnel.

"I will give you great wealth. I will give you great power. All the world will thrill to your existence. The world will worship at your feet. You will be rich beyond anything you have dreamed."

A whimper escaped Snoop. Tarscenian searched through his pockets for something to block his own ears, but he'd lost everything in the lake. His hands would have to do. Covering his ears, he stepped to Snoop's side. He had to remove Snoop from the creature's deadly influence.

"All of Solace will work to indulge your every wish. You will want for nothing. You will enjoy power and wealth that kings would gladly die for."

Tarscenian placed a hand on Snoop's shoulder. Snoop gave a small scream and jumped toward the creature. The slime monster turned slightly and now addressed Tarscenian.

"I will help you attain what you seek, also. Your lady will live again, and Hederick will die. Together, you and your lady will rule Solace. You will have wealth and power. All this will come to pass. You can spread the word of the Old Gods throughout the world, you and your lady. The two of you will never die. Your bodies will become young again; you will be fertile; you will have many children. And these children will worship the Old Gods."

Tarscenian covered both ears. "It cannot be so," he whispered. "It is against nature."

"I can make it so."

Tarscenian pulled again at Snoop's arm. Snoop struck out, sending the older man sprawling back into the mud. The thief lunged toward the monster, but as soon as Snoop touched the creature, he began to scream. In a moment the creature had covered him with ice-blue slime.

Snoop beat frantically at his torso and legs, trying to remove the sticky stuff that gnawed at his skin. Tarscenian held the lance forward, hoping the light at the tip would be enough to dispel the ooze, but Snoop gave one final cry and collapsed, lifeless, on the tunnel floor. The creature hovered over the thief, eating ravenously.

The older man seized that moment to dash around the creature and escape up the tunnel. There had to be a way out.

The tunnel curved. Tarscenian heard the sound of water ahead at the same time the whisper of the creature behind him stroked his mind.

"I will give you eternal life. You will have countless lifetimes to worship your gods, you and this mage woman you love. Your bodies will be young, your lives easy."

Tarscenian bounded around the curve and skidded in the slippery muck. The tunnel ended. Water streamed from two openings in the wall above Tarscenian's head. Between and above them was a trapdoor.

The slime monster came slithering around the curve behind Tarscenian.

And at that moment he remembered what would stop the creature.

"You will be wealthy. And you will be forgiven. All your sins, Tarscenian, will be swept aside at once, like dust. Those years as a Seeker fraud—forgiven. Those years of greed and pride and deception—as nothing. And you will have Ancilla at your side."

The mound of blue ooze slithered toward him and stopped just short of the fresh water that cascaded from the wall. Tarscenian edged back into the space between the waterfall pipes.

"Think of it, Tarscenian, a life of ease. You can rest. Don't you want to rest? Aren't you exhausted, Tarscenian? I can help you."

Tarscenian's clothes were sodden, but the water was clean. He felt the filth of the tunnel slough from his body, and with it, some of his exhaustion. The creature edged aside. Its whisper never ceased, but Tarscenian steeled his mind against it. He bolted through the waterfall and circled behind the creature.

Tarscenian stepped forward and jabbed the lighted lance at the slime creature. Smoke hissed from the ooze where the lance tip touched it, and the monster jerked backward toward the waterfall.

"Your lady will live again. Hederick will die. You will have wealth and power. You can spread the word of the Old Gods. You will never die. You will become young. You . . ."

Tarscenian slammed the lance into the slime creature as hard as he could. Still the hide resisted, even though smoke curled above the ooze. The light in the lance tip made the slime glow like blue flame. Tarscenian braced his feet against the tunnel wall and threw all his weight into his next thrust. The tip did not pierce the creature's hide, but the force of the blow sent the slime monster sliding back into the cascades of clear water.

In an instant, the creature's protective coating of ooze was swept away. The tough hide quivered with shock beneath the force of the pure water.

Then the monster exploded.

Chapter 20

Tarscenian felt for the footholds he'd seen fastened to the wall behind the cascades of water, and climbed. Cautiously, he extinguished the magical light on the lance tip and raised the trapdoor.

The door opened up into a dark hallway. Tarscenian climbed out and flattened himself against a wall. Too late the adventurer realized he was leaving a telltale stream of water. Why not just paint an arrow on the floor with a sign saying "Fugitive This Way"? he thought disgustedly.

His nose twitched. The smell of food and soap came to him. This, then, must be the kitchen and laundry area. And where there was a laundry, there would be dry clothes.

Tarscenian edged along the wall. The rooms he passed had no doors, just curtains to mask their contents from the prying eyes of passers-by. He poked his head into the first room. A small lantern burned. He saw brooms, mops, wooden buckets and shelves holding a lifetime supply of chamber pots, but no clothes.

Nothing but an apron. He snatched up the apron and slipped back into the corridor to wipe up the traces of his arrival.

Just then, a burst of raucous laughter greeted him. Tarscenian froze. It wasn't until a loud female voice sounded, prompting more laughter, that Tarscenian realized he hadn't been spotted.

Footsteps came his way, though. He dived across the hall, behind another curtain.

Steamy air engulfed him. The dim light showed nothing but a row of what looked like two dozen coffin handles. Tarscenian grabbed one of the handles and yanked—perhaps a secret passage?

A drawerlike contraption rolled smoothly toward him on tiny wheels. Inside were wooden dowels that held rolls of white fabric. Hot air rose from some heat source under the floor.

"A clothes-drying room," Tarscenian muttered, intrigued despite himself. "Ingenious."

"Hello, dearie!"

Tarscenian leaped around to see a smiling nymphet of a woman. Her red hair was wild, her grin suggestive, her clothes barely decent. Her feet were bare—no doubt the reason why he had not heard her approach. She laughed coarsely. "Are you one of the new girls, dearie? My, my, Hederick has taken to hiring some *ugly* women!"

"What is it, Helda?" Another woman shoved aside the curtain. "Are you talking to yourself . . . Oh, looky here!"

Tarscenian, for the second time in as many days, found himself speechless before a woman. He clutched his lance and waited.

"Well, man?" asked a black-haired woman. "Are you

one of Hederick's prisoners?"

"Mmmm, not yet," Tarscenian muttered. "Any moment now, though, I suspect."

The women laughed as though he'd said something terribly witty. It occurred to him that they were just this side of drunk. More of them appeared behind the first two. "Do you work here, ladies?" Tarscenian asked.

Another chorus of giggles resounded in the humid room. "Ladies! He called us ladies." "Well, ain't he a sweet one?" "I ain't been called a lady some twenty years or more." "Are you married, sweet man?"

At Tarscenian's hesitant nod, they sulked for a bit, then resumed their chatter. The redhead who'd discovered Tarscenian waved an imaginary fan and curtsied deeply to the black-haired woman. The rest of them went into gales of mirth, and soon everyone was curtsying and fanning someone else.

Perhaps the Seekers were operating a home for lunatics or dipsomaniacs, Tarscenian decided. Perhaps he had stumbled into the main dormitory. He had no idea how far he'd traveled in the discharge tunnels, after all.

He put a hand on the nearest woman's arm. "This *is* Erolydon, isn't it, my dear?" he whispered. "The temple?"

Clearly he'd scaled new levels of hilarity with that remark. The women giggled until one of them, practicing a curtsy in the crowded drying-room, slipped on the damp floor and landed with a yowl.

Then the little redhead was back by his side. "Here, dearie," she said. "My name is Helda. You ain't going to get far running around the temple in those clothes." She shooed all but one of the women into the corridor. "He's mine. I saw him first. So back to work, *ladies*," she said, causing even more hilarity. Tarscenian could see he'd provided them with entertainment for days to come.

With the help of the black-haired woman, Helda hauled on the handle of another drying rack. This one held brown robes.

"You'll make a nice-looking priest, even if you are taller than most of them," Helda said, rummaging through the garments. "So what are you, an escaped prisoner? An assassin? Ah, I *do* hope you're an assassin. I'd stick a paring knife in old Hederick's gut myself, except he pays regular. Not much, but regular. Can't say as I'd mourn long if someone else did him in, though." She didn't wait for Tarscenian's answer. "How about this one?" she asked, holding up a brown robe.

"It's gonna be too tight across the shoulders," the black-haired woman said.

"It's the biggest one in here. It'll have to do."

"I'm sure it will be fine," Tarscenian said quickly. He grabbed the robe. "Don't the temple guards patrol down here?"

"Sometimes," Helda said. "When we're baking pastries, they sometimes come to visit. It don't pay to get 'em mad. We always make enough extra. But they only come down here during baking time, not cleanup. Which is now."

"Isn't that just like a man?" the black-haired woman said with a sigh. "Show up for the goodies, but . . ."

Tarscenian interrupted. "I'd like to try this on."

"So go ahead." Both women stared at him as though he'd suddenly sprouted wings.

"Could you two ladies, ah, that is . . . well, give me some privacy?"

Helda and her friend poked each other, giggling. "That's a sure sign of quality, Helda," the black-haired woman said as they left him alone. "Modesty in spades. Me, I've never had a problem with modesty. Did I ever tell you about the time I . . ."

Eventually the voice faded. The black-haired woman must have returned to the kitchen. Tarscenian pulled the robe down over him. It was tight but dry, and it did have a hood. Tarscenian poked his head around the curtain.

Helda stood outside, leaning against the wall. She held out a dagger, hilt first. "It's mine," she said softly. "You never know when the temple guards'll overstep themselves, and I do maintain some standards." She shook off his thanks. "You'll need it. That lance don't exactly go with a robe, you know. And I gather you're trying to be sneaky." She accepted Tarscenian's lance in exchange for the dagger, slipping it behind a pile of sheets in a nearby closet. "You're sure you're married, now?"

"Absolutely," Tarscenian said, smiling.

"A shame," she rejoined.

"I have no way to pay you for the dagger."

"Do me a favor, then." Helda leaned forward and scooped aside the thin strap that held her blouse in place. She showed Tarscenian her back, which was crisscrossed with welts, some barely healed before they had been retraced. Then her blouse was back in place, and Tarscenian was gazing into fierce blue eyes. "Make him suffer," she hissed. "Make him pay."

He hesitated, then nodded. Helda whirled back toward the kitchen without another word.

Chapter 21

Mynx!

For a short time after Kifflewit deposited her and the Diamond Dragon in his pocket, Mynx continued to fume and drum her fists against her knees.

Eventually, though, she realized the startling fact that someone was calling her name.

Mynx!

She sat up. She could see nothing but the inside of Kifflewit's pocket, lit by the dragon's purple glow.

Mynx!

Outside, then. Someone outside the pocket was speaking to her. Rejuvenated, the woman jumped up and rocked the artifact from side to side until Kifflewit Burrthistle's hand returned to retrieve it.

"My, this thing is lively tonight," she heard the kender

say. He held up the Diamond Dragon and peered at it. Mynx glared back. Couldn't he see her? Couldn't he remember that the Diamond Dragon had enveloped her?

Perhaps the magical artifact ensorceled him.

Mynx looked around. The kender was seated upon the centaur. Night had fallen. The vallenwoods had thinned out until there were vast distances between them. One of the huge trees towered over them.

Mynx did a double take. This tree glowed at the bottom. The voice that called came from that glow, she realized, although she could not have said how she knew. Either the tree was alive, or someone inside the tree was calling to her. Perhaps the Diamond Dragon made it possible for her to hear. Mynx shook her head. She was beyond understanding things by now.

"Thou had best put that thing away, little one, lest thou drop it," Phytos warned. "We shall enter my home glade soon. I do not want to be delayed pawing about in the brush."

"Oh, I'd never drop it, Phytos. I'm really careful with important things . . ."

Mynx! Come here!

That voice again, from the tree. Suddenly Mynx knew that she had to stop them, by whatever means possible, from leaving the vallenwoods. She flung herself from side to side, ignoring the bumps and bruises as she tossed and fell.

The artifact quivered in Kifflewit's hand as he chattered on. "Phytos, I'm really trustworthy when it comes to things like . . ."

As Mynx rocked the artifact again, Phytos cried out in alarm.

Then Mynx and the Diamond Dragon were falling.

It was a long way down from the centaur's back. Mynx made herself go limp, hoping that the landing would not break any of her bones.

Mynx!

The Diamond Dragon crashed into the earth and skittered to one side. Mynx heard the kender call out in dismay, then she blacked out briefly. She awakened as she barreled, end over end, limbs flying, inside the rolling artifact.

Then she caught her balance as the Diamond Dragon came to rest against a stone—an arm's length from the glowing tree. Couldn't the centaur and kender see the glow in the vallenwood? She hurled herself against one side of her prison and then the other, until her head rang with the effort. She had just worked the Diamond Dragon free of the rock when Kifflewit picked up the artifact again.

"No!" Mynx bellowed. Frantically, she resumed her gyrations. She was bruised from shoulders to knees now, but she was determined to succeed.

The kender dropped the artifact again.

Mynx's prison bounced and rolled. It came to rest against the vallenwood's rough bark. "Help!" she shouted, drumming on the side nearest the tree. "Help me!"

She spied Kifflewit bounding toward her again, mouth open and hand outstretched. Phytos leaped behind him, annoyance apparent in his face.

As soon as the Diamond Dragon touched the tree, the humming that had annoyed Mynx for so long grew louder and louder, until she dropped to her knees. She covered her ears and closed her eyes.

Miravel firtas, overli ghacom.

Whatever was inside the tree was chanting. The noise increased. "Stop it!" she screamed. The buzzing drowned out all other sound—Phytos's shouts, the kender's excited squeals, her own entreaties. She smelled smoke and dared to open her eyes a slit. The air around her was ominously cloudy.

Miravel firtas, overli ghacom. Ytanderal limkir od y'd requistandilus.

Then Mynx burst free of the thing. She felt her body soaring through the air, expanding and growing until she thought she must be the size of a vallenwood. She turned over and over, like a stone rolling down a hill.

And landed, soft as a feather. Her hands clutched, not the sides of her head, but pine needles and other litter on the forest floor. She opened her eyes. The tree, Kifflewit, and Phytos swam around her.

She closed them again, then tried once more.

Mynx was back to normal size. The artifact lay at her side on some leaves.

Phytos skidded to a halt, his violet eyes almost starting from their sockets. Kifflewit Burrthistle scooped up the Diamond Dragon and bounced up and down like a cork in a stream.

"There she is, Phytos!" the kender chattered. "I knew she'd find us! See, centaur! I told you all about Mynx. She was here all along, waiting for us. Aren't you proud of me, Phytos?"

Mynx resisted the urge to clobber the kender.

"How . . ." The centaur's voice failed, and he coughed. "How didst thou get here?"

She pointed weakly to the Diamond Dragon. "I was in there." Doubt creased the centaur's face, followed by sympathy.

"Poor thing," he murmured. "She hast gone daft. She must have been wandering in the forest for days. Who dost thou suppose she is, Kifflewit?"

The kender was still hopping up and down. "It's Mynx, I told you, Phytos! She's my friend. She wanted the Diamond Dragon, but I wouldn't give it to her. She probably followed us, huh?"

"That thing swallowed me, Kifflewit!" Mynx shouted at the kender. "I've been bouncing around in there like dice in a tavern, while you two have been breathing fresh air, drinking wine, and eating bread and cheese!"

Soon she and the kender were nose to nose. "It's mine," the kender shrieked. "Your tricks can't fool me!"

"Didn't you remember I was *in* there, you addlepated, dunderheaded kender?"

"Well, maybe so, but if you hadn't tried to steal it from me in the first place . . ."

"We need this thing to help Tarscenian, you little idiot!"

"You could have asked. Not even a 'please'!"

"Tarscenian needs it!"

"Thief!"

Finally Phytos cleared his throat. "I fear there are explanations I am not privy to. But perhaps thou couldst tell me, Mynx."

When the thief appealed to the centaur, words poured out of her. Phytos's expression grew increasingly grave.

". . . So you see," she finished, "Tarscenian is heading into danger, and the Diamond Dragon isn't even where he thinks it is, to help him. Gaveley sold him out, Phytos! They'll kill him. We have to go back and help him." She tugged at his arm. "Hurry. Can you carry us both?"

Phytos grasped her frantic hand and held it. "Calm thyself, woman. I will do what I can. Get thee on my back." He directed his violet gaze at the kender. "Perhaps we should leave Kifflewit Burrthistle here," the centaur intoned, "inasmuch as he has made this task that much more difficult."

"Me?" the kender squeaked. "What did *I* do?"

Mynx climbed up on Phytos's back. Kifflewit, protesting all the way, bounded up to join her just as the centaur launched into his trot. "Wait!" Mynx cried. "Phytos, you're going the wrong way."

"No," the centaur rejoined. "Hand me the horn from my pack. If, that is, the kender did not dent it beyond use when he hid in there."

Mynx rummaged in the pack, passing the horn up to the centaur's waiting hands. "We should be near enough," the man-horse said to himself. The creature raised the horn to his lips and blew a long blast, then two short ones, then another long. He handed the instrument back to Mynx.

In a short time, they were surrounded by several dozen centaurs carrying bows, arrows, and clubs. Phytos rapidly apprised them of recent events in Solace, of the deaths of Feelding and Salomar and their two compatriots, and of the dire predicament of the lone man who might be able to act against Hederick without bringing about a full-scale war.

"Wilt thou go back with me?" Phytos shouted. "Wilt thou join thy strength with him and this woman?"

The centaurs raised a hurrah.

Within moments, Mynx sat upon a well-rested centaur, with Kifflewit perched happily on another. Phytos, riderless, moved into the fore.

They turned their heads toward Solace and moved at a gallop.

Chapter 22

A short time later, Tarscenian hurried up the kitchen steps and darted into another corridor. It was long past midnight. Hederick was old. He would be in his rooms at this hour, resting, if not asleep.

If only Tarscenian could find the High Theocrat's quarters. He cursed silently. Helda had scooted back to the kitchen before he could think to ask for directions, and he'd lose even more time if he went back now to ask . . . assuming the scullery maids would even know.

Footsteps sounded—furtive ones. Tarscenian stepped back into a doorway, reassuring himself that his dagger was still concealed in the sleeve of his robe.

A yellow-robed novitiate came around the corner, up the stairs from the direction of the kitchen, a chunk of sausage in one hand and half a loaf of brown bread in the other. He was busily chewing. Clearly, the novitiate expected to meet no one at this hour. Tarscenian tried to remember what he could of Seeker etiquette.

He stepped out from the doorway and hailed the novitiate. "Little brother, stop a moment!"

The young man stopped, horror dawning on his face. At first he tried to secret the food behind him, then gave up the attempt. "Oh, sir, I was hungry. The fast has been so long. I am sorry. I know thievery is a sin. Please don't tell the high priest . . ."

"Yes, yes." Tarscenian waved away the young man's apologies. "Never mind that. Don't worry. I need your assistance. I was taking an important message to Hederick and lost my balance and fell on this hard corridor. I hit my head, and now, for the life of me, I cannot remember where Hederick's quarters are. Could you direct me?"

The youth, still staring, pointed off to his right. "Cross the main entryway and take the corridor immediately in front of you. The High Theocrat's door will be the third one on your left." The young man resumed chewing. "You're not going to punish me?" he asked hopefully.

Tarscenian was already heading toward the doors to the stairwell. "Why would I punish you, lad?" he said over his shoulder. "You look famished. No one can study well on an empty stomach. Eat up. But hurry, get back to your room, and tell no one." Tarscenian raised a hand to the young man, who dazedly waved back with the hand that held the sausage.

The temple was deserted, except for a few guards posted outside the main doors. In a moment, Tarscenian was at Hederick's portal. The heavy door was locked, of course. Tarscenian knocked quietly. "Your Worship?" he whispered.

Hederick's voice was thick with sleep. "Who is it? Dahos? Is it you?"

"It is . . ." Tarscenian mumbled something that might

pass as a name. "I have a message."

"Come in, then."

Tarscenian heard the sound of soft footsteps, then the bolts clicked aside.

Tarscenian waited for the footsteps to recede, then he slipped through the doorway. He saw Hederick silhouetted on the bed, lying down again, a fire burning in the hearth behind him despite the summer heat.

"What is your message, priest?" the High Theocrat asked sleepily.

"It is . . . it is a written message. It was left at the gate. I did not know if it was urgent, so . . ." Tarscenian fumbled in his pockets as though he indeed carried a scroll with a message for the High Theocrat.

"Put it on my writing table, then. And leave me. Lock the door on your way out."

"Yes, Your Worship." Tarscenian pretended to lay something on the table. Then he stepped to the door and quietly opened and closed it, remaining inside. He stood in the flickering half-darkness, not moving at all. Light from Solinari streamed through gaps in a shutter.

Soon Hederick's breathing evened out. Tarscenian stepped to the bed. The religious leader's face was slack with slumber. His round arms lay straight down at his sides. And around his neck was the thong and its leather-wrapped treasure.

Tarscenian reached for the Diamond Dragon.

A spear nudged his back. A lamp flared. Hederick sat up, laughing, and Tarscenian saw himself surrounded by a half-dozen guards, plus Dahos. In a moment, he was disarmed and held securely.

Hederick chortled, rubbing his hands together. "I have lived decades for this moment," he crowed. "You sought to steal Sauvay's gift, did you, Tarscenian? By the New Gods, I will use that selfsame gift to destroy you!"

The High Theocrat unwrapped the leather.

Then he cried out in shock. He and Tarscenian stared in dismay at the plain gray stone in Hederick's palm.

It was Tarscenian who first remembered the figure of a kender bent over Hederick's body in the western court-yard. And here he thought the kender had given the arti-fact back. He began to chuckle, then laugh out of control.

"I will kill you for this, sinner," Hederick snapped. He rapped out orders. "Dahos, we will reconsecrate the temple tomorrow morning. At the dawn service." He con-tinued speaking over Dahos's protests that there wasn't enough time. "The highlight of the ceremony will be the execution of a false Seeker priest."

* * * * *

"By the gods, Tarscenian is doomed," Olven whispered. "All right, Marya. I am with you."

The woman scribe sprang down from the stool and rushed to his side, but the dark apprentice held up one hand. "I will do it, Marya. Not you."

"Why take that upon yourself?" she demanded. "It was my idea."

"You may have expressed it first, but it was in my mind from the first atrocity I recorded. The man is evil."

"But . . ." Marya's sentence trailed off unfinished. What did it matter who changed Hederick's history, she thought, as long as someone did?

Olven took a deep breath and picked up his quill again. At that moment, however, a rested, replenished Eban entered the Great Library and stepped smartly up to their shared desk. Marya frowned, but stifled a groan.

"I thought you'd want a rest," the young apprentice said to Olven. "I'm anxious to get back to this history to see what hap-pens. Has Hederick been vanquished yet?"

Olven and Marya exchanged glances, their faces all the more tired-looking next to Eban's youthful enthusiasm. "I have a bit more to write," Olven said at last, "and then you may take my place."

"What happened?" Eban asked, finally taking in their glum expressions.

"Tarscenian's been captured," Marya said curtly. "Let Olven finish."

Olven closed his eyes, as though he were going into a trance. Then he opened them, and only Marya could tell that the reverie was a fraud. Eban edged between the other two to see the words as they appeared beneath Olven's pen.

"Suddenly, Hederick clasped his hand to his chest, cried out, and collapsed," Olven wrote. "By the time his aides reached him, the High Theocrat was dead."

"By the gods!" Eban whispered. "Hederick has . . . ?"

The three stared at Olven's words. Abruptly, tears glittered in Marya's eyes, and she reached past Eban to put a hand on Olven's suddenly shaking shoulder. "Olven," she said. "I think we've made a . . ."

Olven cried out at that instant. The quill was scratching again on the parchment, but, judging from the writer's agonized face, not by his own volition. Quickly, the quill's tip went backward over the sentences. As it passed over them, the words disappeared. The parchment appeared as it had before Olven's false trance. The long white feather floated to the library floor, but none of the three paid it any attention.

Marya was the first to speak. "Are you hurt, Olven?"

Tears were streaming down the apprentice's face, but he shook his head. Gently, Marya coaxed him to his feet and, half-supporting him, guided him out of the library. Eban stared, goggle-eyed. The red-haired apprentice hesitated before he moved into Olven's place and took up a new quill.

* * * * *

In his cell in the depths of the Great Library, Astinus nodded as he read the new passage on the page of his own history.

"And at that moment, two apprentice scribes in the Great Library at Palanthas attempted to alter the course of history. However, they soon learned—as had countless Great Library apprentices before them—that one can change history only by living it, not by wishing it."

Chapter 23

One moment, Mynx and her centaur were speeding along over the forest floor with the rest of Phytos's force. The next moment, they had barged pell-mell into a sea of shouting humans, goblins, and hobgoblins.

"What is it?" the kender shouted from his own mount as the centaurs scrambled to assess what had happened.

Mynx recognized several figures. "It's the slave train. They must have stopped for the night."

"What are they doing *north* of Solace?" Kifflewit demanded, being suddenly of a decidedly practical turn of mind. "There's nothing up this way! See, I have the maps to prove it . . ." He rummaged in his pockets.

"I don't know," Mynx yelled back. "Maybe they're heading for the Straits of Schallsea." Or maybe the rumors of armies to the north were true, and the relocation of the slaves was tied in with the military movements, she thought. She would not be surprised if Hederick was cooperating with vermin armies whose rampages had sent all those refugees pouring into Solace.

She had no time to develop her thoughts, however. The centaurs had pitched into battle with the goblin and hobgoblin captors of the human slaves. And before she knew it, Mynx was fighting for her life from the centaur's back. She wielded that creature's short sword. The centaur, meanwhile, swung a club with deadly accuracy, dashing in the skulls of more than one goblin.

The hobgoblins were well armed with maces, spears, and long swords, and although the centaurs outnumbered them, the horse-creatures were limited to using clubs in close quarter fighting. It proved too crowded for bows and arrows.

The slaves, as before, huddled together and begged for mercy. Finally, one of them shook herself free of the crowd. Ceci Vakon was not dressed the part of a warrior. The mayor's widow still wore the frilly nightrobe she'd had on when Dahos and the temple guards had forced her and her family from their home. Her curly brown hair lay tangled on her shoulders, a yellow ribbon askew in the mass of hair. But there was no mistaking the purpose in her flashing eyes.

"People," Ceci shouted, "we lost one opportunity for freedom because of fear. Are we going to throw away another?"

The fifty humans only bunched closer together. No one replied until Ceci's own daughter spoke up. "Mama, what if we get hurt?" the teen-ager asked softly.

"I'll fight!" cried Ceci's ten-year-old son, jumping up. "Give me a sword!" Soon Ceci's other two sons were clamoring for weapons as well.

Then, as the battle raged around them, the other children in the pack called for weapons. The hobgoblins were too busy evading centaur clubs to notice the insurrection growing in their midst.

A man shamefacedly stepped forward. "I can't have it said that my children'll fight for their freedom and I won't," he said. Another man stepped up, too, and a young woman. They joined Ceci Vakon in exhorting Hederick's slaves. "We're with the mayor's wife!"

"Who else is with me?" Ceci cried.

This time all the people roared to their feet, sweeping up whatever they could find in the way of weapons. From a five-year-old lad hurling rocks to a seventy-year-old woman wielding a knitting needle, they tore into their surprised captors.

The hobgoblins and goblins, used to passiveness from the slaves, were thrown utterly off balance. Ceci herself knocked the hobgoblin sergeant down, and Mynx finished him with her borrowed sword.

Soon the centaurs and the slaves had slain every hobgoblin and goblin, at least two dozen of the creatures. A half-dozen humans and several centaurs also lay dead.

Phytos spoke to the freed slaves. "We are on our way to Erolydon to challenge Hederick. Thou art free now to go where thou wilt."

"I'm with you, centaur!" Ceci Vakon called out stoutly. "I'm a widow because of Hederick's greed. I have a score to settle with the High Theocrat!"

Her daughter seconded her. The rest of the slaves, buoyed by victory, shouted their support as well.

Soon most of the slaves were mounted on centaurs. Other slaves ranged on foot, vowing to follow the attacking force as quickly as they could.

Phytos called the charge, and they pounded down the forest trails.

Chapter 24

Tarscenian's cell was next to the materbill's. Even if he had wanted to sleep, the noise of the pacing, growling creature would have prevented it.

The old man's cell, at least, had a small window—about the width of his hand and the length of his forearm. Even though the window faced west, he could tell that it would soon be dawn.

"And so, Great Paladine, it ends this way," he whispered, "with my love dying within the trunk of a vallenwood tree, and the mages who swore to help us similarly doomed. The Seekers, and those of Gaveley's foul sort, have won. I pray that there may come valiant heroes who can vanquish those who embrace evil."

He paused. "The coming years frighten me, my god. I don't know what they will bring, only that it will be fearsome indeed, and I will not live to see the outcome. My heart bleeds for the sorrowing world.

"To you, Paladine, my allegiance remains. From you, all blessings flow."

Tarscenian sat quietly for a time after ending his prayer.

He was exhausted beyond imagining.

He knew, too, that he was ready to die.

Dawn had arrived.

*   *   *   *   *

"I am very pleased, indeed, to be summoned to your presence, High Theocrat. It is an honor."

Gaveley bowed deeply as his hoarse voice rasped out the words. His face glowed with pleasure. He glanced around Hederick's receiving room with appreciation. His quick eyes noted and evaluated the frescoes on the walls, the inlaid pattern in the floor tile, and the steel and silver statues of the Seeker gods that graced the corners of the room. "I am very, very pleased," he repeated.

His hand stroked the arm of a marble nymph that might have been the goddess Ferae. Gaveley wasn't exactly sure who was whom among the Seeker gods; there were so many of them.

"Certainly, certainly, my friend Gaveley," Hederick murmured, inwardly vowing to have the statue scrubbed later. By the New Gods, how the infidel dressed—indecently tight blue leggings and matching boots, orange tunic, and a white hat with a green feather. It was enough to give a godly man like the High Theocrat a headache.

Hederick sipped from his early morning goblet of mead. "You warned me about Tarscenian, and you helped deliver him into my hands. For that I am grateful."

"As am I," Gaveley returned. "I know the Seekers are not prone to admitting those of elven blood to their temples."

Gaveley inclined his head, but he couldn't quite keep the

bitterness—or the sweet triumph—out of his voice.

Hederick only smiled. Better that Gaveley not know the humans-only rule was Erolydon's alone. Anyway, the temple would soon be reconsecrated. The stain of Gaveley's presence would then be wiped away.

"We will make tremendous partners, you and I," Gaveley continued with zest. "With my spies and thieves and your wealth, Hederick . . ." He whistled. "You've already got the network set up. You just need someone like me to manage things. Someone with a bent for this kind of business."

The High Theocrat murmured something indistinct, and the half-elf seemed to realize that he'd stumbled across some boundary of etiquette.

"My pardon, please, Your Worship," the thief whispered smoothly. "The veneration I hold for you, and the excitement of being summoned to your presence, addles my wits a bit, I fear." He bestowed upon Hederick the shining smile that had never failed to disarm Mynx.

Hederick let his lips curve in return. "It's understandable," he said.

"You have business for me, then?" the half-elf asked. "Your messenger led me to believe . . ."

"Ah, yes," the High Theocrat murmured. "Business. But first we must drink a toast to our—what did you call it, my friend?—our 'partnership.' " Hederick indicated a carafe on a table at Gaveley's elbow. "Please join me." His bulging blue eyes glistened as the half-elf thief poured himself a generous portion of the beverage. Some of the mead slopped over the edge of the glass and stained the table, but still Hederick maintained his pleasant smile.

"A toast," the High Theocrat proclaimed, raising his own full goblet. "To a new association." Then, as Gaveley raised the goblet to his lips, Hederick cried, "Wait! No, we must raise this tribute to the beginning day. It is the Seeker way." He ushered the half-elf to the window and flung open the shutters. "In the name of Sauvay, god of power and vengeance, I bless this mingling of minds." He sipped his mead, then placed the goblet aside as Gaveley quaffed the liquid he'd poured from the carafe.

The half-elf died quickly—quicker than he deserved, Hederick decided.

The High Theocrat caught the thief under the arms and tipped him forward through the window. It was but a short distance to the ground. Yellow Eyes and one of his confederates scurried forward to carry the body away.

Hederick downed his own mead—which, of course, was not poisoned—and watched until the blue and orange of Gaveley's outfit disappeared over the marble wall to the north. "You were too ambitious for my liking, Gaveley, my former friend," he whispered. "Much too ambitious. And no one treats High Theocrat Hederick with that kind of familiarity."

He regarded Gaveley's spilled mead with satisfaction. "Macaba root," he purred. "It has never failed me."

* * * * *

The centaurs slowed, then halted once more. Mynx's centaur was forced back among the crowd, and she couldn't see ahead. "Kifflewit!" she shouted. "What is delaying us?"

The kender's mount was near the front of the massed pack of centaurs. "Someone is hurt!"

"One of the centaurs? From the battle? I thought we'd treated all the wounded."

"No," the kender supplied, "a child." He looked around. "It sure is foggy all of a sudden."

A child, alone in the forest in the middle of the night? Mynx wondered. And what about this fog? She checked to see whether the Diamond Dragon was still safe on its new thong around her neck. It was.

Then she flung herself off her centaur and pushed her way through the mass of bodies until she saw what had stopped everyone.

A young boy lay before them. He was unconscious, his head flung back, his small red mouth open. A beautiful peasant woman who must have been the child's mother cradled him on her lap. She wept bitterly. Nearby, a wrinkled crone sat upon a fallen tree and moaned, wringing her hands. The old one appeared not to be in her right mind. She mumbled nonstop to herself and occasionally beseeched the night sky, the vallenwoods, and various boulders for assistance.

Swirls of thickening mist glided between Mynx and the trio, and the thief had to squint to see them. Without thinking, she clasped the Diamond Dragon. The fog suddenly cleared.

"Young woman," Phytos said gently to the mother. "What is wrong?"

The child's mother turned huge brown eyes toward the centaur. Her face was stunning in its pale delicacy. "Oh, pray, sir, don't hurt us!" she implored. "Don't send us back there! My sweet boy is dying."

Phytos blinked several times. "Send thee back where, woman? Thou hast escaped from somewhere? Hast thou been a slave?" He looked at Ceci Vakon and the others, but they shook their heads. No, the trio had not been part of the slave train.

"We escaped from Hederick, sir." The woman's gaze returned to her child's bloodless face. She stroked the lad's cheek before she continued. Sudden wrenching sobs made it difficult to understand her.

"We could not pay our taxes. The High Theocrat sought to sell my husband—this old woman's son—into slavery and take me, my child, and my mother-in-law into custody. See the poor old lady, sir. She's not been lucid since they dragged my dear husband away."

"So I see." Phytos still appeared nonplussed, however. "Young woman, we are on our way to Solace. I suppose we can carry three more as well, but we must move swiftly . . ."

The woman sobbed even harder, shaking her head. "Oh, no, kind centaur! My child is far too weak to stand a ride on the back of a horse. See how much blood he has lost!" She drew back slightly from the child, and the centaurs and slaves gasped in unison.

Only a darkened stump remained of the boy's right arm. The centaurs burst into protests. "By the gods!" "Didst thou see that?" "What monster would do that, and to a child?"

Phytos had to shout to make himself heard. "How did that happen, woman?"

"The boy—such a courageous lad, my Buni—rushed forward to defend his father when the goblins came to take him to the slave yard. One of Hederick's hobgoblins cut him badly. My husband fought them, giving us time to escape with Buni here, but I fear my husband is dead." The woman burst into fresh tears, cradling the child close to her breast, which had the unfortunate effect of making the wound bleed anew. "Oh, my poor, brave, fatherless boy!"

Her tears broke off abruptly. The young woman felt in her pocket and drew out a small gem—muddy yellow and nearly valueless—which she handed over to Phytos. "It's all we have. I will give you this gem in return for safe passage. Please, kind centaur, help us!"

Phytos assured her that the centaurs had no intention of abandoning the bereaved family.

But Mynx was frowning. Something about the woman's story didn't ring true. One man—able to fight off a troop of Hederick's trained minions long enough for his wife to escape with a fatally wounded child and a doddering old woman? She gazed at the trio. Mist swirled around the centaurs, but wherever Mynx focused, there was no mist. She found herself stroking the Diamond Dragon again.

Her thoughts were remarkably lucid, she noted. As clear as the diamonds that decorated the artifact's back.

The centaurs were undoubtedly moved by the family's plight, but centaurs were markedly susceptible in some areas. Being so strikingly handsome themselves, they tended to trust that which was physically perfect. And the mournful young mother was pretty indeed.

The slaves, so recently freed from bondage themselves, also were full of sympathy for a trio who appeared to have suffered at Hederick's hands.

Mynx smelled magic.

"Young woman," Mynx said, stepping around a centaur with black skin and green eyes. "Where did you live in Solace?"

The young mother looked up. Something flashed in her eyes as she surveyed Mynx and the Diamond Dragon; then it was gone. Her voice remained sweet and low, though throbbing with sorrow. "We found a room in the center of town, kind lady. Near the town square."

"That would have placed you next to the Inn of the Last Home."

The woman hesitated, then nodded.

"You are refugees? You would have enjoyed Otik's hospitality at the Inn, then. Otik has a soft spot for the helpless."

The fog deepened. Mynx stroked the Diamond Dragon again, and the cloud was dispelled. The woman glanced at the crone, who nodded almost imperceptibly. "Yes," the younger woman said. "He does. Otik is a kind man."

"Do you remember his specialty?" Mynx went on. She spoke loudly, her words carrying to the centaurs and human slaves. "Otik is noted for his spiced pepper sausage, fried to a crisp and eaten as hot as you can stand it. I remember it well. Did he share some with your family, woman? He usually does with refugees. As I said, he is a generous man."

"I . . ." The woman's eyes brimmed over with tears, and she glanced down at her child. The fog thickened worse than before, except where Mynx stood.

"What *is* this?" burst out a centaur just behind Mynx. The centaur's head appeared hazily through the deepening mist. "The woman interrogates these poor lost souls when what anyone can see they really need is rest and food and some attention to that child's arm. Thou should be ashamed of thyself, Mynx!"

Mynx turned slightly, making sure to keep the crone, young woman, and child well in sight. "These three are not what they claim to be," she shouted to the centaurs. "They seek to delay us! Look!" She pointed to the north, where the straggling group of riderless slaves were just coming into view. "Already we have lost precious time, if those with no centaurs to carry them have been able to catch up!"

Mynx peered into the frowning faces of the centaurs. "I don't know who has sent these three to waylay us, but it is someone whose interests ally with Hederick's. Can't you see they are false?"

Phytos cantered to her side. "Thou would have us abandon these poor folk here, Mynx? They are destitute, as anyone with eyes can see."

"Abandon them? I would have you *kill* them!"

The centaurs, and the slaves on their backs, burst out in fresh protests. The trio in the path did not move, but the two women glared daggers at Mynx.

"Let me ask them just one question," Mynx demanded.

Phytos nodded. "One question, then."

Mynx faced the trio again. "What spice is in Otik's specialty, the one the fried sausage is known for? If you have truly eaten at the Inn of the Last Home, you will know. It is an easy question. Hurry, now."

"I . . ." The women exchanged glances. The crone frowned at the younger woman, who then turned back to Mynx and snapped, "Pepper! The spice is hot pepper. Now can we get some help from you, or will you make us talk all night while my son dies?"

"Well?" Phytos asked quietly.

"Wrong!" Mynx sang out. "It's not pepper. In fact, it's not even sausage. Otik is known throughout Solace for his spiced potatoes. Anyone who had ever been near the city would know that. Moreover, the Inn is *not* next to the town square, as this woman said. You've been ensorceled, centaurs!"

For an instant, the centaurs milled about uncertainly. Some drew their bows, while others fingered their war clubs, and still others continued to counsel patience. The slaves, even Ceci Vakon, likewise seemed confused.

Then the fog melted away.

At that instant, the three fugitives vanished. In their places stood three haggard old women. Two, Mynx's height, had greenish skin, while the third, at least half again as tall as the others, had a deep blue complexion. All bore moles and warts, stringy hair, and withered faces. Their teeth were black. Their hands ended, not in fingernails, but in long claws that looked to be as strong as iron.

"Hags!" shouted one of the centaurs. "An annis hag and greenhags! Fellow centaurs, Mynx is right. We've been magicked! Attack!"

The centaur, a slender male carrying a young man, dashed forward. The largest hag calmly reached out, clasped the man-horse around the torso with both hands, and crushed him. She flung the body away with a laugh, chased down the centaur's rider, and did the same to him.

"Next?" she taunted, her foul breath polluting the air.

Three centaurs let fly with arrows at the same instant. The hags leaped aside.

"By the gods," Phytos cried. "The speed! The strength!"

Another half-dozen centaurs, wielding clubs, leaped toward the hags. The wizened crones deftly outran them, closing and grappling when the opportunity arose. Soon two slaves and three more centaurs lay crushed on the ground, victims of the annis hag. Mynx, caught without a mount in the melee, sought to fight her way to the rear of the surging crowd. Finally Phytos grabbed her by the arm and hauled her to one side.

The other centaurs continued to do battle, but the hags were too quick. They always managed to sidestep the centaurs' clubs.

The hags finally drew back. Another centaur let an arrow fly, but the greenhags merely disappeared. The annis hag deflected the arrow with one hand.

"They don't need to fight us," Phytos said. "They merely seek to delay us. Thou wast right, Mynx. Hederick must have sent them."

"But Hederick hates magic!" Kifflewit cried.

"Unless he has some necessary use for it," Mynx murmured. She probed her memory for information about hags. How to stop them? "Where are the two greenhags?" she asked suddenly.

A cry from the centaurs answered her question. One of the centaurs to Mynx's left suddenly grasped his neck, where invisible hands had crushed his windpipe. He went down, gagging and kicking. The woman who'd been astride him leaped away.

"Phytos!" Mynx shouted. "The gem!"

Phytos looked confused.

"The gem they gave you. It's a hag's eye. It's magical. Destroy it!"

Phytos looked in his hand, where the mud-colored jewel still nestled. Then he flung it to the ground and stamped upon it with his forehooves.

Three screams sounded through the forest. The annis hag clapped her hands over her eyes. "Sisters, I'm blind!"

she cried. The two greenhags reappeared. They, too, were pawing at their eye sockets.

It took but three centaurs armed with clubs and arrows to slay the hags.

Mynx found the female centaur who had been carrying her. "Hurry!" the thief shouted. "We may be too late already!" Her hand reflexively went to her neck, to where she'd placed the Diamond Dragon for safe-keeping.

Her fingers found . . . nothing. Mynx immediately cried out and countermanded her own order.

The centaurs pulled up, protesting, as Mynx groped under her armor for the Diamond Dragon. Perhaps it and its thong had slipped under the armor's gorget, she thought. Phytos caught the panic-stricken look in her eye and understood immediately.

"Thou hast lost it?" he cried. "The magical artifact?"

"I don't know," Mynx returned. "I was pushed and shoved in the battle. Perhaps it fell off."

The centaurs and humans lost valuable time searching for the Diamond Dragon.

Finally, Kifflewit Burrthistle found it, stomped into the mud. "Here it is!" he chirped. He bolted over to Mynx and handed it to her with a flourish. Hands shaking, she retied it around her neck.

"Hurry!" she shouted. "We've no time to waste."

The slaves remounted. The centaurs leaped into a canter, and then a gallop. Trees flew by. To the east, a yellow glow announced the arrival of day. Mynx glanced down; the Diamond Dragon sat serenely atop the gorget of her mismatched armor.

Mynx frowned. One of the diamonds was missing. She found herself hoping it wouldn't make any difference in the artifact's power. At any rate, there was no time to backtrack and search some more.

"Hurry!" she repeated. "Oh, please hurry!"

The longtime thief found herself breathing the first

prayer of her life.

Meanwhile, on a nearby centaur, Kifflewit Burrthistle patted one of his pouches. Yes, the diamond was still in there. It had sure been loose when he picked up the artifact. What a lucky thing he had been there to pry the jewel out of its setting and keep it safe.

Who knew what trouble there might be if it were lost, he thought.

* * * * *

Outside Tarscenian's cell, footsteps scuffled on the flagstones. A temple guard.

Tarscenian stood and faced the door of his prison cell. The footsteps stopped. Hands rattled the tiny window in the door and slid it aside.

Hederick's face peered in at Tarscenian. The older man inclined his head and waited for the High Theocrat to speak first.

"I have come to offer you clemency," Hederick said.

"Ah. But at what price, Hederick?"

"Tell me where the Diamond Dragon is," the High Theocrat ordered. "If you do this, I will let you go."

As near as Tarscenian could guess, the magical artifact was probably waltzing through Krynn in the pouch of a carefree kender, but the old man would die before he'd tell Hederick that. "I do not know, High Theocrat."

"Of course you do," Hederick snapped.

"If I knew where it was, why would I have ventured into the temple? Into your quarters?" Tarscenian asked reasonably. He gazed at Hederick. There was no sign of the frightened boy he once had been.

"Remember the giant lynx, Hederick?" Tarscenian asked quietly. "Remember how we fought it off together? You fought fair, once."

"Don't change the subject," the High Theocrat spat out. "If you came into the temple, it must be because the Diamond Dragon is hidden here somewhere. That's it, isn't it, Tarscenian? Tell me where it is, and I'll arrange to have my minions transport you safely away from Erolydon."

Tarscenian shrugged. "As a dead body, no doubt."

Hederick drove his fist into the thick door. "I will kill you slowly, false priest! I will torture you, I swear. It will take you *days* to die. No one defies me. Everyone in Solace will witness your humiliation."

Tarscenian stood silently.

"If you think your friends will come and rescue you, you are wrong," Hederick snapped. "Even now, three hags devour them in the forest outside Solace."

"Ah, Hederick," Tarscenian chided. "Stooping to using magic. What would your gods think?"

It was the High Theocrat's turn to say nothing.

"I am ready to die, Hederick," Tarscenian told him. "I wish to join Ancilla."

"Then she *is* dead."

Tarscenian declined to admit he wasn't sure. There was still hope of some miracle—and of Ancilla escaping from the tree trunk in the courtyard. "Yes, Ancilla is dead."

"Where is the Diamond Dragon, Tarscenian?"

"I don't know. Nor do I care."

Hederick's tone was silky. "I will have you bound to the vallenwood trunk and torn, limb from limb, by the materbill."

Tarscenian only shrugged at Hederick's threats.

"By the New Gods, Tarscenian, you will beg for mercy before I am through!"

"There are no New Gods, Hederick. I told you that long ago, back in Garlund. There are only the Old Gods, and they will return someday—perhaps sooner than you know. And when they do, Hederick, you will suffer for what you have done."

Hederick snorted. "One last chance. You will not tell me where the Diamond Dragon is?"

Tarscenian shook his head.

"By the New Gods, then, I will tear apart every stone in Erolydon to find it! I built this temple, and I can destroy it if need be!"

"As you will, Hederick."

The High Theocrat slammed the small window shut.

A short time later, the temple guards came for Tarscenian.

Chapter 25

"There's Crystalmir Lake!" Ceci Vakon cried. Her mount and Mynx's led the thundering centaurs as they streamed through a clearing just east of the lake and north of Erolydon.

Then a shadow swooped over the women, and they threw themselves to the ground. "Night hunter bats!" Ceci shouted. "They're the ones who carried us off to the slavers."

"Everyone stay low!" the silver-haired Phytos bellowed. "We are challenged!"

Within moments, the entire force had taken shelter under low-hanging boughs as a half-dozen of the seven-foot bats swooped near the ground. The night-hunters could see well in the dark, but they needed room to maneuver, and the tree branches would hinder their attack.

"Arrows nocked! Bows ready!" Phytos shouted.

Mynx crouched with Ceci beneath a pine branch. The thief felt several small figures nestle against her, and she realized the kender and Ceci's sons had joined them.

"Don't be afraid, Kifflewit," Mynx said soothingly. "The archers will take care of them. The bats certainly make big enough targets."

Kifflewit Burrthistle sniffed with contempt. "Who's scared? Not me," he said. "I just wanted . . . to get closer to the action!"

"Fire!" Phytos cried.

The centaurs let loose with their arrows just as the bats dived into their midst. One night hunter managed to get its claws around a centaur, but the man-horse was too heavy for the bat, which nonetheless managed to rake the centaur with its razor-sharp tail before the bat fell dead, pierced by an arrow from Phytos's bow.

Another night hunter died when it dived heedlessly toward the branch under which Mynx and Ceci Vakon hid. With a shout, Mynx leaped out, stabbed at it, and slit the huge beast from throat to tail. Ceci darted off, herding her sons under a thicker outcropping of pine boughs. Kifflewit Burrthistle let out a war whoop and took off in another direction.

Phytos led a charge of centaurs as the last four giant bats massed to arc down toward the humans and horse-creatures. Clubs beat two of the flying beasts out of the air, and arrows stopped the last pair. Soon the four were flopping on the ground in their death throes. The centaurs roved among them, using clubs to hasten their deaths.

The battle had taken only a short time, but the delay was bothersome anyway. Mynx ran to Phytos. "Look!" she cried, and pointed to the east. "The sun is coming up."

"Hurry!" the centaur shouted to his troops. He cantered, then ran, through the early morning light, while the others rushed to follow. A female centaur gave Mynx a hand, pulling the thief onto her back. The freed slaves quickly found their mounts and chased after Phytos.

Through the vallenwoods, they could just see the northern wall of Erolydon gleaming white in the morning sun.

Chapter 26

Phalanxes of temple guards and priests diverted the crowds of Solace residents and refugees who swarmed toward Erolydon for the dawn service. Instead of the Great Chamber, the spectators were surprised to find themselves herded into the eastern courtyard, into the viewing area between the inner and outer walls.

There was no sign of Hederick. Tarscenian stood bound to the trunk of the vallenwood. Alone in the center of the courtyard, he seemed curiously at peace.

"What now?" the people muttered. "Did you hear what happened yesterday with the black-robed mage?" "Indeed." "My cousin was there. She said the wizard blasted Hederick's heart right out of his chest!" "And yet his gods saved him." "The Seeker gods work mysteriously." "I missed yesterday, so I dared not miss today. Who is today's sinner?" "The old man who was with the lady mage who challenged Hederick two days ago."

Then the voices hushed as novitiates moved among the crowd, cautioning people that the ceremony was about to begin.

Two rows of blue-garbed guards entered the courtyard through the main doors to the temple. Behind them came Hederick, dressed in ceremonial blue velvet, his pudgy chin up, his face resolute. He could not resist a sneer of triumph as he surveyed his longtime enemy helpless upon the vallenwood stump.

He hadn't had Tarscenian gagged. The ex-priest wasn't a formidable enough mage, in Hederick's estimation, to bother with that. Besides, the High Theocrat had long dreamed of savoring the dying screams of the false Seeker priest. Now he was moments away from that experience. Hederick allowed a smile of anticipation to cross his face. Then he resumed his usual emotionless demeanor.

Hederick pivoted on one sandaled heel and stepped smartly to the reviewing stand, erected safely behind a marble wall. He mounted the steps, strode to a velvet-draped lectern, and, with head bowed, delivered the invocation of the Seeker gods that began all Seeker services. Then he looked up and addressed the people.

"This morning heralds a special day," Hederick intoned. "It is a holy time, a time of reblessing, of renewing Erolydon's sacred charge. Of making clean that which has been sullied."

"What?" some people in the crowd whispered. "What happened?" "Some centaurs snuck into the temple." "Ah, no!" " 'Tis true; Hederick's own high priest let them in." "Was he daft?" " 'Tis said he hoped to honor Hederick by sacrificing them within Erolydon itself." "Fool."

"Blessed Seekers of Solace," Hederick shouted, "I present one of the greatest sinners I have yet encountered. Greater than any witch, than any mage, than any spell-caster, indeed. For *his* sin involves . . ." Hederick waited for the crowd's murmurings to die away. "For this man threw away opportunity that prayerful people would gladly die for. Tarscenian, whom you see before you, had the entire kingdom of the Seeker pantheons before him. He was blessed by the Seeker gods and goddesses. He was himself a Seeker priest."

"Ah," several people whispered. "That's the man. I'd heard Hederick was searching for someone." "The goblins have been busy these last few days. I did not allow my children outside at all, for fear of them."

"This man, this Tarscenian, threw off the Seeker faith," Hederick said. "He gave up—tossed aside!—the holy brown robes of the Seeker priest. And, not content with that sin, he went on to find a new altar to worship at—the profane altar of the Old Gods."

The people cried out. Hederick held up his hands, palms outward, until they quieted. "And *still* not satisfied, this evil soul entered into a filthy liaison . . . with a witch. Together they devoted their lives to halting the Seekers. They have sought to impede me for years—unsuccessfully, of course. The woman died as a result of my holy inquisition"—Tarscenian started in surprise at Hederick's explanation of Ancilla's demise—"but the man, Tarscenian, escaped."

Hederick swept his arm toward the figure strapped to the tree trunk. "This man, people of Solace, would have denied you your only hope of salvation! He would wipe the Seekers, and the comforts of their holy order, from the world!"

Again the noise from the crowd rose and ebbed. "But I . . ." Hederick smiled grimly, waiting for the chatter to abate. "I, guided by the hand of my god Sauvay and the rest of the blessed pantheons, I was too clever for one who follows the betrayer gods. Sauvay himself warned me of Tarscenian's plot, and I laid a crafty trap—a trap that, only last night, the unrepentant sinner Tarscenian fell into!"

Hederick held out a hand to Dahos, who had waited silently at the base of the reviewing stand. The high priest climbed the steps and joined the High Theocrat. The Plainsman's face was colorless and set.

"This priest," Hederick said, "has also sinned. He admitted to the holy temple Erolydon those creatures who sullied it by their very presence. He sinned in a great way, but he has sought forgiveness for that sin. Thus, in my generosity, I have acquitted him." The High Theocrat nodded formally at the high priest, who returned the gesture but did not meet his superior's eyes.

"Nonetheless, forgiven or not, it is necessary to reconsecrate the temple," Hederick continued. "We are here today to ask the Seeker gods to cleanse it with their holy blessings. To that purpose you are witness this morning. And to that purpose the blood of a sinner will stain the cobblestones of Erolydon's courtyard."

Hederick turned to Dahos. "Release the materbill," he commanded.

The tall priest hurried to the pulley that controlled the door to the monster's prison. Dahos worked the ropes, and soon the fiery-maned creature appeared, howling, in the doorway between the dungeon and the courtyard.

All of a sudden another sound vied with the materbill's roars. The spectators turned from side to side as the sound of a hundred hooves, thundering toward the northern wall of the courtyard, inundated them.

"What is it?" a woman cried out. "More hobgoblins?"

Then the people screamed in terror, ducking as the first dozen centaurs, led by Phytos, hurtled to the top of the outer wall, then leaped from there to the inner wall. They plunged into the arena with Tarscenian. Another dozen centaurs mounted by freed slaves followed, and a dozen more.

"Halt!" called Phytos.

The mounted slaves jumped off the centaurs then, and swarmed over the inner wall and into the spectators. As the slaves threw themselves at temple guards and goblins alike, the centaurs formed a mass and approached Tarscenian.

There was another roar as the last of the freed slaves, who had traveled more slowly because they'd had no centaurs to ride, came dashing out of the trees and helped each other clamber up the wall. Two of the slaves raced along the wall and tackled a stubborn hobgoblin guard. Two more slaves used the creature's own sword to overcome it. Other slaves sprinted along the inner and outer walls.

Many of the freed slaves, both men and women, fell lifeless to the cobblestones, pierced through by swords and spears. Again as many were able to arm themselves from the bodies of the slain victims and race back into battle against the goblins and guards. "For Solace!" some of them bellowed.

Mynx stood as straight and proud as she could in her armor, riding on the back of her centaur. "Tarscenian!" she cried. "I have the Diamond Dragon!" She broke the thong around her neck and held the glittering artifact up to the morning sun. People gasped at the sheer radiance of the object.

The centaurs formed a living shield around her as Mynx edged her centaur toward the captive.

"Hold it against the vallenwood!" Tarscenian cried. "Ancilla is inside!"

Although she wasn't sure what he meant, Mynx leaned over and placed the warm artifact against the vallenwood's roughness.

"Ancilla, here it is, the thing we sought for so many decades," Tarscenian shouted. "We have the Diamond Dragon now!"

The trunk of the vallenwood began to glow, and Mynx heard the same humming sound that had torn at her when she was trapped inside the Diamond Dragon. Surprised, she fell back. As soon as the artifact broke contact with the tree, the glow died away.

"Hold it there, Mynx!" Tarscenian ordered. "Let nothing pull you away, no matter what happens!"

Mynx did as he instructed. The incandescence and the drone resumed. She closed her eyes and waited.

But nothing more happened. She looked at the old man. One of the centaurs had cut his bonds, and he had mounted the largest of the men-horses.

"Something is wrong," he shouted. "It should have worked by now." A grimace of defeat crossed his exhausted features. "Perhaps Ancilla is dead after all."

Mynx examined the Diamond Dragon. "There's a stone missing," she said suddenly, pointing to the artifact's back. "Could that be it?"

Tarscenian nodded. "Where is it?" he asked eagerly.

She shrugged helplessly. "It was all right before we were attacked by the hags. Maybe during the battle, we lost it somehow . . ."

Tarscenian's face fell.

At that moment, the materbill, who had been all but forgotten in the commotion, leaped forward with a roar, directly attacking the centaurs. People cried out, and the centaurs broke ranks.

"Kill the infidel! Kill Tarscenian!" Hederick shouted to one of the guards flanking him on the reviewing stand. In a moment, the guard's bow was up, an arrow nocked. In another instant, the arrow flew toward the vallenwood tree.

Mynx's centaur sensed its approach and lunged against Tarscenian's mount. And then Mynx, not Tarscenian, was down, lost among the legs of the centaurs, clutching her bloodsoaked right arm, the one that still held the Diamond Dragon.

Tarscenian found the sword of a dead guard pressed into his hand by a centaur. "Murderer!" the old man cried at the High Theocrat. "It is you who are the infidel, Hederick!" Then he was plowing through the crowd, fighting through dozens of guards toward Hederick.

The centaurs let loose a volley of arrows, and the materbill howled in agony. The air was filled with smoke and flames, the screams of dying guards and centaurs, and the terrified cries of hundreds of spectators. The freed slaves were fighting hand to hand with goblins. Some spectators cheered them on, howling whenever a goblin went down and rushing forward to tear the unfortunate creature limb from limb.

Kifflewit Burrthistle darted through the riot to Mynx's side. It was the kender who was able to rouse the wounded thief enough to half-drag, half-push her away from the tumult to the relative safety of the vallenwood tree.

"There's something wrong with it," she lamented, her eyes glassy. "With the Diamond Dragon, kender. We lost one of the diamonds, Kifflewit. By the gods, how could we have been so stupid?"

The kender's head shot up, startled brown eyes searching hers. "Lost it? But I have it, Mynx," he finally said. Kifflewit was uncharacteristically somber for a moment. "The diamond was loose. I . . . I found it. I was afraid we'd lose it." He cheered up. "Lucky I did, Mynx. It's safe in my pouch. Everything will be all right! I have it."

Not for the first time, Mynx had to control an urge to

strangle the kender. "So where *is* it?"

The kender peered through the sea of humans and centaurs, goblins and guards, battling around them. Gouts of flame from the dying materbill lit up the courtyard at odd intervals. "I dropped my pouches when I came to rescue you. . . . There they are! And there's the one with the gemstone! I remember, it was the red pouch with the blue string." He pointed triumphantly but seemed disinclined to budge from Mynx's side.

"Get the diamond, kender!"

Kifflewit scuttled off through the bedlam without a backward glance. Phytos battled nearby, protecting Tarscenian's flank. Mynx shouted until the violet-eyed centaur turned her way. "Help me up, Phytos," she commanded. She put the Diamond Dragon into the centaur's hand and clambered awkwardly onto his back, her right arm dangling at her side. She strained for a glimpse of Kifflewit Burrthistle.

At first nothing but dust and tangled bodies greeted her eyes.

Then there he was, scooting across the courtyard and through the chaos like a rabbit. The materbill writhed not more than an arm's length from the kender's red and blue pouch, but Kifflewit dashed right up and grabbed it. He held up his hand and waved to Mynx.

She raised her left arm. "Throw it, Kifflewit!" she shouted.

The kender may not have heard the words, but he understood the gesture. He flung the missing diamond across the courtyard.

Mynx caught it deftly in her left hand and quickly replaced it in the figurine of the Diamond Dragon.

With Phytos shouting encouragement, she pressed the glittering artifact against the vallenwood. This time the droning and glowing far overwhelmed what they had experienced before. Mynx cast a triumphant look back at Kifflewit—just as the materbill roared one last time and died.

The last Mynx saw of him, Kifflewit Burrthistle was looking bewildered as his clothes went up in flames. "Kender!" she cried.

And then the vallenwood exploded.

Chapter 27

The explosion knocked Tarscenian off the centaur and onto his back. Out of the corner of his eye he saw the Diamond Dragon arc through the noon sunlight, shedding sparks in gold, yellow, and white.

The dragon figurine hovered in midair. Tarscenian realized that its paper-thin wings were moving, beating, and the artifact's head was twisting this way and that. Hederick cried out, and Tarscenian saw that the High Theocrat's gaze was on the Diamond Dragon, too.

Then the tiny ruby eyes of the diminutive steel dragon spied Tarscenian. It dived to his shoulder, its diamonds sparkling in the sun. Hederick called out in fury. Tarscenian drew his sword and once more plunged toward the High Theocrat.

Hederick was looking elsewhere now—nearly straight

up, above Tarscenian. The High Theocrat's face was distorted with anger and horror. Tarscenian spun around.

The stump was gone. In its place rose Ancilla as the Presence—the vision of a woman and a dragon combined. She had the eyes of a snake and an aura of undreamed-of magical power.

The being was twice as tall as Erolydon, and the lance that flowed from her midsection was thirty feet long.

The miniature dragon on Tarscenian's shoulder gave an unmistakable cry of joy and flew toward Ancilla. Soon it was perching on her shoulder, too small to be seen from the ground, except for an occasional flash of yellow, blue, or red from one of its gemstones.

Tarscenian had nearly reached Hederick.

Several dozen guards had joined the High Theocrat on the stand. Under their combined weight, the wooden structure swayed and suddenly collapsed. Hederick dived off one end and rushed into the temple. Tarscenian could see him peering up at Ancilla from behind one of Erolydon's main doors. The Seeker priest hysterically shouted orders to his guard captains, to his goblins, to anyone who would listen.

His bowmen showered arrows on Ancilla, but the Presence shed the projectiles like so much sand.

The Presence raised its mighty spear, described a circle with the tip, and shouted "*On respayhee vallenntrayna!*" Its tail lashed the air, knocking over part of the inner wall.

"*On respayhee vallenntrayna.* Come forth, my brethren!"

The voice of the Presence came from everywhere. People sensed it rather than heard it with their ears.

The tops of the surrounding vallenwoods trembled and jerked. "*On respayhee vallenntrayna.*" Leaves showered the stampeding occupants of the temple. A sudden wind sent the leaves whirling around the courtyard. "*On respayhee vallenntrayna.*"

"Valiant mages of the White Robes, I return your powers.

Let them course for the good!"

Upon Ancilla's call, more than three dozen vallenwoods glowed at their bases. People fighting atop Erolydon's marble walls froze, then pointed at the trees.

"I call you from your vallenwood protectors. I thank
you, venerable trees, for sheltering those who would fight
for the New Gods. But now these wizards are needed
here!

"Carosanden tyhenimus califon!"

Then the courtyard was filled with mages. White robes
swirled as thirty-nine freed spellcasters chanted and
spread their magical powders and herbs. White robes
flashed like sails as the mages unleashed spell after spell.

A goblin exploded near the dead materbill. Another
fell, screaming, beneath a suddenly toppling wall. Freed
slaves killed a hobgoblin, and the crowd another.

Her right arm dangling uselessly, Mynx pushed
through the crowd to where she'd last seen Kifflewit
Burrthistle. She found only a few charred pouches and
the kender's tiny cloak.

There was no time to mourn the kender, however. A
goblin bore down on Mynx with the promise of death in
its eyes. She raised her sword in her left hand. She'd never
fought left-handed, but she'd die trying.

"Cantihgnas f'ir wermen pi!"

A bolt of blue lightning, spitting fire, shot over Mynx's
head and severed the mace-swinging goblin at its midsection.

"Antin mrok mon midled alt'n."

Another bolt, green this time, arced toward Mynx; her
right arm was encased in green fire. When the glow
receded, the wounded arm was bandaged, the pain gone.
Ancilla as Presence was just lowering her claws from casting the spell as Mynx looked back. With her left hand,
Mynx raised her swordtip to her helm and nodded. The
Presence gravely nodded back. The Diamond Dragon

sparkled on her shoulder.

And then suddenly the centaurs and mages had goblins and hobgoblins alike on the run. The few temple guards who survived fled with them.

Erolydon's perimeter fell into rubble.

The Presence's image flickered, so that one moment Tarscenian saw a woman, then a lizard, a snake, then a dragon, and once again a woman.

"Hederick. Face me. I am Ancilla. Face me."

A dragon stood where Ancilla had been.

Hederick remained behind the temple doors. Ancilla sighed, and leaves swirled once more around the courtyard. Her image flickered to that of a snake.

"Hederick, I summon you. I have the power. You no longer have the Diamond Dragon. It is back with me. I summon you!

"Cariwon velpacka om tui rentahten-Hederick."

The temple door opened. The rotund priest stood there, his robe streaked with dust. As he stepped unsteadily through the portal, Ancilla—now a woman garbed in white, but double the height of the crumbling temple—pointed a finger at the entryway. It collapsed behind him.

"Admit your pain, Hederick. Face it, welcome it. And then throw it aside. Your gods are but a figment of this pain. Embrace the Old Gods, the true gods, and you may still be saved. They may forgive, although you have done much to anger them.

She was a dragon again.

Hederick merely stretched a hand toward his sister and shrieked, "Witch!"

"The Diamond Dragon is gone from you now, little brother. It has returned to me, its rightful mistress. You cannot use its charisma to charm and snare the people any longer."

Ancilla's image took on the form of a snake, then a woman, and again a lizard. The image gestured toward

Solace with the lance.

"See how they have left you, Hederick. Even your high priest has fled to the village. Solace has no use for you anymore. Even your guards and aides desert you. Where are your goblins, your other foul creatures? My brother and sister mages slaughtered them as they stood.

Hederick moved toward the huge lizard that called itself his sister. "I am the High Theocrat of Solace," he shouted. "I will be the greatest Seeker on Krynn. There is no one who can stop me! *I will be a god!* And you cannot stop me, Ancilla."

Ancilla's dragon eyes glittered at the man.

"You will stop yourself, Hederick. I will not have to."

"Impossible."

"*Sauveha deitista, wrapaho yt vontuela.*"

Out of the rubble of the temple rotunda rose a curl of mist, and then another. Hederick turned and cried out. The mist coalesced into the figure of a massive man, who grew until he was equally as large as Ancilla. His shoulders were corded, his face broad and heartless. Hederick fell to his knees. "Sauvay!" he cried. "Punish this witch."

Ancilla continued chanting.

The apparition raised its arms above its head and opened its mouth. A new voice throbbed through the courtyard—a deep one, whose words matched the movements of the godlike apparition.

Hederick, Erolydon is foul. You have spread filth upon my name.

"My lord Sauvay?" Hederick stammered. "The temple is a tribute to you. I built it only for your glory."

No, Hederick. You built it for your own glory. And now you must destroy it.

"Destroy Erolydon?" Hederick whispered.

Ancilla's Presence began to flicker faster than ever. Mynx looked at Tarscenian.

The old man, his face haggard with fatigue, nodded

with understanding. "She's weakening," he said. "She's losing control." Even as he spoke, Ancilla took the form of a lizard, then a snake, then a woman, and a lizard again. "She cannot control the god apparition and her own at the same time."

Burn Erolydon, the fake Sauvay commanded. *Destroy it now. Or I will destroy it, and you with it!*

The other mages continued chanting at Ancilla's feet. Hederick's minions were gone by now, either dead or fleeing. Chanting grew louder in the courtyard, and the building shook with a series of crashes. One of the pillars worked loose and toppled between the Presence and Hederick.

Hederick whirled and vanished into Erolydon. Within moments, a new explosion tore through the temple. Flames rose from the back of the building, from the area of the Great Chamber.

"He's setting off the special powders!" Tarscenian shouted. "The ones the priests use to impress their followers."

"Will that be enough to destroy the building?" Mynx asked.

"More than enough."

"Tarscenian, my love."

"Ancilla?"

"I am weakening. The building will explode soon. You must get Hederick out of there."

"Let him die, Ancilla!" Mynx cried. "He has killed hundreds of people."

"Perhaps thousands," Tarscenian said quietly. But his eyes were resigned.

"I will hold the building safe as long as I can, Tarscenian. Get him. Hederick may yet recant. I would not have my brother die a heretic to the Old Gods. I made my vow."

The image of Ancilla began flickering so fast now that it

was visible only as a column of glittering light. Tarscenian raced into Erolydon, Mynx close behind him.

They darted around fallen columns and arches, and were halfway down what remained of the corridor when Mynx screamed and pointed upward. "Tarscenian, look out!" A blazing tapestry detached slowly from the wall. The flaming curtain fell directly toward the two, who threw themselves into a doorway. Soon the corridor was filled with flame.

Ancilla was calling to Hederick from the courtyard, encouraging him to come out of Erolydon now that he'd set in place the powder that would destroy it.

"Never!" came the High Theocrat's voice from the smoke before them. "You are evil!"

"I am the only good you ever knew."

The sound of laughter from Hederick.

"You will die at the hands of evil forces if you do not embrace the true gods now, Hederick."

"I am the embodiment of good. I will die here, in my holy temple," Hederick rejoined. He sounded almost giddy at the prospect. "Sauvay will gather me to him."

Tarscenian threw himself into the hallway and dashed through the blaze. Mynx followed.

The vallenwood Great Chamber was filled with smoke, but the dense wood had not yet burst into flame. The statues of Omalthea and the rest of the pantheons were smoldering in the heat. Mynx and Tarscenian could see the open crates of red and yellow powder that the High Theocrat had piled around each statue.

Hederick stood at the top of the pulpit. His hands were up, his lips moving, but no sounds came out. Then, the silent benediction over, the High Theocrat bowed to the empty benches. He beamed and smiled and nodded like a potentate accepting accolades from adoring subjects.

Then Hederick began to descend the flights of steps, slowly and regally, still nodding to each side as though he were leaving to the roar of a standing ovation.

"Tarscenian! I cannot hold the building much longer."

Goaded by Ancilla's call, Tarscenian and Mynx raced up the steps. Between them, they wrestled the portly High Theocrat onto Tarscenian's shoulders, then fled down the steps and out the lakeside door.

The moment they stepped into the sunshine, Erolydon erupted into a volcano of block, flame, and ash. Mynx and Tarscenian went flying into the trampled grass of the western courtyard. They came to rest against a section of standing wall and burrowed against it.

When the explosion died away, the two lifted their heads. There was no sign of Hederick.

They made their way around what was left of the steaming building. Every now and then, more fires would explode. Soon Mynx and Tarscenian didn't even flinch at the continuing eruptions.

"What are you looking for?" Mynx asked Tarscenian after the old man climbed carefully from one jagged block of marble to another.

The tall man surveyed the littered courtyard. The bodies of Hederick's forces as well as those of a few mages lay sprawled between him and the column that marked where the front gate used to be.

Tarscenian gestured. "There. There she is."

Mynx saw a huddled figure in a white robe. Scars of flame marred the cobblestones on every side but did not touch the body, the robe, or the cascades of curly gray hair.

As they watched, something shiny crept onto the figure's shoulder. The flash of a diamond brightened the battle scene.

With a metallic cry, the tiny jeweled dragon launched into the air. Tarscenian bowed his head. "It would never have left her if she were alive," he said softly. "Not willingly." His gray eyes were haunted.

The Diamond Dragon darted like a silver hummingbird over the desolation. Now and then it dived toward the ground, touched the cobblestones with its clawed feet, and arced back upward again. It performed the act at least twenty times. Then the magical creature moved outside the site of the former temple building and repeated the ritual.

In each spot, a tendril of green appeared. As Tarscenian and Mynx gazed on, each tendril became a thick stem, then a sapling. The saplings stretched toward the sky, thickened, and Mynx recognized the bark of vallenwoods.

The Diamond Dragon circled overhead, alternately swooping down to observe its handiwork, then soaring back up above the rapidly spreading tree limbs. It plummeted once more to Ancilla's body and settled itself into the angle of her neck, nuzzling the tangle of hair.

The metallic creature gave one last cry, and both woman and dragon vanished.

Chapter 28

"Erolydon is destroyed, the priests and novitiates scattered. Even if Hederick has survived, the Highseekers Council in Haven would be fools to give him such power again." Tarscenian paused and considered before continuing. "At least I hope so. That's one of the things I hope to persuade the Highseekers."

Mynx and Tarscenian were making their way along the road to Haven.

"You think Hederick might still be alive, then?"

"Ancilla swore never to hurt him. Her word meant everything to her. Yes, I believe Hederick survived."

Mynx turned that over in her mind. "Do you think they will give you a fair listening in Haven?"

"From what I hear, Elistan will turn me an unbiased ear, but the rest of the Highseekers . . . I don't know." Tarscenian shook his head. "I *am*, after all, a fallen Seeker priest. That will weigh heavily with them, I'm afraid. How heavily, we can only wait and see. Over the years, Ancilla and I grew accustomed to defeat when reason predicted success."

Mynx turned her attention elsewhere. She stroked the armor that Tarscenian had bartered for her before they'd left Solace. It was missing a few pieces, but the pieces that were there matched each other—and fit her perfectly.

"Tarscenian," Mynx said suddenly as she and the swordsman rode on through the late afternoon sunshine. "Hederick and Ancilla were brother and sister. Why were they so different? How could anyone be so evil as Hederick?"

Tarscenian raised one eyebrow. "He believes he is good. What he has never understood is that some of the greatest harm in the world has been done by people convinced that they, too, were doing good."

"Nonetheless . . ."

"Nonetheless, Mynx, you are right. Hederick *has* caused great suffering, as you have said." Tarscenian frowned and gazed at the pommel of his saddle while he sorted out his thoughts.

"At some point in people's lives," the old man finally said slowly, "if they live well, they have to take stock of what is true and what is illusion. They must do this honestly. Once they have gazed at what is darkest within their beings, they must move resolutely on—casting off the shadow of illusion and living as best they can in the light of what they have learned to be true. This takes great courage. I'm afraid Hederick was never brave or honest enough to do that, Mynx."

"And you have done this?"

"I did it in a tiny village called Garlund, on the prairie just west of the Garnet Mountains. And I have done it daily since then."

"I'm not sure I understand this, Tarscenian."

"It's a long ride to Haven, Mynx. We'll have plenty of time to talk."

* * * * *

Tarscenian and Mynx certainly were making fast time, Kifflewit Burrthistle thought as he bounded along the Solace-Haven road. "Won't the two of them be surprised to see me, though!" he said to himself, chuckling.

His pockets were full again. The people rushing pell-mell from the exploding temple had paid little attention to a kender running alongside them.

They'd paid even less attention to their pocketbooks and pouches.

He'd lost most of his own pouches and their contents when the materbill roared fire. It was lucky that he'd found—so soon!—so many wonderful things to replace them with. "Even a few new pouches," he murmured.

* * * * *

A few nights later, red and silver moonlight glinted off the helms of twenty goblins and one hobgoblin as they watched a portly man approach. He carried himself like a king, double chin up haughtily, bulging eyes cold over bulbous nose, and a permanent sneer on his mouth.

"Still thinkhe we servants," one goblin muttered. "Seekerfool."

"Shutup, morefool," the chain-mailed hobgoblin leader snapped.

Hederick's foot caught against one of the chunks of blackened marble that littered the area, and he stumbled. Only a short time after the fire, and already the forest was reclaiming the scarred land. At this rate, within months there would be no sign of what had once been the greatest wonder of the Seekers, Hederick thought bitterly.

"Magic," he said suddenly. "Even in death, the witch ensorcels me, steals back my Erolydon. But she could not kill me. Ha, not she! Sauvay saved me."

Hederick stumbled again.

"Drunksick," the talkative goblin murmured. "All-thetime now, drunksick he. If we atehim, weget drunk-sick, too, certain. He not last long under Highlord, certain." A companion guffawed, the hobgoblin hissed another warning, and both goblin soldiers fell silent. They waited in the ruins and marked the High Theocrat's irregular progress.

Finally Hederick stood before them. He spoke first, slurring his words but eliminating none of the contemptuous tone. "I see you have found reinforcements. Good. I have another task for you: Eliminate Dahos. He has outgrown his usefulness to me. His incompetence brought about the destruction of my Erolydon. I cannot trust Dahos. Or anybody."

"Needmore steel coins then, muchmore."

Hederick lurched against a piece of marble. "I've told you, you idiot, that all my money has gone to bribe the Highseekers in Haven. They *will* rule in my favor. All but Elistan, the fanatic, but he'll be a lone voice. I *will* remain High Theocrat of Solace, and there will be plenty of money to pay you later. But you'll have to wait."

"You notgo away. You owe we! Owe plenty!" The hobgoblin towered over Hederick. "You notgo away."

"Of course not." Hederick hiccoughed. "Where would I go? I shall remain in the old Seeker chapel in Solace. My priests are returning, even Dahos, and a few new novitiates."

Hederick's attention wandered. He seemed to be talking more to himself than to the hobgoblin and its comrades. "I still preach to the townspeople morning and evening, and they support my needs. Sauvay smiles upon me. I have bribe money enough. Imagine: Krynn—a Seeker theocracy, with me at its head! I will emerge victorious yet." Hederick shot them an unfocused look. "You will be wealthy enough then, vermin."

One of the goblins in the back erupted in what could have been a cough or a laugh, hastily muffled. The hobgoblin put a mailed hand on the hilt of its sword and glared equally at Hederick and the goblins.

In response, Hederick's hand went to his chest, felt briefly for something, then fell away empty.

For a moment, his watery blue eyes shone with fear. Then his eyelids drooped, and he staggered away from the goblins without comment or dismissal. A silver flask appeared in his hand.

His words drifted back in the night air.

"So what if it's gone, I don't need it, I don't need her. I don't need anybody!"

Epilogue

Astinus, leader of the Order of Aesthetics, surveyed the scribes before him and permitted a half-smile to grace his face for a fraction of a moment. Then it relaxed again into sternness.

Shortly before, Olven, Eban, and Marya had completed the manuscript, cut the scroll into uniform lengths, and bound the leaves into a book. That now book lay atop Astinus's desk in his private cell. He patted the tome as he addressed the scribes—now two, not three.

"You have done good work," he said. "You are apprentices no longer, but assistant scribes. Welcome."

Eban sighed in relief. But Marya said, "Where is Olven, master?"

Astinus didn't answer right away. Instead, the historian slipped off the stool, picked up the Hederick volume, and placed it on the wooden cart by the doorway. Later in the day, an assistant would list the book in the library's records and assign it a place on the already overloaded shelves.

"Olven decided that he preferred a life out in the world," Astinus said after he returned to the stool. "We talked long. He felt chafed by the strictures he found here. Olven decided that he could not be happy for long if he were merely recording history. He is, I believe, on his way to Solace."

Eban's freckled face appeared mystified, but Marya suddenly smiled.

"And you, Marya?" Astinus asked her gently. "Can you remain here?"

The woman nodded. "For the time being," she whispered. "I have things to learn first, before going my own way. Perhaps eventually I will follow Olven."

Eban looked from one to the other without comprehension. But the historian and the female scribe exchanged glances of perfect understanding.

The PRISM PENTAD
By Troy Denning

Searing drama in an unforgiving world . . .

The Obsidian Oracle Book Four

Power-hungry Tithian emerges as the new ruler of Tyr. When he pursues his dream of becoming a sorcerer-king, only the nobleman Agis stands between Tithian and his desire: possession of an ancient oracle that will lead to either the salvation of Athas – or its destruction.

ISBN 1-56076-603-4
Sug. Retail $4.95/CAN $5.95/£3.99 U.K.

The Cerulean Storm Book Five

Rajaat: The First Sorcerer – the only one who can return Athas to its former splendor – is imprisoned beyond space and time. When Tithian enlists the aid of his former slaves, Rikus, Neeva, and Sadira, to free the sorcerer, does he want to restore the world – or claim it as his own?

ISBN 1-56076-642-5
Sug. Retail $4.95/CAN $5.95/£3.99 U.K.

On Sale Now

The Verdant Passage Book One
ISBN 1-56076-121-0
Sug. Retail $4.95/CAN $5.95/£3.99 U.K.

The Amber Enchantress Book Three
ISBN 1-56076-236-5
Sug. Retail $4.95/CAN $5.95/£3.99 U.K.

The Crimson Legion
Book Two
ISBN 1-56076-260-8
Sug. Retail $4.95/
CAN $5.95/£3.99 U.K.

The Penhaligon Trilogy

If you enjoyed *The Dragon's Tomb*, you'll want to read —

The Fall of Magic   Book Three
A sinister mage unleashes the power of an ancient artifact on Penhaligon, an artifact that drains the world of all magic except his own. In a final, desperate gambit, Johauna and her comrades set out on an impossible quest to stop the arcane assault and save the world of Mystara! *Available in October 1993.*

ISBN 1-56076-663-8
Sug. Retail $4.95/CAN $5.95/£3.99 U.K.

The Tainted Sword
Book One
The once-mighty knight Fain Flinn has forsaken both his pride and his legendary sword, Wyrmblight. Now Penhaligon faces a threat only he can conquer. All seems hopeless until . . . Flinn regains his magical blade. Yet even Wyrmblight may not be powerful enough to quash the dragon! *On sale now.*

ISBN 1-56076-395-7
Sug. Retail $4.95/CAN $5.95/£3.99 U.K.

Novels